W9-BSX-698

# Anthony

## WORDS OF FIRE, LIFE OF LIGHT

# Anthony

## Words of Fire
## Life of Light

By
MADELINE PECORA NUGENT

**Second Edition**

Pauline
BOOKS & MEDIA
Boston

**Library of Congress Cataloging-in-Publication Data**

Nugent, Madeline Pecora.
  Anthony : words of fire, life of light / by Madeline Pecora Nugent.— 2nd ed.
     p. cm.
  Rev. ed. of: St. Anthony. 1995.
  Includes bibliographical references.
  ISBN 0-8198-0777-X
  1. Anthony, of Padua, Saint, 1195-1231—Fiction. 2. Italy—History—476-1268—Fiction. 3. Franciscans—Italy—Fiction. 4. Christian saints—Fiction. I. Nugent, Madeline Pecora. St. Anthony. II. Title.

  PS3564.U348S7 2005
  813'.54—dc22

                    2004013551

*Cover art:* Painting of Saint Anthony holding a lily and book, found in the convent of the Basilica of Saint Anthony in Padua, Italy; with the kind permission of the Messenger of Saint Anthony—Padua—Italy.

*Art section:* With the kind permission of the *Messenger of Saint Anthony*—Padua, Italy: Figures 1–4, 9–10, 15–17, 24; Courtesy of Sergia Ballini, FSP—Rome, Italy: Figures 5–8, 11–14, 18–23.

All rights reserved. No part of this book may be reproduced or transmitted in any form or by any means, electronic or mechanical, including photocopying, recording, or by any information storage and retrieval system without permission in writing from the publisher.

"P" and PAULINE are registered trademarks of the Daughters of St. Paul

Copyright © 2005, 1995, Daughters of St. Paul

Published by Pauline Books & Media, 50 Saint Paul's Avenue, Boston, MA 02130-3491.

Printed in U.S.A.

www.pauline.org

Pauline Books & Media is the publishing house of the Daughters of St. Paul, an international congregation of women religious serving the Church with the communications media.

1 2 3 4 5 6 7 8 9                    11 10 09 08 07 06 05

*To Andy from your godmother,*

*Love*

*Aunt Gin*

# Dedication

————◆ ◆————

To Father Benedict Groeschel, C.F.R., who today is preaching the same message that Anthony preached, which is the message of Christ, namely, "Repent and believe the good news."

# Contents

## PROLOGUE

## PART ONE

## The Beginning of Ministry

## Part Two

— ▬

## Mission to Italy

## Part Three

— ▬

## Mission to France

PART FOUR

—  —

## Return to Italy

PART FIVE

—  —

## The Final Month

# Spain and Portugal

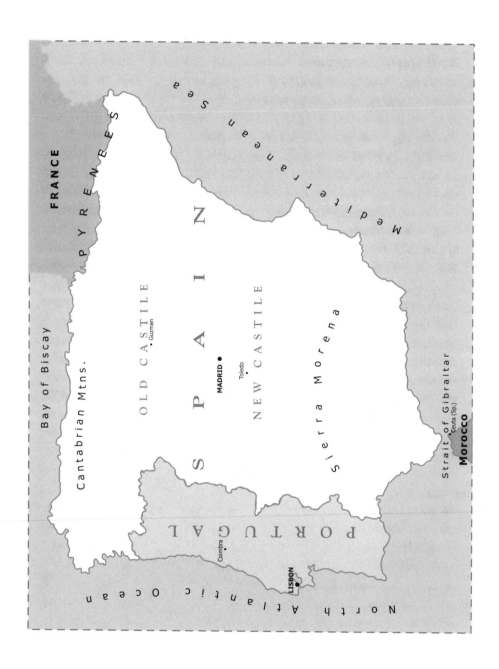

# Italy

# France

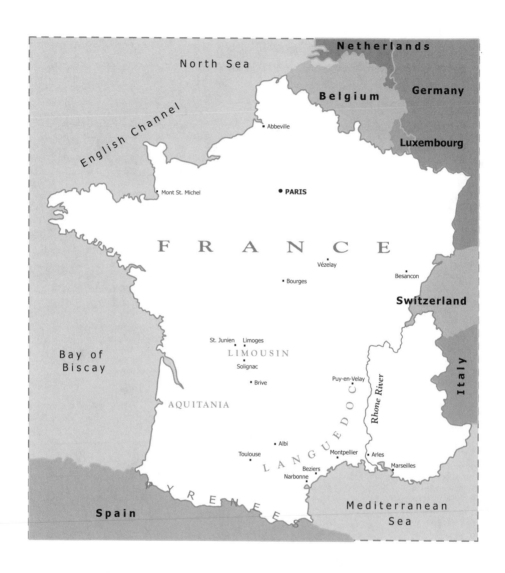

# Acknowledgments

I WOULD LIKE TO THANK the following persons for helping to make this book possible:

Father Leonard Tighe, Father Jack Hoak, and Father Claude Jarmak for reading the manuscript and making invaluable comments. In addition to his written comments, Father Tighe also met with me in person for a lengthy and profitable discussion of my manuscript.

I also thank my husband Jim, and teenage children: James, Amelia, and Frances for their important written and oral critiques of the manuscript.

Paul Spaeth for obtaining for me a pre-publication copy of the translated *Sermons of Saint Anthony of Padua* and Brother Edward Coughlin for giving me permission to quote from this text.

Father Sebastian Cunningham for his help in contacting Father Livio Poloniato, editor of the book: *Seek First His Kingdom*. I thank Father Livio and the *Edizioni Messaggero Padova* editorial staff (Padua, Italy) for granting me permission to quote from this text of St. Anthony's sermons. I also thank Father Claude Jarmak, who translated many of the sermons in *Seek First His Kingdom,* for mailing me additional translated sermons not included in the book and allowing me to quote from them. Father Jarmak also researched for me in non-English texts. He located information that I could not otherwise have found and translated information for me. He gave me copies of his notes regarding the burial of Francis, the translation of his body, Francis' tomb in the basilica, and the chapter meeting of 1230, as well as copies of two bulls issued by Gregory IX. He also mailed me photocopies of articles on the causes of St. Anthony's death and on the 1981 study of his corpse. In addition to all of this, he kindly allowed me to borrow his well-used copy of the translated *Lectio Assidua.*

Father Julian Stead for translating from the Italian a text on the possible causes of St. Anthony's illness and death.

Dr. Alex A. McBurney, Dr. John T. McCaffrey, and Dr. Charles McCoy for studying Anthony's symptoms and physical appearance and diagnosing what could possibly have been the cause of his illness and death.

Marilyn London, forensic anthropologist for the State of Rhode Island, for studying photos of and articles on Anthony's remains and making medical judgments about Anthony's health.

Father Geoffrey Chase for translating into English Anthony's favorite song, *O Gloriosa Domina.*

Sister Mary Francis Hone for her valuable information on the lives of the Poor Ladies of the time and for checking for me some information on Sister Helena Enselmini and Brother Philip. I also thank her for making available to me an English translation of the first biography of St. Anthony.

Father Michael Cusato and Father Claude Jarmak for their insights into events involving Brother Elias.

Therapists Thomas Carr and Sister Katherine Donnelly for their insights into topics pertinent to their field. I particularly thank Mr. Carr for his editing of the chapter on Master John.

Professional artist Joseph Matose who read the manuscript and created a drawing of the saint that, I believe, accurately captures his personality. I also thank Joe for his faithful and fervent prayers as I completed the final manuscript of this book.

Joan and Butch Hitchcock of Signal Graphics for their time and help in reproducing out of print texts for me to use in my research.

Dr. Michael DeMaio for translating for me the beginning sentences of *Quo elongati.*

The library staff at Salve Regina University in the reference and library loan departments, particularly Joan Bartram, Nancy Flanagan, and Klaus Baernthaler, who researched and obtained for me through their interlibrary loan most of the texts used in writing this book.

Reference librarian Theresa Shaffer and others in the reference department at St. Bonaventure's Library for researching Sr. Helena Enselmini, Brother Luke Belludi, Brother Philip, the Second Life of

St. Anthony, and the papal bull, *Quo elongati,* and for photocopying materials and mailing them to me.

All those who prayed for me and for this text, particularly my mother, Amelia Pecora, friends, and acquaintances too numerous to name, the members of my Franciscan fraternity, and my ecumenical prayer group. I also especially thank Leonardo Defilippis and Father John Randall whose prayers enabled me to complete the chapter on Brother Elias, St. Anthony himself, and the Trinity whom I invoked daily. Anything good in this book is the result of powers far more perceptive than my own.

# Introduction

**"Tony, Tony, come around,
Something's lost and can't be found."**

ST. ANTHONY IS THE ONLY DOCTOR of the Church who is invoked when someone loses a pencil. Why? Because St. Anthony cares. And he is effective.

I am executive director of Saints' Stories, Inc., a national, non-profit, tax-exempt organization that distributes one-page stories of the patron saints for all baptismal names. Those wanting stories write to Saints' Stories, Inc. (520 Oliphant Lane, Middletown, RI 02842-4600) and enclose the names of their children, grandchildren, or themselves. Saints' Stories, Inc., provides, for a small donation, the stories about their patrons. One of the saints often requested is St. Anthony.

Anthony was born eight hundred years ago, but his message is as fresh as if he were living now.

Today our Catholic Church is challenged from within and without. Some who call themselves Catholic openly challenge Church teaching on the sanctity of human life, God's divinity, or humankind's redemption by Christ. Some reject the Church's interpretation of certain Bible passages. Anthony faced the same challenges. Society seems to value capable, intelligent, and healthy people more than the incapacitated, mentally deficient, and incurably ill. This was also the society in which Anthony lived and preached.

Anthony was loyal to his Church and fiercely in love with God. His knowledge of and insight into Scripture was phenomenal. Called in his own day "the hammer of heretics" and "the ark of the testament," he battled heresies that questioned the value of all life, the authority of the Church, and the very nature of God. He was eloquent and effective in preaching the truth to a society that was generally ignorant of it. Moreover, he not only proclaimed the Gospel, he also totally lived it so that his very life was a witness to the profound truth of his words.

Anthony tenderly ministered to people whom others considered unimportant. Although he lived at a time when some Catholic clergy were dissolute and avaricious, he maintained his own purity and holiness by constant prayer and vigilance. He spoke out forcefully against sin and offered Christ's infinite mercy and forgiveness to those who repented. Thus, Anthony was one of the most forceful and yet most gentle of saints.

Anthony believed that a preacher's goal must be to bring listeners to repentance and penance, and he designed every one of his sermons with this in mind. Repentance means a total and genuine desire to turn away from sin, not just major sins but all sin. Penance means conversion of the individual's entire spirit, a conversion from sin to goodness, from the world to Christ. Penance necessarily involves contrition, confession, and satisfaction for sin, but not in a superficial sense. Anthony advocated sincere sorrow, thorough confession, and complete and cheerful restitution. Both repentance and penance do not come about by saying a certain number of prayers given by the priest in the sacrament of Reconciliation. They come about by an absolute renunciation of a sinful life (and every person's life is sinful to some degree) and by entirely embracing and submitting to a completely new life centered in God and God's perfect will for each person.

St. Anthony has a powerful message for our time. We need to return to and embrace his values, to experience the breadth and depth of his faith, and to know and love his Christ. We need to totally relinquish our own will as St. Anthony did so that we may wholly do God's will for us. Only then will we truly "repent and believe the Good News."

## Problems with Writing about St. Anthony

St. Anthony is a wonderful saint but most frustrating to write about.

Although he wrote three volumes of sermons as homily outlines for other preachers to use, no stenographer took down word for word what Anthony actually preached. Very few of his spoken words are recorded. When speaking and preaching, Anthony must have often expressed the same ideas that he wrote in his sermons, but just what did he say?

In this book, I have Anthony speaking, for the most part, words he either said on a particular occasion or words that he wrote in his sermons. If Anthony had preached his sermons exactly as he wrote them, his listeners would have been lost in a barrage of references, history, and allegory. Since he must have gone a bit slower, expanding on one point before moving to the next, I have often expanded a bit on his words, too. The chapter notes at the end of this book tell which sermons provided the basis for his counsel, prayer, or preaching in a particular chapter.

St. Anthony is called "the miracle worker." Yet most scholars accept only a few miracles during his lifetime as genuine and different traditions accord these to different locations. Many other miracles took place following his death. Were some of these transposed, in the oral tradition, as taking place during his lifetime? I have had to decide which miracles to include and where and when they took place. The chapter notes refer to any variations on the miracles related in the book.

Biographers during Anthony's time recorded few personal details about their hero. Later writers fleshed out his history, but how accurately? I have had to decide what to include; again, the chapter notes tell of some of the discrepancies in Anthony's story.

This book looks at Anthony through the eyes of those who knew him, thus giving the reader a sense of what it may have been like to know the saint. As much as possible, I have used details and characters who were real. Where details and characters were missing, I have supplied them in an imaginative way and indicated this in the chapter notes. In all cases, descriptions of historical places and events are as accurate as I could make them. I have remained true to history's record of how Anthony looked and spoke, and I have created no miracles or background history for him. Scholars can refer to the references at the end of this book for more in-depth study of what we know and believe about St. Anthony.

This book is about St. Anthony and those whose lives he touched. In that sense, it is a book about us. In many characters, readers will find some characteristics of their own. By identifying with those who knew the saint, readers will meet the saint. I hope that in doing so, they will come to genuine repentance and heart-felt penance that will enable them to more deeply know, love, and serve the Lord to Whom Anthony so totally and freely gave his life.

## St. Anthony's Sermon Notes

Father Livio Poloniato's book, *Seek First His Kingdom,* has excerpts of many of Anthony's sermons and is an excellent introduction to Anthony's spirituality and faith. Father Claude Jarmak translated many of Anthony's beautiful prayers in the book, *Praise to You, Lord: Prayers of St. Anthony.* Both books are available from the Anthonian Association, Anthony Drive, Mount Saint Francis, Indiana 47146.

The Franciscan Institute has translated Anthony's Easter Cycle of sermons, which includes his complete sermons for Easter and the six Sundays following. These are lengthy and intended for the scholar. This book, *The Sermons of Saint Anthony of Padua,* is available from the Franciscan Institute, St. Bonaventure's University, St. Bonaventure, New York 14778.

## St. Anthony's Health

A 1981 study of St. Anthony's skeletal remains and the historical record of Anthony's appearance and health history yield some important information. Anthony was robust and just under 5 feet, 6 inches tall, slightly taller than a medium-sized person of his time. He had a long, narrow face with large, deep-set, penetrating eyes (presumably black or dark brown since he was Portuguese), dark hair, and an aquiline nose. His legs and feet were very sturdy, and his hands were long, with thin fingers. His beautiful, regular teeth showed very little wear for a man of his age. This means that he ate little, probably mostly vegetables.

Anthony's knees showed signs of long hours spent in kneeling. The left knee had evidence of bursitis and osteitis and an infection under the kneecap. This could have been caused by a fall or, more likely, by excessive kneeling on that particular knee. His three lower ribs on the left side were also distended abnormally. This could have been caused by any number of factors: carrying heavy loads on that side (his books and manuscripts, perhaps?), or by kneeling, or by the swelling of an internal organ (perhaps a lobe of the liver), or by pressure of some sort on his corpse.

Anthony is variously described as being a bit stocky as a youth, then growing thin upon entering religious life (presumably from excessive fasting) and then, later in life, as corpulent. His skin is described as being brown, ruddy, bronzed. When he died, it immediately whitened and became like an infant's.

Anthony suffered a severe fever in Morocco; no one knows what this was. However, he was ill off and on during the remainder of his life and many scholars of the saint believe that the fever was responsible for this chronic illness. We do know that, later in life, Anthony suffered from dropsy (edema) which is water retention in the body tissues. This was most likely the cause of his corpulency.

By studying paintings of Anthony by contemporaries, his description in the histories, and his bodily remains, one may make some very tenuous conclusions about the illness that caused this man to die before the age of forty. Innumerable causes of dropsy exist including a poor and unsubstantial diet. Some diseases which cause dropsy are kidney disease, heart disease, some cancers, and hepatitis.

No one can say with certainty what caused St. Anthony's final illness and death. At least one author attributes the cause to asthma and diabetes. I have preferred to describe Anthony's physical appearance without diagnosing its cause. The description that I use, however, does most closely resemble that of a person afflicted with chronic active hepatitis. I believe he may have contracted this disease from unsanitary conditions or contaminated fish on his journey to Morocco.

## Canonical Hours

In Anthony's day, time was divided into three-hour segments. These and the corresponding hours on our modern clocks are as follows:

**Matins:** First prayer of the night recited by monks. Usually combined with Lauds.

**Lauds:** Prayer said at dawn.

**Prime:** 6 A.M.

**Terce:** 9 A.M.

**Sext:** Noon

**None:** 3 P.M..

**Vespers:** Prayer said between 3 and 6 P.M.

**Compline:** Last prayer of day.

## A Note on Capitalization

In this text, all pronouns referring to God, Christ, and the Holy Spirit are capitalized. This is not always the case in the translations of Anthony's sermons. I have chosen to capitalize these pronouns out of respect for the Trinity, which Anthony had and which we all should foster.

## Where to Go from Here

Many who read St. Anthony's life and words feel drawn to a more spiritual way of living. Catholic Third Orders, Lay Associations, and Institutes can provide much guidance in this regard. The group whose Rule is the most closely paralleled modern up-date of that penitential Rule of Life lived by Count Tiso da Camposampiero in this book is the Confraternity of Penitents, 520 Oliphant Lane, Middletown, Rhode Island 02842, www.penitents.org, copenitents@yahoo.com.

May the Lord direct you as you seek to know Him better and serve Him more faithfully!

# Prologue

## Cardinal of the Roman Church

**Bedchamber, Rome, Italy (Spring 1232)** ✣ The old cardinal lay in bed, tossing and turning in the total blackness of his cold, damp sleeping quarters. This room always felt dank. Often he'd considered it a privilege to suffer the chill for the love of Christ, but tonight the nip in the night air of Rome was troublesome.

Or maybe it wasn't the frost in the room. Maybe it was the chill in the consistory. He did not like to make enemies, and here he was, making plenty. The whole city of Padua and its surrounding towns hated him. Who did he number among his adversaries? The common people. The Friars Minor. The Poor Ladies. The priors of several monasteries. The university students and faculty. The Podesta, who governed Padua, and his council and knights. The Bishop of Padua and the Bishop of Palestrina. Ottone, the son of the Marquis di Monteferrato. The Cardinal of San Nicola. He had made enemies of all of them. All because he was cautious. They wanted Anthony of the Friars Minor canonized now. The cardinal wanted to wait.

Over these past days, he had not been the only one, but he had been the most pugnacious, who insisted that canonizing Anthony of the Friars Minor was a bit premature. The man had not even reached forty when he died, a young age to achieve the ranks of sanctity, and he hadn't been dead even a year. Certainly the Church's declaration of sainthood should stand the test of time, not be in response to some fad, some popular movement to canonize a hero. Why, less than a month after Anthony's death, bishops and clergy, government officials and nobility, commoners and knights had sent a delegation to the papal court. They had come with a long list of extraordinary miracles taking place at his tomb and begging the Holy Father to begin the canonization process. Then the letters began to come, and more envoys, month after month in a continuous stream, all begging the same favor. Canonize Anthony.

The old man turned on his pillow, burying the prickly gray stubs of his whiskers into the silk coverlet. If only he could stop reliving the afternoon. The images kept tumbling through his brain like a glass, bouncing, bouncing when it should have shattered. Fifty-three miracles attributed to Anthony's intercession, and approved, all but one of them taking place after his death. That afternoon in the consistory, Brother Jordan, prior of St. Benedict, had read the list orally in his deep, monotone voice.

A hunchback woman straightened at Anthony's tomb.

A man severely crippled in a fall from a church tower able to walk away from the tomb without his crutches.

A blind brother of the Friars Minor, after venerating Anthony's relics, restored to sight.

A man deaf for twenty years hearing laughter again after praying to the dead friar.

A young man, unable to speak his entire life and painfully bedridden for fourteen years, carried to Anthony's tomb, walking away freed of pain and paralysis and singing loud praises to God.

And that image of the glass. That one image that the cardinal could not erase from his mind. After Anthony's death, a heretic knight from Salvaterra had come to Padua. At lunch, his family and friends were praising Anthony's miracles. Angry, the knight emptied his drinking glass in one huge gulp and challenged, "If he whom you call a saint will keep this glass from breaking, I will believe all that you say about him." The cardinal kept seeing the knight flinging the glass against the stone floor. The glass bounced, bounced again, and finally slid to rest. Unbroken. Believing, the knight carried the glass to the Friars Minor where he confessed. Now that knight was proclaiming the wonders of Christ and beseeching the Holy Father for Anthony's canonization.

The miracles were authentic. John of Abbeville of France, Archbishop of Besancon and Bishop-Cardinal of Santa Sabina, and his learned committee had investigated every single miracle carefully.

They had discarded many. But these fifty-three they accepted. Oh, they were authentic all right. But make Anthony a saint? Now?

The haste troubled the cardinal. Anthony had barely died at the convent of the Poor Ladies in Arcella when the nuns and the Little Brothers of Francis who lived in Padua began to argue over which convent should house the remains. What an embarrassing mess that was with townspeople taking up arms and choosing sides. Peace returned only when the Bishop of Padua and the clergy plus the minister provincial of the friars declared that the brothers would get the body because Anthony himself had requested burial at the friars' Church of St. Mary's. Backing up the decision were the Podesta of Padua and his city council.

So Anthony was buried at St. Mary's where the processions to his tomb were outlandish. The numbers visiting choked Padua, and the murmuring of prayers at his grave sounded persistently like the hum of crickets in the swamps at night.

Worst of all were the outrageous candles lugged by pilgrims to the tomb. Each new devotee seemed determined to outdo the others. Many candles were so huge that they had to be lopped off to fit in the church. Others were so heavy that two oxen pulling a cart could barely drag them. Many tapers were ornately decorated with churches or flowers or battle scenes of wax. So much flame surrounded the tomb, both inside and outside the church, that night was as bright as day. It was another miracle that neither the small wooden church nor the town of Padua caught fire. This was not faith. This harbored on superstition and the push toward canonization on hysteria.

The cardinal was old and venerable. His pinched nose had smelled heresy in the air for three-quarters of a century. His dark eyes, once gentle as a deer mouse's, had grown wary as a rat's for having seen the brutal slaughter of an infidel and the equally vicious butchering of a Christian missionary.

He had watched Peter Waldo appear, dressed like John the Baptist and preaching repentance and poverty. His followers claimed to imitate Christ and the Apostles, but after twenty years, the Church denounced Waldo's position. He had blasphemed the Church, its customs and clergy. He claimed that his group alone was the

Church of Christ, obedient to God alone, and refused to submit to papal authority and excommunication.

The cardinal had seen, too, the growing strength of the *Cathari,* another more dangerous heretical sect. They rejected the very foundation of the faith by claiming that Christ had never taken human flesh, for flesh was created not by God, but by Satan.

The cardinal had seen supposedly holy priests fall into sin and generous monks grow greedy. He knew that time is a great test of sanctity and he wondered why so many wanted to rush this particular follower of Francis into heaven. Was it because this Anthony, baptized Fernando, had been the noble son of a Portuguese knight? Had the public been snared by the romance of a young dandy giving up his riches to embrace the poverty of Christ? And had the romance given weight to the miracles and perhaps even caused them through some mass, public hysteria and adulation?

The cardinal had come to see his mission as defeating the canonization. Yesterday he had pressed his points in the consistory. The pope had listened intently. The Holy Father seemed to agree that perhaps he was acting too hastily in canonizing Anthony now. Tomorrow the consistory would meet again. This time ambassadors from Padua would be present. The cardinal would press on. If God knew that he were right, the canonization would wait a few years until the world was certain about the holiness of Anthony of the Friars Minor.

All the cardinal wanted now was a little rest. If only he could relax. Long after midnight, the cardinal fell into a fitful sleep troubled by glasses bouncing through candle flames and knights kneeling at tombs.

Then the quality of his dreams changed. The vision clarified and became a scene. The pope, dressed in pontifical vestments, stood before the altar in a church that had to be new since every stone, every slab glimmered without a scratch, without dust, without the stain of candle smoke. Around Pope Gregory IX clustered cardinals, including the dozing man himself who, in his vision, was awake and alert. The stately prelates in red stood prayerfully as the pope proceeded to consecrate the altar. The pope looked about in confusion. He could find no relics of the saints to seal within the altar.

In the center of the church stood a casket in which lay a body covered with a white veil.

"Take relics from that," the pope said, pointing down the aisle toward the corpse.

The cardinals exchanged glances, their noses wrinkling slightly at the idea. No one moved.

"Your Holiness, there are no relics. Only a body," one cardinal said.

"Take courage and go quickly," the pope said. "Take off the cloth and see what is inside. The body will provide new relics."

Finally, one cardinal pursed his lips and nodded slightly. He bowed to the pope and stepped forward, walking down the aisle with a purposeful gait.

The others followed. The first cardinal lifted the veil and touched the long, thin fingers that lay folded in prayer on the bosom of a patched, gray habit. A fragrance so sweet that the sleeping cardinal could smell it in his dream wafted from the corpse. The scent was of myrrh, incense, and aloes.

"St. Anthony," one of the cardinals said with reverent softness. The word swept through the group. "St. Anthony! St. Anthony!" The cardinals began to pluck at the body, at the wool habit, at the black hair cut in a tonsure, each greedy to snatch a relic to hide away for his personal reverence.

The dreaming cardinal woke in a cold sweat. Too shaken to move, he lay staring into the darkness. He did not fall asleep again until shortly before dawn and the hour of his morning Office.

With pink streaking the sky, the old man secured his breeches and under-tunic, then knelt and prayed the worn pages of his breviary. He tried to focus on the words through the remembered image of the corpse in the coffin. As he read, he felt calmness seep into his soul like broth into newly baked bread. Through a vision, God had made His will known.

Pushing to his feet, the cardinal shuffled out of the bedchamber into an outer room where three clerics, awake and dressed, waited for his orders. As one went to get his cassock and shoes to help him dress, the cardinal caught his arm.

"Wait. I must tell you a vision," the cardinal said. His red-rimmed eyes were stinging with glaucoma or perhaps with tears as he told of his dream. "So God sent me this vision," he concluded as the clerics stared, wide-eyed at him, "to tell me that Anthony is worthy of the honor of the altars."

Later, as he was leaving his residence on his way to the consistory, he met the ambassadors of Padua. Before they could speak, he held up his hand and noticed with wonder how vividly his veins stood out in the sunlight. "I am an old man, beyond my usefulness," he said. "I fully opposed the canonization of Anthony and had resolved to do all I could today to stop it." He watched a shadow of pain cross the face of the plumpest, most highly adorned fellow. He knew that he, like a magician, had the power to change that look with a word. "Today God gave me a dream and I am of a totally different opinion now. I know well that Anthony is a saint and is worthy to be canonized. I will do all in my power to hasten his canonization." He beckoned the ambassadors to follow him, almost feeling on his back the glow on the plump one's face.

The cardinal was as good as his word. Not only did he speak eagerly of Anthony's greatness but he also spent the greater part of the day sidling up to opposing cardinals and persuading them to yield to the judgment of those who favored Anthony's cause.

The cardinals agreed. The pope consented. The Church decreed. The canonization took place in the cathedral of Spoleto on Pentecost, May 30, 1232. The old cardinal sat with the others. Weeks later, he heard from a priest that the bells in Lisbon, where Anthony had been born and baptized Fernando, had rung of their own accord at the very moment that had rung at the cathedral. While the Romans were cheering their new saint, the Portuguese of Lisbon were seized with a strange joy and burst into song and dance to the mysterious pealing of the bells. Only later did they learn of their beloved Fernando's canonization.

When Pope Gregory IX read the decree of canonization, the cardinal allowed himself to grin in public. To him, the words sounded as forceful as if they came from Christ Himself.

"Surely God...frequently is pleased to honor...his faithful servants...by rendering their memory glorious with signs and prodigies, by means of which heretical depravity is confused and masked and the Catholic religion is more and more confirmed.... Of this number was Blessed Anthony...of the Order of the Friars Minor. In order that a man be recognized as a saint...two things are necessary; namely, the virtue of his life and the truth of the miracles.... We have been assured of the virtues and of the miracles of Blessed Anthony, whose holiness We have also experienced...when he dwelt for a short time with Us. We have decided...to enroll him in the number of the saints...and We request that you should excite the devotion of the faithful to the veneration of him and, every year, on the thirteenth of June, that you should celebrate his feast."

The cardinal sighed and closed his damp eyes momentarily. Anthony belonged to the world but lived in heaven. The cardinal had done what God had wished. It mattered little if he died that very moment, for now his mission was complete.

# PART ONE

—•—

# The Beginning
of Ministry

——•——

## ℘ 1 ℘

## *Master John*

**Holy Cross Monastery, Coimbra, Portugal (1220)** ℘ Master John was sitting in his cell at Holy Cross Monastery in Coimbra, Portugal. Before him on a small table lay an open text of St. Augustine's work, *On True Religion*. Next to it lay the Scriptures, open to Matthew's Gospel. Master John was preparing his lesson for the following day when he heard a tap at his door.

"Come in," he said as he pushed his body to standing position and shook out his arthritic knees.

As John started toward the door, his hand outstretched in greeting, he saw that the one who had knocked was a slightly built young priest. John broke into a grin. Even his nearsighted eyes could tell who the young man was.

"Fernando, my star student! Come in." John clasped Fernando's forearm and shook it heartily. Fernando returned the gesture.

"Which philosopher have you come to discuss today? Aristotle? Or the writings of the saints? Bernard, perhaps? Jerome? Gregory? I am working on St. Augustine for tomorrow's lecture. Perhaps you could enlighten me."

Dressed in the white linen rochet and cord worn by the Canons Regular who followed the rule of St. Augustine, Fernando smiled. "I think not, Master. You are the teacher."

"Come. Sit down." John tugged Fernando toward the extra chair that stood beside his desk, waiting for inquiring students just like Fernando. As John eased his bulky body into his own chair, he winced at the pain in his knees. "Don't mind me, Fernando. I'm getting old."

*10*

Fernando settled into his chair, his long hands clasped in his lap. "We are all getting old, Master."

John propped his elbow on the small table. He planted his chin on his upraised fist and made himself comfortable. He always enjoyed Fernando's visits. Their discussions often went far into the evening. "So, you did not come to talk about age. What is it today?"

"Master, I have come to tell you that I have asked the Friars Minor to accept me into their Order."

The news was totally unexpected. John's fist fell to the table and he sat bolt upright.

"The Friars Minor? A mendicant Order? Since when have you been thinking of this, Fernando?"

"For a long time, Master."

"A long time? You, Fernando, who are the son of a noble knight? Those men live more poorly than Christ Himself. What do they have? A patched tunic. A frayed cord for the waist. Not even sandals. God alone knows the condition of their breeches. They are beggars. They plead for alms like beggars, sleep like beggars, smell like beggars."

Fernando was staring at John with that intensely deep look of his. "I know, Master. Here we have a powerful priory, lands, a subsidy from the king. The Friars Minor have nothing but God. That is what I want, Master."

John rubbed his bald head in confusion. "But Fernando. It is poor enough here at Holy Cross. Prior John has kept us all in misery with his mishandling of the monastery finances. His sins of usury have gained him money paid back with unlawful interest, yet he has used none of that ill-gotten money on this monastery. I've complained to the Holy Father. He excommunicated Prior John but has done nothing more to remedy the matter. You are already in poverty. We all are."

"I am speaking of poverty of spirit, Master. This is what I need."

Poverty of spirit? What did that mean? Suddenly John knew what must be the real reason for Fernando's decision. Prior John. Had he accosted Fernando?

Master John fought to keep the fury out of his voice. "Fernando, has Prior John been making advances toward you?"

Fernando shook his head. "No, Master. Not anymore."

John closed his eyes and groaned: "Not anymore. What did he do to you?"

Fernando's voice was steady but pained. "Nothing, Master. His looks at me seemed strange at times. Sometimes he touched my wrist in a way that was too tender, not of God's love but of man's passion. I pulled away. He never tried anything more with me, Master. He has not bothered me for years."

John threw back his head in relief. "Thank God, Fernando!"

For he had touched many, male and female, Christian and pagan alike. Despite being sent into the desert to do two years of solitary penance for several years of these crimes, the elderly prior had not repented. Master John had no solid proof, but he knew. A few canons at Holy Cross too frequently "consulted" Prior John for "spiritual guidance" also. The prior made continual excursions into Coimbra on "business" as well. From that city, gossip about Prior John seeped into Holy Cross.

"Fernando, you do not have to leave. I have written to the pope again. I have asked him to investigate Prior John. You will see. He will be dismissed."

"Master, I am not leaving because of Prior John."

"But you said yourself, in one of your sermons—I remember it so well, I wish I had said it—you said, 'Sham sanctity is a thief that goes about in the dark of night.' I was sure you meant Prior John and those like him. And then I remember, too, in another sermon—how did you put it?—'The false religious are errant stars who, in the dark of this world, lead others to shipwreck.' You are right, Fernando."

Fernando leaned toward John, his palms extended slightly upward, his long, expressive fingers fanned, as if he would hand his Master a message. "Prior John and the others are not beyond hope, Master. Are you not praying for them daily as I am? God's grace and the Church are calling them to repentance. If any one of them responds, the devil will forsake his soul and he will be lifted up by God. As Psalm 27, verse 10 says, 'My father' the devil 'and my mother' carnal concupiscence 'have forsaken me; but the Lord has raised me up.' There is hope for those men. I am not leaving because of them."

"Then why, Fernando?"

Fernando closed his dark eyes and brought his clasped hands toward his bowed chin. When he lifted his head, his gaze at John seemed to plead his words. "Master, please try to understand. It is no longer enough for me to fast and pray, to celebrate the Mass, to preach. I am happy doing these things, it is true, happy, too, with receiving guests in the refectory and scrubbing the kitchen and circling the garden in prayer. But they are not enough. Even my night watches are not enough, although I begged Prior John to be allowed to continue them. I have not given up all, Master. I have held on to my life. I want to give God my life so that I may merit eternal joy."

"Have you prayed about this, Fernando?"

Fernando's voice trembled. "Oh, Master, I have been praying and praying. He wants me to give Him my life."

John groaned. Of course, Fernando had been praying. Ever since he arrived at Holy Cross eight years ago, Fernando had been praying. When John's arthritis kept him awake at night, he often paced through the monastery to walk the pains out of his feet. Countless nights he had caught Fernando deep in prayer in the chapel. Sometimes Fernando would be kneeling before the altar, his eyes fixed somewhere above it, as if looking at Someone no one else saw. Other times he would be before the alcove of the Blessed Mother, his left knee on the floor, his body bent over his right leg, his hands on his right knee. More than once John caught him totally prostrate, face down on the stone floor. Ever since King Alphonsus had placed the silver reliquaries of the five martyred friars into the chapel at Holy Cross, Fernando had prayed there, too, his head pressed against one coffin or the other.

"Fernando," John would say, "go to bed." Always the slight shoulders would droop just a bit with disappointment and the deep-set eyes would look sorrowful. But the words obediently came, "Yes, Master John."

What did all these prayers mean? Could God have truly spoken to the person sitting across from him? John leaned toward Fernando. "God has told you to join the Friars Minor?"

Fernando's gaze was unwavering. "Not in so many words, Master. I heard no voice, if that is what you mean. But I must do it."

"But why?"

"Because I want to give God my life, Master. This is what He wants me to do."

"But can't you give it to Him here?"

"That is what I thought, Master. But I no longer think that."

John leaned back in his chair. "Fernando, have you spoken to Prior John about this?"

"Yes. He said there is a rule. No one may leave the monastery without the permission of all the canons who live here."

"True. They will never give you permission." John placed his arm on the table and leaned into it. "Fernando, you are a priest, one of the youngest we have ever ordained. We had to have an exemption from Church law to ordain you, but it was done because you are full of promise."

As he spoke, John saw the color rise in Fernando's dark face at the compliment. He knew that compliments made Fernando uneasy, but sometimes the truth had to be told.

"We are sixty canons here, Fernando, and you, despite your youth, are the brightest man among all of us. Admit it, Fernando. You love books. I have heard you in your room, studying, reading aloud Scripture, philosophy, and the writings of the saints. You drive them into your brain with your recitations until they become a part of you. You know history, science, nature, all the controversies of our faith. Your memory is phenomenal. Have you ever read one thing that you have forgotten? I think not. You will throw all this away to beg for scraps with men who cannot even write their names? Fernando, that Order's founder, Francis, will not allow the friars to own even a breviary. Your knowledge will be wasted."

Fernando's eyes were downcast at the tirade, their gaze resting on his hands clasped again in his lap.

"You are a preacher. You love to preach. No one else can speak the words of fire that you do. Your words bring repentance and conversion to those deepest in sin. I have never heard of one decent preacher in the Friars Minor. Join them and you will throw away your gift."

John paused. What else could he say?

Fernando's voice came steady, but his gaze remained on his hands. "Master, do not credit me for what others understand through my words. Unless there is inwardly He Who truly preaches, my tongue labors in vain. My preaching is good for preparing the way. But it is the inner anointing through the inspiration of grace, along with the outer anointing of the sermon, which teaches about salvation. When the anointing of grace is missing, my words are powerless."

"They are never powerless, Fernando."

"That can be a great source of pride, Master. And pride keeps a person from Christ."

"Do you want to give up preaching? To protect yourself from pride? Is that it?"

"I don't know if that's it." Fernando lifted his left hand toward Master John as if begging him to understand. "The friars have given God everything. *Everything.* I must do that. I must give God everything. Even my preaching if that is what He wants. Everything. Master, I have not given God my life."

Suddenly John remembered. Fernando had been praying at the tombs of the five friars who were martyred in Morocco. He chose his words carefully. "If you become a friar, you will be a martyr. That is what you think. That is what you desire."

John expected his statement to make the young man fidget. He was wrong. "Oh, if only God would count me worthy to share the martyr's crown! What joy, Master! I have asked the friars to accept me on the condition that they send me to Morocco."

John slapped the table in exasperation. "The friars agreed to this?"

"Yes."

John pushed back his chair with such force that it toppled beneath him. "Well, why not agree?" he shouted at Fernando. "The Order has no form, no rule, no novitiate. It has nothing but Francis. You know yourself, Fernando, had Francis not returned from the East when he did, his rag-tag band of serfs and free men would have splintered into disaster. You have fallen under the spell of a merchant's son, Fernando. Sometimes I think he is a crazy merchant's son."

Fernando looked up at Master John with that penetrating gaze. "I am not joining because of Francis, Master. I am joining because of Christ."

John paced around the table. "Why do you keep saying 'am joining'? You will never get permission to leave here."

"The friars are returning tomorrow to invest me, Master."

"Tomorrow!" John's fist slammed onto the table so suddenly that *On True Religion* jumped and tumbled to the floor. As Fernando bent to pick it up, emotion swelled inside of John's gut and threatened to overcome him.

His voice came shaky but subdued, his back to the priest so that Fernando could not see the trembling of his mouth. "Leave me,

Fernando. And pray. Pray hard. Discern. Does God want you to die? Or do you?"

"I will pray, Master."

John heard the rustle of cloth, the shuffle of sandals, the soft closing of the door to his cell. Turning to the table, John sank to his knees and buried his head in the volume which Fernando had just placed on the wood.

*Fernando, Fernando! You could be all I never was, all I wished I could be. You will go to Morocco and be killed? For what?*

John's breath came in great gulps as Fernando's life sped like a gale through his mind. He was as powerless to stop the recall as a sapling is to impede a tempest.

Fernando was too weak to become a knight as was his father Martino, a wealthy noble of Lisbon. However, Fernando was well educated and good with figures and accounts. So Martino planned, "He will manage my estate and land."

A religious man, Martino attended daily Mass. One day, fifteen-year-old Fernando approached him with the statement, "I want to become a priest." Martino had vehemently opposed him. "Why leave your inheritance? Be holy at home."

Fernando persisted. Martino relented.

Fernando sought out Prior Gonzalo of St. Vincent's Abbey, daughter monastery to Holy Cross, which lay just outside the walls of Lisbon. "I am worried about the world's influence," he had confessed. "I am tormented beyond measure by the allure of marriage and the call of the flesh, yet I wish to live my life for God. Father, if I continue to accompany my friends and do not abandon the world for Christ, I will fall into serious sin and lose my soul."

Knowing well what temptations Fernando was abandoning, Prior Gonzalo had admitted the young man as a novice.

Thus, chubby, pale Fernando came to pray in the dark chapel as well as toil in the sun. His long, pampered fingers grew sturdy pulling weeds in the monastery garden. His fleshly arms thinned and muscled out as he wrestled with hoes and brooms. Within months, Fernando had grown ruddy and muscular and seemed to have conquered the temptations of the flesh.

But he was not content.

After a year or so at St. Vincent's, he asked Prior Gonzalo to transfer him to Holy Cross. "Too many friends and family members visit me here. They are drawing me back into the world. To follow God, I must leave the world and be alone with Him," he explained.

So Fernando was transferred to Coimbra, the capital of Portugal, one hundred miles from Lisbon. Here he had few visits from family and none from friends.

Here, at Coimbra, Master John had met Fernando. In John's class, Fernando proved himself to be insightful, quick, genteel, graceful, a young man whose nobility was evident at a glance. When assigned to the kitchen, he was an efficient cook and housekeeper, equally at home with pots and brushes. At work in the garden, he tilled and planted and harvested with diligence. In his free time, he lived in the library absorbed in books or in the chapel sunk in prayer. When he preached at church, the congregation sat awestruck.

Of the many monastery duties, Fernando seemed best suited to that of guest master. And that was the duty to which Prior John eventually assigned him. In the guesthouse, Fernando distributed alms when the occasion warranted and received visitors from all walks of life including priests, paupers, bishops, lepers, nobles, beggars, Queen Urraca of Portugal, and the Friars Minor.

The Friars Minor lived at the friars' monastery at Olivares, which had been given to them by Queen Urraca herself. Fernando had become friends with many of the mendicant followers of Francis. When one of the martyrs, Brother Questor, died, Fernando confided a vision to Master John. "While celebrating Mass, I saw Brother Questor's soul winging its way through Purgatory, ascending like a dove into glory."

Master John should have attached more importance to Fernando's attraction to the Friars Minor. Fernando had often told him about Francis of Assisi, repeating stories that the friars must have told. Francis had dreamed of being a noble knight. Yet he had given up everything to follow Christ in utter poverty and total love. From the crucifix at San Damiano Church in Assisi, Christ had spoken to Francis, saying, "Go, Francis, and repair My house which you can see is falling into ruin." Francis had begun by begging stones to rebuild the structure. Idealistic men had joined him until Francis had founded an Order to rebuild the Church with living stones, the people themselves who form the Church of Christ. By simple preaching, austere lifestyle, and holy example, Francis and his followers were evangelizing the populace in fields, markets, and public squares.

From Assisi, they were spreading across the world into pagan lands and heretic strongholds. The world was beginning to listen to the message of these friars in robes of unbleached gray or tan wool.

One day, five young Friars Minor from Italy came begging alms. They were on their way to Morocco, they told Fernando, to preach Christ's message to the pagans. Their zeal and exuberance had impressed him. At mealtime, Fernando, in his usual theatrical way, had told his fellow followers of St. Augustine about his encounter with these followers of Francis. "Brother Berard said he was going to die for God's glory. Brother Peter agreed. Brother Otho joked about being food for ravens. Brother Adjutus spoke little but laughed with him. Brother Accursius said that nothing better existed than to die for God Who died for us."

The five friars had gone to Morocco as chaplains to the sultan's soldiers under Dom Pedro, brother of Portugal's King Alphonsus. Dom Pedro was the well-paid head of the sultan's armies.

Father John Robert had gone into exile with Dom Pedro. But when Dom Pedro sent the martyrs' remains to Holy Cross, he sent John Robert along with them. From John Robert, the monks at Coimbra had heard the stirring details of the martyrs' deaths.

In Morocco, John Robert said, the friars had preached about Christ to those who would listen and those who would not. Hearing their rash proclamations, the sultan thought them mad and ordered them either to return to Europe or to be silent. They refused. So the sultan punished them with twenty days of imprisonment, starvation, and excessive torture.

Upon their release, they returned with joy to preaching, thus infuriating the sultan who ordered Dom Pedro to put them aboard ship and send them home. Having earlier tried to persuade the friars to moderate their zeal, Dom Pedro now twice attempted to deport them to Spain. But the stubborn friars would listen to no reason and, eluding their guards, found their way back to the sultan.

When Berard mounted the sultan's chariot to speak, the sultan's sanity seemed to snap. "Enough!" he had cried. He ordered them to be tortured and killed and, thus, the blood of the five friars had been spilled in Morocco.

Moved to tears, Dom Pedro had used his political influence to claim the bodies and encase them in two silver caskets. The remains made their way throughout Spain and then into Portugal, finally reaching the capital city of Coimbra. Not knowing whether to bury them in the monastery at Olivares as befitted their humility or in the cathedral as befitted their martyrdom, Alphonsus' s wife, Queen Urraca, who had gone on foot to meet the procession, declared that the mule bearing the reliquaries be released to go where it pleased. To everyone's surprise, it plodded to Holy Cross where it knelt before the altar until the holy burdens were removed from its back.

Master John had seen this mule's behavior and had thought it odd and yet glorious. God had wanted the martyrs to be enshrined here at Holy Cross. But why? Now he felt angry with God. Had God brought the martyrs here so that He, through their presence, could claim Fernando?

For no one could deny that the presence of the martyrs' bodies had wrought a change in that young priest from Lisbon. His voice cracking with emotion, Fernando had preached at the Mass of the martyrs. Then, many times afterward, Master John had caught him praying at their caskets, his head resting against the gleaming metal, his cheeks often streaked with tears.

Had Fernando been praying to die?

Tomorrow he would leave. God wanted this? *Why, God? Why Fernando?*

John knew that he must pray. He was still kneeling at the table, his head buried in the book. Now he pushed to his feet, pains once again shooting through his knees. He would go to the chapel and pour out his heart to God.

Fernando, however, had beat him there. Before the alcove of the Blessed Mother, Fernando bent almost prostrate to the stone floor.

John slipped into a pew toward the chapel's rear. *Why, God? Why Fernando? Are You calling him, Lord? In every life, You give a call. Many calls. To do Your will is to submit, to obey. Are You calling him to the Friars, Lord? To die? He has such potential. Lord, can You want this? Are You calling him, Lord? Lord, I beg You, if this is from Fernando and not from You, foil his plans.*

Then from deep inside John, like a furtive mouse, poked a thought. *If You are calling, Lord, this monastery will allow Fernando to leave.*

THE NEXT DAY, PRIOR JOHN called together the entire monastery. The men sat in the meeting room, each in his accustomed place on the benches arranged along the walls. Fernando, standing in the room's center, presented his question. Whispers swept along the walls. Although Master John, due to his poor vision, could not clearly see the faces of the men, he had grown accustomed to nuances of speech. He did not hear a gasp of shock as he had anticipated he would. Perhaps Fernando had spoken to the men earlier, one by one. Or perhaps God had.

The men began to cast their votes. One by one they agreed with Fernando. Reluctantly. Sorrowfully. Against their better judgment. But they agreed. With each vote, John's spirit fell. They were voting to send Fernando to his death. He could see the budding lily of Fernando's promise being crushed by a massive, fatal paw.

Now it was John's turn to vote. He stood uncomfortably. "Fernando, I do not understand why God would want your life. But if God truly wants it, then you must give it. You have made it clear that you have prayed, that this desire for martyrdom is not only from your own will but is from God Himself. What we, in our poor understanding, deem folly, God often sees as wisdom. If it is God's will that you go to Morocco, then you must go." John's voice began to quaver as he limped toward the young man with the anxious face. "Fernando, I will not be the only one to oppose you." John extended his arms to Fernando and embraced him. The young man's body was trembling. John's voice was thick. "Go, then and become a saint."

"Oh, Master," Fernando whispered, his voice quivering, "when you hear of that, then you will praise God."

Late in the day, two Friars Minor, one of them the provincial minister, Friar Jean Parenti, came, bearing a coarse gray habit. In the guest receiving room, in the presence of Master John, Prior John, and all the canons of the entire monastery, Fernando removed his white rochet and cord and kissed them. He handed them to Prior John and slipped into the scratchy, floor length tunic. Around his waist he tied a frayed length of rope. "Thank you," he said, embracing each canon present before he stepped out of his sandals, leaving them on the floor behind him as he left barefoot.

After Fernando had gone with the friars, John, still feeling the sting of the rough wool against his palms, knelt in the chapel and lifted his eyes to the icon of the Blessed Mother. For long moments he stared at her. "Be with Fernando," he whispered over and over.

He prayed for Fernando daily for a week before two friars came to Holy Cross with the news that Fernando now bore a new name. The wanderers renamed him after the saint of their convent at Olivares.

John knew much about that saint. Nearly a thousand years ago in Egypt, that man had waged a life-long struggle between a desire for holy solitude and a call to Christian community. He had renounced wealth to become a poor hermit. He had struggled with temptation and the devil and had emerged the victor. He had lived a life of deep prayer and constant penance in utter solitude and yet had founded the first Christian monasteries based on his principles of total renunciation of the world for Christ. The man was a source of encouragement of persecuted Christians, a counselor to lowborn folk and to emperors, a preacher of the Gospel and a champion against heretics who proclaimed that Jesus was not divine. And now Fernando bore his name: Anthony.

From now on, Master John's prayer would be, "Lord, be with Anthony."

$\mathcal{Q} 2 \mathcal{Q}$

## *Maria*

**Lisbon Cathedral, Lisbon, Portugal (1220)** ᛞ The small, stocky lady, dressed in the pale, beaded gown of a noble woman, walked slowly down the aisle of Lisbon cathedral. Some said it was the most magnificent church in all Portugal. Before the main altar, a monk intoned a hymn, his thin whisper magnified in the vastness of the sanctuary. Maria was aware that those kneeling in prayer, more poorly dressed than she, were watching her curiously, but she had learned to ignore their stares decades earlier when she was a child. Conscious of the rustle of her gown in the holy stillness, she made her way to the alcove of the Blessed Mother, to the left of the main altar. There she knelt on the hard marble kneeler, her back straight as she had been taught from her youth to carry it, but her head bowed. She did not pray aloud; she never did. Yet, in her heart, she spoke clearly and, she hoped, poignantly.

*Blessed Mary, my Mother, Mother of my Fernando, look into your tender soul and have mercy on me. Where is my son, Blessed Mother?*

"Take me to Coimbra," she had begged Martino that night months ago as they lay in bed.

"All Lisbon is talking about the miracles of healing at the tombs of the five martyred friars."

Martino had rolled toward her and lightly kissed her cheek. "The five martyred friars are buried in the church of Holy Cross. Is that not where Fernando is?" His voice had a touch of pain that it always had whenever Maria mentioned their oldest son.

"You know I would like to see Fernando, too."

"If he had stayed home," Martino said with a hint of bitterness, "and had taken over the estate as I wished him to, you would not have to go to Coimbra to see him."

Maria flinched at this reminder of her husband's broken dreams for their son. Kissing Martino's cheek lightly, she pleaded, "Martino, the time for resentment is past. Fernando left us years ago. He is happy as a monk. He would have been miserable here."

Martino groaned. "I know. He moves souls. He could have moved men."

"He is doing God's work, Martino."

Martino stroked Maria's hair. "I know my sweet joy. I miss him as much as you do. We will leave once the sowing is done." He had planted a kiss on her lips and continued to love her, a regular occurrence that seemed remarkable to her now that her black hair was flecked with gray and her once firm breasts were sagging. Martino still called Maria the name he had used on their wedding night. His "Venus."

The journey to Coimbra seemed forever as it always did. She had worried if the nurse would properly care for the children she left behind. Would the nurse see that Pedro ate well? Would she be tolerant of Maria's moodiness? Would she insist that Feliciana practice her stitchery?

Martino never worried. "The children are grown," he always told her before these journeys. "They can care for themselves."

But she worried anyway. The Blessed Mother understood. The Blessed Mother must have worried about her own grown Son. Did He not leave their dwelling, challenge the religious authorities, and traipse all over the countryside with no place to call home? Surely, He concerned her. Once, with His relatives, she went to call Him. Jesus ignored her, saying, "Who is my mother and my relatives? They who do My Heavenly Father's will." Grown children can be a worry. The Holy Virgin understood.

When she had arrived at Holy Cross, Maria had encountered the unexpected. Fernando was not there. "He has joined the Friars Minor," the guest master told her. He directed her and Martino to the Little Brothers' abbey of the Olivares.

The abbey was nearby. Queen Urraca, beloved ruler of all of Portugal, had chosen a beauteous spot to give her friars. Maria, Martino, and their entourage of horses, mules, baggage, servants, knights, and nobles wound their way through gnarled olive groves where the delicate lace of the olive leaves brushed Maria's face. With a smile she knew what only a mother would know. Fernando would often stroll under the olives, seeking the leafy softness as another man might seek his lady's caresses.

Then she saw the abbey and her smile died as swiftly as a crushed gnat. The abbey was a hut. Worse. A shack. Fernando here? Against the abbey leaned hovels of wattle. As her horse strode past, she glimpsed two figures inside one of these rude dwellings. One friar lay on a bed of straw, his head on a stone, his bare and dirt blackened feet splayed out beneath a ragged, tan woolen tunic that was splashed nearly to the knees with caked mud. Another friar was bending over him, swabbing the prostrate one's neck with a gray, dripping cloth.

Fernando here? Even as she silently screamed "no," the doctoring friar turned toward her and stood.

*He's no more than a boy,* she thought with a start as she noticed the scraggly beard just beginning to sprout. *Where is your mother, lad? Why did she let you come here?*

He saw the questions on her face but misread them. "He has a fever," he said, nodding at the ill friar.

"We are looking for a priest named Fernando," Martino said.

"Fernando?" The young man was obviously puzzled.

Maria found her voice. "Our son. A friar with black hair, dark skin. About medium height. Well-bred," she added. "He joined you from Holy Cross."

The lad smiled. "You mean Father Anthony. He does resemble you, my lady," he added with a bow. "But he is no longer here. He has gone to Morocco with Brother Philip and Brother Leo. They set sail two weeks ago."

She felt her face go ashen.

"This had been his cell, here in the olive grove," the youth said, "but shortly after he left, Brother Joseph grew ill. Our prior ordered him to come here. Father Anthony's cell was newer than Brother Joseph's. More water tight," he said with a grin.

"He is not here, Maria," Martino had said. He grabbed her horse's reins in his own strong hands and turned the beast back the way they had come.

"God's speed, my lord," the youth called as he stooped into the hut.

*Oh, Blessed Mother,* Maria prayed now in the Lisbon cathedral, *how my own silk sheets and down comforters mock me! Fernando on straw? Oh, Blessed Mother, have pity! And he is not even there at Olivares.* "He has sailed for Morocco," the friar told us.

Morocco. Morocco. There in the olive orchard, Maria had wanted to shriek like a peasant woman who hears that her son has been run over with a plow. If only she could faint like a coward at the sight of his own blood. Or beat the earth with her fists like a knight knocked to the dust in a tournament. But the wife of a court noble does no such thing, so she sat straight in her saddle. The beast under her pulled against the taut rein as the cortege headed back to Lisbon.

"Morocco." Maria whispered the word in the cathedral. The word sounded like the first note of a dirge. She boldly raised her eyes to the icon. The Blessed Virgin's gentle face was tilted to the right. Her dark eyes seemed to look pityingly into Maria's own.

*Blessed Mother,* Maria pleaded, *the pagans in Morocco do not believe in your Son. Nor do they wish to hear of Him. Those who speak of Christ in Morocco die for their valor. The five holy martyrs were killed in Morocco. Is that what Fernando wants? To die for your Son, Blessed Mother? Let it not be, my Mother.*

Maria's gaze wandered to the Holy Infant Who stood in the crook of His Mother's left arm, His chubby hand stroking the Virgin's cheek.

*Was it not enough, Blessed Mother, that your own Son died? Death was your Son's mission. It is not my son's.*

*Blessed Mother, you know how I prayed to you for this child. How I gave him to you from the first moment that I knew he was growing beneath my heart. You accepted my gift. You saw that he was born on the feast of your Assumption, August 15. He is not yet thirty, Mother. Even your Son survived to thirty-three. Can my son not have at least as many years or a few more?*

Maria was weeping in silence as a faint memory returned, suddenly strong, the sweet, sweet smell of slippery, newborn wetness. How tenderly, eagerly her infant had tugged at her breast, his dark eyes fixed on her face as his mouth pulled!

Could she leave those memories in the sands of the desert? Those and other recollections. The young Fernando noticed what everyone else overlooked. Sunlight snagged on the steep terraces and stone walls of his neighborhood. The anguished cries of sea birds that flew between the River Tagus and the Lisbon shore. The peculiar moaning of sea and wind on stormy nights. What would he notice in Morocco but the glint of steel, honed to kill, the shouts of pagans out for blood?

*Oh, Mother of mine, he is worth more than his blood.* Maria remembered him, a chubby, little boy in a tunic too long for his short, plump legs. The sleeves hugged his arms. The low neck was embroidered with golden curls and loops, her design, her art. She combed his hair and sent him to school. So near their house, yet so far for a seven year old.

"Your Blessed Mother will be with you when I am not," she had told him.

"She's as sweet as you, isn't she, Mother?" he asked.

"Sweeter," Maria said, kissing his head and sending him off.

At the bishops' school attached to the Lisbon cathedral, he did very well in his studies. Fernando did not brag about his abilities, but his uncle, Canon Fernando, who taught at the school, frequently told Maria and Martino how brilliant his little namesake was. How quickly Fernando grasped writing on a small wax tablet with a stylus! With what confidence he memorized Old Testament genealogies and lists of vices and virtues richly engraved on framed sheepskin hides! His teachers praised his memory, his behavior, his cheerfulness. As he grew older, the praises increased. All subjects seemed easy to him. Arithmetic. Geometry. Botany. Medicine. History. Philosophy. Music. Rhetoric. Natural science. He would come home from school eager to tell Maria about the precious gems or exotic beasts or diseases of the body which he had studied that day.

Surely, his teachers said, Fernando would make a fine knight, an asset to the king's court. But Martino said no. Fernando was too small, too weak to be a knight. Why waste his brilliance on combat when he was physically more suited to intellectual pursuits? Fernando would write the accounts for his father, manage the castle, inherit the estate. He had the intelligence and grace to rise in society. He would be a noble in every sense of the word.

Martino's plans thrilled Maria. She had not wanted to see her son wield a sword. Better for him to be at home, safe, than risking his life in combat. Better to be respected at court for wisdom than for prowess.

*You know how Fernando loves you, Mother of God. Ever since I sang "O Glorious Lady" to him, over and over as an infant, it has been his favorite song. Every Mass he ever served as an altar boy he dedicated to you. When we would walk the streets of Lisbon and pass a church, he would ask to go inside and pay you a visit. Even the cathedral school that educated him bears your name.*

*Why has he gone to Morocco, Blessed Mother? Is the devil drawing him there to be rid of him?*

Maria had thought that he was done with demons. Years ago, when he was praying before the Blessed Mother's shrine at St. Mary's cathedral, he had encountered a devil, a hideous creature that had appeared at the altar. Frightened but not frightened off, Fernando remembered the Son of God. The boy traced a cross on the marble step on which he knelt, whispering as he did so the precious name of Jesus. The creature vanished. Fernando raced home to Maria to tell her, to pull her back to the church and to show her the spot of the apparition.

*Oh, Blessed Mary, I thought I had lost him when he told us that he wished to join the Canons Regular of St. Augustine. The convent of St. Vincent was nearby, but it might as well have been in Germany for he was giving up all his life to enter there. He was not yet twenty.*

Maria had dreams. She had envisioned Fernando's wedding, his wife, his children on her lap. She had seen him riding across his estate seeing that the serfs who worked his land had food and goods. She pictured him endowing cathedrals and schools with his funds.

A priest had no place in Maria's daydream or in Martino's. They told their son that he was throwing away his life. He told his parents that he was saving his soul. They showed him what he would be losing. He told them all that he would gain. In the end, Maria and Martino relented. Fernando accepted the white robe and black, hooded cloak of the Order.

Maria and Martino saw him often. So did his friends. He was hardly a man when he asked to leave St. Vincent's monastery and Lisbon. Martino promised that his family would visit him wherever he went.

*Oh, Blessed Queen of Heaven, beg your Son not to take mine. The monks at Coimbra praise Fernando's preaching. He has a gift, they say. Let him use it, Blessed Mother. A brother in religion told me that Fernando cured him of an obsession by praying with him and covering him with his mantle. Is this not a gift, too, Blessed Mother, that should not be poured out on pagan sand? The prior once told me that Fernando was even gifted at languages.*

*Perhaps he thinks that he can learn a new language quickly enough to speak to the Africans of the wonders of Christ. I have no doubt that he can speak and tell well the wonders of God. But will the pagans listen? They did not listen to the other five followers of Francis.*

*Sweet Mother, have mercy on the tears of this mother, your daughter. Fernando, I know, is praying to you, too. He is begging to die for his faith. Merciful Mother, I am older and wiser than he is. I know his gifts even if he wishes to disregard them. Will he not do you more good alive than dead? Do not listen to his prayers, dear Lady. Answer mine. Spare my son.*

$\backsim 3 \wp$

*Emilio*

**Ship Bound for Portugal, Mediterranean Sea (Early Spring 1221)** ℘
Emilio raised his gnarled fist to the sky and shook it at the swirling
black clouds. From the moment he had arisen an hour before
dawn, until now, the wind had crested from a moan to a roar. The
ship was pitching in the tempestuous Mediterranean Sea. Much as
he wanted to shave the gray stubble poking out on his weathered
face, he'd not risk the razor today. On the rolling ship, he'd likely
slice himself deeply and add another scar to cheeks that had sustained too many wounds in bar room brawls.

Emilio hated storms because his unshaved beard always itched
during them. For all the pain and discomfort he'd experienced at
sea, he didn't know why the facial irritation bothered him so much,
but he accepted it just as he accepted the knee cramps that seemed
almost constant now that he was getting too old for life at sea. He
must be past forty, he thought, but how could he return to the land
after twenty-six years on the waves?

Of course, if he gave up sailing, he could sit indoors during
storms and maybe even enjoy a warm fire. Right now that sounded
mighty inviting. Any moment, he expected to be pelted with rain
and, perhaps, hail. "Cursed be all ye demons in hell," he muttered
as he strode across the narrow, shifting deck of the ship.

He paused at the hold in the ship's belly from which wafted up
the sweet odor of lemons and limes from Morocco, piled in bins for
sale in Lisbon.

"Hey, ya friars down there? Ya'wake?"

"We are," a sturdy voice called out of the darkness.

"And a good morning t'ya, though ya'd not know it from the sky," Emilio yelled above the wind. He shoved his head down into the narrow opening. "I'll help ya git the good Father on deck, Brother Philip."

A young friar's face appeared in the gray circle of light at the foot of the ladder. Then the priest's ashen face moved into the glow. He was young, too. Emilio could tell that, but the flush on his sunken cheeks aged him.

"Ya look peaked ta-day, Father Anthony," Emilio shouted. "Ya better get up here and take some air before she starts ta rain."

The tall young friar supported the shorter priest from below as Anthony climbed the ladder. Emilio's muscular arms grabbed the priest's thin ones and pulled him out into the light.

"Don't know why the captain took ya on," Emilio said to Anthony who stood unsteadily on the pitching ship. "He knew ya was sick. How ya going ta work your way ta Lisbon?" He looked at the young brother who was now standing on deck, too, staring at the angry sky.

"Now, Brother Philip. Ya kin work for your passage all right. I seen ya yesterday, hoisting them sails like an old sea dog when ya ain't hardly even old enough ta be a man yet. Swabbing the deck like ya was born with a rag in yer fist."

Emilio gave his arm to Anthony to steady him. "I know. Ya try, Father Anthony. Ya do a passable job. Don't know how ya keep yer legs under ya. I seen ya a couple times, leanin' into the railing, sick with fever. Ya don't eat, not much anyway. How ya gonna git strong if ya don't eat hearty?"

He sat Anthony on the deck between a pile of rope and a creaking mast. "Course, maybe ya don't wanna muscle up. Maybe ya wanna die. Hey, I heard the stories. The whole ship knows the two of ya and your friend Leo sailed ta Ceuta ta die. Course only Leo got his wish."

Emilio avoided looking into the priest's eyes as he fished around under his grayish shirt for the bread he'd stashed there.

"All right. Ya didn't go there ta die. Ya went ta preach about yer Savior. But the sultan wants nothin' ta do with yer Savior. He made vulture bait of five other of ya guys who came here. And yer friend Leo, too. Ya knew what would happen when ya came. Aren't those first five friars buried in yer city? I don't think King Alphonsus cared much about the friars, the king bein' out of the pope's graces and all that. But his brother Dom Pedro welcomed their bones like they was angels, I hear. Stuffed their dust into silver boxes. Silver! Is that what ya two want? Silver don't do no good unless yer alive ta spend it."

Emilio found the loaf and, squatting on the deck before the two friars, tore at it with his greasy hands.

"Look. Ya wanted ta die. Ya might get yer chance. Naw, the captain wouldn't touch ya. He claims he's a follower of yer God. So yer God don't mind if the cap'n's got a woman in every port, sometimes two? A God like that I might believe in. Might, ya hear. Don't go preaching ta me again. I ain't ready ta hear it."

He tossed a hunk of bread up to Philip who was standing as sturdily as a column beside him.

"Naw, ya needn't worry about the cap'n. It's yer God ya need ta worry about. Ya, Father Anthony, ya told me that He got the sea and the sky in His hand like I got me this bread. He does what He wants with them, ya said."

Emilio put a hunk of bread into Anthony's hand.

"He's doin' a rotten job right now, Father. Us out of port just barely a day and this wind comes up outta the west. Wind? This ain't no wind. This is a gale. A maelstrom. We're barely through the strait, so close ta land yet. So intense. Seems unearthly. Ya been praying ta go back ta Portugal, back ta your community, ya told me. Ya better pray harder, friars. This ship ain't going nowhere near Portugal in this storm."

He looked at the two friars who were still holding their bread. "Why don't ya eat? When the rain starts, the rest o' the bread will rot."

"First we pray," said Anthony, bowing his head.

Emilio didn't listen to the words. He heard instead the first splatters of rain thrown across the ship like pellets of ice.

—▶ ◀—

THREE DAYS LATER, EMILIO FOUND a length of soaked rope behind one of the water barrels and went looking for the friars. He found the two of them kneeling in the hold, wedged one behind the other in the narrow walkway between two bins of fruit, their heads bowed in prayer. The boat was pitching from side to side and the ankle deep water in the hold washed from one side to the other, flowing up against the friars, around them and down with each toss of the vessel. The lemons and limes were shifting first to one side, then to the other, straining against the wooden slats that kept the fruit in check.

Water sloshed in Emilio's boots as he waded over to the friars. He didn't care if he interrupted a holy hour. "Listen, ya guys. Where's yer God? Three days in this tempest. Not even the cap'n knows where we are. Ya better pray. We're goin' down if this keeps up."

Then he felt a tinge of remorse. He was used to storms, though he had been in few as violent as this. These men were only on their second sea voyage.

"Yer holdin' up in this, ain't ya?" he asked more tenderly. "Ya all right, Father Anthony?" Emilio grabbed the shoulder of the friar closest to the ladder.

"Hey! Wake up!"

Anthony lifted his head and looked at Emilio. Emilio felt as if the priest could see his innards and, even worse, his sins. He thrust the rope at Anthony, knowing that the priest would look at the tether rather than at the sailor.

"Cap'n told me ta give ya this. He's afraid these bins is gonna bust open. An' if they do, ya won't be able to stay down here. Ya'll have ta be on deck. If that happens, Father, ya lash yourself ta the mast. Brother Philip, he's sturdy enough ta hang on. But you? Ship's heavin' too much, pitchin' worse. Yer red with fever. Cap'n's afraid ya'll wash overboard. Bad luck for us all then. Tie yourself ta the mast, ya hear?"

Anthony nodded. Just then, a shriek came out of the west, an ungodly scream of wind, and the ship rolled almost completely over. The lemons and limes heaved against the wooden slats and a horrible crack burst through the hold. The fruit to the left of the three men came pouring out upon them in an avalanche and bumped across the hold. Suddenly, the water was a soup of green and yellow fruit. The three men pushed toward the ladder. As Emilio lost his footing, two pairs of wet wool-covered arms reached out for him and heaved him erect.

"Thank ya, friars," he managed to sputter as he spat out the water he had gulped.

As the men reached the deck, Emilio grabbed Anthony and pulled him toward the central mast. The ship pitched again and threw the priest against the upright wooden log. Emilio snatched the rope from the friar's hands and swiftly began to lash him fast.

"Now don't ya preach ta me," he said as Anthony began to speak. "Ya didn't git to preach to the Saracens, so don't preach ta me." Then he felt a wince of pity at the man's lost dreams and changed his mind. "Well, go ahead, preach. Ya didn't see an infidel in Morocco, did ya, but I'm pretty close ta one in belief anyhow. I heard ya was sick with fever when ya landed in Ceuta 'bout the start of the year. Ya'd have got yer wish ta die there if it weren't for yer friend. Him runnin' around, gittin' ya eats, bathin' yer fiery body, that's what kept ya alive."

"And his prayers," Anthony said. "He prayed, too."

"Yes, Father, and his prayers, too. If ya say so. I seen these fevers. Seen lots a sailors die from 'em. Sickness hits the weak ones. Why'd ya think ya was strong enough ta stand the desert? But then, maybe ya didn't care if ya snuffed out like a candle."

Emilio cinched the knot. Twice.

"Have you ever loved anyone enough to die for them?" Anthony asked.

"What kind of stupid question is that? I live fer me self, Father. If I die, it'll be fer me."

The ship lurched again and a swell of water washed up over the prow, burying the deck.

"Yer fast now, Father. You'll not roll. I'll be back with a tarp for ya if the sea don't git me first. Cap'n wants ya to have it. Course I don't know what good it'll do. Ya already look like a drowned rat."

"A drowned rat must look more handsome than I do." Those black eyes were twinkling. "Or than you do. Or Brother Philip."

Emilio chuckled. "We're drownin' 'n yer jokin'. Yer all right, Father Anthony. Say yer prayers. Prayers is all we got left."

➤ ◆

THE NEXT DAWN, just as the blackness of night was reluctantly yielding to the thick grayness of day, a sickening scrape ripped through the wind and the boat shuddered like a horse in its death agony. Emilio had felt this once before on a vessel bound for France. The ship had run aground. They were going down. He had half a mind to jump and save himself, but he couldn't leave the friars.

Pulling his knife from his belt, he worked his way up the tipped deck to where Philip was frantically trying to untie the priest's ropes.

"Ya need a knife, boy," he said, pushing the young friar aside. "Father, I'd not leave ya here. I'll have ya loose quick now." One of Emilio's gnarled hands grabbed the swollen cord, thick as a sausage, while the other worked the knife. The blue veins on his wrists protruded and throbbed like worms.

"We two will stay with ya, won't we, Brother Philip? Ship's goin' down. We struck something. Damn night. Sorry. Didn't mean to offend yer sensibilities. Cap'n couldn't see a thing. Couldn't avoid the reef if he had. Sails no damn good in this wind."

The rope split. "Yer loose, Father." Emilio pulled the cord away from the woolen habit. It had stuck fast to the waist. "When we go down, grab yerself a plank, Okay? You'll wash in an' maybe yer God'll keep ya from grinding ta pulp on the reef."

The ship was tilting more dangerously now but no longer pitching so violently. The wind seemed quieter, as if the storm were breaking up.

"Uh, Father, if ya don't mind. Could ya, like—uh, bless me, Father. I been baptized. My mother saw ta that. Ain't done nothing with my faith since then. But bless me now. I don't want ta die without a blessin'."

The ship shuddered and sighed. A rush of water flowed up over the dipping prow. "Quick," Emilio commanded. "She's shiftin'. What do I say?"

"In the name of the Father, and of the Son, and of the Holy Spirit."

Emilio repeated hurriedly. "In the name of the Father...."

—▶ ◀—

EMILIO HAD WASHED IN WITH THE TIDE. So had the lemons, the limes, the captain, the crew, and the friars. He and Philip had found Anthony lying face down in the sand at the edge of the tide. They dragged him out of the water's reach to an outcropping of granite where Emilio had left them while he went in search of civilization. After walking inland about a mile, he found a village where people who spoke a strange dialect clustered about him. They told him that he was in Sicily. He told them about the wreck and about the two friars, one of them ill. Was there any place around here that they could stay?

The crowd of men, women, and children all nodded and spoke in a jumble. He was able to comprehend that a few miles up the beach in the town of Messina was a community of Friars Minor. A lanky, black haired farmer with a cart volunteered to take the friars there.

Anthony and Philip were still sitting in the shelter of the rock when Emilio and the farmer arrived.

"Naw, I ain't goin' with ya," Emilio said as he hoisted Anthony into the straw. "Cap'n wants me ta stay here with the ship. See if we can salvage anythin' before we outfit again for Portugal."

Then he had a thought. It had been nagging at him ever since the storm started, really. But he had been able to crush the idea pretty well until the ship broke up. Then he'd made that promise.

"Look, Father Anthony, before ya go, would ya hear me confession? I mean, I kinda promised God I'd go when I was out there fightin' the sea. Promised I'd go if I lived, that is. Don't like ta break promises, I don't. I mean, any man who's blown 1,500 miles off course and survives the deep should keep his promises, don't ya think? Do ya mind, Father? Ya folks with the cart can wait 'til I'm done, can't ya?"

The farmer and Philip nodded and considerately walked off along the beach, leaving Anthony sitting in the straw and Emilio leaning awkwardly on the cart.

"Climb up," Anthony said with a smile.

Emilio had sat in lots of places, places he knew a priest would never go. None of those bars or brothels had embarrassed him like being in this cart did. But he climbed in obediently and attempted to kneel before the priest.

"Sitting is fine," Anthony said.

So Emilio sat. "How da I begin, Father? I got probably twenty-eight years ta talk about."

➤ ━

EMILIO HAD NEVER FELT SO LIGHT or pure in all his life as he felt after that confession. He thought he could skip across the sky as the white clouds in the wake of the storm were now doing.

The cart was ready to leave. The two friars sat in the straw and the farmer took up the reins. "Look, Father, ya take care," Emilio said. And he meant it. "Yer fever's still warm. Git better now. I don't know much about prayin', but I'll put in a word fer ya. Thanks fer hearin' my confession. My mother, rest 'er soul, mustta prayed from heaven fer this day. God knows, she prayed enough fer me while she walked this earth.

"God bless ya two friars," he called after the bumping cart. "God knows this ain't Portugal, but ya'll be okay here. Pray fer me."

He hadn't had to ask. Anthony's hand was already tracing the sign of the cross in Emilio's direction as the cart rounded a dune and disappeared from sight.

❧ 4 ❧

## *Brother Philip*

**Portiuncula, Assisi, Italy (1221)** ❧ Tall, eighteen-year-old Philip leaped across the grassy meadow and arched into the air. His palm solidly met a small ball and whacked it upward over the heads of his French teammates and across a crude net strung between two saplings. The ball sped downward on the other side of the net where a sturdy young friar raced toward the hurling object, slammed it with his palm, and sent it back across the net.

The ball plunged to the right of the net in Anthony's direction. Anthony took a running jump and slapped the ball just as it dipped toward the ground. His strike was solid but short. The ball flew over the net and dived earthward so close to the net that no friar on the opposing team could reach it before it bounced through the grass.

A cheer shot from the opposite side of the net, loudest of all from Philip. It rang across the meadow and through the glades where other friars were sitting, watching the game, or exchanging words with each other.

The winning teammates bounded together and began to pound each other's backs in hearty appreciation. Then, as one group, they hurried over to the losers and patted their backs, too.

"Good game."

"Luck."

"We prayed harder."

"Like fun."

"You got more Romans on the winning side and this is Roman territory. We French aren't used to the soil here."

"You Frenchmen taught us this game of the palm. You ought to know how to play it."

Gradually the banter ended. The French friar who had painstakingly knotted the net untied it from the saplings and, rolling it up, tucked it under his arm. Taking the ball he'd brought from France, he bid farewell to the other brothers. He'd be setting out for his new mission soon, this one in Toulouse. The friars wandered off in various directions to do what they pleased until the final Vespers of this chapter meeting.

Philip and Anthony, his thin face flushed red from exertion, meandered across the clearing, found a grassy knoll and sat down. Anthony lay back and stared up at the sky. Philip joined him.

"Do you ever miss home, Father Anthony?"

"Yes."

"I've been thinking a lot about Spain. About the girls in flamenco dresses at festival time in Castile. Is that wrong, Father?"

"I would say that is normal."

"I bet you never think about women."

Anthony chuckled. "Friars are not to bet. And if you did bet on that, you'd lose."

Philip sighed. The warm sun on his forehead felt like a soft maiden's palm. "Did any woman ever tempt you, Father?"

"Yes. Once."

"What did you do?"

"I sent her back to serve her mistress."

"So she was a servant girl. I used to like a girl once, too. She tended pigs. Sometimes I still think about her. Do you ever think about that servant girl, Father?

"Sometimes."

"What do you do when you have these thoughts?" Philip watched the clouds.

"I do what Father Francis told us to do. I use the discipline. Or run. Or plunge into an icy stream."

Philip sighed. "I've done that, too. It does work." He was silent for a while, then asked, "Do you ever miss your family, Father?"

"Yes."

"What do you do about that?"

"I've written to them."

Philip had never thought of that. His parents could not read, but the lord of their estate could. He would write.

Oh, what he could tell them! How could he make them understand what joy he felt at following Christ and at preaching about Him crucified? For Francis had taught all his friars how to preach.

"When you approach a town," Francis had instructed, "and see the church spire, kneel and pray." The prayer was to be Pope Innocent's prayer. He composed it in honor of the crusaders' victory over the pagans at Toledo in 1216, just before his untimely death. Philip could hear Francis intoning this cry of victory: "We adore You, O Christ and we bless You, because by Your holy cross, You have redeemed the world." Philip had intoned it many times himself.

Upon nearing the city gate, the friars were to chant aloud: "Fear and honor, praise and blessing, thanksgiving and adoration be given to the Lord God, Almighty One, Father, Son, and Holy Spirit, Creator of all things." Then the friars would call out: "Do penance! Bring forth fruits worthy of penance, for be sure that soon you will die. Give and it will be given to you. Forgive and you will be forgiven. If you do not forgive others their offenses against you, the Lord will not forgive you your sins against Him. Blessed are those who die penitent, for they will go to heaven. Alas for those who die impenitent for they will be children of Satan whose works they do and will go into eternal fire. Take care and refrain from all evil and persevere to the end in doing good."

The homily was fixed and straightforward, easy to remember. Philip had seen it convert a peasant here and there when he, a simple man, had recited it with fervor. Father Anthony had exhorted the people, too, in similar words spoken with deep conviction. But when Anthony spoke, Philip always felt a sense of uneasy longing, as if Anthony had within him so much more to speak and was holding back. Philip shook his head. Perhaps Anthony was not holding back. Perhaps he was simply not yet well enough to say more.

What good fortune that the storm had blown Anthony to Sicily! The two months of spring weather there had been beautiful and healthful, restoring most of the ill man's vigor. Anthony had even felt well enough to plant a few cypresses and citrons in the monastery garden. Then he had left after Easter by boat with Philip and the other friars who had come to the chapter meeting. Anthony's newly regained health had sustained him on the short boat trip. It also persisted throughout the rigorous weeks spent hiking nearly the entire length of the kingdom of Sicily into the duchy of Spoleto to attend this chapter meeting. It was Philip's first since joining the Order at age sixteen.

As they drew near Assisi, Philip felt that he was coming to a fair. Dusty friars clogged the roads. Knights and ladies rode by on horses decked with colorful ribbons and small, furled banners. The townfolk of Assisi had readied their homes for the influx of friars, but so many thousands had come that the houses had not enough room. So the friars went into the meadows and woods and constructed wattle huts in which to stay and reed mats on which to sleep. For a week Philip and Anthony and friars from across Europe had slept and prayed and feasted out in the open. And Philip had loved every minute of it.

Francis had called this meeting of his friars to draw together his splintering Order. All came to see the short, frail father of their Order who, even though he had resigned as minister, was still their beloved leader. After Francis had gone East to preach to the heathen, rumors of his martyrdom had filtered back to Europe. But Francis was alive. He had returned, weak and with his eyes diseased and burning, but his love of Christ as sturdy as ever.

The first Mass of the chapter was High Mass on Pentecost, May 23, celebrated by a bishop under the direction of Cardinal Rainero Capocci, who presided over the gathering. At the solemn Mass celebrated by the richly robed prelate, shabbily dressed Francis had proclaimed the Gospel and preached in his thin, high voice. "Little children, you have promised great things to God; still greater things are promised us by God if we keep to what we have promised Him and firmly expect what He has promised us."

Every day Francis preached to the friars and to those peasants, ladies, and lords who came to hear him, too. "The lust of this world is short, but the punishment which follows it is endless," he reminded. "The sufferings in this life are short, but the glories in the other life are endless!"

The chapter officially lasted a week, but here it was Tuesday and the friars were still present. They had to stay, Francis said, to finish the good food brought to them in such abundance by the people of the area. Philip had never seen anything like these meals with lords and ladies serving the poor friars all the delicacies of their castles. Francis, who was known for his fasting, ate heartily and bid the friars to feast as well.

And out of this joyous time of fraternity had come a mission to Germany and a new Rule of life that all the friars could follow. The original Rule, some had complained, had been too difficult. Brother Elias, the new minister general of the Order, would see that the men followed the Lord as the Rule dictated. The new period of novitiate, which had been instituted after Philip and Anthony had joined the Order, would insure that those who sought to become friars would know what they were about. And what they were about was total joy, selfless love, limitless patience, supreme compassion, and utter poverty in imitation of Christ Himself.

"Father Anthony." Philip caught himself in mid-sentence and glanced at the priest whose eyes were closed and mouth slightly open. Anthony was asleep.

Philip smiled. Perhaps he should nap, too. He would hear the call for Vespers. And soon he did.

Philip and Anthony brushed the dust from their habits and hurried toward the chapel for the evening prayer. When it and Compline were over, the sun was low in the sky and the breezes of the day had gone to sleep. The two friars strolled through the lengthening shadows to the wattle hut that they shared and lay down on their mats.

"Father Anthony, I am going to Città di Castello tomorrow. They say it is not far from here. I may never see you again. Where are you assigned?" Philip asked.

"I am not assigned, Brother Philip."

"Not assigned? But didn't you ask the provincials to take you? I saw you asking when I did."

"No one accepted me."

Philip stared at the figure curled up in the darkness. No one accepted Father Anthony? Why? Then he thought of how the rather average-sized, frail priest, still thin from his bout with fever, must have appeared to the provincials. Not capable of the rigors of the Order. They no doubt thought he would be a burden.

"Didn't you tell them you were a priest?"

"No one asked."

"What did you tell them?"

"I asked them to instruct me in spiritual discipline and I offered to clean the kitchen for them and do household work or beg."

Anthony's humility frustrated Philip. "You can't stay here with nowhere to go."

"Philip, I went to Morocco because I was certain that God wanted me there. I still feel that He did. Yet He resisted me all winter by striking me with that fever. Thus God foiled my desire to die for Him, the desire that I was certain was His will."

Philip groaned. Anthony had spoken to him several times about the confusion that he felt over his desire for martyrdom. If God had truly called Anthony to Morocco, then why did the Lord not allow him to preach there? If God gave Anthony the burning desire to die for Christ, then why was that desire not fulfilled?

Anthony gazed at Philip with eyes that seemed pained. "I don't understand, Philip. Did I misread what I thought the Holy Spirit wanted me to do? Was the desire to die for Christ from me and not from God? Please try to understand, Brother. I did not think that I wanted my own will then, but maybe I did. I know now that I only want God's will. I will wait here until God puts me where He wants me."

Philip fell asleep praying that God would find a place for Anthony.

The next day, many of the friars had left well before sunrise, following the prayers at Matins and Lauds. Philip was scheduled to leave at dawn with the band for Città di Castello. That would be immediately following the prayers at Prime. Between the two offices, he looked around anxiously for a provincial, any provincial, and found one, Father Gratian of Romagna.

"I have a friend, a priest who is not assigned," Philip told the square jawed, big eared priest.

"A priest? Who is he?"

"Father Anthony of Portugal."

Gratian squinted a moment in thought. "I know of no Father Anthony of Portugal."

"He has been a member of our Order less than a year. He had been ordained at Holy Cross monastery in Coimbra, under the Rule of St. Augustine."

Gratian ran his hands over his thick, black beard. "I may have use for him."

When Philip found Anthony, he was kneeling at prayer in the Portiuncula, the little church that Francis had repaired in the early days of his conversion. Philip knelt in the back of the chapel and prayed as well until the hour sounded for Prime. At the sound of the call for the office, he waited for Anthony and met him coming out of the chapel.

"I have found a provincial who may take you," Philip said. "Will you ask him?"

"If you wish," Anthony said.

As the friars gathered for prayer, Philip looked for Gratian and found him in the crowd. "There he is," Philip said, "the big man with the black beard. Go and ask him to take you."

Anthony smiled. "You still are taking good care of me, Brother."

"Go ask."

Nodding, Anthony approached Gratian. "I am Brother Anthony," Philip heard him say. "I am not assigned. Will you accept me in your province and assign me to a hermitage where I may learn spiritual discipline?"

Gratian glanced at Philip, then at Anthony. "So you are a priest?"

"Yes," Anthony said.

"If Minister General Brother Elias approves, you are welcome in my province. I have there a small hermitage, Monte Paolo, in the Apennines, about four miles from Forli. You will learn spiritual discipline there. The six brothers there have been going to Forli or Cesna for Mass and the sacraments. They have repeatedly asked me for a priest, but I have had none to send them. Are you willing to go there and celebrate Mass for the brothers?"

"I am willing to do whatever you tell me, Father."

"Good. Then I shall ask Brother Elias at once. I am sure that he will approve."

Following Prime, Philip looked about for the group bound for Città di Castello. He spied them off to the right of the assembling friars.

"Good-bye, Father Anthony," Philip said. The two men hugged each other warmly, Philip's chin resting lightly on Anthony's shaved scalp.

"The Lord give you peace," Anthony said. His voice was thick with sorrow. "May Christ bless you, Brother, for all you have done for me."

Philip tightened his embrace on the man whose life he had saved. "You are my brother," he said, his voice trembling. Then, in a firmer tone, he returned the greeting that Francis had taught his friars. "The Lord give you peace."

## ❧ 5 ❧

## *Superior*

**Monte Paolo Monastery, Between Arezzo and Forli, Italy (1222)** ❧
"Brother superior? You called for me?"

The deep whispered voice at the door sounded like a purr. The big boned superior of Monte Paolo was wedged into a tiny wooden chair at his desk in the cramped cell. He was reading for the third time Anthony's commentary on the Psalms. If he had not been so engrossed by the words before him, he would have realized how cramped his thick muscles had become.

As a squire, the superior had learned to read. As a knight, he had enjoyed stretching out in his large chair by the fireplace to study by candlelight his single, precious text of Scripture. Since becoming a friar and retiring here to Tuscany, to these mountains between Arezzo and Forli, he had nothing to read at all. This poor, out of the way hermitage owned not a single manuscript. Then Father Anthony had arrived and requested writing materials. The superior had given him permission to beg for them provided that the young priest submit his work to the superior's scrutiny. He would have preferred to read the commentary outdoors where he could prop his bulky back against a huge oak, but the mountain breezes were tricky. The superior feared that a gust would catch one of the carefully penned pages and snatch it forever from him.

So he remained in his cell. He stretched against the wooden chair and realized with a start that his neck and rib cage felt stiff.

The superior pushed back his chair too abruptly, catching it swiftly as it nearly toppled to the floor. He arched his back and flung his arms wide. They nearly touched the two walls of his cell.

Then he sighed. The friar at the door had not moved. "Come in, Father Anthony," the superior bellowed. "I have been reading your work."

The friar walked softly into the cell and stood before the superior. He looked tiny compared to the huge man next to him. "They are only my thoughts, Brother superior. I don't know why you asked to see them."

"Father, this is the first material I have been able to read since joining the Order."

"My words are better than nothing. Correct?"

"Better than much that I have read. You have tremendous insight. I had never applied to myself Psalm 127, verse 3: 'Your children around your table like new olive plants.' I had thought that verse was for families. Right here you have written," the superior said, picking up the page and reading, "'Your children, dear Jesus, are Christians whom You have given birth to in the labor pains of Your passion.' And here," the superior said, flipping a few pages, "you wrote, 'These children are indeed Your children since You have redeemed them with Your own Blood, O Lord. Would that they really be Yours and not their own, that is, given up to their own flesh.'" He put the page back onto the table and smiled at the priest. "I do not think that I will ever again see an olive shoot without thinking of myself as a child of God."

"Did you call me here to discuss my work?"

Glancing down at Anthony's pages, the superior stretched again. "You don't mind a walk along the mountain, do you?"

Anthony laughed. "Do I mind going to God's garden?"

"So that is what you call these glades," the superior said as he led the way out into the sunlight and in the direction of Anthony's cell. He said no more until the two men had moved beyond the small cluster of cells, past the cleared ground and cultivated garden plots where two brothers, bent over their hoeing, paused a moment to nod at the pair. When the two arrived in the thick of the forest where the sound of the hoes could no longer be heard, the superior spoke again.

"Are you happy here, Father Anthony?"

Anthony stopped short, threw up his arms as if to embrace the wood and turned about slowly, his hands and face upraised to the branches above him. "Are the sparrows happy here?" he said, pointing to a few who winged above from branch to branch. He paused, then knelt and scratched apart the pine needles at his feet. When he stood, an earthworm crusted with dirt squirmed in his palm. "Are these happy here, Brother?" He bent to drop the worm back onto the soil, then sprinkled dirt and dry needles over it again. "All creatures are happy in the Creator's garden including me."

"The cell that you have been using? It suits you?"

Again the smile. "Brother Artisan was very kind to let me use it. For me, he removed the tools he stored there so I could replace them with myself, this hunk of obstinate metal and unbendable wood."

"And is the metal becoming malleable and the wood pliable?"

"I would hope so."

"May I see your cell?"

Anthony led the superior to the narrow cave not far off.

Someone, perhaps another hermit, had hewn with a great deal of difficulty, no doubt, the cramped cavern from a huge rock thrusting out of the mountainside. Near the opening stood a rough looking table and rustic stool. "You made those, Father?" the superior asked.

"Brother Artisan let me use his tools."

The superior laughed. "Brother Artisan, is it? That is your name for him? A good name, too."

In the rear of the cell lay a mound of straw with a stone for a pillow. Against the wall, at the head of the pillow, leaned a scourge of tufted marsh plants. Stream rushes. Pliant. Sturdy. When used to lash one's flesh as a discipline or as a deterrent to temptation, they stung like slender whips.

The superior saw all these things in a glance and knew what they meant. His smile disappeared. He turned and looked directly at the priest. "The brothers tell me that you take no bread or water with you to this cell and sometimes, when the bell rings for the evening meal, you are so weak that they must support you as you walk."

Anthony returned the gaze. "I have never missed a meal."

"Nor a prayer either. You are faithful and prompt." The superior looked again at the rushes. They were green, yet shredding, a sure sign of frequent use. "I want you to relax the discipline. And I want you to eat more, if not in this cell, then at table." The superior squeezed Anthony's right arm through the sleeve of his habit.

"You are bones, Father Anthony. You came to us barely recovered from illness."

"You were good to take me. I am better now."

"Barely recovered from illness," the superior repeated as he lightly shook the thin arm. "You are no good to us dead, Father. A dead priest cannot celebrate Mass. Less discipline. More food."

Anthony's shoulders, always so regally carried, fell just a bit. "Yes, Brother Superior."

"Is not obedience better than sacrifice to God?"

"Obedience purifies the soul. First Peter, Brother Superior. Less discipline. More food."

The superior released his arm and turned away from the cell. He began walking again into the forest. "The kitchen has been spotless, Father. Every pot and pan is scrubbed and in place. You do well with this job you asked for."

"Thank you."

"You feel better about eating now that you are a servant?"

Anthony grinned.

"You were not born a kitchen drudge," the superior said, turning back toward the hermitage.

"What makes you say so?"

"The carriage of your back. Your steady gaze. Your confident and clear manner of speech. These are part of you. From infancy, serfs learn to act as serfs, nobles as nobles. You bow, Father, and avert your eyes as a serf might do, but you do these consciously. These mannerisms are not part of you, Father Anthony, just as they are not part of me."

"I am sorry that they are not."

"Never be sorry for what God has created in you."

"Thank you for that. 'For we are God's creation. What we shall later be has yet to come to light.'"

The two walked in silence, listening to the birds twittering and the breeze soughing through the pines. Soon the hoes sounded in the woods. "I am glad Father Gratian sent you to us to celebrate Mass," the superior confessed.

"So am I."

"And I am glad that you allowed me to read your commentary. It has opened my eyes as nothing I have ever read before, except perhaps Augustine."

The superior glanced sidelong at the priest to see how he would receive his compliment. A bit of color rose to his cheeks as Anthony said, "I am no St. Augustine, Brother Superior."

"If only Father Francis could see this. Perhaps he would change his mind about allowing the friars to be educated. Father Francis wants us to preach the truth. You have explained our Lord's teaching well."

"It is easy to do so, Brother. The Gospel is the kiss of God."

The superior nodded. The kiss of God. Only Father Anthony would think of a term like that. And so true and beautiful a phrase, too.

The sound of the hoes was much nearer, just beyond the next thicket when the superior stepped over a huge toppled tree trunk and sat down. Anthony sat next to him.

"Father Anthony, in Ember Week there will be an ordination at Forli. Some of our brothers and some of the Friars Preachers will receive Holy Orders. I am requested to go and would like you to be my traveling companion."

"I would like that, Brother Superior."

Brother Superior clasped Anthony's two long hands in his own huge paws and shook them heartily.

"Then we have a pact. To Forli."

"To Forli."

## ✑ 6 ✒

### *Father Gratian*

**Convent of the Friars Minor, Forli, Italy (March 19, 1222)** ✒ Gratian
always enjoyed an ordination because the ceremony meant more
priests for his Order.

That morning, the convent of the Friars Minor at Forli seemed
to Gratian to be a bit shabby for the Friars Preachers who had been
ordained there with the followers of Francis. However, the tasty
meal that they were now enjoying compensated for the poverty of
the surroundings. The visiting friars would excuse the simple, tiny
portions; after all, this was the season of Lent. But what had been
prepared had been prepared well.

Gratian was just now relishing pan-cooked spring greens seasoned with olive oil and garlic. As a yeoman, he had observed with
what delicacy the noble lord whom Gratian once had served ate his
meals. In attending to him, Gratian had picked up some of the re-
fined eating habits of the nobility. He hoped he had not forgotten
them by becoming a follower of Francis. Right now he was sharing
his table with Bishop Albert. He did not want any of his table man-
ners to appear coarse to the prelate.

As the men chattered and filled their stomachs on roasted nuts,
Gratian swallowed his last delicious mouthful and pushed away
from the table. The meal was ending and the men were growing
louder. Now seemed the best time for the dinner speech. One of
the Preaching Friars who belonged to the Order founded by the
forceful Dominic of Guzman had been assigned to prepare the message. Gratian would find out who was to speak and quiet the men.

Gratian located the provincial of the Friars Preachers, a stern looking gentleman with a pointed white goatee.

"Father, who has been appointed to preach at this time?" Gratian asked. "I will introduce him now."

The black robed friar opened his hands wide. "No one asked us to provide a speaker. We assumed that, since the ordination was at a convent of the Friars Minor, you were providing the preacher."

Gratian scowled and then immediately tried to smile. He knew his tactic was fruitless. He had never been able to make his face move into contortions that his emotions warred against.

"We are not prepared, Father," Gratian said in desperation. "Would you care to speak?"

"I am only good at preaching when I am prepared," the father said, his beard bobbing up and down with his words. "Why not ask some of my friars? Perhaps one will agree."

With a glimmer of hope, Gratian moved along the table, sending the question before him. Would one of the followers of Dominic be willing to preach? They all had the same excuse. No one was prepared.

As Gratian moved back toward his own brothers, Bishop Albert waved him in his direction. Gratian came reluctantly to the bishop. "Is something wrong?" the prelate asked. "By comparison to your face, a prune would look handsome."

Gratian could not hold back a grin. "Your Excellency, do not bother yourself about my problem."

"Come. Tell me what it is. We can't have your sourpuss ruining this delicious meal."

"Your Excellency, no one is prepared to speak."

"Aren't you provincial? Choose someone."

"We are all brothers here save a few."

"Preach yourself. You are a priest."

Gratian moaned. "I am not prepared."

Bishop Albert propped his chin upon his fist. "Do you not have one who will preach out of obedience?"

Gratian glanced around the room. His gaze fell on Anthony seated at the rear table, speaking softly to the superior of Monte Paolo who sat across the table from him. This was the thin, sickly looking young priest whom Gratian had sent to Monte Paolo last year. Since then, the friar's face had plumped out a bit. Monte Paolo has restored his health, Gratian thought. Then he remembered something else about that friar.

"Back there is a priest who once told me that he would do whatever I said," Gratian told Bishop Albert.

"Call him up here," the bishop ordered.

As Anthony knelt before the bishop, Gratian looked with dismay at the priest's rough, chapped hands, clasped before his chest. Obviously, the superior of Monte Paolo had made him a kitchen drudge.

*I have brought a man who washes pots and sweeps floors to the bishop as a speaker,* Gratian thought.

"Can you preach?" the bishop asked Anthony.

"Yes, Your Excellency."

"Then I order you, under obedience, to give a toast."

"But, Your Excellency..."

"Under obedience."

"Yes, Your Excellency."

"You are to take as your text, 'Christ became obedient unto death, even to death on a cross.'"

"Yes, Your Excellency."

"And speak whatever the Holy Spirit may give you. I bless you now in the name of the Father and of the Son, and of the Holy Spirit." The bishop made the sign of the cross over Anthony who blessed himself with the words. Then Bishop Albert lightly touched the top of Anthony's head. When he removed his hand, Anthony looked up at the prelate who said, "You may begin."

Gratian prayed rapidly as the rather average-looking friar made his way to the front of the table, all eyes on him. *Holy Spirit, give him the words.*

Anthony stood still, his head slightly bowed but his back straight, as a murmur sifted through the room and died. The men shifted in their seats and then the sounds of creaking faded. Anthony lifted his head and looked slightly upward, as if to Someone he alone could see.

"'Christ became obedient unto death,'" he spoke. His voice seemed to quiver before gaining strength, "'even unto death on a cross.'" His gaze spanned the men before him. "In the name of the Father and of the Son and of the Holy Spirit."

The friars crossed themselves.

Anthony's voice came again, louder. "Christ." A pause. "Became." Pause. "Obedient." Pause. "These words find their first expression early in Scripture in Luke, chapter 2, verse 51. After Mary and Joseph found Jesus in the temple, 'He went down with them and came to Nazareth and was obedient to them.' He came to Nazareth, that garden of humility and 'He was obedient to them.'"

Anthony paused and gazed from one attentive face to the next. Suddenly he called out, "Let all boasting cease, let all impudence disappear in the face of these words: 'He was obedient to them.' Who was He, Who was obedient? He Who has created everything from nothing."

Anthony raised his eyes and stretched out his arms to heaven as he spoke. "He 'Who' as Isaiah says, 'has cupped in His hand the waters of the sea and marked off the heavens with a span; Who has held in a measure the dust of the earth, weighed the mountains in scales and the hills in a balance.'

"Who, as Job says, 'shakes the earth out of its place, and the pillars beneath it tremble; Who commands the sun, and it rises not, Who seals up the stars; Who alone stretches out the heavens and treads upon the crests of the sea; Who made the Bear and the Orion, the Pleiades and the Constellations of the south; Who does great things past finding out, marvelous things beyond reckoning.'"

Anthony lowered his arms and gazed again at the friars. "He Who does all these things 'was obedient to them,' Whom did He obey? A carpenter." He held out his left hand. "And a poor, humble virgin." He extended his right hand. "He Who is the Beginning and the End, the Ruler of angels, made Himself obedient to human creatures. The Creator of the heavens obeys a carpenter, the God of eternal glory listens to a poor virgin. Has anyone ever witnessed anything comparable to this? Has any ear heard anything like this?"

Anthony drew his hands to his chest, placing them over his heart. "And we would hear even more profound wonders, for He, the Christ, the Creator, became obedient, not only to Mary and Joseph who nurtured His life but to death, death on a cross."

And so he spoke. Gratian lost all track of time. He had heard many friars preach in the simple, straightforward way that Francis had taught. Many had Anthony's conviction. Some had his grace. But no one else he had ever heard possessed such depth of knowledge or breadth of spirituality. Anthony was opening up the Scriptures, shining on the word "obedience" a radiance that could only come from God Himself.

"And thus the Son, obedient to His Father's bidding, ran to meet death, death on a cross." Anthony stretched his arms at his sides. "Therefore, 'He stood with His hands outstretched' on the cross 'between the living and the dead.' He was stretched between two thieves, one of whom was saved and the other condemned; He stood between those who were being kept in prison in the netherworld and those who were living in the miseries of this world's exile. All of these the Son delivered from the blaze of diabolic persecution when He offered Himself to the Father in the sweet fragrance of sacrifice."

Gratian felt himself to be a witness to something wonderful, something unfolding and rising like the wings of the Spirit filling the room.

"In his arms outstretched on the cross, Christ gathers us." Anthony's arms reached to encircle, as it were, the friars and to lift them to his chest. "He lifts us to the bosom of His mercy as a mother takes her child. He nourishes us with His Blood as if it were milk. And He has carried us in His arms extended on the cross. Therefore, rejoice because Christ has died for you."

Anthony's voice rose as he called out, "To the ends of the earth, O preachers, proclaim this word of joy. Proclaim it not only to the just who are in the Church's midst, but to the outer bounds of the Church, outside the precepts of the Lord within which we must live. Let the world hear the word of joy so that all people might obtain the full joy which has no bounds. For Christ became obedient unto death for us, thereby bringing us to eternal life. Let us become obedient unto Him and proclaim to all that He, our obedient and merciful Savior, is to be praised. He is the beginning and the end, wonderful, ineffable for all ages. Amen. Alleluia!"

On the very edge of Gratian's consciousness, he watched Anthony return to his bench and sit. No one else stirred. After a lengthy silence, a murmur broke across the room. Gratian could feel excitement stirring his soul.

The bishop was smiling at him. "An excellent choice, Father Gratian. He must be a great asset to your province."

Gratian grinned. He pushed out of his bench and ordered his legs to walk, not sprint to where Anthony was surrounded by a cluster of congratulating friars. He drew aside the superior of Monte Paolo who was sitting quietly, staring at Anthony and the friars around him.

"You have kept him to yourself for nine months," Gratian said eagerly. "Now he belongs to our entire province. He must go throughout the Romagna to preach."

"Father Gratian, he never preached for us. We thought him incapable and never asked."

"I will send a message to Minister General Brother Elias this very night," Gratian continued. "Rimini is rife with heretics. First Father Anthony shall make his way there, preaching as he goes."

# PART TWO

# Mission to Italy

$\mathcal{A}7\mathcal{D}$

*Benedetto*

**Shore of the Marecchia River, Rimini, Italy (1222)** ⌒ Benedetto was squatting along the shore of the Marecchia River. His toes dug into the cool wet sand. His skinny hands swiftly plucked fish from the netted mass directly in front of him. In the near distance where the Marecchia met the Adriatic Sea, the dull roar and crash of the tide broke on the beach. To avoid being blinded by flinging sand, Benedetto had turned his back to the brisk sea breeze that now whipped his thick, black hair around his face.

Even though the eastern sky was just beginning to turn pink, Benedetto could see clearly enough to sort the saleable from the useless fish and drop them into the proper tubs. He had been fishing for fifteen years and probably could have sorted the fish by touch.

Right now he was not even thinking of fish. Perhaps the last time he had been truly conscious of the fish was when he was twelve, seven years after he'd begun working the nets with his father. When he was twelve, he began to think of girls. Then, his thoughts had been deliciously new and strange and, as he grew older, forbidden. But he had tried to censor those lewd ideas, for God would disapprove.

When he was seventeen, his thoughts had turned to fifteen-year-old Ginevra. She was the one his father had chosen for him, the daughter of a fishing acquaintance from Pesaro. Benedetto had seen others more beautiful than Ginevra, for her nose was a bit too big for her slender face, but he noted in her an inner loveliness.

Ginevra loved the good God and the Church as he did, an unusual attribute in this area.

Today, as he sorted the fish, he was thinking of Ginevra, big with their third child. Would Ginevra be calling the midwife even now? Would he return home to a third son? His first two boys, as custom dictated, had been named after his and Ginevra's fathers. A third son would bear Benedetto's name. Benedetto's heart swelled at the thought.

But when the child did come, he would be unable to share his joy with the men who fished the sea with him. Benedetto glumly thought of Giuseppe and Rodrigo whose boat flanked him on the right, and Isidoro who was sorting his fish to the left. All three were *Cathari,* believers in that sect that was destroying the Church not only in the Empire but also all over the world. The *Cathari,* whose name meant "the pure," were called Albigensians in southern France where they were especially strong in the city of Albi. They went by other names in far distant lands like Germany and a place at the end of the sea called England.

The *Cathari* saw all sexual union as sinful because, they said, all sexual appetite was of the devil. The good God was pure spirit and the Creator of everything spiritual and good. The evil god had created the visible world and every living thing in it including human bodies. In human bodies, Satan imprisoned apostate spiritual beings who once rebelled against the good God. These souls had to do penance and free themselves of all flesh if they were to enter heaven. To his fishing buddies, Benedetto was in league with Satan because he fathered children in whom spiritual beings were held.

Not that Giuseppe and Rodrigo lived lives of purity. Unlike the *perfecti* in their sect, whom the rogues called the "Good Men" or, even more blasphemously, "Good Christians," the two scoundrels had not yet received the *consolamentum,* the secret rite of baptism into the *Cathari.* Thus the men were free to live loose and licentious lives, for the sacrament, they claimed, would purge them of all sin. Once they took the *consolamentum,* which they planned to do on their deathbeds, they were assured entrance into heaven. Should they die too swiftly, their souls would be reborn in the bodies of other humans until they would do sufficient penance and become *perfecti.* The souls of Benedetto and Ginevra, who believed in the

Roman Church, were condemned to endless cycles of rebirth and death until they, too, embraced the *Catharist* truth.

Benedetto had no patience or love for Giuseppe and Rodrigo. To him, they were *Cathari* because, by so believing, they could sin without the guilt they would have to face were they Roman Catholics. At night, the men's raw, drunken laughter would echo through the Rimini streets as they made their way to the town brothel. Their beastly existence held no lure for Benedetto.

Isidoro was different. In the red bearded teen's presence, Benedetto felt sinful and confused. Isidoro embraced his faith as fully as if he were a "Good Man" himself. He killed no birds or four-footed animals for, he said, that was sinful. He ate no meat, not even the fish he caught for a living. He drank no wine, courted no woman. Three times a week he fasted on bread and water. Having received the first part of the *consolamentum*, Isidoro was now worthy to pray the "Our Father" several times daily. Once a month, he attended a service presided over by the "Good Men."

Isidoro's holy life mocked Benedetto who sometimes felt too exhausted to attend Sunday Mass, even though he always went, and who often resented fast days and the hunger pains that accompanied them. Would God take him to heaven despite his faults? The idea of receiving the *consolamentum* and being assured of eternal reward was appealing. Increasingly, he began to wonder if he were holding onto his Roman faith only because he had been raised in it.

Isidoro pitied Benedetto, so he often tried to convert him. Isidoro's words echoed those of the black robed *Catharist* preachers whom Benedetto had frequently heard sermonizing in Rimini's squares. The *perfecti* put their faith in the good God, they said, and not in the false sacraments of the Roman Church. They praised poverty, chastity, and charity, and they practiced all three virtues. They owned nothing, lived on alms, and fasted, and prayed much. They refused sexual relations of any kind and were quick to offer solace, help, and encouragement to those in need. Truly, they were selfless, good men.

The *Cathari* declared that true Christians must trust the true church which they claimed to represent. The Roman Church, they said, had gone astray.

"Look at Canon Alonzo," Isidoro said more than once. "Do you think he is following Christ?"

Benedetto had to admit that Canon Alonzo purchased sweets with money collected for the poor. The house he occupied was far superior to Benedetto's. Benedetto also saw him working his way home from the local tavern.

"You see," Isidoro would say, "things the Church claims are true are not. You say that you go to Mass for the Eucharist, but would the holy Christ associate His Body with such earthly matter as bread and wine? Even if He did, would He come at the bidding of a sinful priest? Believers can pray anywhere. A barnyard is as good as church for calling upon God. And, where Canon Alonzo is concerned, maybe better."

Isidoro made Benedetto think. Sometimes he felt as stupid as the fish that lay exhausted at his feet. He tossed a plump fish into one basket to save and sell, and a tangle of seaweed into another to discard. Which basket was he in, God's or Satan's? How about Isidoro and the "Good Men?" Whose basket claimed them?

"Hey, Benedetto! Here comes your new priest!" shouted a deep, raspy voice from the next craft.

The call of squat, muscular Giuseppe punctuated the soothing lap of the river's waves against the smooth hull of Benedetto's boat. Benedetto strained his eyes to stare down the beach.

Far away, just emerging from the spot where night and dawn merge in a man's vision, was the silhouette of a man who walked with the straight carriage and purposeful gait of a noble, but who was clothed in coarse beggar's wool. Friar Anthony.

"I hear that priest is even holier than you and Isidoro," Rodrigo called.

"Then maybe he is Christ returned," Giuseppe roared. Benedetto's ears burned at the blasphemy.

Anthony had arrived in town two weeks ago and had been preaching about the city as the *Cathari* did. Audiences would gather to listen. Benedetto himself had listened several times. Anthony was not from the Romagna—Benedetto could tell that—yet he spoke the language well. Even more than that, he spoke of God as forcefully as the *Catharist* preachers. Benedetto had never before heard any priest speak like that.

On Sunday, Benedetto, Ginevra, and the children had gone to Mass at which Anthony presided with Canon Alonzo assisting. There Benedetto participated at Mass as never before. Although he did not fully understand the Latin that Anthony used, Benedetto knew that the words differed in pronunciation and perhaps in meaning, from those Canon Alonzo spoke.

Anthony preached. Benedetto had never heard anyone preach at Mass. He had learned his faith from his parents, from the paintings on the walls of the church, and from the prayers the Apostles Creed and the Our Father that Canon Alonzo had everyone recite. But until Anthony had spoken, Benedetto had not really thought about the love of Christ. Once at Mass Friar Anthony had said that Jesus's disciples were fishermen. As Benedetto continued to sort the fish, he wondered if Jesus could call someone as sinful as himself to follow the Lord. Now Benedetto's gaze was following Anthony as the friar made his way down the beach. Anthony was pausing at each boat, taking time to speak to each man. Benedetto suddenly reddened over his uncultured manner, his clothes and body reeking of fish, his hands covered with slime. He wanted to run and hide, but his fingers kept up their mechanical task of sorting the fish.

Now Anthony was standing beside Isidoro's boat. The two men were speaking so softly that Benedetto could not hear. Then Anthony nodded and moved down the beach toward Benedetto.

"I am Brother Anthony," he said with a smile and a slight bow toward Benedetto.

Benedetto did not know what to do with his hands. They seemed unable to leave the fish.

"I know, Father. I have heard you speak."

"Then you know how proud you should be of your occupation. Jesus chose men who fished to tell the world about Him. He made one of them the head of the Church."

Benedetto blushed.

"What is your name, my son?"

"Benedetto, Father."

Anthony smiled. "'Blessed' is the meaning of Benedetto. A good name for you, too. God has blessed you with a sturdy back and a good wife and family. Soon to be increased."

Benedetto grinned. "How did you know, Father?"

Anthony laughed gently. "My eyes work as well as yours, Benedetto. I saw you and your wife standing in church on Sunday. In so small a crowd, how could I miss you?"

"This is a poor town for preaching," Benedetto said bitterly. "They are all *Cathari* here." He glanced sidelong at Giuseppe and Rodrigo. "The true faith is almost gone."

Anthony shrugged. "Gone? You know, Benedetto, a fish symbolizes faith."

Benedetto squinted in confusion. "Faith?"

"Faith. Like a fish that is born, nourished, and lives in the deep waters of the sea, faith cannot be seen with the human eye. Like a fish, faith in God is born in the dark recesses of one's heart. It is sanctified by the invisible grace of the Holy Spirit by the waters of Baptism. Have you been baptized, Benedetto?"

"Yes, Father," Benedetto said with pride.

"Good. Then you have faith. But you must allow the invisible help of Divine Providence to nourish that faith lest it grow weak. For true faith, like a fish pounded by the sea's waves, is not destroyed by life's adversities. Ask God for this faith. Say, 'Give me the grace to live and die in the faith of the holy Apostles and of your holy Catholic Church.'"

Benedetto pursed his lips. Did this friar know that he had been questioning his faith? "There are many in this town who do not care about the holy Catholic Church, Father. Their reasons are sometimes convincing."

Anthony looked toward Isidoro. "I know."

"They are hopeless, Father."

"Hopeless? So it is as hopeless for the *Cathari* to return to true faith as it is for these fish before you to return to the sea?"

"They are snared," Benedetto shrugged, "just like these fish."

Anthony reached down at Benedetto's feet and picked up a squirming fish. "May I have this one?"

"Of course."

The priest held the fish firmly, walked down to the waves and waded into the river. Benedetto saw the water creeping up along his robe to his waist. Then he dropped his hands into the water and, when he lifted them up again, the fish was gone.

"Swim, fish!" the friar called out. "Swim to the sea, your source and sustainer of life!" Then he turned back toward the shore and his voice swept over Benedetto like a breaker on the beach. "We are all snared. But God gives up on no human being. Christ can set you free to seek the Source and Sustainer of your life. But first you must know that you are caught and helpless. Then you must trust the nail-pierced hands of the One Who can release you. In the world, all freedom is slavery. With God, all slavery is freedom. Do you wish to be snared by the world? Or do you wish to be free in Christ? Today I will be preaching here at the hour of Sext. Will you come?"

Benedetto would be here at Sext, mending his nets and rubbing down his boat. So would the other men. The friar would have a captive audience.

— • —

AT SEXT, THE SUN WAS HIGH OVERHEAD, but the wind blowing off the water moderated the heat of its rays. Benedetto was scraping the hull of his boat. He had sold his fish. He had visited Ginevra who assured him that today she would not give birth. He had told her about Father Anthony coming to the beach to speak. Ginevra had wanted to come, too. Benedetto scanned the small crowd that was gathering along the shore. Men. Women. Children of the town. He knew most of them. A smattering of people, about equally divided between Catholics and *Cathari*.

"Daddy!"

Benedetto broke into a grin as two pudgy arms from behind twisted about his neck. He stood up and swung around in a circle with four-year-old Alfredo clinging to him for dear life. Two more tiny arms grabbed his left leg. Benedetto swooped up Pascal and swung him into the air. Benedetto plopped Pascal into his boat and then peeled Alfredo from his neck and placed him beside his brother. He looked down the beach. Ginevra was trudging toward him, a basket weighing on her arm. Benedetto knew what it held. Bread and cheese, dried fish and wine. They would not be hungry while Father Anthony spoke.

— • —

"'YOUR CHILDREN AROUND YOUR TABLE, like new olive plants.'" Anthony's voice resonated like a loud trumpet as he repeated the text from Psalm 127, verse 3, the verse he had been discussing for the past hour. About fifteen yards from Benedetto's boat, the priest was standing on a rock that jutted above the beach, the small crowd spread out along the shore like the shells that dotted the coast. Ginevra was comfortable in the boat, the empty basket at her feet and Alfredo and Pascal dozing in her lap. Benedetto was knotting a net and listening while he worked. He was mildly surprised that the *Cathari* in the group had given the friar this much courteous attention.

"We can speak of three different kinds of tables," Anthony called out, his voice resounding easily above the slapping of the waves. "Each of the three tables offers its own proper nourishment. The first table is that of doctrine, of the teachings of the Church that Christ founded upon Himself. The second table is that of penance, the payment back to God for our wrongdoing against Him and against one another. The third table is that of the Eucharist where the faithful partake of the Body of our Lord and Christ at Mass."

Benedetto became aware of a murmur, a rustling, a shuffling. The sound of people ill at ease, shifting. He looked up from his nets. Isidoro's slow easing to a standing position in the hull of his boat caught Benedetto's eye.

"The first table is that of doctrine," Anthony continued. "'You have prepared a table for Me, against those who afflict Me,' the Psalmist said in Psalm 22, verse 5. The verse refers to Christ. Those who afflict Christ are heretics who choose what they will believe of the teachings of the Church. They are much like pampered children who choose their sweets from the plate held before them. God wishes us to have all good, not only part. Christ is truth and truth does not change, truth does not divide."

From behind Benedetto, Giuseppe rasped. "Hey, Rodrigo, we have heard enough, eh? This work can wait until tomorrow. Let us go home and have a nap."

Twin dull thuds of feet hitting sand told Benedetto that the men were leaving. The two companions were part of a momentum that was slithering through the crowd. Certainly the focus on doctrine, Eucharist, and penance, all three of which the *Cathari* denied, was causing the break up. Benedetto saw the people begin to move apart as bread slowly drifts into crumbs when thrown into water. Isidoro himself seemed transfixed between Anthony's stare and Benedetto's, as if he wanted to hurry off yet wished to stay.

"So I have said things you do not wish to hear," Anthony's voice rang out above the dispersing crowd. The friar lifted his eyes heavenward and paused for the briefest moment. Then he leaped off the rock and strode toward the river.

"Hear the word of God, you fish of the sea," he called out, facing the waves, "since heretics and infidels do not wish to listen to it."

Benedetto stared at the friar. The sun and the disappointment at which his words were received must have made the priest feverish.

"My brothers the fish, you are greatly indebted, in as much as you are able, to thank your Creator for having given you so noble an element to live in. At your pleasure you have both fresh water, and beyond it," Anthony stretched his arms toward the sea, "salt water. God has given you many shelters against storms and food by which you may live."

The friar was attacking the very foundation of *Catharist* belief. He was saying that the good God, the only God, and not Satan had created the physical world. This world embraced the sea and the fish in it; God's Holy Spirit resided in these lowly creatures of flesh.

Benedetto heard a surging that he recognized. His gaze flew automatically beyond the friar to the river. There a swarm of fish surfaced, their shiny heads emerging, their mouths open as if to feed. Up and down the river, as far as he could see, fish were surfacing. The smaller fish were closer to the shore and bigger, brawnier fish farther out in deeper water. They were all the way out to the mouth of the Marecchia where it merged with the Adriatic.

"God, your courteous and kind Creator, when He created you, commanded you to grow and multiply. He gave you His blessing. When the great flood swallowed up all the world and all other animals were destroyed, God preserved only you without injury or harm. He has almost given you wings so that you may roam wherever you please."

Benedetto heard another sound, this one from the shore. Here and there among the dispersing people were excited mumblings, tugging at departing friends, pointing to the water. Some scattered folk turned on their heels and ran in the direction of Rimini.

"To you, God gave the command of preserving Jonah who was tossed into the sea and, after three days, one of you cast him upon the shore safe and sound. One of you held in your mouth the tribute needed by our Lord Jesus Christ, which He, poor and lowly, could not pay had you not given Him the coin. You were the food of the everlasting King, Christ Jesus, before the resurrection and, again, after it by a strange mystery when our Risen Lord ate fish on the beach with His apostles. For all of these favors are you bound to praise and bless God Who has given you so many benefits."

Benedetto did not know where to look. To the beach on which the fickle crowd was beginning to surge toward the priest. To the water which was shimmering with rows of slender fish. To Isidoro who had turned in his boat and was staring at the river. Or to Anthony whose gaze swept the gentle waves from east to west as if he were exhorting reasonable creatures to the praise of God.

"Blessed be the eternal God, since fish of the water honor Him more than people who deny his doctrine. The unreasoning beasts more readily listen to God's word than faithless humanity."

Then Anthony turned ever so slowly back toward the gaping crowd on the beach. The curious came running from the direction of Rimini toward the friar.

"Even the beasts of the earth recognize the table of the Lord's doctrine. They believe Christ's teachings in their entirety for they recognize the holiness of the One Who created them and Who taught us. But only those made in God's image have been invited to God's second and third tables, those of penance and the Eucharist. For beasts, unable to sin, have no need of repentance. And beasts, unable to be saved, have no need of the Bread of Life."

Suddenly, Benedetto felt his boat shift. His worried glance caught Ginevra. Her falling to her knees had caused the craft's drift. Beside her, Alfredo and Pascal stared over the water. The dancing ribbon of fish was so close to shore, dangerously close, where gulls could have easily snatched them.

The gulls. Where were the gulls? With so many fish this close to the surface, the white predators should have been swooping into the river in massive, winged clouds, their raucous shrieks knifing the air. Where were the gulls?

"'The rest of your table shall be full of rich food,' God says in Job 36:16. The rich food of God's forgiveness comes when we cry out our sins to our Father and beg His mercy. And who among us has not sinned? Have we sinned with money, with lust, with pride, with possessions? Have we neglected our Father or our families? Have we turned from Christ, true God and true Man, to follow the heresies of mere men? Have we, like Pharisees, thought ourselves better than the rest of humanity? No sin can come into God's presence. 'All have sinned and fallen short of the glory of God.' Oh, what rich food we consume when we admit our sins and beg God's mercy. Then God feeds us with the grace of forgiveness until our souls are full."

As the priest continued to speak, people here and there began to kneel. Benedetto sank into the sand, his head in his hands. How quick he had been to see the sins of others while remaining blind to the darkness of pride and a judgmental spirit in his own soul! Didn't *Catharist* doctrines tantalize him? Yet Anthony had shown that God was in control on this very beach in the fish He had created. If fish knew and bowed to the Lord, why not Benedetto?

"We receive God's forgiveness. Then we are worthy to receive in abundance at the table of the Eucharist where 'you cannot be partakers of the table of the Lord and of the table of devils.' For God and demons are enemies and those who do not serve the One surely serve the other. At which table do you wish to be seated? The food served at the first table, the table of doctrine, is the word of life. The feast at the second table of penance is the food of groanings and tears. The meal at the third is the Body and Blood of Christ. Must you choose your table? No! God calls you to all three."

Benedetto stayed on his knees, his soul weeping softly as Anthony continued to speak. He dared not look up at the holy priest, for he felt that, if he did, the whole town would see the tears glistening on his cheeks.

"So come like children 'around the table,' seeing all that God has to offer, taking all that God wishes to give you. Come. Believe firmly. Approach reverently. Admit the unworthiness of such great grace given to you. Eat of the tables of God with humility. Oh, Christ, may we nourish ourselves at Your three-fold table so joyfully, humbly, and trustingly that we may merit to be nourished at Your eternal table in heaven. Amen."

As Anthony's words faded, soft sounds of weeping people and splashing fish mingled.

"My good people and my dear fish, thank you for listening with your hearts. Now return to your homes in peace."

The waters surged and gurgled. By the time Bendetto wiped his eyes and could see through their glaze, the river surface was covered with rapidly widening eddies where thousands of fish had dipped below the waves.

On the beach another surge rippled through the crowd. Open weeping. Scattered cries of "God have mercy." Anthony could not be seen through a cluster of people who thronged around him.

Benedetto turned to Ginevra who was still kneeling, staring at the mob around the priest. "Ginevra," he choked, "I must go to confession. Today."

Ginevra nodded. "I, too, Benedetto."

They waited. As the sun was dipping behind Rimini, they finally reached the father and confessed to him beside the Marecchia River. They would have had longer to wait, but Isidoro, who was in front of them, saw that Alfredo and Pascal were getting drowsy. He gave Benedetto and Ginevra his place in line.

$\mathcal{C}8\mathcal{D}$

*Bononillo*

**Saddle Shop, Rimini, Itlay (1222)** ◌ Bononillo's bulbous nose loved the smell of leather. In his saddle shop, he was stooped over a saddle, tacking the softest leather to the bows. Even to his weathered hands, which had worked on saddles for fifty years, properly tanned leather still felt softer than the skin of an infant. Bononillo liked to work with materials that he could see and touch. Wood that he could carve. Leather that he could coax into shape. And sometimes, for a duke or a lord, rich paints that he could delicately dab onto the pommel and cantle and create a work of beauty.

A shadow fell across the saddle and Bononillo looked up. Anthony stood in the doorway.

"Ah, my friend, what a beautiful job you do during this holiest of weeks," Anthony said. "God has given you an eye and a hand to do this work well."

Bononillo's sharp, black eyes looked up at the holy priest. "My hands are as strong—even stronger—than they were when I was twelve and opened this shop."

"Then I bet you thought you were in your prime. You thought you knew all there was to know about making saddles. And about life in general as well."

"How did you know that?"

"Because all youth are the same."

Bononillo nodded his nearly bald head. "You are a young man yourself. When you get old like me you will realize how little you know now."

"True. There is always so much more to know about God. This is a very great week to learn."

Bononillo pressed into the leather with his cloth, rubbing briskly. He had picked up the young friar's second hint about Holy Week. "You are hoping that I will confess this week and go to Eucharist on Easter, are you not?"

"Is that such a bad hope?"

"I have not been to confession and Eucharist in thirty years."

"It is not yet the hour of Terce. I have all day to listen."

Bononillo lifted the saddle to the morning sun. The buffed leather shone in the rays. "It is not sin that keeps me from confession, Father Anthony. You know that it is the Eucharist. We had this conversation several times since you came to Rimini. Your arguments are no more convincing than those of Canon Alonzo where the Eucharist is concerned. Canon Alonzo is a lax priest. Why would the holy Christ agree to rest in Canon Alonzo's hands, even in the form of bread and wine?"

Anthony groaned. "Canon Alonzo holds the office of priest. He has been ordained to consecrate bread and wine into the Body and Blood of Christ. His sins do not affect this function."

Bononillo scuffled through a pile of fresh rags that lay in a tub at his feet. "God allows scandal if He permits men like Canon Alonzo to consecrate His Body and then distribute it to others."

"May I come in?"

Bononillo shrugged.

Anthony sat on a wooden stool beside the saddler. "That ring on your finger, Bononillo, it's made of gold, isn't it?"

"Are you hoping I will donate it to the Church, Father?"

Anthony burst out laughing. "If you want to, Bononillo, I will sell it and give the money to the poor. But, no, I was not thinking of that. I was thinking of a story in the Passion of St. Sebastian. The story tells of a king who had a gold ring adorned with a precious stone, much like yours, which he liked very much. One day the precious ring fell into a sewer. The king was heartbroken. What would you do if you were the king, Bononillo?"

Bononillo was buffing the saddle. "Get someone to get it out, Father."

"And suppose no one would."

Bononillo rubbed the pommel. "I am not stupid, Father. I would go in myself and get it."

"And so the king did in my story. You will notice, Bononillo, that the sewer did not deter the king from seeking the ring. Why not?"

"Because the ring was valuable."

"Correct. And if your ring fell into just such a sewer, wouldn't you retrieve it? Wouldn't you wash it clean and treasure it?"

Bononillo turned the saddle over and gave the underside a hearty buff. "I told you, I am not stupid."

"So you are not, Bononillo. The ring is of the same value and luster whether or not it lies in refuse or encircles your finger, correct? In the same way, the office of a priest does not change even if the priest is defiled by sin. It is a permanent office, just as gold is a permanent metal. Defilement changes neither gold nor the priestly ability to consecrate the Eucharist."

Bononillo turned the saddle upright again. "Are you defending Canon Alonzo's lifestyle?"

Anthony rose so abruptly that the stool toppled. The friar stood it in place as he spoke. "You have heard me speak, Bononillo. You have heard me say more than once that those who abuse the inheritance of Christ by their immoral lives shall be cut off from the kingdom of God. They are like idols in the Church, fit only for hell. I do not defend immoral clergy. I defend the Eucharist."

Bononillo angrily threw the rag into the dust. "The Eucharist. The Eucharist. Suppose you are right about Canon Alonzo and his priestly office. But the Eucharist?" Bononillo thrust the saddle toward the friar. "You can see this. Feel it. Smell it. It is leather. You claim that the Eucharist is the Body and Blood of Christ. Yet I can see it, feel it, smell it. It is bread. Wine. I had eaten it myself for twenty years before I realized what foolishness it was to believe. Then I could receive the Eucharist no longer or I would be pretending to believe what is so obviously false."

Anthony took a deep breath. "Bononillo, I have told you before. Christ said, 'This is My Body. This is My Blood.' Do you not believe your Lord?"

Bononillo groaned. He picked up the rag and shook out the dust. "I want to believe, Father, but I simply cannot. I have spoken to my sons about this and to my grandsons who are now having sons. None of them can explain it to me. Canon Alonzo cannot explain it. The

*Cathari* say there is no sacrament. I don't believe much of what else they say, but they are right about the Eucharist. I know you are a holy man, Father, but you are mistaken. I see bread. I see wine. I eat bread. I drink wine. I know what flesh is, Father. The Eucharist is not flesh."

Anthony clasped his hands behind his back and slowly paced the short length of Bononillo's shop. Bononillo went back to polishing his saddle.

"Even the beasts recognize the Creator."

"I know, Father. I heard you speak at the river. I saw the fish. I believe in God. I believe everything you say. But the Eucharist. It is unbelievable."

"The form of the bread, of the wine, remains the same. The substance changes. The substance is Christ."

"God asks us to believe that? That is absurd."

"You are as thick-headed as a horse, Bononillo."

"A horse is smarter than you, Father. A horse knows bread from flesh."

Anthony stopped pacing. He stood facing the doorway, his back to Bononillo, his head bowed, his hands clasped behind his back. Bononillo watched him curiously. Abruptly, Anthony raised his head and tilted it backward as if he were gazing at something transfixed in the sky. He maintained this posture for so long that Bononillo stopped watching him and returned to buffing the saddle.

Suddenly Anthony called out, "If your horse recognized Christ in the Eucharist, then would you believe?"

Bononillo giggled. "My horse?"

"Would you believe?"

"Yes! I would rejoin the Church and take my entire family with me."

Anthony turned toward Bononillo. "Starve your horse for three days. Then, on Holy Thursday, after Mass at Prime, bring her to the village square along with some oats and hay. I will bring the Eucharist. We shall see what the horse will do."

Bononillo shrugged. "She will eat the hay and oats."

"If she does, then the fault is mine, not God's. Just remember that. My sin, not God's lack of presence in the Sacrament."

"You really do believe, don't you?" Bononillo felt a tinge of pity for the young, idealistic fool. "All Rimini will be there to watch. If your test does not work, you will lose the town. The church will be empty for your Easter sermon."

The friar smiled thinly. "If the test does work, God shall resurrect your soul and perhaps a household of souls. I will let God take charge of the outcome."

Bononillo nodded. "To God, then."

—  —

"POOR ENRICA," BONONILLO SAID gently as he led the horse out of the stall. "No food for three days, Enrica. Is the good friar fair to you, my lovely one?"

Enrica seemed a bit shaky. Her big eyes were watery and trusting. Across the mare's back, Bononillo flung two packs, one of oats, the other of hay. He had chosen his best saddlebags to display to the crowd.

"Soon you will eat, my good worker." He patted the beast and led her out into the street that was flooded with light from the rising sun.

"Here comes Bononillo!" shouted a child to some playmates. "Come on!"

Bononillo felt as if he were leading a parade. All Rimini had heard about the challenge. Neighbors drifted out of their homes and shops and clustered about him as he made his way to the village square. Everyone liked a good prank and this was one the visiting friar was about to play on himself.

Besides, this was Holy Thursday, the day on which Christ first changed bread and wine into His Body and Blood. If the first miracle were true, perhaps the people would see a second such occurrence today. The potential of such an occurrence seemed slim, yet what if it did happen? Who would want to miss seeing it? Bononillo felt the tiniest thrill of fright shiver along his body. What if the miracle took place?

The square was crowded with people when Bononillo arrived. He and Enrica stood awkwardly among the people who made a tiny circle of space around them both. How wise he had been to choose his best saddlebags!

The restless crowd began to murmur. "Where is the priest?"

"I saw him in church."

"He's been in church the past three days, praying."

"Oh, that is why we have not heard him preach."

"Where is he now?"

"Someone, run to the church and tell him that Bononillo is here and his horse is hungry."

A young boy sprinted away from the crowd in the direction of the town chapel. Twenty minutes later, he bounded back to the crowd. "He was saying Mass. But look, he's coming." The boy pointed down the street from which he had just run.

Sure enough, coming around the corner, were Canon Alonzo and one of his young assistants bearing candles and a third swinging a censer. Behind them walked Anthony, a small, cross-topped silver tower held high above his head. Bononillo had not seen one of those since he had left the Church, but he remembered what they held. The Eucharist. Following the procession were people, mostly women, who probably had been at Mass. The procession walked silently and slowly. As the tower approached, many in the crowd fell to their knees and made the sign of the cross. As the priest moved into the cluster of people, he nodded to Bononillo.

"Put down the hay and oats."

Bononillo pulled the bags off Enrica's back and tore them open. He tumbled the hay before the mare and then spilled the grain on top of the pile. As he did so, Anthony walked next to the pile of food. His gaze was fixed on the little tower held high over his head. Enrica turned toward the friar. First one knee and then the other buckled under the horse until the beast was kneeling before the Eucharist. The animal's head bowed.

Bononillo felt as if he were no longer in his body. He seemed to be watching a drama or a dream. A massive feeling of relief swept his soul. The Eucharist was true. How it was true, Bononillo did not know. Anthony's words about substance and form still made no sense. But he could see Enrica. Enrica recognized Christ. Bononillo crumbled to his knees, his arm around Enrica's neck, his eyes looking at the elevated tower, his soul seeing Jesus. He was again free to believe.

"Come," said Anthony, "it is time for the hungry to be fed. Enrica, you may rise now and eat."

The horse sprang to her feet, shaking off Bononillo as she did so. Her mouth dipped into the hay and oats and a loud "crunch" broke the quiet. Spontaneous laughter rang through the crowd.

Anthony was grinning. "For hungry beasts, oats and hay. For believers in Christ, the Bread of Life. Enrica has been without food for three days and see how famished she is. Bononillo, you have been without the Food of Life for thirty years. Are you famished, too?"

Bononillo's voice was too thick to answer. He merely nodded.

Anthony held the Eucharistic tower toward the crowd and moved it in an arc around them. Many of those still standing fell to their knees and hurriedly crossed themselves. "And you, how hungry are you? How long has it been since you have feasted on the Body and Blood of Christ? 'Unless you eat of the Flesh of the Son of Man and drink His Blood, you shall not have life in you.' 'Come, you who are hungry and eat. For My Flesh is food indeed and My Blood is real drink.' Come and confess your sins. Then your souls will be pure to receive the risen Christ on Easter."

That morning, Bononillo and a long line of other penitents went to confession. On Easter, they received the Eucharist from Anthony's hand.

## ❧ 9 ❧

## *Brother Giusto*

**School of Theology, Bologna, Italy (1223)** ❧ Brother Giusto lay on his straw mat, staring wide-eyed into the darkness as if, by looking hard enough, he would see his turbulent thoughts take on demonic form. The calm night mocked his anguish. The soft snoring of peaceful friars came from nearby huts. Crickets chirped. Night frogs croaked their love songs to each other.

The same thoughts had come so many nights before. During the day, when the twenty-seven-year-old brother begged alms or bent his muscular arms to hoe the friars' vegetable patch, he could push the thoughts deep inside. At night, when his body and mind were too tired to fight them any longer, the questions would emerge to terrify him. What if the Bible were wrong?

Such a blasphemous thought should not even enter a friar's head. Yet he had asked an even more heretical question. Did God exist? And, if He did, why was He so cruel?

*Why do you fast, pray, discipline yourself when it is to no avail?* his mind would ask. *Can't you see that the Bible is the product of men's minds? Look at those around you. Brother Giovanni goes about with lowered eyes and appears so pious. Yet how many times have you seen him dropping candle wax on the heads of those below him in choir? And Friar Bertrado. How can he follow Father Francis when he must daily have five boiled eggs for breakfast?*

*Even yourself. The others look at you and say, "Giusto is a model of virtue." They say this because you, a baron, left all your inheritance to follow Christ, thinking to gain a greater reward in eternity. They say this because*

75

*they do not know how often you cheated your serfs of their just produce from your meadows or how disdainfully you treated your grooms and squires. They know nothing about Lady Elena whom you courted while her husband fought the crusades. They had never seen how you squandered money on fine silk stockings and fur capes when it should have been given to the poor. How proud you were, Giusto! Your pride will damn you to hell. If only the other friars knew the real you, they would expel you like a dog. How wisely Jesus spoke of you—outwardly white like a marble tomb, inwardly full of uncleanness and corruption. Was it not this way with those who lived years past? Those who wrote the Scripture chose pious words, but their deeds were far different. Didn't David pen the Psalms yet sin with Bathsheba? Didn't Moses write God's commandments yet kill an Egyptian? Even the books of God were written by such men who looked holy but committed evil deeds. Certainly if God existed, we would see no such wickedness. God would not allow these questions to torment you nor would He allow evil to exist in the world. The very presence of doubts and disasters prove that God is merely an idea created by men to pacify others.*

Pulling his thin, woolen blanket with him, Giusto rolled over on his belly and thrust his face into his hands. *Stop!* His mind shrieked. *The torment must stop!* His mind would crack if these questions continued.

"God," he whispered, "if You do exist, tell me Who You are and show me what You can do. I cannot bear these trials much longer."

"Go see Father Anthony." The thought was gentle yet firm.

*Father Anthony is asleep,* Giusto argued.

"Go see Father Anthony."

How could he go to see Father Anthony? Compared to the priest, Giusto considered himself dung.

Francis, who had founded the Friars Minor, had himself commissioned Anthony to teach the brothers theology. He had given no other friar such a mission. "You may teach while maintaining the spirit of prayer and devotion," Francis had written.

Before coming to Bologna, Anthony had spent time in Vercelli with Abbot Thomas of Gaul. Abbot Thomas had come from the famous St. Victor's abbey in Paris to be superior of St. Andrew's monastery in Vercelli, whose canons followed the Rule of St. Augustine. Thomas was a saintly mystic and author, the greatest living doctor, some said, in all the world. Reportedly, he soon realized that his attempts to teach Anthony theology were unnecessary.

"He is aided by divine grace," he declared, "and draws most abundantly from the mystical theology of Divine Scripture."

In Vercelli and Milan, Anthony's preaching had reclaimed heretics and nourished the faithful. Now at Bologna, Anthony was teaching the brothers.

Giusto had never spoken to Anthony personally. How could he? At Vercelli, the story went, the priest had expounded so thoroughly on the different orders of angels that his fellow students and even Abbot Thomas had felt as if they were in the very presence of the angels themselves. Francis, whom Giusto considered angelic himself, lovingly called Anthony his "bishop" and had chosen the priest to accompany him to the papal court to discuss the new Rule of the Order. Giusto felt unworthy to breathe the same air that sustained a man like that.

The former baron was so wicked that God would most surely never pardon him. God was a righteous judge. Didn't Scripture say that the righteous would scarcely be saved? Jesus, who claimed to be the very Truth, said, "He that is able to receive it, let him receive it." Didn't that mean that not every person can receive the faith or do good? Surely Giusto was one of those who would never be saved. And God, should God exist, saw these torments and tears and cared not at all. How foolish it was to persist in useless prayers! Ezekiel said, "The soul that sins shall die."

Giusto had sinned exceedingly and still sinned by his doubts. Even Scripture states that "all have sinned and fall short of the glory of God." God, if He existed, was just and must punish wickedness. If God were a mere imagination, Giusto had no hope. If God were real, he still had no hope. Why was he here with these followers of holy Francis?

"Go see Father Anthony."

How could Anthony understand Giusto's torment? The man was totally devoted to God, totally devoid of all unclean desires. Just today he had spoken about the name of Jesus.

"Let me tell you briefly what Pope Innocent wrote about the name of Jesus," he had said. The students were seated beneath a huge oak, clustered around the saint. The gnats and flies were especially annoying, so Giusto and the others, including Anthony, had pulled their hoods over their tonsured heads to discourage the insects.

"The name of Jesus is made up of two syllables and five letters: three vowels and two consonants."*

"The two syllables in the name Jesus are symbolic of the two natures in Jesus, the divine and the human. The divine nature comes from the Heavenly Father, the human nature from His earthly mother.

"Note that a vowel is a sound that can be pronounced by itself, while a consonant needs another sound with it as it cannot be pronounced alone. The three vowels in Jesus' name signify the divinity which, although One in itself, exists in Three Persons. In First John 5:7, we read, 'There are Three who give testimony in heaven: the Father, the Word, and the Holy Spirit. And these Three are One.'

"The two consonants—both s's—in the name of Jesus signify humanity. Although humanity is made up of two substances, that is, body and soul, nevertheless, like the consonants, neither body nor soul can stand alone. Each must be joined with other substances to form the unity of a person.

"Just as a rational soul and body form one person, so God and man form one Christ. Christ is both God and man. He can subsist by Himself in as far as He is God—part of the Trinity—but He cannot subsist by Himself in as far as He is human, that is, body and soul. Acts 4:12 tells us, 'There is no other name given to us whereby we must be saved.' May we be saved by God through the name of Jesus Christ Our Lord, Who is blessed above all things throughout all the ages. Amen."

"Go to Father Anthony. Only in the name of Jesus can you be saved. Go to the priest."

Giusto pushed back his blanket and felt to his left for his breeches and coarse worker's tunic, the order of dress for a Friar Minor. He could see the ghostly glow of a faintly moonlit fog just beyond his door.

Anthony's hut, five away from Giusto's, looked as if it were dissolving into the mist. Outside the priest's cell, Giusto stood motionless. Now what? How dare he wake the priest? Should he call out? Tap lightly? Go in and wake the man?

---

* The name Jesus is spelled *Iesus* in Latin. Anthony uses this spelling in his explanation of the Holy Name. The two consonants are s and s; the three vowels are I, e, and u.

Inside the still hut, coarse cloth rustled. Soft footsteps. Anthony stood in the doorway.

"I thought I heard someone. Brother Giusto, what troubles you?"

Giusto's knees crumbled beneath him. He was kneeling in front of the priest, sobbing uncontrollably.

He felt two firm hands on his shoulders.

"If we speak here, we shall disturb the sleeping brothers. Come."

Anthony helped the man to his feet and guided him away from the cells toward the winding road that led to the town fields. The night was perfectly still, wrapped in a vaporous shroud. As the men's bare feet scratched the dust, crickets in the tall weeds on either side of the road momentarily ceased chirping. The mist opened before the men and closed behind them.

For a long while, Giusto poured out his sins, fears, and questions. The priest listened without speaking. Finally, when Giusto had no more to say, they walked on in silence. At last Anthony turned off the road and pushed through a ribbon of high, dew soaked grass until he stood at the edge of a newly plowed field. Giusto obediently followed.

"Brother Giusto," the priest began, "this field represents the body of Christ. God says in Genesis 1:11, 'Let the earth bring forth vegetation.' This cannot happen unless the soil is first broken."

Anthony stooped to the earth and scooped up a handful of rich, moist soil. Still stooping, he gazed up at Giusto. "The earth is Christ, crushed for our sins, pierced by a lance and nails. Just as the earth, ploughed and broken in springtime, produces abundant harvest, so the bruised and broken body of Christ gained for us the harvest of heaven."

Anthony rose and pressed the soil into Giusto's hand. It felt delightfully cool, almost alive. "This field, Brother, is also you. When a person is contrite for his sins as you are, he is like a piece of soil that has been reduced to dust. Crushed by sorrow for his offenses, the sinner can turn his mind to God and make of it a delightful garden. What other possible pleasure or joy can satisfy a man when he stands before God, from Whom and in Whom everything that exists is true? You have stood before God, Brother Giusto, and have admitted that you are nothing in yourself.

"When have you done this? In the desert of your questioning." Anthony rubbed his hands on the moist grass to cleanse them.

"Brother, there are three stages in our spiritual life. God describes them through the mouth of the prophet Hosea. 'I will nourish her; I will lead her into the desert and speak to her heart.' With God's grace, a beginner in the spiritual life is 'nourished,' becoming stronger and stronger in the practice of virtue. This you have done by overcoming your carnal desires.

"Now you are passing through the second stage of spiritual development. In this stage, God 'leads the soul into the desert.'"

Anthony led the way back to the road and began walking again, going deeper into the pasture land areas. Giusto thought momentarily of the robbers on the roads at night, then dismissed the thought. Robbers would not harm the friars. They knew the followers of Francis had nothing to give but their tunics and breeches.

"Where did God speak to John the Baptist? In the desert, 'parched, lifeless, and without water, where I have gazed on you' as Psalm 62 states. John came as 'a voice crying in the desert.' A voice is a preacher and the desert is a symbol of the cross on which Christ died, abandoned, naked, and crowned with thorns. From the desert of the cross, Christ cried, 'Father into Your hands I commend My spirit.' Thus we must do as well, when we are in the desert of our own questioning."

"It is so difficult, Father, to give my soul to God when I question His very goodness and existence."

"Ah, very difficult. Most exceedingly difficult. For Satan's influence is always present in the desert."

Giusto clutched the soil in his fist. "Are you saying, Father, that my thoughts have come from Satan?"

"This may well be, Brother. Yet God has permitted these thoughts, has He not? They have clouded your mind just as this mist clouds the night. And you wonder why God has permitted your torment. Because one stage of the spiritual life is the desert. In the desert, when one submits to God, one can also find peace and quiet, away from the tumult of internal unrest. Here God 'speaks to her heart' the way a loving mother speaks to her child. Can you hear God speaking to you in the desert of your thoughts?"

"I believe God told me to come to you, Father."

"Perhaps to help you see that what you are experiencing is neither unusual nor evil, for it will bring you to the third stage of spiritual development. In this third stage, the soul experiences the complete joy of God's presence within it. What a superabundance of love, joy, and zeal a soul experiences when it possesses God! Certainly, Brother Giusto, you are looking for that joy."

"Who is not looking for it, Father?"

"But you think that you must have faith without reason. No, Brother. To have faith is to exercise the most reason. St. Peter in his first letter writes, 'As newborn babies, desire the rational milk without guile.' Something is rational when it is done according to reason. Reason is a faculty of the soul which recognizes truth. It also means the contemplation of truth or the truth itself. Jesus said, 'He who knows the truth listens to My voice.' He said this because He is the Truth, as He said, 'I am the Way and the Truth and the Life.' We are to be 'rational' toward God, always seeking the truth. Truth does not come except to those who seek it. One way of seeking is through questions."

"But I have questioned the very existence of God and His goodness."

Anthony stopped and moved his arm in an arc. "What do you see, Brother Giusto?"

"Just a bit of the road, Father and some grass beside it, an edge of meadow beyond. Nothing else, Father. It is too dark and misty."

"And do you question if all that you see is all that is?"

"Of course not. I know that meadows extend to the left and right as far as the eyes can see and beyond them the Apennine Mountains."

"How do you know?"

"I have seen them before."

"And is that everything that exists? Or is there more to the world than you can see at any one moment?"

"Bologna lies behind us and beyond that all of the Romagna. Then, to the north, France, and to the south, the sea, and beyond that the ocean and other nations."

"Have you seen them?"

"I have never left the Romagna."

"Yet you believe. Why?"

"Others have seen and written of these places or brought back tales of them."

"And you believe them. Then look at the Bible, Brother. It was written by those who saw, those who witnessed. Look at Jesus. He is the writing of the Father. St. John calls him the 'Word of God.' Read that 'Word' for your answers, Brother Giusto, and be 'not unbelieving, but believe.' I will pray for you."

Anthony swung around on the road and headed back through the fog to Bologna. The men walked slowly and in silence. Giusto knew that the priest was already praying for him and he sensed a strength and calm coming from those prayers. To know Anthony was to know a man who understood and loved and lived the "Word." To be in his presence was to meet the Truth. The Truth was the Son, rising now in Giusto's soul to warm away the fog of doubt. Giusto was glad that he had gone to see the priest.

# ꧁ 10 ꧂

## *Father Vito*

**Rectory, Bologna, Italy (Early 1224)** ༄ As he approached the hearth in the poorly built hovel that served as his rectory, elderly, stooped Father Vito stepped over Cidro, the skinniest beggar in Bologna. Cidro lay on the floor, snoring and curled up before the dying embers. His big, sooty feet were so close to the fireplace that if there had been any flames they would have singed them.

With his bony fingers, Vito drew the huge, black kettle toward himself. Stepping over Cidro again, he carried the kettle outdoors to the well.

Through the thin rags that wrapped his feet, old Vito's toes curled at the cold of a delicate, fresh layer of snow. With hands already tingling from the dawn's chill, Vito let down the water bucket. He heard a feeble crackling as the wood smashed through the fragile ice that had formed on the water overnight. Then he drew up the water, poured it into the kettle, and lugged the kettle indoors.

On the small, rickety table on which he ate, he found the wrinkled carrots, sprouting onions, and softening garlic that he'd brought up late last night from the root cellar. Yesterday a matron had brought him a gigantic cheese.

He had shared it with the six men and women who were sleeping in his room just now and then saved some for today in the little larder near his bed. When Vito took out the cheese, he noticed that it was smaller than when he had put it in.

The gray-haired priest glanced around the room at the rag-covered bodies on the floor and at the curled up form on his bed, that of crippled Maria, her infant asleep in her arms. Who had sneaked a night nibble? Crooked nosed Donte, the leper? The big-eyed orphan girl, Tazia? Or old Cidro? No matter. Vito crumbled the remaining cheese into the kettle, then sliced the vegetables and added them as well. He brought the kettle to the hearth and added wood to the embers. As a tiny flame leaped up, Vito tugged at Cidro' s feet, dragging them out of danger of the heat.

From the mantle above the hearth, Vito took a thick, well-worn book, its pages neatly penned in small script. Kneeling next to Cidro, he opened the breviary and began to silently recite his morning prayers. By the time he finished them, the beggars would be up.

As VITO WALKED INTO CHURCH, the beggars who had slept in his house overnight had already clustered at the doors to beg alms from those going into Sunday Mass. They would remain there, begging, until Mass began, then creep in to huddle at the rear of the church. After Mass, they would scurry outdoors again to beg of the worshipers as they left. After begging, they would slip into the streets of Bologna and, if the night were warm, sleep there. But if it were cold, as it had been last night, they would be back at Vito's door. He would give them soup to eat and a place to sleep, for in them he saw Christ.

Vito had been in church but a moment when the visiting friar arrived. Father Anthony taught theology to the Friars Minor at their little convent in the city. He was, Vito had heard, a mighty preacher. He and Anthony would celebrate Mass together. Anthony would preach the sermon.

MASS HAD BEGUN. ANTHONY NOW stood in the pulpit while Vito sat to the side of the altar and gazed at his motley congregation. On the floor in the back of the church, the beggars clustered. In front of them on wooden benches perched the well-dressed lords and ladies of Bologna. Some of the wealthy listeners were responsible in part for the wretched plight of those who huddled behind them. Every

Sunday Vito looked down at this congregation while his soul seethed. How could the usurers sit there in comfort while the poor whom they swindled stared at their backs?

Every week, it seemed, Vito spoke out against the crimes of the rich and the plight of the poor. Today Anthony was speaking of it himself.

"The Psalmist says, 'This vast ocean' which is the world, 'stretches its arms wide. In it, innumerable reptiles swarm. Here live creatures small and great, swimming in the waters as ships sail by.'" Anthony had called out the text of Psalm 104, verses 25 and 26. "The sea is the world, full of bitterness, yet vast in riches, wide and teeming with delights. Its arms are open wide to gather in the greedy." Anthony threw open his arms to their fullest breadth.

"St. Matthew says it well. 'Wide is the way leading to destruction.' Who goes this way? Certainly not Christ's poor who enter by the narrow gate. The way to destruction is a wide sea through which the usurers swim on their way to hell. These greedy people swarm throughout the entire sea, having the whole world in their grasp."

*How could those most insidiously guilty listen with ears of stone?* Vito wondered. How could they listen week after week and not be moved? The poor of Bologna were in misery because of usury. Swindlers loaned the needy money at thirty, fifty, even eighty percent interest. How could the poverty stricken, wasting away in wretchedness, possibly pay it back? Sometimes, in desperation, the borrowers hired assassins to slay the men to whom they were financially bound. Meanwhile, the usurers grew fat and drunk on choice wines that might well have been distilled from the sweat and blood of the destitute.

"Look at the usurers. Look at the hands that dare to come to church and offer alms. Such hands are dripping with the blood of the poor. Oh, there are innumerable reptiles in the great sea of this earth. One kind, most plentiful," Anthony said, lowering his voice to a hissing sort of whisper, "hide themselves from sight as best they can, crawling and groveling in the shadows. These furtive yet loathsome creatures are those who practice usury in secret. This very day, they sit among us with their ill-gotten coins lining their pockets. Then there are those more visible, small creatures of the ocean. These are the swindlers who practice usury openly," Anthony's voice rose, "but who charge moderate rates of interest. How generous they seem, how merciful! Let your mercy be that of Christ, Who gave to all freely, expecting nothing in return!"

He paused and then his voice trumpeted through the church. "Finally there are those powerful and vicious animals of the ocean from whom all other life flees in terror. These usurers are evil, lost, professional souls who ply their trade unashamedly in the full light of day."

Ah, there in the congregation sat thirty-year-old Signor Zaccaria and his wife Signora Odilia. Comfortably warm in his gray fox cape, raven haired Zaccaria was one of those powerful and vicious animals of the sea of which Anthony preached. Vito had many times spoken to him about the evil in his life. His words had left as much an impression on Zaccaria as an inchworm leaves on the bark of an oak.

"These miserable persons care nothing for the realities of life. They never think of how they entered this world in utter nakedness, nor do they think that they will leave it wrapped in a few rags. How have they come to possess so many things?" Anthony paused. "Through theft and cheating."

Anthony held his left palm toward the congregation. "Can you see what I hold here? Probably not, for it is less than an inch long, so small that, to you, it appears to be only an insignificant husk. And so it actually is the husk of a dung beetle." Anthony moved his hand slowly from left to right, allowing all to peer into his palm.

"Who has not seen a dung beetle? This creature, when alive, is cloaked in an iridescent shell. What finery of black, purple, blue, green, bronze, or gold he wears! Why, he gleams in the sun like a precious metal. How beautiful and impressive he seems! And what does this vivid creature do? He spends his entire life collecting great quantities of dung. How long he labors to roll it into balls! What effort! What toil! And for what? For one day a donkey passes by and his hoof falls on both beetle and dung ball." Anthony brought his fist down upon the dried up beetle. "Thus, both beetle and ball are squashed in the same instant."

*He is as superb as they say,* Vito thought. *I am glad I invited him to preach.*

"In the same way, the greedy person toils at length to gather the dung of money and then death comes and crushes him. And what is left of the man who thought himself so fine and important? The usurer's flesh goes to the worms, his money to his relatives, and his soul to the devil. Thus will it happen unless each guilty person restores ill-gotten goods and then does penance."

Anthony curled his fingers around the dead beetle and dropped it on the pulpit.

"The usurers and all greedy, cheating people will come to the same end as the dung beetle. But does God abandon those who swim about the vast sea of the world in so much foolish confidence and unconcern? Not at all. So that they might do penance, the ships, that is the preachers of the Church, pass by." Anthony turned and nodded at Vito who amiably nodded back. "They need only approach the ships to be lifted out of the water of temporal greed and into God's kingdom."

Anthony raised his arms and face upward. "'Lift up your eyes on high,' says the prophet Jeremiah." He lowered his arms and his gaze. "Sea creatures do not lift their eyes on high. Their eyes are so placed that they must look to the side or below. But Jeremiah says, 'Lift your eyes on high.' Who looks on high? The person who acknowledges the malice of his deeds and confesses them openly, sincerely and without reservation."

Vito could see Anthony peering into the congregation, catching first one face and then another in his gaze. "Therefore, lift your eyes on high. Do not cast them down or sideways. Do not be ashamed. Do not fear. If you lift your eyes on high and acknowledge your sins, you will 'surely live and not die.' Abandon yourself completely to the judgment of the priest. Make your words those of Saul, who became the Apostle Paul, 'Lord, what will you have me do?'"

Vito sighed. If only the priest's words could penetrate the oaken hearts that listened! If only tears of repentance would flow! As Anthony continued to exhort his listeners to repentance and confession, Vito lifted his heart in prayer. *Lord, let Friar Anthony's words penetrate the heart of this congregation. Let them have an effect, Lord, so that the dignity of the poor may be restored.*

"Let us give thanks, then, to Jesus Christ, the Son of God, Who cast out the devil and Who can save us from the deep and carnal waters of this earthly life. Let us devoutly and humbly beg Him to give His grace to each of us, to enable us to acknowledge our sins, to confess them, and to faithfully obey the counsel of our confessor.

May the Lord Jesus Christ, to Whom be honor, majesty, power, praise, and glory throughout all ages, grant this to all of us. And let every creature who swims in the sea of this world answer, 'Amen!'"

As Anthony descended from the pulpit, Vito pleaded, *Lord, let his words bring fruit.*

—▶ ◀—

VITO SAT IN ONE CORNER OF THE CHURCH and Anthony in the other. Both had penitents lined up. In Anthony's line stood Signor Zaccaria and Signora Odilia.

As Vito listened to the sins of skinny Chico, a great bubble of envy swelled inside the old priest's soul. For years he had urged Zaccaria to confession. For years he had preached the very message that Anthony had preached today. Zaccaria had never once confessed. Today he was.

Vito had prayed for this moment. Prayed fervently. Had even prayed today. He thought Zaccaria would come to him to confess. Instead, he had gone to Anthony.

Anthony was young, good looking, straight and noble in carriage, with eyes so large and deep set that they seemed to probe a person's soul. He was articulate and intelligent, his voice strong with youth and conviction. In contrast, stoop-shouldered Vito was nearly seventy-five years old, his face dotted with warts and brown age spots. Vito's voice was high and shrill and his small eyes red-rimmed and watery. He often fumbled for words for his education had been minimal.

Anthony and Vito had preached the same message, but the preacher and the delivery were different. Today Zaccaria was confessing to the young priest. And Vito knew, beyond a doubt, that what he had suspected for several months was true. He was too old to be effective.

Vito absolved Cidro who had confessed to stealing the cheese. Then he listened to Maria's sins. All his beggars, he noticed, were in his line. Precious people. They trusted him. Anthony's line was a colorful thread of fur capes, jaunty caps, and high boots. Why was Vito even a pastor of this church if only the poor came to him? A younger priest should take over. A younger priest could get the response that this young priest got today. Vito knew God and loved

Him, but he was too old to influence the young. Vito could exhort. But a young priest, full of the fire of faith, could convert.

Confessions continued until the final beggar was absolved. Anthony still had two more richly dressed penitents. Vito would wait. He wanted to thank Anthony for preaching today. He wanted to congratulate him on his success with Zaccaria.

Vito closed his eyes briefly and laid his head back in the pew. He had slept on the floor last night beside Donte, having given his bed to Maria and the baby who had fussed with fever throughout the night. The fussing had disturbed Vito's sleep.

Now Vito dozed. As he napped, he saw Anthony approach him. "Why are you jealous of me? There is no need," the friar said. "Come and speak to me."

Vito woke with a start. Anthony was nowhere near him. He was in the far corner of the church, dismissing his final penitent. As the plump matron started toward the door, Vito knew what he must do. He had long ago learned to distinguish a mere dream from a God-given vision. This was a vision. God wanted him to speak to the friar. He would not argue with God. Pushing erect, he approached Anthony, his arm outstretched in friendship.

"Friar Anthony, your words are powerful," Vito said. He grasped Anthony's forearm and embraced the friar. "My church is poor. Yet you came to speak in it. Thank you. You have converted people I could not reach."

Anthony shook his head. "Father, I speak words. The Lord grants conversion."

"Your words brought it about. I am envious."

"I have seen you with your poor. I, too, am envious."

"No, Friar. I really am envious. I have tried to reach Signor Zaccaria for years, to no avail. Today, for the first time, he confessed to you."

"Signor Zaccaria? The usurer in the fox cape?"

Vito nodded.

"He told me that many times you had spoken to him about his crimes." Anthony glanced toward the door of the church. "Father, come with me."

Vito followed Anthony to the door where Anthony stepped outdoors into a lightly falling snow. As his bare feet left toe tracks in the whiteness, Anthony stooped beside a patch of ground to the right of the church door. "On my way into church, I noticed the garlic here popping up through the snow. Did you plant them, Father?"

Vito looked at the little green shoots pricking like tiny blades through the snow. "I always plant garlic, Friar. In the fall."

"Like all good farmers and gardeners do." Anthony stroked one of the tiny plants. "You don't expect to eat the garlic today, do you?"

"I couldn't even get them out of the frozen ground," Vito said. "And they are not grown."

Anthony looked up at Vito. "But they will continue to grow in the early rains of spring and the late rains of summer until harvest."

The friar stood. Vito observed the young face, the snow alighting on dark lashes and black hair. "You are a good farmer, Father. St. James writes in his letter, 'The farmer waits for the precious fruit of the earth, being patient over it until it receives the early and late rain.' The farmer is the preacher, Father. A preacher such as yourself sows the seeds of preaching and implants the desire for eternal life in your listeners. In the meantime, there is need for patience. Sometimes a soul is in winter, as it were, when no growth occurs and grace seems ineffective. But life in the soul is still present, just as it is present in your garlic."

Vito gazed at the tiny green shoots and nodded.

"Then comes the 'early rain,' which is premature grace through the hearing of God's message. It is premature for it comes too soon for harvest. This is the grace that your words have given Signor Zaccaria and several others who confessed today."

"But you are the one who brought about their confession, Friar."

"I was merely the 'late rain,' coming at a later time. Through my words, God's Spirit brought conversion today." Anthony reached out and laid a firm hand on Vito's shoulder.

"You will bring late rain, too, Father, if you are patient. When you bear your trials with patience and joy, you will receive the 'early rain' of grace yourself and you will be able to dispense it to others. You will receive the 'late rain' of glory in the future when those whom you have been tending and watering with your words convert and when you yourself enter eternal life. You have planted and watered the seed for years, Father. I have appeared only at harvest time."

Vito disagreed. "But I have been unable to harvest anything. The young merchants and usurers will not listen to me. I am too old. A younger man like yourself would be much more effective."

"Youth means nothing, Father. Faith means all. I say to you, Father, what Paul said to the Galatians, 'So let us not grow weary in doing what is right, for we will reap at harvest time if we do not give up.' Do not give up, Father. You will reap."

Vito shook his head. "Friar, I want to believe that you are right." Anthony, Vito saw, was growing white with snow. He glanced at Anthony's bare feet. "Would you like to come into my house, Friar? I have a fire on the hearth and some soup in the kettle."

"I would like that, Father."

Vito's house was just five steps away. The two priests shook the snow from their tunics as they entered. Vito pulled two scratched wooden bowls from a shelf and ladled the bubbling soup into each. As he and Anthony sat at the table, a knock sounded at the door.

"Come in," Vito called.

The door pushed open and snow-covered Maria crept in on her knees, her useless, twisted legs dragging behind her. The woman's whining baby, wrapped in a tattered length of wool, was clutched to her chest.

"Maria," Vito said. "I'm glad you came. Come have some soup with us."

The woman smiled, the wide spaces between her teeth showing.

"Take my chair, my lady," Anthony said, rising. He reached out his hands toward her infant. "May I hold your sweet child?"

"He's got a fever, Friar," Maria said, handing him the baby.

"So I see," Anthony said as he pulled back the dirty blanket and stroked the infant's forehead. Anthony made the sign of the cross over the infant and then over Maria who signed herself and then pulled herself into the chair.

As she sat, Vito placed a bowl of soup before her and noticed that her stubby, twisted feet were raw and bleeding. He fished beside the hearth for some rags and dipped one into a pail of water that he kept filled beside the hearth. Squatting beside Maria, Vito began to swab her bloody toes.

"Maria, where are the shoes I gave you yesterday? Lady Serena gave me only that one pair."

Maria blushed. "Donte said the lepers hadn't any, Father. I told him to give them mine."

Vito sighed. Beggars. Some of them were more generous than the wealthy could even imagine being.

Vito dried Maria's feet and returned to the hearth for some additional rags. As Maria lifted the bowl of soup to her lips, Vito wrapped her feet snugly in the tattered cloths.

"Maria," Anthony said, "you have given away your shoes. You are as merciful as the Virgin Mother of Christ whose name you bear." Hugging the whimpering child to his chest and rocking back and forth, Anthony smiled at the tired looking mother. "You are blessed to bear the sweetest name of any woman on earth."

Maria put her soup bowl down and grinned at the priest. When a smile flooded Maria's dirty face and huge mouth, she looked almost pretty, Vito thought as he sat in the chair opposite the woman.

Anthony smiled back. "Jesus loved His mother more than all women, Maria, since He had received from her His human body. She found more grace and mercy in Christ than any other woman. Oh, what a blessed name is Maria!"

"My mother named me, Friar. After the Virgin. That was what she always told me."

"So your mother was faithful as was our Lady's mother, St. Anne. Do you know that your name, Maria, means 'star of the sea'?"

Maria shook her head. "I didn't know it meant anything."

Anthony spoke as he rocked, his words louder than the fussy cries of the infant. "The name is most appropriate for our Mother in heaven. Mariners watch the North Star for safe passage while sailing. It is a fixed star in the heavens and, by watching it, they are able to find their bearings in any sea. Mary is like this star. She is a star which indicates a clear path to all those tossed about on the turbulent waters of life. Mary is a name beloved by angels and feared by devils. I imagine, Maria, that you often find life difficult." Anthony was rocking the infant more slowly now. The whimpering had stopped.

"Yes, Friar. But Father Vito helps. He is good, Friar."

Anthony glanced at Vito and smiled. "So I can see. And Father Vito often finds life difficult, too. That I can also see."

Vito blushed and turned his eyes away from the friar's.

"I'd like to teach you both a prayer to our Lady, a prayer that will guide you through difficult times."

"I would like that, Friar," Maria said.

Anthony held the child in his arms, pressed close to his chest. The infant was quiet, possibly asleep. Bowing his head, Anthony began to pray in a soft, gentle voice. "We pray to you, our Lady, our hope. We are tossed about by the storm of life's seas. May you, Star of the Sea, enlighten and guide us to our safe harbor. Assist us with your protective presence when we are about to depart from this life so that we may merit to leave this prison fearlessly and reach happily the kingdom of endless joy. We hope to receive these favors from Jesus Christ, Whom you bore in your blessed womb and nursed at your most holy breast. To Him be all honor and glory, forever and ever. Amen."

"Friar, would you repeat the prayer again so that we may learn it?" Vito asked.

So Anthony, gazing at the sleeping child, repeated it. At the end of the third repetition, with Maria and Vito praying the words with Anthony, the baby began to wriggle and whine, his little mouth rubbing back and forth against Anthony's tunic. Anthony laughed and held the child toward Maria. "I cannot give him what he wants now. You take him and nurse him."

Maria bubbled with joy. "If he wants to nurse, he will get well." As she enfolded the infant in her arms, she grinned. "He is no longer hot. The fever has broken."

"Thank God," Vito said. Then he added, "Maria, perhaps if you lie down and nurse him, he will fall asleep." He pointed to his bed which he always gave to beggars when they visited. It was the only luxury Vito had, but when the needy slept at Vito's, Vito slept on the floor.

Clutching the baby who was rooting eagerly at her chest, Maria crawled to Vito's bed and climbed in, lying down with her face to the wall.

Anthony smiled as he sat at the table. "I envy you, Father. Your name Vito means life and you have given life to so many people. How many of the poor in Bologna love and need you? You not only speak to them of Christ. You show them Him in who you are. Without an exemplary life, Father, no one can assemble the people, since a preacher's words have no effect if his life is held in contempt."

"Yes, people like Maria listen," Vito said. "But those who confessed to you today do hold me in contempt, Friar. They do not listen at all. Some speak against my taking in people like Maria."

"Father, I constantly find people who spare neither the saint nor the sinner from their detraction. These people perversely claim that good is bad and that bad is good. They call darkness light and light darkness. They turn what is bitter to sweetness and what is sweet to bitterness."

"Friar, some pastors in this city do that very thing. I see their fine churches and the alms they gather. If I spoke as they do, I would not anger men like Signor Zaccaria. Then perhaps people like him would give me money to care for the people who come to me for help."

Anthony, who had been sipping the soup, lowered his bowl. "Father, Christ said of Himself, 'I am the Truth.' Those who preach the truth give witness to Christ; those who do not preach the truth deny Christ. 'Truth produces hatred.' This is why some preachers, rather than incur the wrath of people, desist from saying anything. When you preach the truth as it really is, something that truth itself demands and Sacred Scripture prescribes, you incur the anger of carnal-minded people. Correct?"

"All the time, Friar."

"Do not fear the people, Father. Truth must not be abandoned out of fear of opposition. Because blind preachers fear opposition, they incur blindness of soul. They are 'blind men leading the blind.' Some wealthy men will give to preachers the dung of worldly goods in order to escape rebukes. But, Father, I beg you to be an authentic preacher who thinks nothing of silver and gold. St. Peter admonishes, 'Feed and tend the flock of God; take care of it willingly as God's shepherds, not under constraint. Do not do it for shameful profit. Care for the flock because your heart is in it. Be an example to the flock, not lording it over those assigned to you.' Serve not with your own strength, but with the very power of God, so that in all you do, God may be honored through our Lord Jesus Christ."

"Friar, I have tried to do this, but the fruit is small."

Anthony drained the soup from his bowl and then turned it upside down. "What is this little tunnel, Father?" he asked, pointing to a thin, serpentine groove in the wood.

"The gnawing of a worm, Friar. It was in the wood when I carved the bowl. I am sorry I have no better bowls to offer."

"The bowl is fine, Father." Anthony pointed to the tunnel. "You say a worm made this. A worm bores and gnaws away at wood. So must a preacher bore and gnaw away at hearts hardened by sin which bear no fruit. Nothing is harder than a worm when it bores into wood. Yet nothing is softer to the touch than a worm. So must a preacher be tender, treating repentant and humbled souls with compassion and mercy. Thus, when you preach the word of God, preach with determination and firmness to move the hearts of your hearers. But if those listeners hurl insults and affronts at you, remain soft, forgiving, and friendly."

Vito nodded. He had tried to do this all his life.

"Mercilessly kill all sins in yourself so that you may show mercy toward others. Thus, you will fulfill the precept of Jesus, 'to be merciful as your Father in heaven is merciful.' For you, Father, must show mercy to those who confessed today. You are the one who must nurture their faith."

Anthony placed the bowl on the table and touched Vito's hand. "Late last year, Pope Honorius wrote to our universities and religious houses commanding them to send preachers to France to combat the heresies there. The minister general of my Order is sending me to France, Father. I will be leaving as soon as winter is over. In Bologna, Father, the newly born in Christ will come to you, not to me."

A knock sounded at the door. "Come in," Vito called.

Zaccaria stood in the doorway, his fox cape flecked with snow. The usurer shook the snow from his cape, then stepped inside the house and knelt before Vito.

"Father Vito, I have come to make restitution and to ask your forgiveness," he said, his head bowed. "You have spoken to me for years and I did not listen. Forgive me, Father, for cheating the Church and the poor."

Vito swallowed the amazement in his voice. Placing his hand on Zaccaria's shoulder, he said, "I forgive you, Signor."

Zaccaria looked up at Vito, his eyes glistening with tears. "Thank you, Father." Then he turned toward the door and called, "Bring in the coins."

A stocky youth in a black fur cape walked into the room, carrying with him a fat leather pouch. Rising from his knees, Zaccaria took the pouch and dumped its contents onto the table before the startled parish priest. Coins of all denominations bounced against the wood until a great heap lay on the wood.

"There will be more, Father Vito," Zaccaria said. Then he took Vito's hand in his right hand and Anthony's in his left. His grip was firm as he said, "Thank you both. You have given me life."

Then, dropping his grip on the hands, he unfastened his cape and stepped over to the bed. Gently he draped the fur over Maria and her sleeping infant. Silently Zaccaria walked to the door and out into the storm. The groom followed, closing the door behind them.

Anthony touched Vito's wrist. "That is your first newborn, Father. Nurse him well with the milk of God's holy word so that he may grow up strong in Christ."

# PART THREE

# Mission to France

# ࿇ 11 ࿇

## *Friar Monaldo*

**Chapter Meeting, Arles, France (September 1224)** ࿇ Friar Monaldo sat on a wooden bench in the very back of the room. His arthritis was bothering him as it always did, but he refused to lean up against the wall. No one must know that he was in pain.

Monaldo had chosen this seat as the one best fitting his station. Here no one would notice the tiny, old man whom his fellow friars lovingly called Brother Mouse. With his patched, gray tunic hanging loosely over his stooped shoulders and his brown eyes bright in his thin face, Monaldo resembled the furtive little creatures that he frequently brushed off his body at night.

Arles was suffering under a mid-September heat wave. Had there not been a light rain today, the friars would have assembled outdoors under the grape arbors that surrounded the monastery. It would have been pleasant there, with the breeze rippling through the wide grape leaves, the thick, purple clusters almost ripe enough to pick.

As it was, Monaldo's superior thoughtfully rearranged this room at the convent so that the benches for those who would address the chapter were directly in front of the open door. Here his guests would catch any breeze that might filter through the arbors to relieve the stifling humidity. Other benches were arranged to face the two in the front. Monaldo, being at the rear of the room, caught very little fresh air. He did not mind. With age had come a perpetual chill in his bones. Today, while many other friars periodically wiped the sweat from their foreheads with the sleeves of their tunics, Monaldo, except for his arthritis, felt quite comfortable.

Monaldo marveled at how fortunate he was to be present at this chapter meeting. Only his Order's younger, more vigorous provincials and delegates were invited. Had he and his convent mates not actually lived here at Arles where the chapter meeting was being held, they never would have been asked to attend. As it was, their superior allowed them to sit in on the meeting. However, they were not to speak unnecessarily to the important delegates. They were to sit only after everyone else was seated. They were to assist any visiting friars if asked.

The brothers agreed. A few of the dignitaries had asked some brothers for drinks of water. No one had asked Monaldo for anything. The brothers had obediently allowed the visitors to sit first, then took the best seats left. Monaldo sat down last. Let the younger men claim the seats that afforded a better view of the proceedings. They were more able than he to absorb the fire of Francis and healthy enough to bring it to the world.

Monaldo had seen Father Francis a few times at chapter meetings of his entire Order. Joy and holiness radiated from the scrawny, short man who had founded the Friars Minor. Once a merchant's son courting dreams of knighthood, Francis was a poet and dreamer whose simple exhortations to his friars proved beyond a doubt how totally and deeply he loved the Lord. Monaldo had never spoken to Francis personally nor even approached him. Between Francis and him, he felt, lay a chasm of difference, the one man with a foot already in heaven and the other no holier than the dust beneath his feet.

Francis himself was not at today's regional chapter meeting. As the Order of Friars Minor grew, so did the number of such regional gatherings and Francis, whose stamina was giving out, could no longer attend them all. In fact, he was ill in Assisi at this very moment and, the friars knew, burdened with worries over his Order. How fervently they offered daily prayers for Francis and for themselves!

Not everyone agreed with the reforms begun in the Order by the current minister general, Brother Elias. The friars whispered that Father Francis feared that his simple Rule of poverty, chastity, and obedience would be destroyed and with it the very soul of his

Order. Yet Francis had submitted himself to Brother Elias in strict obedience. Monaldo could only imagine the struggle and pain Francis felt as Elias worked to bring structure and direction to the friars. Francis, who to Monaldo seemed as free as a lark, could only have seen Elias' efforts as trying to cage a flock of sparrows.

Where did Brother John Bonelli of Florence, their provincial who had called this chapter meeting, stand regarding the Rule? No one was certain. He had not discussed the Rule, although the chapter had already covered many issues on which the friars held differing opinions—disciplining lax brothers, owning convents, teaching theology, battling heresy, ministering to lepers and the poor.

Before the men grew too burdened with dry and discouraging problems, Brother John called a brief recess. Monaldo remained in his seat, content to rest. Despite the drizzle, many other friars ventured outdoors to walk briefly under the arbors. When they reassembled, the room smelled of wet woolen tunics and sweat.

"Before we begin our discussion again, we need to return our thoughts to Christ," Brother John said. "He must be the Beginning, the End, and the Means by which we do all. I have asked Brother Anthony to address you on the inscription on Christ's cross, 'Jesus of Nazareth, the King of the Jews' and on His sufferings for our sake."

Anthony was one of those young, vigorous men whom Monaldo admired. When Monaldo had been Anthony's age, he was working in obscurity as a serf on a baron's estate. And so he continued until he was past fifty when he heard some followers of Francis speak. Then he left the nothing he had to embrace the Everything the friars offered. With them he begged, prayed, and tended the poor in obscurity. Obscurity was all he knew, all he wanted, all he merited.

In contrast to Monaldo, the young man who knelt before Brother John to receive a blessing was becoming a legend. Some said that he was closer to Francis in his beliefs than any other friar. Some wanted him to be minister general of the Order. Many friars, including Monaldo, had never heard him preach, but they had heard that the fire of God burned in him as he preached the true faith here throughout the area.

In his rain-splattered tunic, Anthony stood to face the gathering. His tonsured hair and eye lashes glistened with mist as he bowed his head and lifted his hands in prayer.

As Anthony began speaking, Monaldo swelled with warmth and devotion to the Son of God. He lost track of time and forgot his pains as Anthony progressed with his sermon.

Now Anthony's gaze was steady on a spot just above the heads of his listeners, as if he were seeing the One he described.

"Let us raise our eyes and fix them on Jesus crucified, the author of salvation. Let us contemplate our Lord pierced with nails and suspended from the cross." He paused before continuing. "How can you not believe when your life is hanging before you from the cross?"

Anthony looked at the faces lifted toward him, his own face beaded with sweat. "What is more important than a man's life? The life of the body is the soul and the life of the soul is Christ. Here, then, your very life hangs from the cross. How can you not feel any pain? How can you refuse to identify yourself with His suffering? If Christ is your life, as He truly is, how can you keep from following Him, ready with Peter and Thomas to be thrown into jail and to die at His side?"

The priest's gaze focused on Monaldo. "Christ hangs from the cross before you to invite you to share in His suffering. He never stops calling to us, 'Come, all of you who pass by the way, look and see whether there is any suffering like My suffering.'"

Anthony bowed his head and raised his hands skyward. "How easily do they fall away, they who were redeemed at the cost of so much pain!"

Again, his head lifted as if he were gazing at Christ Himself. "His passion was more than sufficient to redeem all humanity and still many head toward perdition. What could cause greater grief when no one recognizes or worries about this tragedy?"

Anthony's voice trembled. "It is truly frightful that the God who once regretted having created us will one day feel sorry for having redeemed us."

He turned to face the doorway, his hands sweeping toward the grape arbors that were dripping with rain. His voice rose above the patter on the roof and filled the room. "If after working all year long in his vineyard a farmer is disappointed because he cannot find ripe grapes, how much more bitter will be God's disappointment at our fruitlessness. God lamented in Isaiah 5, 'What more was there to do for my vineyard that I had not done? Why, when I looked for the crop of grapes, did it bring forth wild grapes?'"

Anthony turned back to the friars. "God is deeply disappointed when instead of justice in conversion and penance, He finds iniquity. He expects righteousness and honesty to be practiced toward one's neighbor, but instead He hears the cries of the oppressed."

He clenched his fists, then opened them and looked at them as if they held the grapes about which he spoke. "This is the bitter fruit that the vineyard yields after the passion of its Divine Landlord." His fingers curled around the imaginary grapes. "It deserves to be ripped out at its roots and thrown into the fire."

The priest's hands swept outward and then upward. Again, he raised his eyes. "Your Life hangs before you on the cross so that you might see yourself as in a mirror. You can thus see how serious were your wounds and that they can be healed by no other medicine than by the Blood of the Son of God. And, if you pause to reflect deeply, you can also come to understand how sublime is your dignity. How lofty is the greatness of your human person for which it was necessary to pay so incalculable a price. The 'mirror' of the cross shows you what you are in the present; it teaches you to what depths you must lower your pride, how you must mortify the desires of your flesh, how you ought to pray to the Father for those who persecute you, and place your spirit in His hands."

Monaldo noticed the slightest flicker of movement in the doorway behind Anthony. A figure entered the room. Monaldo broke into a grin. Father Francis!

Even as he smiled, he squinted. Francis was not wet with rain. Monaldo saw the little man fling his arms open wide in the form of a cross and then rise until his head and shoulders were above those of Anthony. Anthony continued to preach as if totally unaware of Francis' presence.

"But you do not believe in Christ, in your Life, Who assures you, 'Just as Moses raised the serpent in the desert, in the same way the Son of Man must be raised up, so that whoever believes in Him may not be lost but have eternal life.' To see and to believe is the same thing because, in this case, you see only as much as you believe."

Francis brought his arms before him and, with his right hand, blessed the friars over Anthony's head. Then he smiled and traced a cross directly above the shaved scalp of the friar who preached beneath him.

Anthony was gazing intently at the friars, his voice a plea, "Believe firmly in Jesus crucified, the Life of your life, so that you may be able to live with Him, Who is Life itself, forever and ever. Amen."

Anthony bowed his head and walked back to the bench on which he had been sitting. Behind him, through the doorway, Monaldo saw the wet arbors. Francis was gone.

In the hushed, prayerful silence, Monaldo struggled with a holy torment. "Tell the vision," the Spirit was saying to his heart.

How could he, a nobody, have been granted such a divine favor?

*I am not worthy to have seen it,* Monaldo argued. *Let the others who have seen it speak.*

"I determine who is worthy. No one has seen my beloved Francis but you. Tell the vision."

No one moved. All were deep in prayer and meditation.

"Tell the vision."

Finally Brother John rose. "Thank you, Brother Anthony. Has anyone anything to share regarding what our brother preached?"

"Tell the vision."

No one spoke. Each seemed to be waiting for the other.

"Tell."

Monaldo stood. His legs felt weak. "Father Anthony, while you were speaking, Father Francis came in the doorway and blessed us and you." He sat down.

"Did you see this, Brother?" Brother John asked.

"Yes, Brother," Monaldo said in a squeaky voice.

Some friars turned to look at Monaldo. Others knelt in thanksgiving. Anthony dropped to his knees, his head bowed to the floor.

Brother John spoke, a tremor was in his voice. "I had been praying for the spirit of Francis to strengthen and guide this meeting. Praise the Lord for having granted my prayer."

## ∽ 12 ∾

### *Novice*

**Road from Montpellier to Arles, Montpellier, France (Spring 1225)** ∽
The theft had been almost too easy. The young novice had lagged behind while the other friars assembled for choir, then he slipped into Anthony's cell. Here he quickly found what he was seeking: Anthony's personally hand-penned *Commentary on the Psalms* lying on a small table near the priest's sleeping mat. The novice had left the convent immediately, giving the impression to anyone watching that he was hurrying to join his brothers at prayer. Instead, he had skirted the church and then, on long, thin legs, raced through the streets of Montpellier. He ran until he reached the road that followed this tributary of the Rhone River, a road that led to Arles. In Arles, he would sell the *Commentary,* purchase some useful clothing, and give the tunic he now wore to a beggar.

He realized how odd he must appear to travelers who walked the road with him. The Friars Minor always traveled in pairs, and he was alone. Yet no one stopped to ask, "Where is your companion?"

He had been too young to enter the Order, he told himself, and too wicked. He was, after all, the son of beggars, a beggar himself. He had slept with the beggar women of Beziers and paid them with coins or food he had stolen. Perhaps he had even fathered a child. Then he had seen the holy beggars of Father Francis and he longed to be like them. They possessed a peace and joy that he knew came from God. He had longed to possess that peace and joy within himself. How could he have been so foolish to think that he, a sinner, could become a man of Christ?

The friars welcomed him lovingly. The Order had been good to him. He had food to eat, not much, it was true, but then he didn't need much. He was used to eating little. He had a place to sleep, only a mat of straw, but he needed no more. His needs were met and he had begun to learn of the God for Whom he hungered.

When he had come to Montpellier to learn from Father Anthony, everything had improved. Anthony's teaching had deepened his faith and knowledge. How little he knew, but he was learning. How poorly he believed, but he was trying. And, in Montpellier, the convent was comfortable and the food plentiful. That was because Montpellier, unlike many other cities in the Province, had never gone over to the *Cathari.* Remaining faithful to the Church, Montpellier was quick to house and sustain any true sons of Christ.

And so the thin-armed beggar had become the thin-armed novice. But now he knew that donning a tunic could not change a sinner into a saint. True, he had worked at his faith. True, he had not stolen or been with any woman since he had joined the brothers five months ago. But as the months went on, he grew weary of begging and repairing chapels and praying and fasting. Out in the streets as a beggar, he had been destitute and maligned, but he was free. In the Order, he seemed always surrounded by other friars, hemmed in by doctrine, constrained by holiness. Sometimes he felt as if he was suffocating. Finally, he came to realize that he could never be a friar. Sin was too entrenched in his soul and the desire for freedom too keen.

Right now, it felt good to be walking down this road, a stolen book hidden in the folds of his tunic, his eyes gazing longingly at each woman who shyly passed him. He knew that he should not feel this pride, this lust, but they were there, surely as much a part of him as his fingernails. They proved to him again that he was not meant to be a friar. Father Anthony might be a good friar. But not the novice.

Then the thought struck him. Father Anthony had received orders to preach against the heretics at Toulouse. Within days he would be leaving and he would want to take his book with him. Most likely he would be back in his cell by now, searching for the volume. Suppose he appeared to the novice. The novice shivered with fear and shook his head. No, such a thing would not happen. Still, what had just happened on Easter? Didn't Father Anthony seem to be in two places at one time on that day?

On Easter, the youth and several other novices and brothers were chanting their prayers in the convent choir while the faithful townsfolk were with Anthony as he celebrated Mass in the cathedral. When the moment for chanting the Office arrived, the brothers waited expectantly for the one designated to begin. It was Anthony's turn. Surely he had found a replacement. The men's heads were bowed in respectful silence when suddenly they heard Anthony's gentle song. From the corner of his eye, the novice could see the friar standing in his usual place, singing the *alleluia*. Mass must have ended extremely early for the priest to return to choir. Once Anthony finished singing, the friars resumed their prayers in unison. When they finally disbanded to return to their cells, they heard the clamor of worshipers leaving the cathedral. The Mass Anthony celebrated was just over.

Just a few days ago, while Anthony was teaching the friars theology, one of the brothers who had served Mass with the priest spoke up, "Father, you say that we must have silence in which to pray. Is that why, on Easter, during your sermon you so abruptly drew your hood over your face and sank back in the pulpit? It was such a long silence, Father, those at worship began to fidget. But when you drew the hood back and resumed your sermon, you said nothing about it. Were you expecting that we, during that time of silence, would reflect on the glory of the risen Lord?"

Anthony had smiled. "That would have been a worthy reflection."

The incident on Easter seemed spookier each time the novice thought about it.

By now, the sun was high overhead and the lad's legs were growing weary. Directly ahead was a bridge across the Rhone River. How cool and comfortable appeared the shade underneath it! There, before continuing his journey, he could rest a bit. That is, he could rest if the frogs that lived along the banks would cease their incessant croaking.

As the novice picked his way down the slope to the shade under the bridge, he thought of Father Anthony. If Father Anthony were here, he would have begun noon prayers after asking the frogs to maintain silence. At the Montpellier convent, Anthony had blessed the water of a pond and asked the noisy frogs in it to be quiet. Ever after, they no longer croaked. One friar claimed that he had taken a few frogs from the Montpellier pond and brought them to another pond where they began to call out. So he took a few from the opposite pond and brought them to Montpellier where they maintained perpetual silence. The frogs were quiet in the Montpellier pond but noisy anywhere else. Strange. A lot about Father Anthony was strange.

The novice was not about to silence the frogs or to pray. He was totally exhausted. The previous week of restless nights had drained him. He had never before planned a theft with so much agitation. If he lay down here on this bed of thick grass, he would most likely fall asleep no matter how loudly the frogs croaked.

He had not been sleeping long when the silence awakened him. Why were the frogs still? He knew. Someone was here. Or something. He leaped to his feet. Perhaps a bandit. Then, to his right, obscured by the arch of the bridge, a dark bulk moved. In a moment of confusion, he thought it was Anthony. Then he saw bristly, black fur and a thick black snout. The novice scrambled up the bank and made for the bridge. The huge monster was on the bridge.

"Take the book back to the priest," a voice seemed to command as the unidentifiable beast lunged toward the novice. "Take it back or I shall kill you and throw your body into the river."

The novice had never seen a demon, but he knew such creatures existed. Only a demon could speak. The black monster must be the devil himself. The novice spun on his heels and bolted back the way he had come, not sparing one second to see if the beast were lurching after him.

The sun was dropping in the darkening sky when he returned to the convent. How would he get the book to the priest? He would simply leave it on the chapel step and someone would discover it and return it to its owner. He did not plan to stay at the convent himself. Tales of discipline in other convents had reached this one. He was certain that Anthony would act as other priests did. Was this man not nicknamed the hammer of heretics? Had he not silenced opposition in the provinces of Aquitania, Narbonne, and Languedoc? A man as forceful as he would punish the crime of theft. Anthony would strip the novice naked and beat him nearly unconscious while the other brothers watched in horror.

As he laid the book on the chapel step, the voice came again. "Take the book to the priest. To the priest."

The novice drew back. What was that shadow just around the corner of the chapel?

He grabbed the book and, forcing himself to walk to preserve the rule of Order, entered the convent and tapped at the door of Anthony's cell.

"Come in."

The novice knew he had better look contrite. Opening the door, he fell on his knees, his head bowed.

"So. You have returned my book," a kind voice said. "God has answered one of my prayers." The priest put his hand on the youth's trembling shoulder. "Why are you so frightened? I am not going to hurt you."

"Father, I am a wretched sinner." He hoped he sounded sorry. Very sorry. "Forgive me, Father."

The priest sank to his knees before the novice, his bowed head touching the ground, his voice almost a sob. "Lord, I realize that, if you were to remove your compassion from me, I, too, would become a victim of my own wretchedness." Then Anthony raised his head and placed his hands on the youth's shoulders. The novice flinched at the unexpected touch, but the grip was gentle instead of severe. With his face lifted heavenward and his eyes closed, Anthony whispered, "O Lord, our protector, look upon the face of Your Anointed. O Lord, do not look upon our sins, but look at the face of Christ, Your Anointed, covered with spittle, swollen with bruises, and covered with tears on our behalf. Have mercy on us, O Lord, because of the face of Christ. Be merciful to us who have been the cause of His suffering."

Then Anthony released his gentle touch and raised his arms to God, his prayer continuing to flow as smoothly as a placid stream.

As the astonished young man listened, the weight of his own pretended contrition crushed him. He was a sinner. He deserved to be beaten to within a breath of his life. The novice pulled the too wide tunic over his thin shoulders. The garment slid down, crumpling about his knees, its sleeves clinging loosely to his wrists. The young man knelt, bare backed and still, his eyes downcast and closed, while Anthony continued to pray.

A beating would feel good. A beating would thrash the guilt and deceit away.

He heard the priest shift before him. He was rising, he knew. He heard soft footsteps circle him to the right. Without thinking, he tightened his back muscles, then flinched at the first touch on his shoulders. It was his tunic being gently lifted back into place.

"The wounds of Christ on the cross speak to the Father of forgiveness, not vengeance, my little one." The priest tucked the garment into place. "I had prayed to have my book back. And I had prayed for you to return with it. The book has returned. Have you?"

The novice could not bear to look up. With bowed head, he whispered hoarsely, "Father, I cannot. I'm not like the others. I'm wicked, Father. If you knew.... I feel trapped here."

The youth felt a tender touch on his hand, warm fingers enclosing it, a gentle tug upward.

"Come with me."

The novice rose and followed the priest out of the convent. Why was he going with Anthony? The novice only knew that he must go.

In silence, the two friars wound their way through the streets of Montpellier with Anthony pausing to chat with or bless several townspeople who stopped him.

*This man is the hammer of heretics?* the novice thought. True, to crowds Anthony spoke forcefully against sin. Yet, he urged mercy toward the sinner. No crusader could use Anthony's words to justify the slaughter of heretics. His correction began and ended with love. What had he counseled the brothers? The novice struggled to recall that class. "With a fallen brother, we must show ourselves neither too tender nor too hard, neither soft as flesh nor hard as bone; in him, we must love our own human nature while hating his fault. St. John exhorts us to fraternal charity, comparing it to and wishing us to model it on the charity that God has shown to all of us. 'By this has the charity of God appeared to us, that God has sent His only begotten Son into the world, so that by Him we may have life.'"

How had the novice forgotten those words? He should not have feared this man.

When the two men arrived at the outskirts of the town, Anthony commented, "We have just preached a good sermon, my little one."

The comment startled the novice. "But we have not said anything."

"Our peaceful manner and modest looks are a sermon to those who have seen us. It can often be more influential to be than to say. Now, look." Anthony pointed to the peaks of the Cevennes Mountains thrust across each other far in the distance. "When did Jesus go up to a mountain, taking with Him Peter, James, and John?"

The novice reached into his memory for that lesson that Anthony, the teacher, had given. Finally, the answer came. "At the Transfiguration, Father."

Nodding, Anthony struck off the main road and led the way along one of the many winding paths that shepherds used to drive their flocks up to higher pastures.

"The three apostles, Peter, James, and John, were special friends of Christ. These three men represent three properties of a soul. Without these properties, a soul cannot ascend 'the high mountain of light.' It cannot establish a relationship with God. Do you want a relationship with God, my brother?"

"I do, Father. But for me, it is not possible. I don't fit in here, Father."

"Let us see if you fit in or not. Peter, James, and John were coarse fishermen. They did not 'fit in' to an order either. Yet they followed Christ, did they not?"

The novice agreed.

"Nor were they without sin. What can you tell me about that?

Again the novice searched his memory for the knowledge that he had gleaned in class.

"Peter cut off a servant's ear. He denied knowing Christ. James and John—they argued about who would be greatest in heaven. And...and they wanted to call down punishment on a town that would not accept them. Is that right, Father?"

Anthony grinned and playfully slapped the youth's shoulder. "You have a good memory, my little one. Now let's look at the names of these three men. Each name has a meaning. Peter means 'an admission.' James means 'a conquest' and John 'the grace of God.' Do you believe in Jesus and hope for salvation, my brother?"

"Yes, Father. But is salvation possible for me, Father? I am so wicked."

"There you go calling yourself wicked again," Anthony said. "We are all wicked. Did not Christ come to save sinners?" Anthony pointed to the mountains which seemed no nearer the closer they approached. "Only sinners may approach God on His high mountain of prayer. If sinners could not come to God, no one would go. Suppose we asked all the saints ever born on earth, with the exception of the always sinless holy Mother of Christ, whether they were without sin? What do you think they would answer if not to repeat with

John the Apostle, 'If we say we have no sin, we deceive ourselves and the truth is not in us.'"

Anthony smiled at the novice. "So do not be afraid to approach God. When you do, take with you Peter as Jesus did when He went up to the mountain. Take Peter and admit your sins, as did Peter. What sins? All of them. The pride in your heart. Your lust of the flesh. Your greed for material possessions. These are sins of which we all are guilty."

The novice hung his head. No one was guiltier of these sins than he.

Anthony continued to walk across the vast meadow toward the peaks. "Take James with you also. James is a conquest. Overcome and conquer these sins. Destroy the pride in your heart. Mortify the carnal desires of your flesh. Curb the vanity of a deceitful world."

"How can I do that, Father? I have just stolen your book. On the road, I have just looked lustfully at women."

"You can curb your sins if you take yet one more person with you when you ascend to God's transfiguring presence. Take also John, the grace of God who 'stands knocking at your door.'" Still walking, Anthony turned to the novice. "God is ever ready to enter your heart, my little one. And He will enter it. You need only to open the door of your spirit. God has revealed to you the evil that you have done and that you still struggle with inside. That revelation is the gift of grace. Now, in God and God's grace, preserve the good which you have begun. What good, you say? You have returned my book. And you have returned yourself."

"But, Father, I cannot stay."

"Do you wish to be happy, my little one?"

"With all my heart, Father."

"Do you recall the Book of Tobit in the Bible? Take to heart the words that Tobit spoke to his son on his deathbed. 'Remember the Lord our God all your days!' All your days, son of Tobit. Remember the Lord all your days and then you will be happy."

"Father, is it possible to be truly happy?"

Anthony smiled. "It is possible. Look around you."

The men halted. They were standing in the center of a field cropped low by countless sheep and goats. Far off to their right, a herd of white, black, and speckled ewes and lambs bleated intermittently. Two shepherds were seated beneath a tree at the edge of the clearing.

"This is a beautiful scene. Surely God dwells here. When God dwells in the soul, the soul becomes even more beautiful than all of this. For who can be more blessed or more happy than one in whom God has set up His dwelling place? What else can you need or what else can possibly make you richer? You have everything when you have within you the One Who made all things, the only One Who can satisfy the longings of your spirit, without Whom whatever exists is as nothing."

Anthony took the novice's hands in his own and raised their arms skyward. The novice, following Anthony's example, lifted his face to the heavens growing dusky with evening. Anthony's voice rang out with joy, "O Possession Which contains all things within Yourself, truly blessed is the person who has You, truly happy whoever possesses You because he then owns that Goodness which alone can make the human mind completely happy.

"But, dear God, what can I give to come to possess You? If I give away everything, do You think that I will have You in exchange? You are much higher than the highest heavens. You are deeper than the deepest abyss, longer than the longest distance, wider than the widest ocean.

"How then can I, a worm, a dead dog, a tiny flea, a son of man, come to possess You?"

Anthony paused and the novice felt the anguish of the priest's cry echoing in his own heart. How could he, a simple sinner, possess the happiness that comes from possessing God?

With his arms and face still stretched heavenward, Anthony continued to cry out, "Job rightly says, when he speaks of divine wisdom, 'It cannot be valued in the gold of Ophir, in precious onyx or sapphire. Gold and glass cannot equal it, nor can it be exchanged for jewels of fine gold...the price of wisdom is beyond pearls.' O Lord God, I do not have these riches; what, then, can I give to possess You?"

The boy's hands were stretched to their uppermost limit and then slowly lowered. As Anthony lowered his hands, he also dropped his voice. "O Lord, I already know Your answer. 'Give Me yourself,' You say, 'and I will give you Myself. Give Me your mind and you will have Me in your mind. Keep all your possessions, but only give Me your soul. I have heard enough of your words; I do not need your works; only give Me yourself, forever.'"

The men's hands were dropped before them, still joined. *Lord, let me give myself to You,* the novice prayed. *Take my poor gift, Lord and make me happy.*

The question came softly. "Do you want to have God always in your mind?"

The novice's voice trembled. "Oh, Father, I want it. I want it so much."

"Then obey Him. We must be obedient to Christ than to our own whims, for we must not serve our Lord only with words. If the heart is humble, the body is obedient. Humility begets obedience. Father Francis whom we follow knows that humility is best supported by poverty. Father Francis calls us to follow Lady Poverty, for whoever possesses poverty is rich and wealthy. Where there is real poverty, there is found abundance. Do you understand this?"

"I want to understand it, Father."

Anthony raised his eyes heavenward. "O inestimable worth of poverty! Who does not possess you, possesses nothing, even though they may possess everything. What joy there is in you! For when we are poor and humble, we empty ourselves of all that we possess. Then we are hollow, able to contain anything poured into us. Into us, O God, pour an infusion of divine grace until we overflow with joy."

"Lord, let me have nothing so that I may have everything that is You," the novice whispered.

The joy in Francis's followers had attracted the novice. The joy in Anthony inspired him. If only he could possess God! Then he would need nothing else, neither the freedom of the streets nor the love of women nor the assurance of gold. God alone would be totally sufficient.

The novice squeezed Anthony's hands. "Father, how can I return to the Order?"

Anthony, who was still gazing upward, lowered his glance. His dark eyes found the novice's.

"You have never left the Order. The book is back. You are back. No more needs to be said."

The youth knelt before the priest. "Father, forgive me." This time, his sorrow was genuine. Placing his hand on the boy's shoulder, Anthony pronounced absolution. "For your penance, you must daily practice emptying yourself to be filled totally with God. When you have done this completely, you must speak to the people of

Montpellier about the possession of God. Find those who will listen, even if there are only one or two. Tell of the Possession Who will possess you. Urge them to empty themselves to the One Who can fill them. Will you do that?"

The novice nodded. The joy in his heart was bubbling up, overflowing.

"God, empty me of myself and fill me with You," he begged.

The joy in his heart began to thaw the iciness in his spirit, melting out of him greed, lust, and desire, and spreading in its place a tiny, warm glow of the Son. A great ledge of ice still clung to his soul, but he would beg God to melt it all. When the Son totally filled him, he would spread His brilliance to others. He would illuminate Montpellier with the light of Christ.

# ∂ 13 ∞

## *Lord Varden*

**City Square, Toulouse, France (Summer 1225)** ∾ Under a high summer sun, Lord Varden perspired in his black robe while he preached from a wooden platform at the edge of the main square of Toulouse. His tall, slender stature and white hair accurately gave him the look of austerity and holiness. Like all *perfecti*, he fasted three days a week on bread and water and never ate meat, eggs, cheese, and milk. Several times daily, he recited the Lord's Prayer sixteen times in succession. He considered the world's goods and attractions to be little better than a dog's vomit.

When he had become a *perfecti*, he had deeded his small estate and castle over to the elders of his faith. They had retained him as landlord, but he now owned nothing but his faith. His life, he realized, had not begun until he had joined the *Cathari*. Prior to that time, worries about his family and his lands had consumed his attention.

Lord Varden's grandfather had owned a huge estate here in the Languedoc, but the custom of dividing inheritances equally among descendants had sliced his lands into smaller sections. Each of his eight sons had to share in the property.

Lord Varden's father had sired nine surviving sons, so Lord Varden's inheritance had amounted to only seven acres near Toulouse, part of it swamp and much of it forest. For all his married life, he had struggled to keep his wife decently clothed and his children fed. But how to divide his minuscule inheritance among his own three sons? What could they do with little more than two acres of ground apiece? And what dowry could his two daughters bring to a marriage?

One June market day many years ago, when Lord Varden had not solved these difficulties, he had ridden into Toulouse to visit Renault the weaver. Renault was a huge man with hands as thick as turnips, yet he wove the most delicate kerchiefs. His prices were steep, but the lord wanted to purchase something lovely for his lady's feast day.

Lord Varden had looked at Renault's wares and then asked, "Have you anything more?"

"I have more precious goods than these," Renault had replied. "Would you like to know more of them?"

Lord Varden was curious. "Of course."

"My goods are from God and you may know God as well." Renault spoke softly, "Such goods will kindle in your heart the love of God."

"I attend Mass every Sunday and Holy Day," Lord Varden had said.

"Is that enough?" Renault had asked. "If you would like to learn more of what I have to give, come to me today at the hour of None and I will teach you."

Thus had begun Lord Varden's conversion. Two years later, with Renault at his side, he received the *consolamentum* and became a *perfecti*. Later he had deeded his castle to the *Cathari*, enrolled his daughters as *perfecti* to live there in the hospice, and watched two of his sons and his wife also become believers.

Through his frequent preaching, the lord had made many converts among the people of Toulouse. He knew that his way of life meant as much as the words he spoke. Both together might convert another soul in the cluster of people who today had come from market to listen attentively. If any expressed an interest in learning more, either the lord or Renault, who was part of today's crowd, would teach them.

The crowd was attentive but obviously minding the sun. Here and there some folks fanned themselves with their hats or even their bare palms. Those near the market stalls hugged the shade. Lord Varden decided to be brief.

As he spoke, he noticed a gray-robed friar slip into the crowd not three yards from Renault. The difference in size between the two men made Lord Varden envision a black bear about to pounce on a gray mountain goat. The comical image did not humor the lord. The friar had not come to be converted. He came to refute.

The lord felt a surge of bitterness. Ever since he had become a *perfecti*, Catholics had been warring against the *Cathari* in the name of religion. He well remembered 1206, the year of his *consolamentum*. Not two months after, the preaching friar, Dominic of Guzman, had walked barefoot into Toulouse to preach against the *Cathari*. Dominic had called the "Good Men" Albigensians after the town of Albi in which many of the *Cathari* lived. Lord Varden had listened attentively to public debates between preacher and *perfecti*. Often these culminated in angry verbal exchanges in which each party accused the other of being the Antichrist.

In 1208, the easily disliked preacher, Peter of Castelnau, was murdered, and Pope Innocent III called for the first Albigensian crusade against the "Good Men." Warfare consumed the territory of the Languedoc, with many towns around Toulouse falling to the crusaders. Tales of massacres, rapes, mutilations, burnings, and dismembering on both sides filtered into the city. Battles became political with counts vying for whatever territories they could conquer, no matter what religion their inhabitants espoused.

Twice Toulouse had been viciously assaulted. Twice it had repelled the enemy. Now the *Catharist* sympathizer, Count Raymond VII, held nearly complete control of the area. Despite the count's promise to the pope not to protect the sect, the *Catharist* bishop still remained safely in the city. Any gray-robed friar who tried to stir up Catholics against Lord Varden would instead rally the *Cathari* to the lord's defense.

Lord Varden decided to assume the offensive. He would turn the crowd against the friar.

"The Catholic clergy tell you that serving God consists in attending Mass," he projected his voice to the farthest corners of the square. "But listen to John 13: 'Jesus rose from supper and laid aside His garments and took a towel and girded Himself. After that, He poured water into a basin and began to wash the disciples' feet.'"

The lord walked back and forth as he preached, his hand and head movements emphasizing certain key points. "He said to them, 'Do you know what I have done to you? You call Me Master and Lord and you say well, for so I am. If I then, your Lord and Master, have washed your feet, you also ought to wash one another's feet. For I have given you an example, that you should do as I have done to you.' So we must humbly serve one another as Christ commanded."

The lord gestured toward the friar. "But do the Roman clergy do this? Listen to Matthew 23 and Mark 13:38–40." As the lord plunged into Christ's long denunciation of the evil and hypocrisy of religious leaders, he was certain that his words would be effective. During his own conversion, Renault had quoted him these very passages. Lord Varden then asked the crowd the same question that Renault had asked him.

"To whom do these passages refer?" And he gave Renault's answer. "They refer to the clergy and the monks."

The crowd shifted and several turned to stare at the friar. Those standing near him, including Renault, sidled away until he was left standing alone in a small, cleared space.

"The doctors of the Roman Church are proud of their dress and carriage. They love honor and to be called Father, but we do not have such Fathers or such honor. They frequently visit women of the town, for reasons that you certainly can imagine, but we each have a wife and live chastely with her.

"The clergy are rich and want more, taking even the money of poor widows to support their ceremonies and buildings. But we are content with simple food and clothes and want no more. Look at the Catholic knights and the bishops who send them to battle with the Church's blessings. They fight and war and burn and kill the poor, but Christ said, 'He who takes the sword will perish by it.' We suffer from them for our righteousness, for, as you well know, they have killed several of our members and warred against our city."

A cry of support rose from the crowd as they recalled the bitterness of their city's siege and their own united, desperate struggle to beat back the crusaders.

"Their clergy do nothing, but we work with our hands. Only their clergy may teach and no one else, but among us women as well as men may teach. In fact, a disciple of seven days may instruct another."

Lord Varden paused as he swept his arms before him as if to encompass the entire city. "Hardly a teacher among them knows by heart three connected chapters of the New Testament, but nearly all among us can recite the text in our own tongue, for we have our own Scriptures written in the language that we speak. And because we have the true faith of Christ and teach a holy life and doctrine, the Roman Church persecutes us without cause, bringing some of us even to death."

A murmur of assent swept through the crowd. A swift motion near the friar caught the lord's eye. Two brawny youths pushed toward the man, but Renault leaped in front of them and, with outstretched arms as thick as clubs, blocked their path. Like all *perfecti*, Renault opposed violence. The youths backed off, and the lord continued to speak.

"The Catholic clergy say much but do nothing. They bind heavy burdens and place them on their followers, but we practice what we teach. They insist that traditions of men be followed more than the commandments of God, to observe their fasts, festivals, Masses, and other human institutions, but we persuade others only to keep the doctrines of Christ and of the Apostles. They load penitents with the most grievous penances which they do nothing to relieve, but we, following Christ's example, tell the sinner, 'Go and sin no more,' and remit all his sins by the imposition of hands, therefore paving his way into eternal life in heaven. On the other hand, they, by their rigorous teaching, send almost all souls to hell. Think which faith is more perfect, ours or that of the Church of Rome?"

The lord paused. "If you wish to learn more, come and speak to me now. I, as well as other Christians, will teach you." With that, he turned and descended the platform, the wild applause of the crowd sounding in his ears.

As the applause died, a deep, firm voice shot forth, "Who among you destroys his entire garden because worms and rot have ruined five cabbages?"

A hush fell over the crowd as heads turned toward the friar. He was speaking even as he walked toward the platform.

"The Church was commended to Peter by Christ with the words, 'Feed My lambs,' not once but three times. Not once did he tell Peter to shear them or to fleece them. It is as if Jesus said, 'If you love Me because of Myself, feed My sheep, not your sheep but Mine. Seek My glory among them, not yours; My gain and not yours, since the love of God is proved by the love of one's neighbor.'"

The friar bowed to Lord Varden as he climbed the steps to the platform. As he reached the flat planking, he turned to the lord and called out, "The lord who just addressed you was right in condemning the corrupt clergy."

A whistle of amazement swept across the square. Even Lord Varden, who had heard many Catholic preachers, had not heard one condemn other members of his Church.

"Woe to that shepherd of the Church who does not feed his sheep even one time, but shears and fleeces them three or four times. To such a shepherd, God says in Genesis, 'The king of Sodom,' who is the devil, demands, 'Give me their souls. The rest you can keep for yourself.'"

The friar's gaze was locking onto individuals in the crowd. "I ask you again. Do you destroy an entire garden because worms and rot have ruined five cabbages? Do you not pluck the cabbages and throw them on the dung heap, then return to cultivate and enjoy the good fruits of your garden? God agrees with the lord who just addressed you. The rotten clergy will be plucked out of God's garden that is the Church. God will give their souls to the devil who will throw them into hell to rot."

He paused momentarily. "Come here tomorrow at this time and learn about God's garden of true faith that can become for you the garden of paradise whose fruit is eternal life."

The friar descended the steps, bowed to Lord Varden, who still stood by them, and walked off in the direction of the convent of the Friars Minor.

As the friar disappeared, Renault touched Lord Varden's shoulder. "Your speech almost got him beat."

"Who is he?"

"They say his name is Anthony."

— —

THE NEXT DAY, UNDER A HOTTER SUN than the day before, Lord Varden and Renault joined a small crowd in the main square of Toulouse. When they had come within three yards of the preaching platform, they stopped. Here a few other *Catharist* believers congregated.

The day was sultry. Every inch of shade was crammed with bodies. Those standing in the sun fanned themselves with scraps of cloth. Beads of sweat glistened on nearly every forehead when the news rippled through the group, "Here he comes."

Two friars, dressed in patched, gray tunics, approached the platform from a tiny side street. The heavier one remained at the steps while the one who had spoken yesterday ascended the platform, raised his hands over the crowd for silence, and then bowed his head. After a few moments, the friar raised his eyes to heaven and, in a sturdy but gentle voice, began to pray.

"O Light of the world, infinite God, Father of eternity, Giver of wisdom and knowledge and ineffable Dispenser of every spiritual grace, You know all things before they are made. You Who make the darkness and the light, put forth Your hand and touch my mouth. Make it like a sharp sword to utter eloquently Your words. Make my tongue, O Lord, like a chosen arrow to declare faithfully Your wonders. Put Your Spirit, O Lord, in my heart that I may perceive. Put it in my soul that I may retain. Put it in my conscience that I may meditate. Lovingly, holily, mercifully, clemently, and gently inspire me with Your grace."

As the friar continued his prayer, the lord surveyed the crowd. The fanning and shifting had decreased as if Anthony's prayer had been a gentle breeze to drive back the heat.

"'God said, "Let there be light and there was light."' Genesis 1:3. In the name of the Father and of the Son and of the Holy Spirit." Anthony crossed himself as he spoke and those Catholics in the crowd did the same.

"Let us examine the seven days of God's creation, beginning with the first, and apply them to our life as followers of Christ."

Lord Varden nodded. Anthony was going to directly attack *Catharist* beliefs. He was speaking from the Old Testament which the Cathari knew was written by Satan. He stated that God created the material universe when Satan, not God, had done so.

"The first day represents the Incarnation of our Savior. Without our Savior, we would be faithless and lost. Without light, our world would not exist. The light is Christ, 'Who dwells in unapproachable light' and 'gives light to every person coming into the world.'"

The *Cathari* knew that only those of their faith had God's true enlightenment.

"When the Father said, 'Let there be light,' He was also speaking of His Son's Incarnation. St. John expresses this more succinctly: 'The Word became flesh and made His dwelling among us.'"

Renault leaned toward Lord Varden. "As I expected. He claims that Christ was truly human flesh instead of spirit alone."

"When the prophet Ezekiel writes, 'the hand of the Lord came upon me,' he is referring to the Son in Whom and through Whom the Father created all things."

Lord Varden tried to calculate how many teachings of his faith Anthony was disputing. Was this the fourth or fifth? The Father created only spiritual things. The Father created the Son.

"God said, 'let there be light,' and the Light of the world was born of the Virgin Mary. 'The darkness which covered the abyss,' that is, the hearts of men, was dispelled."

*Six. Christ's birth through Mary was an illusion. God would not have entrapped himself in human flesh to be born in a human way from a woman's womb.*

"On the second day, God said, 'Let there be a vault in the middle of the waters, to divide the waters in two.' The vault is Baptism which, like a vault, divides the deep from the shallow waters, believers from unbelievers."

*Following the example of the evil John the Baptizer, Catholics espoused water baptism, even for infants. The "Good Men," knowing that water was material, and therefore the creation of an evil god, followed Christ who baptized with fire and the Holy Spirit.*

"God set a vault between the waters to divide them. This vault is Baptism. Sinners, however, break the pact which they made with God at Baptism. The earth, laboring under the sins of greed, lust, and pride, merits the curse pronounced upon it in the Book of Revelation, 'Woe to the inhabitants of the earth.'"

As Anthony continued to expound the sins of humanity, Lord Varden glanced about the crowd. The friar was speaking to Catholics now, for they were the ones consumed by these vices.

"On the third day, God said 'Let the earth bring forth vegetation, every kind of plant that bears seed and every kind of fruit tree on earth that bears fruit with its seed in it.' The earth, plowed and broken up in springtime, produces abundant fruit at harvest. Thus, the earth represents the Passion of Our Lord Whose bruised and broken Body, 'crushed for our sins,' produces the abundant fruit of the heavenly Kingdom."

*Christ had not really suffered and died, for He had no real body. The Passion was but an illusion.*

"On the fourth day, God said, 'Let there be two lights in the dome of the sky.' The sky is the risen Christ, resplendent like the sun in the glory of His resurrection and incorruptible in His Body like the moon. Thus, the fourth day prefigures the resurrection of our Lord."

*As Christ's death was illusion, so was his resurrection and incorruptible body, for He never had and never would assume evil flesh.*

"On the fifth day, God made 'birds of the air.' This text recalls the mystery of the Ascension when the Son of God flew like a bird to the right side of His Father."

*Where did this friar get these comparisons? His theology was heretical, but his knowledge of Scripture and its applications were stunning.* As a preacher, Lord Varden recognized and admired talent when he heard it. If only this man were a *Cathar!*

"On the sixth day, God said, 'Let us make people in our image, after Our likeness. God blew into the man's nostrils the breath of life and so the man became a living being.'"

*Satan had taken apostate spirits who had rebelled against the good God and, forming bodies of earth, had imprisoned those spirits in them. The devil and not the good God had made humanity.*

"The image of God in humanity, deformed and obscured by sin, was restored and illumined by the Holy Spirit Who breathed the breath of life into each person. Thus, the sixth day represents the sending of the Holy Spirit into the world at Pentecost. The Holy Spirit, given at Pentecost, impresses on our hearts the Spirit of God and so makes of each of us 'a living being.' Due to the gift of the Spirit, we can recognize the Father in the face of the Son and we can follow that Son through the light of faith."

*Not everyone possessed the Holy Spirit. God granted this gift only to those who had received the* consolamentum.

"'Since on the seventh day God was finished with the work He had been doing, He rested.' On the last day, the faithful will also rest from all their work and suffering and God 'shall wipe every tear from their eyes.' The seventh day is the gift of eternal life. On that day, the Church will be welcomed by Christ, her spouse, who will 'give her a reward of her labors and let her works praise her at the city gates.' Those gates are the final judgment at which Christ will say, 'Come, you have My Father's blessing.' May each of us be counted worthy to enter those gates and forever 'feast in the Kingdom of God.' Amen."

Cheers rose from the Catholics in the crowd as Anthony descended the platform. Some surged toward him. Renault and Lord Varden remained like statues of stone in the shifting mob.

"He is forceful," Renault said.

To Lord Varden's right, three *Catharist* believers were kneeling, their backs bowed. "And effective," he added. "Apparently, he has made some converts."

The two men worked their way toward the kneeling trio. They must be won back to the true faith before they succumbed to the friar's words.

That night, in the coolness of the castle's sitting room, the talk was of Anthony. *Perfecti* and believers who lived in the hospice tore apart his speech as wild dogs rip to shreds a fallen stag. As one of the elders, Lord Varden took the lead in the discussion. Only past midnight did he and two other remaining *perfecti* finally surrender to weariness and retire for the night.

Lord Varden lay awake a long time. Anthony troubled him. The friar was sincere in his heresy. How could he so firmly believe falsehood? The lord would listen to the friar preach again and find the holes in the fabric of this man's faith.

Four days later, Lord Varden was again preaching. He had decided to attack head on the core of Anthony's speech, namely that God created the world. The sky was overcast and the day pleasant. The crowd was ample. Again Anthony was in the gathering.

"It is perfectly clear from the Scriptures that the god and lord who is the creator of the world is different from Him to Whom the blessed commend their spirits," the lord began. "Our opponents say that according to Genesis the Lord is the creator of the visible things of this world: the heaven and the earth, the sea, men and beasts, birds and reptiles."

The lord looked at Anthony. Several listeners did the same.

"But I say that the creator of the visible things of this world is not the true God. And I prove this from the evil of his words and deeds and the changeable character of his words and deeds as described in the Old Testament. Where should I begin? The whole Old Testament is filled with the evil of this god.

"Abram, who was called by this god to leave his homeland, gave his wife Sarai to the Egyptian king and said that she was his sister. The king intended to commit fornication with her because of this lie. This same Abram committed adultery with a slave woman so that he would father a son."

Lord Varden continued to name men and women who served the Old Testament god but whose lives were sinful—Jacob, Rachel, Rahab, David. He gave examples of slaughters of many innocent people, all done in the name of this god.

"It is evident enough to the wise that the true God could not be the creator who mercilessly tempts men and women to destruction. The good God is the God of the New Testament, the God of the Spirit, the God of Jesus, the God we serve. To Him be all praise and glory and honor. Amen. *Alleluia!*"

The following day, while Lord Varden and the other residents were taking a light breakfast in the lord's castle turned hospice, a servant brought him a message.

"A friar is here to see you, my lord."

The friar could be none other than his rival. The lord wished to speak to him privately. "Lower the drawbridge and bring him into the sitting room," Lord Varden commanded.

With a sip of wine, he washed down his final bite of bread, then bid good day to his fellow *perfecti* and believers.

In this sitting room dwelled ghosts of memories. Here, before joining the *Cathari,* the lord had often sat to work on accounts and ledgers. Here his sons had shown him little boats they'd made of wooden planks and his daughters had sung their childish songs. After the castle had become a *Catharist* hospice, the lord's wife, little more than an enfleshed reed, had lain upon a bed here. Here she had received the *consolamentum* and had every sin forgiven. Then to insure that she would sin no more, she had voluntarily begun the final, suicidal fast called the *endura.* After five days of bloodletting in warm baths and eating and drinking nothing, she had entered eternal life from this very room. Here, not two weeks ago, the lord had presided at the *consolamentum* of the city coppersmith whom he had sent to Carcassonne to preach. Now he would confront the friar whose faith he had rejected.

Lord Varden was alone with these thoughts when the servant and Anthony appeared.

"You are dismissed," Lord Varden nodded to the servant who bowed and exited the room.

The friar and the lord both bowed to each other, then broke into grins. "So each of us recognizes the other's breeding," Lord Varden said, extending his hands.

Anthony grasped the lord's hands in his own. "Your hands are as rough as mine," he said. "It seems that we have both exchanged breeding for weeding."

"I have plucked a few rotten cabbages out of my garden," the lord remarked.

Anthony laughed.

Lord Varden nodded toward a small side table around which three wooden chairs were arranged. "Have a seat."

As the men sat, the lord asked, "Have you come to convert me?"

Anthony was still smiling. "I cannot do that, my lord. Only My Lord can convert."

"He seems to work effectively through you."

"Any victory is His, not mine. But I did come to speak to you about Him, if only to satisfy myself that I have done so."

"The Catholic Church is in heresy. It abandoned the way centuries ago. We have returned to faith as it was meant to be."

"You have made yourself superior to God." Anthony's voice was gentle but firm.

The lord had submitted himself to God. "What do you mean?"

"God is the author of our life and our freedom. God has given us laws which we must follow. Do you agree?"

Of course the lord agreed.

"God gave us those laws so God can dispense with the laws if He wishes. Yesterday you questioned the Old Testament's apparent evil done in the name of God. You concluded that the God of the Old Testament cannot be the God of the New. By denying the goodness and wisdom of the Old Testament God, you deny the goodness and wisdom of Christ who quoted the Old Testament extensively."

"Christ commanded us 'Love your enemies. Do good to those who hate you. If someone strikes you on one cheek, turn to him the other also.' He said, 'Anyone who is angry with his brother is liable to the fires of Gehenna.' The killings, fornications, and deceits of the Old Testament, done in the name of God, do not follow these dictates of love."

Anthony nodded. "My lord, what is this at which we are sitting?"

"A table, of course."

"What is a table useful for, my lord?"

"As a place to serve food, to gather around, to write on."

"You had this table made for those very purposes, did you not? Let us now suppose that it was the dead of winter and the castle was under siege. Every bit of firewood was gone. You had no way to obtain more. Is it lawful for you to break up this table," Anthony said, rapping on the wood, "to burn in the fireplace?" He held his hand toward the bare hearth.

"Of course."

"Why?"

"Because it is my table and because it is needful to burn it."

"No one could say that you do not know the function of a table since you used it for firewood, could they? In like manner, God, Who created the laws against killing, deceit, fornication, and so on, can dispense with those laws to fulfill His will. Just as you would not burn this table except in extremity, so God does not dispense with His moral law except in extreme and rare cases."

"You are saying that God can will killing."

"God may sometimes will it, but no one can justify killing or any other sin against the moral order unless God absolutely wills it in times of extremity."

"Your theology is dangerous, Father. You frighten me."

"No, my lord. In the Old Testament, when God drew His people from those who worshipped demons, He willed extreme measures to make the Jewish nation holy and His alone. When the time was ripe, Christ came to a nation separate from the world. He gave us laws of love and mercy which we must now follow."

The lord protested, "Any fanatic could kill someone and say God told him to do so."

"Fanaticism attributed to God is blasphemy. No one is authorized to break the moral law unless one is certain beyond a shadow of a doubt that God so wills it. This comes through prayer, consultation with the clergy, and absolute and total submission to the will of God not only in the matter at hand but also in all matters. To do what is wrong in God's name is a frightful responsibility, for to do so incorrectly makes one guilty of grave sin. God broke His Own law against killing by delivering Himself up as the Son to be crucified. He did this for our total and greater good."

The lord interrupted, "Christ's death was an illusion, not a fact."

"So you say. By denying Christ's death, you deny His humanity. Thus you negate the very foundation of Christianity."

"God Who is all good would not have taken to Himself sinful flesh."

"The beginning of the Gospel of John, which you quote, states, 'The Word was made flesh and dwelt among us.'"

The lord knew the answer to that objection. "This illusion is pointed out by St. Paul in his letter to the Philippians where he writes, 'Christ Jesus, Who, being in the form of God, did not think equality with God something to be grasped, but emptied Himself taking the form of a slave.' The word 'form' is used."

"The verse continues, '...taking the form of a slave, was made in the image of humankind and being formed as a man, He humbled Himself and became obedient unto death, even the death of the cross.' In his first letter to the Corinthians, St. Paul writes, 'If there be no resurrection from the dead, then Christ is not risen; and if Christ is not risen, then our preaching is in vain and your faith also is in vain.' You deny the actual death of Christ and His actual, bodily resurrection. How can you deny the eyewitness accounts of the Gospels?"

"The apostles and St. Paul were deceived by what they saw. They could not differentiate between illusion and reality."

"You were married, were you not?"

The lord nodded at this sudden change in subject.

"A wedding celebrates the union of two people, a bride and a groom. Many times weddings are arranged between two contending families to produce peace between them, the man taking a bride from his rival's family. In the human race, dissension existed between God and humanity. God wished to establish peace. All the messengers and legates sent by God could do nothing, so God the Father consented to send His Son who united Himself to our human nature in the womb of the Virgin Mary. Thus, the union of God and man was complete in the Son. Two disparate natures joined. In Christ, we are granted union with the Father, forgiveness of sins, and a share in eternal life."

"You must know that you will never convince me of your heresies."

Anthony stood. "God enlightens souls, my lord, not I."

Lord Varden stood as well.

"Do not trouble yourself, my lord. I can find my way out."

"Nonsense. I will walk with you to the gate house." The lord smiled weakly. "Have I disappointed you by not rushing to embrace your God?"

Anthony laughed as the two men came out of the sitting room. "With God there is always hope that misguided souls will know the truth. I am only to tell of His truth." Anthony turned to the lord as the men walked into the sunlight. The friar's black eyes were bright with earnestness. "There is truth, my lord. Christ said, 'I am the Way, the Truth, and the Life.' John 7 tells us that 'in Him is no falsehood at all.'"

The friar's gaze was unsettling. "Father, I admire your sincerity."

"And I admire yours. But it often happens that sincere people are sincerely wrong." Anthony bowed to the lord. "I will continue to pray for you, my lord."

"And I for you."

At the gatehouse, the two men grasped hands again before bidding farewell.

Weeks passed. Lord Varden preached. Anthony preached. Usually they were in each other's audience. Sometimes sentiment supported one, sometimes the other.

Anthony's crowd was swelling. Certain shopkeepers closed their doors on the days the friar spoke and came to hear him. If he were speaking at noon, women would begin to arrive at nine in order to claim a spot near the platform. Always after he preached, Anthony would be mobbed. The lord often thought of approaching him, but he had no reason to do so. He did not believe the friar's theology. Nevertheless, he could not discount the holiness of the man's lifestyle. He was teaching the Little Brothers theology at their convent. He was said to have cured paralysis and epilepsy with the sign of the cross. People claimed that he spoke in strange languages.

Where were the holes in the fabric of his faith?

One warm Saturday, under a clearing gray sky, Anthony was on the platform preaching. Lord Varden stood about ten yards from him in a crowd that was packed so tightly in the square that a horse and rider would have had great difficulty pushing through. With all eyes on him, the friar said, "And so, my people, today will be the last time that I preach to you. Tomorrow after Mass at dawn, I will be leaving for Castres."

A cry went up from the crowd. The friar raised his hands for silence.

"So I want to leave you with this final message."

*Here it comes,* the lord thought. *Now he will pit them against us. The Catholics will want to show him how deeply they love him and his God. Trouble will begin with this speech.*

"The apostle John tells us that, following Christ's resurrection, 'when the doors were shut where the disciples were assembled, Jesus came and stood in their midst and said to them, "Peace be with you." When He had said this, He showed them His hands and His side.' St. Luke, who describes the same incident, says that Christ told the apostles, 'Look at My hands and feet. It is really I. Touch Me and see, for a spirit has no flesh and bones as you see I have.' When He had said this, He showed them His hands and His feet."

Anthony looked squarely at the lord. "It is my opinion that Christ showed His apostles the wounds in His hands, feet, and side for four reasons. First, He showed the wounds to prove to them that He had really risen."

Anthony looked across the crowd as he held his long, expressive hands, palms outward, toward them. "By showing His wounds, Jesus intended to demonstrate that the faith of His disciples had nothing to do with current or popular opinion about Him. It had nothing to do with theories or interpretations of Scripture. Faith was based instead on the direct knowledge and experience which His followers had gained through their familiarity with Him. By showing His wounds, He wished to remove all doubt from their minds. May He remove doubt from the minds of any of you present."

*I have no doubt,* the lord thought. *My faith is secure.*

"Second, he revealed His wounds to the Church and faithful souls because within those wounds is a place of refuge." Anthony raised his left hand skyward and brought it down gracefully to rest in the palm of his right hand. "Just as a dove builds its nest in a safe place to protect itself against the attacks of a hawk, so Christians find shelter from the attacks of the devil by constructing for themselves a nesting place within the wounds of Christ." He held his hands, one nesting within the other, toward the crowd. "Nest there, and find solace."

*In wounds that are illusory, solace is impossible.* The words that came from nowhere pricked Lord Varden's soul.

"Third, Christ showed His wounds to impress on our hearts the signs of His sufferings, and fourth, to evoke in us compassion so that we would not crucify Him again with the nails of our sins."

Anthony's voice rose with fervor as his eyes sought each person present. "Christ shows us the wounds in His hands, feet, and side and says, 'See the hands that made and formed you; see how they have been pierced by nails. Behold My side, pierced by a lance, from which came forth My Church, like Eve who came from the side of Adam. The angel, stationed at the gates of paradise after Adam's sin, has been washed away by the blood flowing from My side. The water, flowing from My side, has extinguished the flame of his fiery sword."

Anthony's gaze again caught Lord Varden's. "Do not crucify Me again. Do not pollute the blood of the covenant by which you have been sanctified."

He paused and lowered his voice. "When our Lord had shown the Apostles the wounds in His hands, feet, and side, He repeated, 'Peace be with you.' Only if we keep in our hearts the memory of Christ's wounds and listen to His words will we find true peace in our hearts."

Lord Varden had found peace with the *Cathari*. He had been assured of eternal life through the remission of his sins. He had provided for his children. He had friends and supporters in the faith.

"May the true Lord, Who is true God and true man, grant you the peace that comes from knowing, loving, and obeying the truth. Amen."

Today no wild cheers swept the crowd. Instead, a hush punctuated by quiet sobbing lay like a shroud on the audience. Anthony was mobbed by people who threw themselves on their knees before him.

Lord Varden heard their cries.

"Don't leave us, Father."

"Before you go, bless me, Father."

"Bless me, too, Father."

"My child, Father."

"May the Lord have mercy on me."

"Father, forgive me."

The pleas of stricken individuals around Anthony gradually grew fainter as the lord and a good portion of the crowd slowly pressed out of the square. The lord had found the holes in the fabric of Anthony's faith and they were not mere holes at all. The holes were the wounds of Christ. Had the lord believed, as Anthony did, that those wounds were real and not mere illusions, he would have proclaimed the Catholic faith to the world.

## ∝ 14 ∽

## *Lord of Chateau-neuf-le-Foret*

**Chateau, Limoges, France (Early Spring 1226)** ∽ The Lord of Chateau-neuf-le-Foret knelt and prayed before a candle-lit tapestry of Christ's agony in the garden. Only two flickering candles illuminated the tiny private prayer closet that the lord had constructed in his castle, just down the hall from his own bedroom chamber. The chilly spring air nipped at the baron's thinly bearded face and seeped through his brown stockings. The cold penetrated his auburn, tight-sleeved linen shirt over which hung a loose, wide-sleeved, brown outer garment.

The lord remained still, his head bowed, his thick black curls falling over his neck. At his sides, his arms hung utterly relaxed as Anthony had taught him. In his prayer, he was probing deeper into the Heart of Christ.

When he was a boy, he had loved things boys love—parties, surprises, and feasts. As he grew older, his tastes included lovely damsels. But he had always had a serious side, one that told him that things of the world could never fill the longing in his heart. In his mid-twenties he turned more completely to the One Who could fill him. He retained a priest to celebrate daily Mass in his chateau's chapel. He gave away his silks and began to live as simply as he could.

Then Anthony had left the convent school at Toulouse where he had been a teacher for a short time and went to Limoges as custodian of the Poor Brothers in this region. In Limoges, the brothers lodged in a small house belonging to St. Martin's Church and under the auspices of the monks who followed the Rule of St. Benedict. The lord had gone to hear Anthony whenever he preached in Limoges or nearby. When Anthony was visiting other convents under his jurisdiction and preaching in those towns, the lord continued to send food twice weekly to the brothers at St. Martin's. They always told him when Anthony would be returning to Limoges.

Sometimes they told him stories, like the time Anthony had fallen ill in Solignac. The followers of St. Benedict had a monastery there where Anthony convalesced. One of the monks suffered from a temptation so severe that he despaired of life. Intending to kill himself, he confessed to Anthony, who told the monk to put on the tattered, worn-out tunic that the holy men insisted Anthony discard. When the distraught man clothed himself, his temptation vanished.

Anthony recovered and returned to Limoges where the lord had spoken with him several times. How might he get closer to God? How might he pray more deeply? Anthony had always counseled him wisely, but the counsel that he best remembered had been given here, at the lord's own chateau.

The lord invited Anthony to his house for a meal and the priest had gladly come. After dinner, the two men strolled outdoors into the castle courtyard where the lord had spoken frankly.

"Father, I pray and ask God to guide me. But I still do not have the peace that you have. How do I find this peace, Father? Is it possible?"

Anthony had lifted his gaze to one of the many turrets of the castle on which a flock of gray doves perched. "'Who will give me wings like a dove that I may fly and be at rest?' David asked in the Psalms. It is your question, isn't it?"

"Yes."

Anthony pointed to the birds. "David's cry is the cry of a soul that is weary of this world and longs for the solitude and peace of life in a cloister."

"Father, I have thought about the religious life. Yet I have obligations here. Many people are in my employ. If I abandon all this and sell it, where will these people go?"

Anthony smiled at the lord. "It is possible to have a cloister in the heart."

"The heart?"

Anthony pointed to the castle walls and gestured beyond them.

"Jeremiah said, 'Leave the cities and dwell in the rock, you that dwell in the country of Moab; and be like the dove that makes her nest in the mouth of the hole in the highest place.' 'Leave the cities' refers to the sins and vices that dishonor, the tumult that prevents the soul from rising to God and often even from thinking of Him."

Vice had never really tempted the lord. He never engaged in drinking, gambling, or licentiousness. But tumult? His responsibilities were many. Always tools were breaking, serfs were ill, weather was uncooperative, household helpers were arguing. Tumult. The word described his world well.

"'Moab' is the world. The world is a place of pride. All is pride in the world. There is pride of intellect which refuses to humble itself before God, pride of the will which refuses to submit to the will of God, pride of the senses which rebel against reason and dominate it. Do you see yourself in any of this?"

The lord saw himself juggling ledgers and extracting tithes from the peasants. He saw himself caught up in his own knowledge, insight, and administrative talents, efficiently running his estate. He prayed much, but he left God in the chapel. Pride.

"To leave the world, to live remote from the tumult of cities, to keep one's self unspotted from their vices is not sufficient. Therefore, the prophet adds, 'Dwell in the rock.'"

Anthony turned and pointed to the cross that rose over the chateau's small chapel. "This rock is Jesus Christ. Establish yourself in Him, my lord. Let Him be the constant theme of your thoughts, the object of your affections. Jacob slept on a stone in the wilderness, and while he slept he saw the heavens opened and conversed with angels, receiving a blessing from the Lord. So will it be with those who place their entire trust in Jesus Christ. They will be favored with heavenly visions. But the soul that does not repose upon this rock cannot expect to be blessed by the Lord."

The lord ran his long fingers through his thick, black curls. "I want to do this, Father. But how can I trust God? How can I abandon myself that completely?"

Anthony moved toward a thick staircase that led upward to the highest walls on the chateau. The lord walked along with him. "Scripture holds the answer, my lord. 'Be like the dove that makes her nest in the mouth of the hole in the highest place.' Doves do not nest on the ground as hens do, or in low shrubs like sparrows. You know where their nests are."

"In the turrets, Father." As the two men ascended the staircase, startled doves perched on the heights flew before them.

"Yes, in the nooks in high, rocky places. Jesus is the rock and the hole in the rock is the wound in Christ's side. That wound is the safe harbor of refuge to which Christ calls the soul in the words of the Canticle: 'Arise, my love, my beautiful one and come!... My dove in the clefts of the rock, in the hollow places of the wall.'"

As the men continued to climb, Anthony's hand swept across the span of the castle walls. "The Divine Spouse speaks of numberless clefts in the rock, but He also speaks of the deep hollow. There were indeed in His Body numberless wounds and one deep wound in His side. This wound leads to His Heart, and here, my lord, He calls you. He extends His arms to your soul. See how He opens wide His sacred side and Divine Heart so that you may come and hide therein."

Abruptly, Anthony paused and pointed ahead and to the left. There, in one of the battlements through which archers might shoot in a siege, a dove was nesting. "By retiring into the clefts of the rock, the dove is safe from birds of prey while also enjoying a quiet refuge where she may rest and coo in peace. So you will find in the Heart of Jesus a secure refuge against the wiles and attacks of Satan and a delightful retreat. But you must not rest merely at the entrance to the hole in the rock of Christ. You must penetrate its depths. In the depths you will find the Precious Blood which has redeemed us. This Blood pleads for us and demands mercy and calls us to Its very source, to the innermost sanctuary from which It springs, the Heart of Jesus. There your soul shall find light, peace, and unimaginable consolations."

A warm love seeped over the lord's spirit like blood from a fresh wound. How he wanted to find that Precious Blood, to find his peace in the Heart of his Redeemer!

The men continued their climb while the dove watched them warily, but without taking flight. Farther along, Anthony pointed to another cleft in which a flattened nest lay.

"What is a dove's nest made of, my lord?"

"Little bits of straw, Father, and grasses."

"And where does she get them?"

"Anywhere. Wherever she finds them. The stable. The pasture. The garden."

Anthony bent down and picked up a few straws that had fallen from the nest to the step on which the men stood.

"The dove uses these little bits of straw that the world tramples under its feet to build a secure and comfortable nest," he said as he stood.

He pointed to the nest. "The virtues we must use to nest in Christ are like these cast off, simple grasses. The world despises them and, indeed, never notices them, yet Christ Himself used them to submit to His Father."

Anthony turned back to the lord. "What are these virtues?" Taking the lord's hand and opening his fingers, Anthony tapped the lord's palm. "Here are the virtues we must use to nest in Christ." Anthony began to place one straw after another into the lord's palm as he spoke. "Meekness. Humility. Poverty. Penance. Patience. Mortification." Anthony tapped the little mound of straw in the lord's hand. "For the soul, these are nesting materials for life in the hollow of the rock, in the Heart of Jesus."

Anthony closed the lord's fingers around the straw. "Make your nest away from the tumult of this world. Make it deep in the Heart of Christ and build it of the virtues of Christ. Dwell there and you shall have the peace you seek. In the hollow of the Rock, you shall know God."

So the lord had constructed this private prayer closet for his own use. It was his cloister in which he hid in daily prayer. Now the lord was no longer conscious of the tapestry before him or of the flickering candles or nippy air. He was deep in the cleft of Christ's Heart. Each time he penetrated that Holy Wound, he found himself meditating on something different. One time it would be Christ's passion. Another time, His mercy. Or His love. Tonight the Heart of Christ had opened and the lord had found himself in that very Heart. Christ held him, with all his sinful imperfections, in the very center of His love. And not the lord alone but every human soul ever to have lived and to live still. The lord's head bowed almost to the floor as he thought of Christ's great humility not only to become human Himself, but also to nurture every other human in His own Precious Heart. God in human flesh loved humans whom He had made in His own image for no other reason than love.

*Lord, make me grateful to You for Your love,* he prayed. *Lord, please make me more like You.*

So his meditation and prayer continued until he felt the images fading and his body chilling in the cool, night air. With a deep sigh of longing to be one with Christ, the lord opened his eyes and raised his head. He pushed upright and shook the stiffness out of one knee and then out of the other. Leaning forward, he kissed the tormented face of Christ on the tapestry, bowed, and left.

The hallway leading to his bedchamber was dimly lit with a single torch in the center. Just prior to the lord's room was a guest room in which Anthony was staying. Anthony's superiors had instructed him to write his Easter sermons so that other priests might use them. Anthony had agreed to the lord's invitation to stay in the chateau because here, in the evening quiet and solitude, away from the crowds who pressed him by day, he could spread out the Scriptures and write.

Therefore, the lord expected to see the flicker of candlelight under Anthony's door. What he noticed instead was a flooding radiance. At the same moment, he heard the babble of a child in the room.

How puzzling! None of the household servants had a small child. The serfs who did would not be in his castle at any time, much less at this hour near midnight. Had a mother come to see the priest? But why would she come at this hour? No one had asked the lord about admitting a woman and a child to the chateau, and no one should have been admitted without his permission.

Now the child was giggling. Who had come to see the priest without the lord's knowledge or approval?

The lord bent down and peeked in the wide keyhole. He caught his breath. Anthony was kneeling at the ample writing table that the lord had provided for him. On the table lay two open books, one of which appeared thick enough to be a Bible. A sheet of writing paper and a reed pen were pushed to one side. Off to the left, a candle flickered.

Anthony was bathed in light and the light was coming from a chubby-legged infant that was sitting a bit unsteadily on the thickest book.

As the lord watched, the friar held his hands in front of the child, his two pointer fingers extended toward the infant. The child reached up and grabbed one finger in each fat fist, then, with the priest's help, pulled himself up on tiptoe. The baby's legs danced up

FIGURE 1. *Exterior view of the Basilica of St. Anthony of Padua.*

FIGURE 2. *Rear view of the tomb of St. Anthony in
the Basilica of St. Anthony of Padua.*

FIGURE 3. *Eighteenth-century painting of the Christ Child appearing to St. Anthony by Francesco Zugno, found in the museum of the Basilica of St. Anthony.*

FIGURE 4. *Painting (1518) by Vittore Carpaccio of the Madonna and Christ Child with (to her right) Saints Francis, Peter, Ambrose; (to her left) Anthony, Catherine of Alexandria, and George, found in the museum of the Basilica of Saint Anthony.*

**Figure 5.** *St. Anthony's vision of the Christ Child by the Italian artist, Antonio Arrigoni.*

FIGURE 6. *A traditional portrayal of St. Anthony*
*lovingly embracing the Christ Child.*

FIGURE 7. *St. Anthony reflecting on Sacred Scripture in a painting by the Italian artist Girolamo Romanino (1484–1559).*

FIGURE 8. *The enraptured St. Anthony and St. Francis at the feet of the Crucified Christ, by the Italian artist Gian Battista Moroni (1518–1520).*

FIGURE 17. *Sanctuary of the Walnut Tree, Camposampiero (Padua), Italy.*

FIGURE 18. *This twentieth-century painting of St. Anthony with Demons, by Italian artist Pietro Annigoni (1910–1988), is found in the Basilica of St. Anthony in Padua, Italy.*

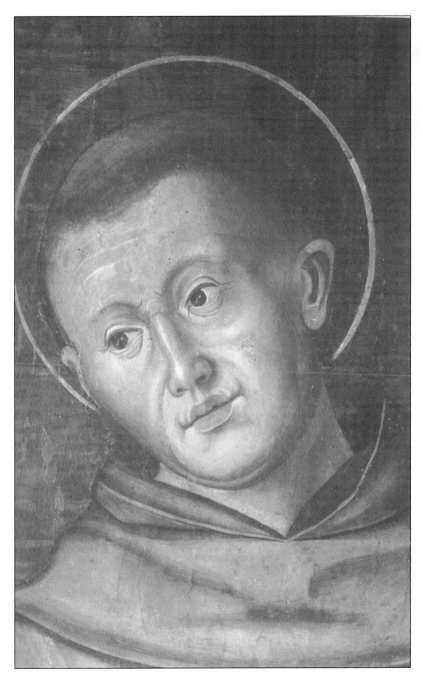

FIGURE 19. *A painting of St. Anthony, detailing his characteristic gentleness, by the Italian artist Andrea da Murano (1462–1502).*

FIGURE 20. *The highly symbolic painting by El Greco (1541–1614), in which St. Anthony tenderly holds the Word Incarnate on the Word of God.*

FIGURE 21. *Altar piece depicting St. Anthony carrying the Sacred Scriptures and flame—perhaps representing the intensity of his zeal for the Word of God—by the Italian artist Antonio Vivarini (1418–1491).*

**FIGURE 22.** *Giotto's fresco of St. Anthony, the teacher and tireless preacher of the Gospel, in the Basilica of St. Anthony in Padua, Italy.*

FIGURE 23. *Saints Anthony and John the Baptist in a painting by the Italian artist Piero della Francesca (1415–1492).*

FIGURE 24. *Lower crypt in the Church of Saints John and Anthony.*

and down while the child laughed with delight. Then, suddenly, one toe slipped and the boy lost his balance. Swiftly, the friar scooped the baby up in his arms before the plump cheeked, dark haired head could strike the table. The child laughed and kicked against the friar's habit, then reached up toward the priest's grinning mouth and fingered the friar's lips. The priest kissed the tiny fingers.

With one hand gripping the priest's lower teeth and the other the neckline of his tunic, the child pulled himself erect in the priest's arms. Then the boy tugged at Anthony's ear, bringing it down to his mouth as if to whisper into it.

The priest turned his face to the door as the child suddenly thrust his arms directly toward the lord. As the child stretched in the lord's direction, almost tumbling out of the priest's arms, the lord bowed his head in awe for just the briefest second. When he looked up again, Anthony's arms were empty and the only light in the shadowy room came from the flickering candle.

The lord bowed his head and dropped to his knees. He was too startled, too overwhelmed with deep joy, even to weep. The door in front of him opened. The lord raised his head. "Father, what was He saying to you?"

Anthony took the lord's right hand in his palm and raised him to his feet. "He said that your house will flourish and will enjoy great prosperity as long as it remains faithful to Mother Church. But when it goes over to heresy, it will be overwhelmed with misfortune and will become extinct."

The lord caught his breath at the prophecy. He had expected nothing like that.

"My lord," the friar said softly, "Christ has permitted you to see Himself and to receive His message. Praise Him for this vision, but tell it to no one. I beg you. Tell this to no one, at least not while I live."

The lord's voice was tight with joy and sorrow, wonder and fear. "Yes, Father. I will tell no one. Until its telling can no longer draw the curious to you, I will tell no one."

## ❦ 15 ❧

## *Notary*

**Saracen Encampment, Jerusalem, Palestine (1226?)** ❧ The notary lay in a small, sturdy hut abuzz with swarms of flies. Outdoors beneath the sun, the sand of the Holy Land had been hot beneath his feet when he had been taken, stripped, to be scourged. Now the sand in the hut's shade felt cool to his quivering cheek. Cool and wet from the blood that oozed out beneath his half closed eyelids. How feebly those eyelids fluttered to keep the grains from the now hollow sockets. Until an hour ago, those sockets had held his eyes. Now his eyes and fingertips were gone.

Outside the hut, voices muttered in a language he could not understand. Guards. Why would the head Mahomet post guards at his door? Certainly the notary was going nowhere. The torturers had broken both his legs.

"Jesus," he choked through a throat parched with thirst. For three days he had been given nothing to eat or drink. Now what moisture he had left in his body was seeping into the sand along with his life.

The world had condensed to a pulse of pain. Despite spasms of agony, images played in his mind. At the judgment, one's whole life races swiftly before one's mind. Was this his judgment?

He saw himself as a child in Puy-en-Velay, France, tagging along with his parents to Mass and being enthralled by the incense and the strange language of the priest. Then as he aged, religion had grown boring and annoying.

He had become a notary by studying hard and earning higher marks than other students in his class. He began settling suits between this Christian and that one. Up close, he saw backbiting, scandal, and greed. How many men had he represented who were ready to cheat and lie to get money or land? Nearly all of these went to Mass and piously dropped small sums into the poor box.

How sick he became of religious hypocrisy! He had begun to believe that the Church and its doctrines were a farce. The Eucharist no longer made sense. He had been taught that God was loving and just. But God seemed vicious and unjust. God struck everywhere with pain, suffering, and death. The notary had seen his brother's children die of a strange, spotted fever. He had watched his saintly grandmother linger painfully for months, barely able to eat, until death finally claimed her. He had held his dead sister's matted head against his breast while the stillborn baby whom she had been struggling to give birth to lay cold and blue in a blanket at her side. His mother had prayed and lit candles for each of these people. What good had come of her hours spent in his family's chapel before a tapestry of Christ's birth? God was deaf, if God existed. Or else God was cruel and unjust.

He preferred to believe in no God than in a cruel, insensitive, and unjust one. He began to say that those who believed in God were stupid. Unlike himself, they refused to admit that the God of their belief could not be the God of the world.

Since God did not exist, the notary could do as he pleased. He started by ceasing to pray. Then he stopped attending Mass. He began to frequent taverns and brothels and he made his work his god. He craved success more than money.

If he had to cheat and lie to win his case, he did so. And he was successful. Merchants, barons, and counts came to him with their quarrels. He nearly always won.

In early October 1225, Anthony came to Puy-en-Velay as Guardian of the convent of the Friars Minor. Soon the notary heard some of his clients speaking about the new priest. "He speaks words of fire," they said. "Everyone is going to hear him."

The notary had no desire to hear him.

But meet him he did. The notary had been riding home after visiting one of his more prosperous clients, a baron who was squabbling with his brother over a portion of the family estate. Each claimed that

their recently deceased father had promised them the choicest fields
and manor house. The father had died without a will. The family had
summoned the notary in an attempt to prevent bloodshed.

The notary liked to be neatly dressed, for the better dressed he
was, the more his clients trusted him, and the better they paid. So
that day he had worn his blue and yellow button cap with blue stockings and yellow outer bliant skirt, slit in front and back so that he
looked quite fashionable astride his black steed. He had chosen his
cherry-red cloak and fastened it at his shoulder with a large, round
brooch of gold. A steady breeze was blowing the cloak behind him
like a banner. How impressive he looked to the rag-a-muffins who
were playing toss with fruit pits in the garbage-strewn streets!

He turned down one street when he saw an unfamiliar gray-
robed friar walking toward him. As the notary drew near, the friar
gazed at him, then dropped to his knees and bowed with his head to
the ground. The notary rode on.

*The new friar must think I am a king,* he thought.

Within a few days, the notary again met the friar. This time the
notary was reeling, half-drunk from the local tavern with one of the
town whores clinging to his arm. Again, Anthony knelt and bowed
his head to the ground.

The next day, when the notary's mind cleared, he thought of
the priest's second act of respect.

*Perhaps he is mocking me,* he thought.

Twice more the same sort of incident happened. Now the notary began to feel uneasy. He watched where he walked or rode.
And if he saw any gray-robed friar on the same street, the notary
took another route.

One day he was playing dice with the town candlemaker when
he idly remarked, "You are more challenging at this game than
Julio."

"You won't have any more easy wins with him," the candlemaker
said, rolling the dice. "He's gotten holy and given up the game."

"Julio? No."

"I win this round," the candlemaker said, sweeping the notary's
coins into his pile. He gave the notary the dice. "Julio's been converted by Father Anthony."

"Julio told me he never wanted to hear or meet Father Anthony." The notary rolled the dice.

"Nor did he want to. His wife wanted to go to hear him preach and Julio refused. He was sick in bed with some sort of stomach upset and told her that she had to stay home to care for him."

"Most likely too much sour wine." The notary watched his opponent sweep a few more coins away.

"Most likely. His wife was upset but she opened her window to see the friar at least. You know you can see straight down into the valley from their home, and the friar was preaching in the town square. She could see the two miles quite well."

"How stupid! The friar would have looked no bigger than a gnat."

"Are women known to be smart?" The candlemaker rolled the dice again. "Not only did she see him, but she also heard him. And so did Julio."

"Heard him? How?"

"I don't know how. But hear him they did. And Julio gave up drinking and dicing. Now he brings wood to the convent. Father Anthony, you know, is guardian there." The candlemaker slapped his knee when he saw the dice. "You have had ill luck today. That last coin of yours is mine."

Over and over, the notary asked himself the same question. How could Julio convert? He and the notary had been in a contest of sorts to see who could lead the most dissolute life. And now the notary had won because Julio had converted.

The following Sunday afternoon, on a day too cold for late October, the notary rode through a forest swept with colored leaves to Julio's house on the mountain. He must see if the candlemaker's story were true.

The big woodcutter invited the notary in and they both sat, warming themselves in the fire's glow.

"You must go to hear Father Anthony." Julio's black eyes were earnest with pleading.

"The clergy are all hypocrites. You know what they do in the dark. You have seen it yourself."

"No. His is a life of light. Even in the dark."

"How can you be sure what he does in the dark?"

"Because I can tell by his works," Julio said. "You know Old One Eye, the crazy beggar?"

The notary nodded. Who did not know the man who, often times naked even in winter, begged, and moaned in the town square?

"Last Sunday, during Father Anthony's sermon at Mass, Old One Eye wandered in. He began moaning and begging in that loud voice of his. Father Anthony came down from the pulpit and made his way to him. He touched Old One Eye's arm and asked him to be calm and quiet."

"As if Old One Eye would understand."

"He did understand. He said, 'I will be quiet if you give me your cord.' So Father Anthony smiled and gave it to him. And Old One Eye tied it around his waist and then sat down and listened to the rest of the sermon in perfect quiet. Go see him tomorrow, my friend. He only begs now. He no longer moans. He is no longer crazy. Through the priest, God has cured Old One Eye."

"You are crazy," the notary said. "You yourself agreed that God does not exist."

Julio grabbed the notary's arm. Through the warm woolen sleeve of his green tunic, the notary felt Julio's too tight grip. "I used to believe that. Then I heard the priest. I have seen Old One Eye cured. My friend, if God does not exist, whether you live a good or bad life, when you die, that is the end of you."

"I prefer a bad life. It's more interesting."

Julio's fingers tightened. "But if God does exist, you will live forever. If you love and serve God, you will rejoice for all eternity in the bliss of heaven. If you hate and reject God, you will suffer for all eternity in the flames of hell. Life on this earth is short, my friend. What are fifty or seventy years or less in comparison to eternity? If eternity does exist, would you rather spend it in bliss or in anguish?"

"If eternity does exist, there may not be a hell. Or God may send no one there."

"But if He does, where are you going, my friend?"

The notary had rode home, more troubled than ever. The next day, he combed the streets looking for Old One Eye. When he found him clothed in a ragged, filthy cape and sitting beside one of the town wells, the notary purposely rode directly up to him. He fully expected to see the scrawny, dirty man weaving back and forth, moaning, and holding out his trembling hands as he had always done.

But not today. Today, with his head cocked upward toward the notary, Old One Eye spoke the first words that the notary had ever heard him speak. "A coin for a beggar?"

"I have none today," the notary said.

"Then God bless you anyway," Old One Eye said, winking his one good eye.

The man was sane.

Not many days later, the notary was summoned to a cloth merchant's house. The man was having difficulty collecting payment from a certain noble who had ordered but never paid for several bolts of fine silk and linen. The merchant wanted his money.

The notary was riding through the crowded marketplace when he rounded a farmer's stall and met Anthony face to face. Again, the priest knelt and bowed.

At the suppressed giggling of two daintily dressed young ladies, the notary snapped. "Priest, I ought to strike you with the sword to punish your mockery. What do you mean? Why do you bow to me and make of me a public fool?"

The young ladies gasped. The notary could feel the stares of many curious eyes.

Anthony raised his head and peered at the notary. But he did not rise. "O, brother, you do not know the honor that God has reserved for you. How I envy your happiness! I became a poor Little Brother of Francis because I wished to be a martyr for God's glory. I even journeyed to Morocco but became so ill that I had to be sent home before preaching one word about my Lord. It was not God's will that I shed my blood for His name. Yet God has revealed to me that one day you will achieve the dream that I had for myself."

The notary burst out laughing. "How ridiculous!"

"When your blessed hour arrives, I beg you to remember me."

"Priest, you are deluded." The notary spit in the friar's upturned face and spurred his horse on.

"May God bless you," Anthony called after him. "And when your hour comes, pray for me."

When the notary arrived at the cloth merchant's house, the merchant greeted him cheerfully.

"Come in," the young, bearded man hailed. "You will get my money for me and I shall use it to host a huge baptismal party for my first-born son. Come. Let us drink a toast to him." He led the notary into his ample kitchen.

The notary grinned. "So your child has been born. I had not heard."

"Oh, no. My wife has not yet given birth. It is too early." The merchant summoned a servant. "Wine for us."

"Then you and I may be toasting a daughter instead of a son."

"No. He is a son. Father Anthony said so."

The notary felt the blood drain from his face and he knew that the merchant noticed it.

"My wife has been going to hear him preach. Surely you have heard him, too. Just two weeks ago, she asked him to pray for her and her child. So he began to pray at once. Then suddenly he paused and told her that we would have a son who would become a Friar Minor like himself and a martyr for Christ. We are naming him Philip and we will gladly give him to our Lord."

The cloth merchant's tale and the notary's own encounters with Old One Eye and with Anthony tormented him for days. Then there was the nagging reality of Julio's conversion. And other things, too. Yes, the brothels and taverns and dicing tables were still busy. But something seemed somehow different. One day, while ordering a new pair of shoes, he knew what it was. The squabbling in the streets had decreased. He had not seen a beggar taunted for weeks. And, on Sunday mornings, the streets were quite empty. Nearly everyone was in church.

Days passed. November arrived and with it the chill of autumn. The notary did not change his lifestyle, but something inside of him had changed. Then one day, he knew why.

Anthony must be praying for him.

So he rode to the convent to see the friar and to tell him that he needed no prayers.

"He's not here. He's gone to Bourges," he was told.

Three weeks later, the cloth merchant invited the notary to his newborn son Philip's baptismal feast.

The banquet was full of well-bred guests. The merchant bragged about his son and retold several times Anthony's prophecy of his martyrdom. One noble after another spoke of conversion because of Anthony's words. But their words were not as powerful as the lusty cry of a little newborn boy. The notary gazed at the child in awe. He had never before seen a martyr. Then he was brought back to the present, to the little hut in Jerusalem, the voices of the guards were growing louder. The notary heard a clamor. The bishop's deep voice, considerably weaker, preached still. There were voices of other crusaders, some pleading for mercy, others preaching Christ. *They are gathering us together to kill us,* the notary thought. What sweet relief!

Conversion had come slowly, like the incessant dripping of water wearing an impression in stone. After Philip's baptism, the notary began having difficulty sleeping. Images troubled him. Images of his childhood, his life, his faith, of Father Anthony and Old One Eye, of the converted Julio and newborn Philip. In this turmoil, winter passed and spring arrived.

In the cool dawns of spring, the notary rose early because he could not sleep and rode out into the quiet country where he wandered among vineyards bursting forth new buds and fields freshly plowed for seed. Always he returned to the same question. What if God did exist? What if God were just? Where would he spend eternity?

One morning, when the birds were full-throated with mating lust, he stopped his horse beside a clear stream and prayed while the animal drank deeply. *Lord, if you do exist, let me know what to do.*

Every day for a week, he rode to that same spot and prayed the same prayer.

Then the bishop came to Puy-en-Velay. He preached fiery words to the people. He exhorted them to join him on a crusade to the Holy Land to convert the Saracens to true faith in Christ. Those who went were promised an indulgence remitting all their sins.

Those who died there in the cause of Christ, the bishop said, were assured of heaven.

This was his answer—a chance to remit his sins. Deep in his soul, he knew that he would not return from the Holy Land. Hadn't Anthony predicted it? So he sold all his property and joined the crusade. On the way there, at daily Mass and in prayer, his faith coalesced and deepened. He marveled at how blind he had been when he had not believed.

When the band of Christian knights and believers reached Jerusalem, the bishop began to preach. To the notary, his words seemed too kind and soft, the moderate words of a man who had never lived evil but who had only seen or read of it.

Unable to contain himself, the notary silenced the bishop and began to preach himself. He told the followers of Mohammed of his own life and its wretchedness and proclaimed the greatness of

Christ as true Son of God. "Those who know of Christ and reject Him reject God," he cried out.

Angry shouts rose from the infidels. Rough hands grabbed him and hauled him and the others away. They had all been tortured. And now they all would die.

Strong hands grabbed the notary's ankles and spun him around. As he was dragged out of the hut and across the burning sand, his body shrieked with pain. *Jesus,* he screamed through the anguish. *Remember me. Forgive me. Take me home.*

Then he remembered. *Father Anthony asked me to pray for him.*

With a petition for the priest on his lips, he was thrown onto the sand. Someone shoved a block of wood under his neck. *Lord, bless the priest. Bless his mission,* he prayed as he heard the motion of a sword thrust toward his neck.

# ❦ 16 ❧

## *Maid*

**Manor House, Brive, France (1226)** ❧ The fifteen-year-old kitchen maid banged the wooden bowls in her mistress' pantry as loudly as she could. She didn't care if they scratched or if their noise disturbed her poor lord's headache. They might as well know that she was angry. How could they send her out to the garden to pick vegetables in this violent rainstorm and then have her scurry all the way to that friary through the drenched fields? *What do they think I am? A fish?*

"What's going on in there?" bellowed a cook in the adjoining kitchen. "Get those leeks to the saint. He told the mistress that the friars have nothing to eat."

The saint. All she ever heard about was the saint. She tossed her head with such anger that her thick, black braids whipped around and struck her in the face. *If he's such a saint, why doesn't he make his own vegetables appear?* Some saints miraculously fed multitudes with bread or rice, or so the ballad singers sang. But not this saint. This saint had to send her out into a storm to get his food. The miracle would be if she returned without catching a deathly chill.

The maid slipped into her rain cloak and grabbed the biggest wooden bowl she could find and a long blade knife.

When she threw open the door, a wet blast of wind slapped against her. Pulling the door shut behind her, she pushed out into the storm.

The wind was whipping her master's pear saplings nearly to the ground and whistling like a demon through the well-ordered vines of his grape arbors. Heading directly into the gale, she hustled toward the vegetable garden. Leeks. She pulled their muddy, white bellies from the ground and threw them into the basket. Parsley. Dill. She plucked huge handfuls and tucked the feathery tops under the leeks so they'd not blow away. Carrots. Beets. Garlic. She sliced away their tops with the knife, then tumbled the muddy roots into the bowl. Cabbage. Its heavy, outer leaves were bobbing in the wind. She sliced two heads and wedged them between the muddy beets and carrots. *So what if the friars have to wash the mud off the cabbages,* the maid thought. *Serves them right for asking for food in this weather.*

When the bowl was full, the maid ran back to the kitchen to return the knife, then headed across her master's uncut hayfield with the bowl. She'd taken this route many times. Didn't her master love to tell of another of his fields, this one near the saint's convent? Her master had sown it with fine wheat for his mill. One moonlit night, a few friars, who were coming out of the oratory in quiet meditation, saw a host of marauders rampaging through the field, trampling and plucking the wheat. The friars ran to find their founder, Father Anthony. He was at prayer. *Of course,* the maid thought. *What else for a saint?*

"Don't be afraid," he had told the friars. "This is only a trick of the devil to distract you from your meditation. The field is not harmed."

And the next day, it wasn't.

Thinking of the story made the girl shudder. Demons, it seemed, must be in this very storm. *Lord, don't let me see one,* she pleaded.

At the end of the hayfield, the maid took a sharp right to a footpath that led through a forest. The path would eventually bring her to a narrow lane that led to the friary.

As she entered the woods, she thought of Anthony living like a hermit in a narrow cave in these very woods. People were certain that he had gone there in order to pray more and to more severely discipline his appetites. What did discipline his appetites mean? Did he whip himself or roll in thorns or beat himself with rocks? What manner of distasteful things did he do? *One thing, for sure, he's not disciplining his stomach. No, he wants vegetables. Leeks. I hope they're strong enough to sear his throat,* the maid thought.

Folks said he had hollowed out a fountain by his little grotto to receive water which gushed from a rock. He wouldn't need water today. If he put a pot outdoors, it would be full of water in an hour. If only he could do that for vegetables. The maid imagined Anthony invoking vegetables and having leeks and parsley and carrots fall from the sky like rain. She grinned at her silly vision.

The girl lifted her skirt to hop over a fallen branch. That had not been down the last time she'd walked this path. That was last week. The wind must have brought down the bough. *God, don't let some falling tree limb hit me,* she prayed.

How many times had she pattered through these woods? If her mistress paid her extra for every trek she'd taken to the friary, she'd have be able to buy cloth for a new chemise by now.

All she ever heard about was Father Anthony. Father Anthony needed this. Father Anthony needed that. *Why hadn't Father Anthony founded his little monastery of friars in Limousin instead of coming here to Brive? Because Quintus de Falcici had built them a house here, you fool,* she chided herself. *Oh if Lord de Falcici were not so pious!*

*Well then, why isn't Father Anthony at his convent in Guienne on such a bad day?* If he were, another maid would be out in this downpour instead of her.

*And why didn't the mistress stay home today in this storm? Why did she have to ride all the way out to the friary to attend Anthony's early morning Mass?* Her mistress had returned home, soaked through her cape and proclaiming that the friars had no food.

*Why don't the friars plant their own vegetable garden? Bah, they have planted one. Little good it does them. They give away all produce to the poor. Saints. They have no sense at all. They live in another world.*

The maid bounded out of the woods and onto the flooded lane. Three knolls and she would be at the friary.

Was it true that Father Anthony raised a dead child to life in Limoges? His mother had left the baby in the cradle, the rumors went, while she went to hear the friar preach. When she returned, the child was dead. Shrieking, she ran to the saint who was detained speaking to those who had lingered behind after his homily. "Go, for God will show you His mercy," the priest told her. When the woman insisted that the priest accompany her, he told her again, "Go now. God will show you His mercy." When she hesitated, he sent her on her way with the same words. As she arrived home, she saw her son playing in the yard with some pebbles.

A second miracle had made its way through local gossip from Limoges to Brive. Another woman, this rumor said, had gone to hear the priest preach and, when she returned home, she found her son playing in a pot of boiling water, yet he was unharmed.

*What is the matter with the mothers in Limoges? Do they care more about a supposed saint than about their own children?* The maid tossed her head. When she married and bore children, she would not leave them unattended even if Christ Himself came to Brive to preach.

Then this Father Anthony sometimes seemed almost like Christ Himself. Just three weeks ago, the mistress had returned from a shopping spree to Limoges. She had gone there to purchase new pottery for the kitchen. While there, she had heard a young novice friar preaching in the square. Of course, she sent a message to her carriage driver to rein the horses so she could listen.

The preacher was a young, lightly bearded novice from Limousin, named Brother Pierre. He was preaching about the Holy Spirit when he related a curious incident. As a friar in the convent at Limoges, Pierre had been tempted to leave the Order. One day, while he was thinking of this, Father Anthony happened to meet him on the grounds of the monastery. Without any questions, Father Anthony cupped in his hands the tall friar's cheeks. Then, tipping the youth's head toward his own, the saint had done what Christ had done to His apostles. He had breathed into the novice's mouth and said, "Receive the Holy Spirit." Smiling at Brother Pierre, the saint had released his grip.

*The saint had better not breathe on me,* the maid thought. *If he likes leeks as much as the mistress says he does, he probably smells like them.*

Brother Pierre, so the mistress said, was now fully convinced of his vocation as a friar. "And so," the mistress had concluded her story, "we must beg God to send His Holy Spirit upon each of us with the same power with which He conferred it on Brother Pierre. For he preached forcefully, almost as good as the saint."

The maid groaned. To hear constantly about one saint in the area was bad enough. But two?

There, up ahead, was the friary. Quite breathless from her scurrying, the maid skirted the main door and swung around to the kitchen. Anthony himself answered her knock, his tunic sleeves rolled back and his hands glistening wet.

"Pardon my casualness," he said. "I'm on kitchen duty and I am nearly done scrubbing the floor." The maid noticed a pail of water and a brush to the right of the door.

Anthony grinned at the bowl of soaked vegetables. "And once I finish scrubbing, I shall have something to cook."

"Just give me back the bowl and I'll be on my way," the maid said. *Let me go before you breathe on me, too.*

"I've made you some mint tea. Why don't you come in and warm yourself before you return home?"

The maid felt exasperated. *Couldn't the saint see anything?* "Father, the storm is growing worse. I'll be soaked to the bone by the time I get home."

"Are you wet now?"

*What a stupid question.* The maid shook her rain cloak. It was dripping with water. But her gown beneath it was dry, even at the hem which had several times swept the underbrush in the woods, not to mention dragging through tall grass in the hayfield. Her toes felt dry and warm in her boots, too.

A bit confused, she replied, "Well, I guess I am not wet. Not much."

Anthony pointed to a small table with a steaming wooden cup on it. "Have your tea." He carried the bowl of vegetables to a sideboard where he dumped them into a tub of water.

"How do you think carrots would taste with," he picked up the dill, "a touch of this?"

The maid gulped the warm tea. "Very good, Father. Especially if you add a bit of leek and steam it all together."

"Fine. We shall have that tonight." The priest began rinsing the roots in the tub. "And the cabbage? I usually braise garlic in a bit of olive oil and then add the leaves."

"You might add a few carrots to it as well. It makes such a pretty dish."

"Good idea. You have picked us such an abundant supply of food. Please give your mistress our deepest thanks."

The cup was empty. "I've got to be going, Father."

Anthony rinsed the bowl and wiped it with the sleeve of his tunic. After handing the bowl to the girl, he raised his hand over her in blessing. Alarmed, she turned her head aside, wrinkling up her nose in anticipation of a breath. But none came.

"In the name of the Father, and of the Son, and of the Holy Spirit," the priest said, making the sign of the cross over her head.

The maid signed herself at his words.

"May the rain spare you on your return trip as well."

"Thank you, Father."

The girl opened the kitchen door and felt the full force of the wind in her face. Drops as huge as acorns pelted her rain cloak. With the bowl firmly tucked under her arm, she raced the long route to her mistress' manor house. When she arrived, her gown and her feet and her thick black braids were still completely dry.

# ✑ 17 ✑

## *Minette*

**Brothel, Limoges, France (November 1226)** ✑ Plump Minette tugged her chemise down over her head and smoothed out its skirt as big, heavy Roland, sitting beside her, laced up his shirtsleeves. Now that he was dressing, having taken what he paid Minette good money to give, he would talk. Roland spoke before he undressed and then after he dressed again. During the heat of passion, he said nothing. Such was his habit. Other men had stranger habits, the strangest of all being Minette's father who had used her ever since she was a child. "A beautiful Eve, my daughter, you be" he recited each time he came. "She made Adam to sin and you make me." Until she was nine years old, she endured his sick rhymes and sicker passion. Then she ran away to live in brothels. She was still a sinful Eve, she thought, making men sin.

Roland pushed Minette's long hair, the color of field mice, away from her face and kissed her. "Tomorrow I will not see you," Roland said. "Tomorrow is All Souls' Day and Celestine insists that I take her to hear the saint."

Minette pushed him away playfully. "Celestine again."

He tickled her chin. "Minette. She is my wife."

"So what saint is this? Every month there is a new saint in Limoges."

"You have not heard of Father Anthony? He is custodian of the friary. He stays in Limoges but travels about preaching. No one you know speaks of him? I am surprised."

Minette struggled with a memory. "I think Janine did mention him. She said he restored Claudine's hair after her husband had pulled it out."

Roland teasingly pulled Minette's hair. "Is she the one who was bringing meats to the friars while her husband was away? And when he caught her, he beat her?"

Minette tossed her head. The pulling pinched. "Yes. Claudine. She is a good woman."

Roland let off pulling her locks and began to caress them. "Minette, there are no good women unless they be saints. Claudine was disobedient to her husband. She deserved to be beaten. "

Minette shuddered, remembering the blows her own father had rained on her. "No one deserves to be beaten," she said bitterly. "The saint did not think she deserved it. She sent for him, and he restored her hair and healed her bruises. That is what Janine said."

"The saint thinks more like a saint than a man. And now he has her husband thinking the same. I have heard that he accompanies Claudine to the friary to bring them meats."

"What is wrong with that?"

Roland shrugged. "Nothing, I suppose. He does penance while I have fun." He pressed Minette close, squeezing her.

"But no fun tomorrow. Tomorrow you have to hear the saint. Why does Celestine not obey you and stay home?"

Roland bellowed with laughter. He was so close to Minette that her body shook along with his. "She would obey me, but I would have to live with her nagging tongue and pouting face. It is better to hear the saint. And perhaps he will speak out against the sins of the clergy like he did at the synod in Bourges. That I would like to hear."

"A priest would never speak against the clergy."

"You have never heard Father Anthony. They say his sermon at the synod made the clergy blush. There were hundreds of them there, all prim and proper in their mitres and copes. Father Anthony shouted out in his sermon, 'You there in the mitre!' Then he told them all their sins."

"*All* their sins?" Minette giggled.

"Yes, my dove. And they say some came to him afterward and confessed. Archbishop Simon de Sully was one."

Minette laughed as she thought of the finely dressed clergy, parading about as if they were lords. How she would love to hear someone openly reproach one of these men!

"What did he confess, Roland?"

"Only his mistrust of the Poor Brothers who follow Francis and the Preaching Friars who follow Dominic. He said he would now welcome them into his diocese."

Minette groaned. "Is that all?"

"It was a lot to the saint. He follows Francis, too."

Minette folded her arms and turned her shoulder to Roland. "So I will not see you tomorrow because you want to hear the saint. And then you will follow Francis, too."

Roland guffawed. "If I follow Francis, I cannot have you." His thick hands pulled Minette back to himself.

— —

WHEN ROLAND RETURNED two days later, Minette was curious.

"How was the saint?" she asked while he sat on the side of her bed and removed his cap. Minette was sitting, fully clothed, beside him.

Roland dropped his cap to the floor. "The saint was good. He preached in the cemetery of St. Paul."

Minette shrieked with glee. The cemetery. What better place for an All Souls' Day sermon!

"He preached on a line from the Psalms. Something about in the evening, weeping shall take place, but in the morning gladness. He said there were three evenings and three mornings. The evenings were the fall of Adam and Eve, the death of Christ, and our own death."

Minette wrinkled her nose. "Not a sermon I would like."

Roland was peeling off his inner shirt, loosening the tight sleeves to slip over his thick wrists. "He said the three mornings were the birth of Christ, the resurrection of our Lord, and our own resurrection."

"That is more cheerful."

"I suppose," Roland said, dropping the shirt to the floor, "if one is going to the right place." He turned to Minette and put his hands on the shoulders of her gown. "But we can have better than heaven here tonight, can we not, Minette? And when we die, we shall both go to hell and then we can continue to enjoy each other."

When Roland slipped on his shirt again, Minette spoke first. She knew that she had better speak quickly or Roland would begin to talk. Then she would not have an answer to the question that was troubling her.

"Do you really think I am going to hell?"

Roland burst into laughter. "Where else, Minette? Purgatory? Purgatory is for people who are at least trying to be good. You do not even try."

Minette felt hurt. "But I am not a bad person."

Roland cupped her face in his huge, hard-skinned hands. "Minette, all women, except the saints, are bad persons. Who do men sin with, if not with women? Look at where you live. Look at what you do. I have come out of here many times with fewer coins in my pocket than I should have had after paying you."

Minette blushed. "Perhaps you lost them on the way."

He pinched her cheeks. "Perhaps you took them, my dove. But I do not care. I have learned to carry only a few coins when I come here. But you will not need any coins in hell."

Minette grabbed Roland's wrists and pulled his hands from her face. "You are not a priest. You don't know where I am going."

Roland laughed again. "Then next time Canon Jacques comes to visit you, ask him." Roland teasingly attempted to wriggle out of Minette's grasp.

"I will visit the saint. I will ask him."

"Him? Then you will know. For you, Minette, and for me, God has no forgiveness."

━ ━

"FOR YOU, MINETTE, God has no forgiveness."

The words stuck in Minette's mind like carriage wheels in mud. For the next several nights, after the men had left her room, Minette tossed in her sleep. The pouch of pilfered coins hidden under her bed seemed to swell until they poked her back. All night she wondered if hell were a raging inferno of flame or a frozen wasteland of ice. Sometimes she dreamed herself in one place or the other, with the men who came to her. The men would beat her as her father had done. And they would call her, not Minette, but Eve.

Was she going to hell? She had to know. The saint could tell her. But he had left Limoges to preach in St. Junien.

After several days of inquiring of her lovers about the saint, Roland told her, "Father Anthony is going to preach in the old Roman amphitheater tomorrow afternoon."

"Then do not come to me," Minette said, "because I will be there to hear him."

—▸ ◂—

UNDER GRAY, THREATENING SKIES, Minette made her way to the amphitheater. She pushed through the haggling crowd at the many market booths to the clearing in the center of the square where an immense crowd, possibly a thousand people, had gathered. Minette, feeling too unworthy to draw any closer to the saint, stood at the very back of the gathering. She could see that a wooden platform had been erected. Near her, two men were pointing to the platform.

"The devil made the one they built for him in St. Junien collapse," one man said. "Father Anthony predicted it would happen. But no one was hurt, as he said no one would be. The man lifted his shirt and pointed to a hammer stuck in his belt. "I came prepared to help remake this one if it falls. That's what the men of St. Junien had to do."

Minette looked curiously at the platform. The devil? All her life, she believed that the devil used her to harm men. Now the devil was after the saint?

When Father Anthony arrived about noon, he mounted the pulpit and the restless crowd settled into silence.

"O Light of the world," the saint called out in a clear voice that betrayed just the slightest hint of accent. "You are the infinite God, Father of eternity, Giver of wisdom and knowledge, and ineffable Dispenser of every spiritual grace. You know all things before they are made. You have made darkness and light. Put forth Your hand and touch my mouth and make it a sharp sword to utter eloquently Your words."

Anthony's eyes were raised to heaven as he prayed. Minette bowed her head. Despite her distance from the platform, she heard clearly every word of the prayer.

"My dear friends," Anthony began, "thank you for coming. A church would have been more comfortable for you, but it would have taken you much longer to enlarge it to hold all of you than it took you to build this platform for me."

Minette giggled as laughter rippled across the crowd.

"Do not be alarmed at the threatening sky. You will be dry if you remain here. And so, let us begin. 'I am the Way, the Truth, and the Life,' John 14:6. In the name of the Father, and of the Son, and of the Holy Spirit."

It had been so long ago that her mother had taught her, yet Minette remembered how to cross herself. She and the crowd did it in a smooth, sleek motion.

The friar's voice rose, gentle yet strong. "'I am the Way,' said Jesus, 'the Way' without error for those who search for it. Isaiah the prophet spoke of this way. 'A highway will be there, called the holy way. No one unclean may pass over it, or fools go astray on it.'"

The word "unclean" leaped out. Minette thought of all the men who came to her and she felt the filth of her many sins. "No one unclean may pass over it." That meant her.

"Christ's message consists in not giving importance to the things of this world. No, the wise appreciate and savor those of the next world, those that belong to God and to eternity."

Eternity. Where would Minette spend eternity? Roland said she was going to hell. Her father had said the same.

"The righteous do not walk across the cursed fields of worldly thoughts and they avoid the vineyards of carnal and wanton desires."

Minette felt weak and conspicuous. Surely everyone around her could see that she was a woman of wanton desires who satisfied those same desires in men.

"The righteous walk straight along the public and well-trodden road that is Christ Who said 'I am the Way.' The way of Christ is public because it is open to everyone. It is well beaten because it has been followed by persecutors and has been stepped on and despised by almost all feet."

She had despised the Way. She had trodden on Christ.

"Only the righteous walk the way faithfully and humbly. They follow it faithfully until death and enter into the Promised Land. Thus, Christ is this Way.

"Christ is the 'Truth.' He is 'Truth' without falsehood for those who find Him. 'The truth is great and stronger than everything else. All the earth invokes the truth and the heavens bless it. There is no truth in wicked kings or wicked women or in all the offspring of iniquity. There is no truth in their wicked words. They will perish in their very sinfulness. But truth remains and grows strong into eternity. It lives and reigns forever.'"

So he had given her the answer that she sought. She was a wicked woman and, as the bastard child of a thief, the offspring of iniquity. She would perish in her sinfulness. Long ago, while yet a child, beaten by her father, she had forgotten how to cry. She wished she could remember for she wanted to weep now for the loss of her soul.

"Yes, even if the temptations of the flesh and impurity are strong, the truth of Christ is stronger and conquers all these sins.

"Christ is Life, for those without life. 'Because I live, you will live also,' Jesus said."

Was she hearing clearly? Was there hope? Would Jesus save her from sin, bring her to life eternal?

A crackling split the air, and Minette shuddered in the lightening that arched across the amphitheater. A ripple of panic swept the crowd.

"Fear nothing," Anthony called out. "I have asked the One Who creates storms to protect us. The storm will pass by."

A few people raced toward the exits of the amphitheater. Most pulled cloaks over their heads but did not move. Minette drew up her hood and huddled, waiting for the rain.

"You who are going out through the gates to this amphitheater!" Anthony called out, "You will pass directly into the storm! Go instead through the gate that is Christ and He will protect you. For He said, 'I am the Gate. Whoever enters through Me will be safe. That one will go in and out and find pasture,' pasture in the eternal fields of heaven. For Christ's days are eternal and the days of His elect will also be eternal. 'I am the Life' means that Christ is our life in example, truth in promise, life in reward; a way that is straight, a truth that does not deceive, a life that never ends. He is the gate to glory through Whom all must pass on their way to the Father."

How could Minette enter the gate of Christ? Surely there must be a gatekeeper, an angel, who would bar her entrance.

"There was a gate in Jerusalem called the 'eye of the needle.' It was so narrow that a camel could not pass through it for a camel is a proud and haughty animal. It refused to stoop low enough to pass through the gate. This gate is the humble Christ. The proud and the greedy, those burdened with false pretensions and riches, cannot enter through this gate.

"Those who wish to enter must humble themselves by stooping. They must kneel in humility before Christ, the humblest of all, and admit their sins. Then they will enter through the gate and will be saved as long as they persevere."

Minette felt wetness on her face. Tears? Thunder crackled. The wind rose with a howl. The wet drops were rain. Minette pulled her cape more tightly around herself. She had been in storms before. She would leave only when the friar did. He continued his sermon, his voice rising above the wind. The crowd remained, waiting for a deluge that never came. That first smattering of drops was all the rain that fell in the amphitheater. By the time Anthony was completing his sermon, the thick, black clouds were thinning out, revealing patches of limpid blue.

"Praise be to You, my Lord Christ, the 'Way, the Truth, and the Life,' the 'Gate' through which the humble sinner may enter the kingdom of God. Amen."

As Anthony's voice faded, the crowd surged toward him. Minette quickly lost sight of him for he had been swallowed in the mob. Her mind was in turmoil. She must speak to him, but what would she say? As the crowd around her thinned, she was left standing alone. Unsure about what to do, she turned away from the crowd at the platform and, through muddy streets strewn with the storm's hailstones, skirted puddles and rivulets until she reached the brothel.

But when she opened the door to her room, she saw it with new eyes. Behind the hanging, rich brocades, she knew that the walls were gutted with rot and stained with rain. Her bed, nest for many men, repulsed her. Under her bed, pushed out of sight in the dust, a small pouch of pilfered coins testified to her greed.

She paced her room. She did not know what to do, for living as she had always lived suddenly sickened her. But she knew nothing else. Suddenly in an act of unthinking desperation, she pulled the pouch of coins from under her bed and, clutching it like a mad woman, ran out the door and into the sodden streets. If she hurried, she might get to the amphitheater before the saint left.

She need not have rushed. Many waited before her and Minette stood in her muddy shoes, leaning against the platform, for several hours.

She had time to study the saint's long, narrow face, his large, deep-set, black eyes and the gracious smile that seemed a living part of his face. Obviously he was well bred. Whatever made her think that she could approach him?

She studied the crowd. Barons, nobles, peasants, serfs, women, men from every walk of life. Even two canons. Many wept. Several threw themselves on their knees before the priest. Others gave him purses or spilled laps full of coins at his feet. Some handed him their daggers and swords. Three other gray-robed friars, who stood near him, silently gathered the booty into pouches while the priest spoke to the penitents and sent each home with his blessing.

A few went away disgruntled. "All I asked him for was a thread from his tunic and he refused," one woman muttered.

"Why wouldn't he give it?" her waiting friend asked.

"He said the faithful take relics from saints and he is not a saint."

Minette's ankles were weakening and the sun was sinking through the dispersing clouds when the friar finally approached her as she leaned against the platform.

"You have waited all this time," he said, "and now there is no one left but you. What is your name, my child?"

"Minette."

"And what is troubling you, Minette?"

"Father, I...." Minette stumbled over the words. She bit her lip. Two bitter tears squeezed out of her eyes. The first real tears in over a decade.

Anthony noticed the moisture, she knew, but he turned from her to the three silent brothers behind him. "Leave now with what you have been given today. Sell the weapons and then distribute the money for them and the other coins to the poor. Return to the friary when your pouches are empty." Raising his hand in blessing over the three men, the priest sent two away. The third walked out of ear shot, and sat on a hunk of stone facing the priest, waiting.

Anthony touched Minette's elbow and pointed to the platform steps. "Minette, let's sit down here."

She obeyed. She had never sat so close to any man who had not looked at her with lust. She recognized compassion in this man's face, a look she had seen occasionally on other faces, but on none directed to her. Minette turned her head away from his, her eyes smarting too much even to stare at the pebbles at her feet.

"My sister," Anthony whispered in a tremulous voice, "do not be afraid. I confess to you and will always confess it, if the Lord had not been my helper, my soul would have fallen into every sin. Take courage. The Lord will console anyone who mourns for his own sin."

Minette nodded. How desperately she wanted consolation! She tried to speak. But the words would not come. She tried again. The words stuck in her throat. Her sins were too horrible to be spoken to this holy man.

"Minette," Anthony said, "can you write?"

She nodded. Yes, she could write. A little.

She heard the rustle of a robe and then blank parchment and a pen pressed into her hands. Puzzled, she looked up through her tears and saw Anthony holding a vessel of ink.

"Write your sins," he said softly. He guided her hand to the wooden steps, placing the parchment onto it. Then he dipped the pen into the ink, releasing Minette's hand.

Shaking, she laboriously wrote. "I lie. I steal. I make men sin. I am going to hell."

Weak with fear of his rebukes, she handed the pen and parchment to Anthony.

Anthony glanced at the parchment, then spoke. "Minette, imagine that the platform behind us is Mount Calvary and you, like Mary Magdalene, are sitting here, exhausted with grief, at the foot of the cross. Can you see, Minette?"

She closed her eyes and imagined a huge wooden stake looming above her head, her back thrust up against it.

"Do you see Christ hanging naked on the cross of shame?"

Minette nodded. The gentle voice came again, "That is how Mary Magdalene saw Christ. Now look at the face of Jesus, swollen and bruised and covered with His tears. He suffered 'though He had done no wrong nor spoken any falsehood.' He 'prayed at all times for sinners' even on the cross when He asked His Father to forgive those who persecuted Him."

Minette's tears came faster. *Was he praying for me? Will He forgive me?*

"The Blood of Christ brings forgiveness and life to His persecutors. Can you see Him, Minette? Can you hear His prayerful cries?"

She could see, hear. *Oh, Lord, forgive me.*

"Now look again, Minette. Do you see the Mother of Christ weeping beside you at the feet of her Son?"

She could see her, a woman three decades older than herself, her face grimy with dust, streaked with tears, its beauty twisted with unbearable grief.

"Minette, you think that you are going to hell. But why despair of salvation since all here speaks of mercy and of love? Behold the two advocates who plead your cause before the tribunal of Divine Justice: a Mother and a Redeemer."

With a clearer vision than she had ever possessed, Minette could see the scene. The Son. The Mother. Herself.

Anthony's voice was like salve. "See before us Mary who presents to her Son her heart transfixed with the sword of sorrow. See Jesus who presents to His Father the wounds in His feet and hands and His heart pierced by the soldier's lance. Take courage. With such a mediator, with such an intercessor, Divine Mercy cannot reject you." He paused. "You say that you have stolen. Are you sorry for this?"

Minette fished up her sleeve for the purse and slid it into Anthony's lap.

"These are the stolen coins? And you wish me to give them to the poor?"

"Yes, Father." Her voice was barely more than a squeak.

"And you lie? So did St. Peter. He repented and was forgiven."

"It is so hard for me to tell the truth, Father."

"I know, Minette. But in Christ all things are possible."

"I am sorry for those lies, Father. I will try harder."

"Then the lies are forgiven."

"Father, I make men sin. The things I have done—to tell you would make me sick. I make men sin. I am evil."

Anthony pointed to Minette's words on the parchment in his lap. "You do not make men sin. Men who sin with you sin of their own accord. Who told you that you were evil?"

She breathed deeply. "A man. Men."

"Were these men Christ? Or his true followers?"

Minette started at the question. Anthony was smiling at her. "I thought not. Then why believe them?"

"But aren't women like me evil, Father? Am I not going to hell?"

"God created women. God does not create evil."

"But look at me. You know what I am."

"I know what you used to be. What you are now is between you and God."

"But, Father, I have sinned in ways that even God cannot forgive."

"Remember, Minette, that all sin that has gone before can be forgiven the one who wishes to make a new beginning. Is this what you wish? To make a new beginning?"

"Oh, Father, more than anything."

"Then leave the men who come to you and strive for purity. Our worst enemy can be our flesh. We must conquer lust and must keep it under control by wholesome penance for it is a most dangerous foe."

Minette dared to look directly into the priest's dark eyes. She found no condemnation and no false pity there. Only acceptance and purity that is love.

Anthony's voice was soft. "Minette, in Christ's new covenant, even our thoughts come under judgment. How much more our actions! Sexual sin allows the unworthy to enter the heart and faith is lost. The life of the soul is faith, Minette. Fornication puts to death the soul that God formed in His likeness. Fornication robs the heart of faith and thus of life."

How could she gaze so intently at this pure man? He knew all about her. How ashamed she felt! She turned her head away from those eyes that were probing her soul.

Anthony's soothing voice continued: "We must prefer to die rather than sell our inheritance in heaven. We must prefer suffering any hardship rather than surrender our eternal glory for carnal pleasure. If we do this, any sorrow that we feel at denying our own flesh will turn into joy. Do you understand, Minette?"

Without looking at the priest, Minette nodded.

Anthony put his hand under Minette's chin and turned it so that the two were again looking eye to eye. "Would you like to learn a prayer that I use very often myself whenever impure thoughts or temptations come?"

"Is there such a prayer? That works?"

Anthony smiled. "There is. Now sign yourself." Minette did so clumsily. "Now say, 'Behold the cross of the Lord.'"

"Behold the cross of the Lord." Her voice was trembling.

"Fly, you hostile powers!"

"Fly, you hostile powers!"

"The Lion of the tribe of Judah, the Root of David has conquered. Alleluia! Alleluia!"

Minette repeated the words softly. Anthony had her cross herself once more and repeat the prayer. Suddenly she grinned. She imagined shouting out this prayer the next time Roland came to her door. That would frighten him off!

"Minette, look at me." Anthony made the sign of the cross over her as he spoke. "In the name of the Father, and of the Son, and of the Holy Spirit. I absolve you of all sins of your past life. You are not evil and you are not going to hell, Minette. Your sins are forgiven."

He handed Minette the parchment that still lay in his lap. The words Minette had written on it were gone.

"Father, the words," she stammered.

"You are not going to hell. Your sins are forgiven," Anthony repeated. "Your soul is as clean as that parchment."

Minette stared at the blank sheet. A sigh from deep within thrust up her throat and escaped like a frightened bird. With it went the vicious words of her father and of the other men. She was not evil. She was forgiven.

"I am not evil, Father?"

"Anyone reborn of Christ is good, Minette." Anthony paused. "But still, I am obligated to give you a penance."

"Even if it were to wear sackcloth the rest of my life, Father, it would not be harsh enough."

Anthony shook his head. "No, Minette. For your penance, I want you to pray daily the prayer I taught you. Pray it often, in every temptation. Think of Christ Who gave His life in exchange for yours. He will help you. Will you do this?"

"It is too little to ask. Yes, I will do that."

"In addition, you must leave behind your lifestyle and you must never return to it. Would you like me to send you someplace where you can find work and live a good Christian life?" When she nodded, he handed Minette the purse. "On our way, I want you to distribute these."

Through muddy streets trekked Anthony and the woman, accompanied by the friar who had waited silently in the amphitheater. Minette gave two coins to a blind beggar, a handful to a man on crutches, and the remainder, along with the empty purse, to a thin woman whose three children clung to her stained gown. How good to give the coins away!

Quite suddenly Anthony stopped at a small house and knocked. When a chubby, young woman, broom in her hand, opened the door, the priest spoke.

"Minette, this is Madam Beaudoin. She is one of our friary's benefactors. Madam, this is Minette," The woman smiled pleasantly at Minette who squirmed at the unfamiliar good will. *She knows what I am,* Minette thought. *Yet she seems kind.*

"Would you kindly let Minette stay the night with you? Tomorrow I will send two brothers from the friary for her."

"Certainly, Father," the woman said pleasantly.

The priest turned to Minette. "Minette, with your permission, the brothers shall accompany you to a convent. There the nuns will love, shelter, and instruct you in weaving cloth. If you stay and do as they teach you, you will learn to make a living. You are not to take the habit unless it is your will and the nuns test your vocation. I will ask them to keep you in their employ until you wish to move elsewhere. Are you willing to go to such a convent?"

Minette's mind was swirling. A convent? She in a convent? There she would be safe. There she would never again have to use her body sinfully.

"It will be difficult for you to change your life, Minette. But with Jesus, all things are possible."

Minette smiled. She thought of Christ gazing at her from the cross and of His mother.

She thought of the saint's gentle words and of the blank parchment. She thought of learning to weave cloth in a convent and of a new beginning.

*With Jesus, all sin can be forgiven. With Jesus, all things are possible.*

# ❧ 18 ❧

## *Peasant Woman*

**Cottage, Marseilles, France (Late 1226)** ❧ The peasant woman had been kneading her bread dough for perhaps two minutes when she heard a soft rap at her cottage door. At least she thought she heard a rap. With the wind whipping a chill December rain across the countryside, she could not be sure if she had heard a knock at the door or the tapping of a tree branch against the roof. So she shrugged and went on kneading. If she had visitors, they would knock again. And they did.

Wiping her hands on her apron, she waddled over to the door. She'd invite them in, of course. If they weren't heretics, that is. The *Cathari*, often called Albigensians in this region, were fleeing the French armies, directed by the boy, King Louis IX, and his mother, Blanche. The war, she had heard, was vicious. She herself had seen little of the fighting, but she had often watched armies of mounted knights and foot soldiers marching up and down the roads and, sometimes, scurrying bands of fleeing heretics.

Today the weather was horrid, but if these visitors were heretics, she would send them on their way with a curse. But what *Cathar* would be bold enough to knock at her door? The heretics had secret networks of their own supporters, she had heard. Surely a heretic would go to a house known to be sympathetic.

Most likely, her visitors were not heretics. Most likely they were pilgrims on their way to a shrine in Le Puy, Mont St. Michel, Vezelay, or any number of other spots in France. If they were true followers of Christ, she would offer them some bread if they were willing to wait for it to rise and bake. Did not Christ say that those who welcomed strangers welcomed Him? The woman fancied that some day she would open the door and, perhaps, the Savior Himself would be there.

Today there was no Savior. But close enough, she smiled to herself. There were two poor friars, drenched to the bone.

"My lady, we've come a long way," the shorter one said, who was just about her height. She recognized a certain tired heaviness in his voice that comes with a deep, deep grief. Her own voice had carried that thick tone for months after her husband had died.

Quickly she ushered them into her one room cottage. She had very little, but what she had was dry.

She could tell at a glance that they were followers of the poor little man of Assisi, Francis, who bore the name of her own country. So she knew what their grief was.

Holy Francis, she had heard, had died in Assisi. These men were mourning their founder. Who could not mourn for him? He was a legend. Tamer of wolves, preacher to birds, poet of prayer. And, she had just heard, bearer of the wounds of Christ. She had heard that upon his death, the larks had flown up, forming a cross in the sky. With Francis had died a special love, gentleness, and humility that had been sung in song and told in story even here in France.

How the woman wished she could ease the friars' grief! If only she had dry clothes to offer them, but she had nothing but her own thin, patched cloak and one extra chemise, hung on a peg by the fireplace. She could not ask them to remove their wet clothing to dry over the flames. She knew that these friars wore nothing beneath their tunics but their breeches.

With a start, she realized that she had rolled back the sleeves of her chemise to knead her bread. Never had any man except her deceased husband seen her bare arms. Embarrassed she plucked at her sleeves to pull them down. What would she do? With them down, she could not knead the bread without dirtying her clothes. If she did not finish kneading, she would have nothing to offer the two men.

The shorter friar touched her lightly on the hand. "Do not worry, my lady. I have kneaded bread myself." He raised his hand in silent blessing over her.

The woman smiled and curtsied awkwardly. "Warm yourselves by the fire while I finish. The bread will rise soon and bake. You shall have that and wine."

"Thank you," the friar said.

The woman went back to her kneading. The friars sat silently before the fire, their tunics pulled out before them. Water dripping from their clothes formed muddy puddles on the floor.

"How far have you come?" she asked.

The taller friar turned toward the question. "From Brive," he answered.

*How young he is!* The woman thought. *Not yet twenty.* "Will you stay the night?"

The tall friar looked at the other for an answer. The shorter friar turned toward the woman and smiled. "Thank you, my lady. With your good pleasure, we will stay until the rain stops. Then we must be on our way to Assisi."

The woman grinned with pleasure. At least until the rain stopped, she would have company to relieve her loneliness and boredom.

Abruptly, the taller brother asked the shorter, "What do you think will happen at the general chapter, Father? Do you think Brother Elias will again be chosen as minister? Who will take Father Francis' place?"

The priest, for now she knew the shorter one was a priest, placed his hand on the youth's arm. "Father Francis created this Order at God's command, and in God's hands it must remain. We must continue to pray that God's will be done. Father Francis is praying with us, you can be sure."

The woman plopped the two loaves of bread onto a board and covered them with a scrap of linen. She placed the loaves on the floor near the hearth and glanced sideways at the friars. Thin, glistening lines of water squeezed from their eyes. She averted her head.

Something about the shorter one made her pause. She seemed to have seen him somewhere. Heard that voice.

"Do you think Brother Elias will have you preach in Spoleto?" the younger friar asked.

"I will do whatever he tells me. With Francis gone, we owe Brother Elias obedience."

The woman gasped, then caught herself. This was Father Anthony. She had heard him preach four times, but each time she had been far back in the crowd. Her eyesight had grown so poor with age, that she had never seen him clearly. But the voice. Yes, the voice was his.

Father Anthony held some sort of important position in Limousin, custodian or something, she had heard. This Brother Elias, whoever he was, must have called all the important administrators of the friars back to Assisi to work on details of their Order now that holy Francis was dead.

Oh, dear, with such an important man in her house, what was she to do? He was so fatigued with travel and grief and all she had to offer him was bread and wine. Her cheese was moldy in a leather pouch by her bed. She might nibble it herself, but she could not offer such a poor scrap to the friars.

She owned only simple, scratched wooden cups and plates on which to serve a meal. If only she had something fine to bring a bit of joy to these men. Her neighbor had a wine goblet. Father Anthony must drink from a goblet. Certainly he was used to such niceties. Had he not called her "my lady" and been as polite as a noble?

The woman pushed herself up from the hearth and reached for her hooded rain cloak. "I have only poor cups to drink from, Father. My neighbor has a fine glass goblet. I shall go and borrow it from her so you may drink from it, Father."

Anthony looked startled and dismayed. "My good lady, do not trouble yourself. I have been living in a cave at Brive and drinking stream water with my hands. I need no fancy goblet."

"A cave? Father, do not tease me. No, you shall have your goblet. Her cottage is just over the hill."

Anthony leaped to his feet. "It is a wretched day. Do not go. It is not necessary."

"My cloak is old but does not leak," the woman said proudly.

"Then let me wear it and go for you," Anthony offered.

"Certainly not, Father. Stay here and I will be back shortly. By then the bread will be ready to bake." The woman hurried out the door before the good priest could protest further.

The cloak did keep her dry, but her shoes were a muddy mess when she returned to the cottage. No matter. She sloshed happily around in them while she slid the bread into the fire and then set the table, the delicate wine glass gracing it as if waiting for a bishop, or for the Savior Himself. She invited her guests to sit down on the bench.

*I have so little to offer,* the woman thought again. *The bread and wine will have to do.*

The woman placed the bread, along with a knife, on the table, then threw her rain cape over her head. Taking a pitcher, she bustled outdoors to draw wine from the single cask in her wine cellar. When she returned with a full pitcher, the younger friar met her at the door. His anguished face told her that something was desperately wrong.

He held his two hands out to her. In one lay the goblet, in the other its stem. The woman nearly shrieked.

"I am so sorry," the young man said in a high-pitched, trembling voice. "I was only looking at it and it slipped."

"My neighbor's glass," the woman moaned. "Her most precious thing. I can never replace it. Holy Mother of God, have mercy. What shall I tell her? Holy Mother of God, have mercy."

The boy looked helpless and about ready to cry. Why had she spoken so quickly? She should have stopped her mouth.

"Don't worry about it," she said almost too swiftly. "We are friends. She will forgive me. I asked for it for Father Anthony. She will forgive me."

A bit unsteady, the woman walked to the table and placed the pitcher on it. Anthony was seated on the bench, his elbows propped on the table, his face in his hands. In the fire's glow, his tonsured head gleamed.

"Father, are you ill?" she asked.

As he shook his head, she suddenly remembered something.

"Dear Mother of God, I've forgotten to turn off the tap!"

She rushed outdoors to the cellar. The wine was running full tilt to the floor, dyeing the mud deep black. The woman turned the tap and leaned against the barrel, groaning. She began to tap the wine barrel from the bottom up. She had not yet reached the middle of the cask when she heard the thin echo of empty space. The barrel had been nearly full. Now it was nearly empty. The earth had drunk almost her full winter's supply of wine.

She plodded back into the house. She would have to be cheerful for her guests. They were feeling enough sadness, and she was the only one here to comfort them. And one of the two the famous preacher. Oh, she almost wished he had gone to her neighbor's cottage rather than her own. First the wine glass. Now the wine. Is this how God rewarded those who served His servants?

The woman trudged indoors and hung up her cape. She tried to smile so as not to worry the friars. She would ask Father Anthony to give a blessing and then she would serve them. First she went to her cupboard to bring out her second wooden cup.

As she turned toward the table, Anthony smiled weakly at her. "I am glad that you decided to join us, my lady. Only I will be glad to use that wooden cup that you have taken out for yourself. I think you, as our gracious hostess, deserve to use the fine goblet."

He held out his hand to her. Astonished, she took the goblet from him. It was unbroken.

His voice, tired and thick, continued. "Now, so we may enjoy our meal together, may I ask you to check your wine cask again? I think, my lady, you will find it full. We will wait for your return before praying together."

"Yes, Father," the startled woman said. Without even bothering with her cape, she ran outdoors to the cellar and tapped on the wine keg. First the bottom. Then higher. Then the center. Then near the top. Each time, she heard the same dull thud that meant only one thing. Wine.

# Part Four

—◆—

# Return to Italy

—◆—

## ❧ 19 ❧

## *Pope Gregory IX*

**Lateran Palace, Rome, Italy (1227)** ❧ In the early dawn, Ugo woke slowly, remembering who he was. He had followed this process of self-examination nearly every morning for the past three and a half weeks. To the world, he carried many titles. Cardinal Ugolino dei Conti di Segna. Grandnephew of the deceased Pope Innocent III. Previous Cardinal Bishop of Ostia and Velletri. Recently, chief counselor of the ailing Holy Father, Honorius III. Once, long ago, Count of Anagni in the Patrimony of St. Peter. Now Pope Gregory IX, Vicar of the holy Roman Catholic Church. But, before God and himself, he was Ugo, pilgrim on a journey to eternal life. And to the doves cooing on the roofs and turrets of the papal residence, the Lateran Palace, he was merely another white bearded Roman stirring awake.

As he lay beneath his blankets, watching the darkness beginning to lighten, Ugo relived his election as if it were happening again. Honorius had died on March 18. After his burial the following day, the cardinals had assembled in the monastery of St. Gregory to celebrate the Mass of the Holy Spirit and then to elect the new pontiff. Ugo had been praying for guidance in making his choice, but, when all the votes were cast, he himself had been the choice.

"No!" he had screamed. He had seen first hand how the papacy had devoured Honorius and Innocent. Was he to be consumed with worry and responsibility, carrying the Church until his death?

"I am not worthy!" he cried. "I am not capable."

As two cardinals, holding the papal mantle, approached him, the nearly eighty-year-old Ugo had bolted toward the locked door.

Hands caught him. Anguish and horror erupted in his soul. Shrieking, he grabbed his cassock, his arms trembling with the strength that comes from unbearable pain.

"No!" His fingers clutched the red garment over his heart, pulling violently as if to wrench out of himself the overpowering fear and grief. As the cassock ripped across Ugo's chest, he felt the papal mantle forced over his shoulders.

"Do not resist the will of heaven," an interior voice seemed to say. Ugo's arms fell to his side as he surrendered to the unavoidable will of God. Two days ago, on Easter Sunday, he had been crowned. The mitre still felt heavy on his head. The papal throne on which he sat still seemed too large.

"Lord, why have You given me this office? I am neither worthy nor capable," he prayed as he lay in bed. "Lord, Your Church seems to be crumbling. Many of your clergy ignore the teachings of Christ. They are greedy, lustful, proud, dressed like peacocks when the poor are in rags. Even some of the cardinals fall into these sins. Thus, the people are without guidance, and the faith is dying. What do You wish me to do?"

Ugo sat on the papal throne, clothed in the robes of Pope Gregory IX. All morning, following Mass, he had hosted audiences with this or that cleric. Now the large doors before him were opening again and the next two figures, barefoot and dressed in tattered, gray tunics, were being ushered into the room.

Ugo broke into a grin. He recognized one of the men even before his name was announced. He had met him four years before when he, with Brother Francis, had conferred with Ugo to discuss the Rule of Francis' Order.

The canon who was acting as a page called out, "Brother Anthony and Brother Jerome of the Friars Minor."

The two friars walked briskly up to Ugo and knelt before him, their heads bowed almost to the floor. Ugo traced the sign of the cross over their stooped shoulders. Something about Brother Anthony looked different. Age, perhaps?

"Rise, Brothers."

Ugo first embraced the lanky, dark-eyed young man with the sparse black beard. "Brother Jerome, I am pleased to meet you. Welcome."

Then he turned to clean-shaven Anthony. "Brother Anthony, it is so good to see you again."

As he embraced Anthony heartily, his joy turned to perplexity. Four years ago when Ugo had embraced both Anthony and Francis, he had felt their ribs through their tunics. Today, only Jerome was lean. Anthony's stomach felt bloated.

Ugo released Anthony slowly. "Let me look at you." He studied Anthony, from the grinning face down to the slightly protruding stomach to the bare, somewhat puffy feet. Ugo had seen cardinals and bishops who were plump with eating rich food. Fat did not look or feel like this. This was different. This was swelling.

"Are you well, Brother?"

"Yes, Your Holiness."

"Perhaps you should see a doctor."

"I am well."

"Do not be too certain. Those like yourself who live your Rule to the letter die young. You are too harsh on yourself. Look at Brother Francis. He was not yet fifty when he died."

Anthony's grin faded. Ugo caught sight of the slightest trembling around the friar's lips. "The wounds of Christ killed Father Francis," Anthony said softly, "just as they killed our Lord."

Ugo looked at the young man's downcast eyes. The sudden wetness glistening on Anthony's black eyelashes embarrassed him. He swallowed the lump that had risen in his own throat and, by doing so, forced inside his own tears. "I loved him, too, Brother."

How Ugo had loved him! Francis was a passionate man who had given all to God. Ah, if only Ugo had the commitment and courage to make that total submission to the Almighty! How he envied Francis' faith! And now he envied even more the faith of this man, fifty years his junior, who stood before him with the love of Francis welling up in his dark eyes.

While Francis had been a merchant's son, not a noble, Anthony had come from a background much like Ugo's. But as Ugo had reached up in the hierarchy of the Church and had obtained the highest office of all, Anthony had reached down to become an unknown servant. God and not Anthony had raised the man to prominence. God had given him a limitless knowledge, a golden voice, and a deep, personal holiness.

*Yet he has no idea,* Ugo realized, *how truly great he is.*

"So you have come to me from France. I understand that you have been serving as *custos* of Limousin. How are the friaries doing there, both the established ones and those that you created during your term? Did the novices and friars grasp the theology which you taught? Will they be able to preach the Good News of Christ and combat heresy effectively?"

"They are good men, Your Holiness. They love Christ and serve Him. That alone will make their words effective."

Ugo nodded. "So it will. And how do those friars in the province feel about Francis' Rule?"

Anthony shook his head. "Some think it is too strict. Others embrace it."

Ugo nodded. "It is the same here. Brother Francis' way of life is still dividing the friars. And Brother Elias sent you to speak to me about the Rule prior to your Order's chapter meeting. As if I could solve the disagreement."

"We are obedient to the Church, Holy Father," Anthony said. "We will abide by your decision."

"When is the chapter meeting?"

"It will begin May 30 and extend into June."

"Ah, in June you will be in Assisi and I will be in Anagni. Rome is unbearable in the summer. Unhealthy. Never come here in the summer, Brothers."

Ugo led the two friars to a large oaken table around which twelve chairs were arranged, six on each side, with one large, ornate chair at the head. In this chair, Ugo sat. He motioned for the friars to sit down, one to his left and one to his right.

Anthony's deeply bronzed cheeks were puckered, as if he were biting them on the inside. "I know," Ugo said, tapping the friar tenderly on the wrist. "This time, it will be difficult to discuss the Rule without Brother Francis."

"I have been praying that the Holy Spirit would guide us," Anthony said quietly, "as the Holy Spirit guided him."

Ugo nodded. How well the Holy Spirit had guided Francis! That chapter meeting in Assisi in 1217 stood in Ugo's mind as a testimony to that Spirit. Determined to attend the chapter daily, Ugo, as cardinal, had ridden up to the plain around the poor little Church of St. Mary of the Angels. There he met clusters of sixty, a hundred, three hundred friars, all bound as solidly together as a battalion of knights. He saw them praying, heard them speaking together of God, noted the straw on which they slept.

*This is Christ's army,* he had thought. *If men can live like this before God, how will things go for those of us clergy who take our ease in comfort and luxury?*

When the friars recognized their visitor, they had begun to surge around Ugo, cheering and blessing him. Tears had welled up in his eyes as he dismounted his horse, threw his luxuriant red cloak over the saddle, and removed his soft shoes. Barefoot as the friars around him, Ugo walked to the chapel to celebrate Mass. Francis preached the sermon.

Ah, Francis was unmovable. One day, some friars had persuaded Ugo to urge Francis to follow a set Rule, perhaps that of St. Augustine or St. Benedict or St. Bernard. When Ugo, whom Francis called his "Pope," approached Francis with the idea, the thin-faced little friar had taken Ugo's hand and presented both of them to the chapter.

"Brothers, Brothers," he had cried. "The way that I have entered is one of humility and simplicity. It was taught to me by God Himself, and I will follow no other. So do not speak to me about St. Augustine or St. Benedict. The Lord wishes me to be a new kind of fool in this world and will not lead me by any other way."

Later, Francis had gone to convert the Sultan and, in his absence, those in the Order more worldly than he began to drift back to the world. When he returned in 1220, dissension among the friars threatened to destroy the Order. Francis turned to the pope for help. "So that I need not continue to bother you," he had said to Honorius III, "grant me the bishop of Ostia as the protector and defender of the Order." Honorius had agreed.

But Ugo, the bishop of Ostia, could not attend the chapter of 1221. At this chapter, Francis presented his expanded Rule, one that he, assisted by the learned Caesar of Speyer, had painstakingly written. The Rule was lofty, poetic, heroic, a clarification of the first Rule. The friars who wished to live as Francis did pushed it through. But those opposed would not rest. By 1223, the friars were splitting into two camps: those who wished to keep the original Rule of absolute poverty and total day-to-day reliance on God's will, and those who felt that a growing Order needed more direction and stability.

That year, Brother Elias, minister general of the Friars Minor, had sensed a split. He sent a physically weakened Francis, with Anthony as his traveling companion, to Ugo to hammer out a new Rule. While Anthony had listened and occasionally commented, Ugo and Francis had argued.

"Your Order has outgrown its original Rule," Ugo had insisted. "You cannot demand heroism of your many followers."

"Christ lived in absolute poverty," Francis had contended. "The Gospel is our Rule. God gave it to me through a priest. He read the passage for me in the chapel of the Portiuncula on the feast of the Apostle St. Matthias."

"I know. The Gospel of Matthew, chapter 10, verses 7 to 13: 'Take nothing in your purse, neither have two coats or shoes.'"

Francis had looked directly at Ugo. Despite the painful disease that was destroying his sight, the little man's sharp eyes gleamed with fervor. "Our Rule is the message Christ gave to His disciples. If Christ could live it, why can't we? It is sufficient. For fifteen years, the friars and I have lived by this Rule."

Ugo, equally insistent, had stared back. "For the disciples it was sufficient. For you and for your first followers it was sufficient. But not now. Your Order is growing, Brother Francis. Your brothers and Friar Dominic's preaching friars are the hope of our Church. Together, your followers will transform the world. Friar Dominic is dead, but his Order is secure because his friars follow a reasonable Rule. To expect your brothers to live solely on alms, to own no property, to have nothing is too unreasonable. You must have structure or your Order will crumble and be of no value to the world or to God."

In the end, Francis had submitted. Ugo rewrote the Rule, attempting to keep Francis' spirit and implementing some of Anthony's suggestions. Nevertheless, he insisted on wording that permitted those less than heroic to live and obey. The Rule was accepted, but Francis was not pleased. Ugo had quenched the fire in his words.

Francis' health declined. Anthony was sent to France. Ugo continued to advise the pope. Now all had changed. Francis was dead. Anthony had been recalled to Assisi. Ugo himself was pope. And the Rule that the three of them together had written was still the source of controversy. Some friars interpreted Ugo's carefully crafted clauses one way, some another.

So now Anthony and Ugo sat while Jerome listened and occasionally commented. Point by point, they went over the Rule of

1223. What did this mean? That? How should Anthony present the pope's interpretations to the chapter?

The men worked until late in the afternoon. Finally, Ugo was satisfied. Rising from the table, he escorted the two brothers to the door. "Before you go, Brother Anthony, I ask of you two favors. Tomorrow, I wish you to preach to the cardinals in their assembly. The following day, you will preach from the steps of the Lateran to the crowd that has come here for the Easter indulgences. The Church is in need of reform. Perhaps your words can begin to make some changes."

Anthony shook his head. "Your Excellency, the Church is made up of individuals. If the Holy Spirit converts individual souls, then the Church will change."

Ugo nodded thoughtfully. "You are thinking," he said, "who, in the end, is going to heaven? The institutional Church or the individuals within her? Converted souls will, of a certainty, reform the Church in line with the will of God." Ugo placed his right hand on Anthony's shoulder. "Brother, will you preach for me? And who the Holy Spirit touches, He touches. Then you will be free to return to Brother Elias."

Anthony bowed. "With your blessing, Holy Father."

Ugo again traced the sign of the cross first over Jerome's head and then over Anthony's.

"Brother Anthony, see a doctor," Ugo said, dismissing the friars.

—◾ ▬

EARLY THE FOLLOWING AFTERNOON, Anthony again knelt before Ugo's throne. Again, Ugo blessed him.

"I have seen a doctor," Anthony said, raising his head. "He told me to eat more and drink more."

Ugo sighed. "I could have told you that myself. And are you doing it?"

"I have begun today." Anthony smiled. "Do not worry about me, Your Holiness. I am well."

"I pray so." Ugo rose. "Come, Brother Anthony. The cardinals are assembling."

Under the high, ornately carved ceiling of the papal court, sat an assembly of the cardinals. Ugo sat behind the pulpit in which Anthony now prayed eloquently for God's inspiration. Ugo had a commanding view of the red robed prelates who were studying the barefoot friar in the patched tunic.

*They are skeptical,* Ugo knew. A smile played on his lips. *Soon they shall see that Anthony deserves his reputation.*

Anthony's voice rang out as a herald. "'The word of the Lord was made known unto John, the son of Zachary, in the desert and he came into all the country about the Jordan. John came preaching the baptism of penance for the remission of sins, as it is written in the book of the prophet Isaiah, a voice of one crying in the desert.' Luke 3, verses 2 to 4. In the name of the Father, and of the Son, and of the Holy Spirit."

As one giant crimson organism, every member of the entire assemblage crossed himself.

Anthony stepped away from the pulpit as he began to speak, his clear voice reaching easily to the farthest corners of the room. "The name Zachary means 'a remembrance of the Lord.' John, the son of Zachary, symbolizes a prelate or a preacher who ought to remember, to remember constantly, the memorial passion of our Lord Christ."

He moved among the prelates, gazing at one after another as he spoke. "The book of Exodus admonishes us, 'It shall be as a sign in your hand and as a memorial before your eyes.' Thus, Christ's passion must be a memorial and a sign for us." He raised his long hands toward the prelates. "It must be a sign in our hands as we use these hands to touch others in the name of Christ and to consecrate bread and wine into His Body and Blood." Moving his arms outward and upward, he continued, "Likewise, the passion of Christ must be ever before our eyes as we pray and as we see in others the figure and the creation of God."

Pausing, Anthony raised his eyes heavenward, then called out, "Are we true sons of Zachary? If a prelate or a preacher is a true 'son of Zachary,' the word of the Lord will be 'made known to him,' as it was made known to John. The word is a word of life and peace, of grace and truth. It will be a sweet word, offering hope and solace to a sinner 'as cold water to a thirsty soul,' 'like good news from a far country.' So says Proverbs 25, verse 25."

Anthony turned and looked directly at Ugo. "To the true son of Zachary, 'God will make known His word,' as it says in First Kings, 'like the whispering of a gentle breeze.' So softly comes the inspiration of the omnipotent God."

The friar turned back to the cardinals. "Job 32, verse 8 says it well. 'It is a spirit in man, the breath of the Almighty, that gives him understanding.'"

Ugo's throat tightened with emotion. *Oh, God, You have spoken to me and I have fought the gentle breeze of Your word. Let me accept this office in which You have cast me. Let me embrace Your words and accept the will of heaven.*

"Fortunate indeed was John the Baptist to have the word of the Lord made known to him!" Anthony again raised his eyes and arms to heaven. "I beg you, Lord, 'since Your word is a lamp to my feet,' may Your word be revealed 'to your servant, according to Your word in peace.'"

Anthony continued his sermon, admonishing the prelates to make haste in spreading Christ's message and to preach repentance and administer penance in love. They must be examples of Christ, he proclaimed, as they bring Christ's message to the world.

"What can I say about the enervated prelates of our times?" he called out. "Like young women about to be given in marriage, they clothe themselves in finery, dressing themselves in leather; their excesses evident in pretentious painted sedans, in the elaborate ornamentation of their horses, and their spurs, stained red with the Blood of Christ."

Ugo studied the cardinals who stared at the beggar priest. He saw some faces turning a shade of crimson somewhat lighter than the color of the gowns the prelates wore. He saw some eyes turning away from Anthony's penetrating stare that seemed to single out each cardinal in turn.

"Take a look at those to whom the bride of Christ is entrusted, the same Christ Who was wrapped in swaddling clothes and laid in a manger. These in sharp contrast to Christ, wantonly loll in their ivory beds and bedeck themselves in leather. Elijah the prophet and John the Baptist girded their loins with skins. Let this be a sign for you, O prelates of the Church, 'You will find an infant wrapped in swaddling clothes and lying in a manger.' You who live from His patrimony, sign yourselves with the seal of the humility and abstinence of this Infant, with the seal of His priceless poverty. Mortify the skin of your body which is destined for death. Then you will receive it glorified in the general resurrection."

Anthony spoke as he walked slowly back to the pulpit. "Descend to minister humbly to your downtrodden neighbor. Descend to assist and condescend to raise up your fallen brother. 'Men should regard us as servants of Christ and stewards of the mysteries of God,' Paul writes in the first letter to the Corinthians. Isaiah says in chapter 61, 'You shall be called the priests of the Lord, ministers of God.'"

He stood now before Ugo, gazing at him again. "The ministers and stewards are prelates and preachers of the Church who attend to the word of God and who preach the baptism of penance for the remission of sins."

From the pulpit now, Anthony turned to face his audience. "Concerning these ministers, Isaiah says, 'How beautiful' since they are free from the filth of sin. 'How beautiful are the feet of him that brings good tidings and that preaches peace!' The good tidings is the message of salvation offered through the peace that God Himself made between Himself and humanity. May we 'show forth good' and 'preach salvation' so that we may proclaim to every soul, 'Your God' and not sin 'shall reign' in you. Amen."

As Anthony stepped from the pulpit, he turned to Ugo and bowed. Ugo leaped up and embraced him, then turned the friar to face the court again. "Behold, the ark of the testament!" Ugo called to the assembly. "Should the Bible be lost, Brother Anthony could write it from memory."

A thunderous cheer rose from most of the cardinals and legates and swelled the hall. Ugo noticed immediately that those who were merely politely clapping were the very ones whom he had seen riding about the city in their painted sedans or on the backs of expensive steeds. Anthony's words had penetrated deeply. Ugo beamed at the red cheeked Anthony.

"I speak God's word, Your Holiness," Anthony said softly, "not mine. God's. To Him belongs this praise."

ON A WARM AND SUNNY APRIL MORNING, the square outside the basilica of St. John Lateran was jammed with pilgrims from every conceivable nation. As Ugo and Anthony walked together out of the basilica, a cheer rose from the crowd. Ugo raised his hands for silence, then introduced Anthony. Another cheer swelled. Ugo stepped back into the shadow of the basilica while Anthony walked forward to the edge of the top step and bowed his head.

After his opening prayer, Anthony called out the text that he had chosen. "Jesus said to Simon Peter, 'Simon, son of John, do you love Me more than these?' John, chapter 21, verse 15. In the name of the Father, and of the Son, and of the Holy Spirit."

Ugo watched the sweeping motion of the cross pass over the crowd. These people, travelers from many lands both near and far, were his children who dwelled in the house of his Church. Could he be a good and holy Father to them? Would their Church stand?

Anthony's voice rang forth. "Jesus did not ask Peter the question only once, but a second and a third time. 'Simon, son of John, do you love Me more than these?'

"Three times the Lord heard Peter answer that he loved Him. 'Yes, Lord. You know that I love You.'"

Anthony paused. "Why, you may ask, did Jesus ask three times instead of only once? Because Peter had thrice denied his Lord." Anthony raised his left hand with three fingers held up to the crowd. To Ugo, the rising sun was visible just beneath his arm, its rays caught against the friar's dark habit, holding him in a glow. "Following Christ's arrest in the Garden, Peter had three times denied knowing Christ." The friar now held out his right hand with three fingers visible. "Now he three times proclaimed his love." As he spoke, he brought both hands together until the fingers of each touched the other. Sunlight gleamed around the two meeting arms, making Anthony's body into the shadow of a cross. "Peter's threefold admission of love parallels his triple denial. Peter thus shows that the tongue ought to be prompted no less by love than by fear."

Thus Anthony's sermon developed, contrasting Peter's denials, his repentance, and his admission of love. Ugo again found himself swept up in the friar's words.

Suddenly, Anthony turned toward the Lateran and flung open his arms. "Behold the Church!" Then he turned to the crowd and extended his arms over them as if to embrace them all. "Behold the Church! The Church from the least of her members to the most noble of her hierarchy was commended to Peter by Christ with the words, 'Feed My lambs.' For we are the lambs of Christ. Christ cares for us. He, as the faithful shepherd, 'laid down His life for His sheep.' Having bought us at so high a price, He wished to commend us to Peter in His stead."

Anthony dropped his arms and turned directly toward Ugo. "Jesus commanded Peter, 'Feed My sheep.' Feed them with the words of your preaching. Feed them with the help of your devout prayers. Feed them with the example of a good life."

Anthony's direct message to him startled Ugo and broke his concentration on the message the friar preached. Now he noticed the sun again, considerably higher in the sky than when Anthony had begun preaching. How long had every face in the crowd maintained uninterrupted focus on the friar? Certainly those who understood the Roman dialect that Anthony was speaking would follow his words. But many in the crowd were from Germany, England, Portugal, and other nations. How had he managed to hold their attention? Ugo could not spot one inattentive face.

Anthony turned again to face the crowd. "Where does Christ feed His lambs? In the Church. Here in the Church the sinner is readmitted by means of faith and repentance. Here the repentant one can share in all the spiritual goods which abound in the Father's house."

Anthony flung his left arm backward to indicate Ugo. "Who is to lead the Church but Peter?" Drawing his arm forward and bringing his right arm up to meet it over his head, Anthony joined his two hands in a tight fist. "Jesus declared to Peter in Matthew 16, 'You are "Rock" and on this rock I will build My Church and the jaws of death shall not prevail against it.'" Anthony opened his arms over the crowd. "Jesus did not say that Peter would be called a rock but that he is truly a rock." Now he drew his hands together, again forming the fist. "Peter was made a rock by Christ. He was made a sharer in the only foundation which is Christ and on which the Church is built." Releasing his grip, he lifted his hands and face heavenward. "Indeed, St. Paul writes in the first letter to the Corinthians, 'No one can lay a foundation other than the one that had been laid, namely, Jesus Christ.'"

Anthony turned and looked at Ugo for a brief moment, then again faced the crowd. "We need not therefore fear for the Church's stability. Even if the raging persecution of the devil and of human persons beats against it; even if heretical currents, like overflowing rivers, rip through the dike; even then we must not fear that devastation will come to our Church."

Again he raised his arms and joined his hands above his head. "Our Church will always stand firm because it is built upon a rock."

Ugo bowed his head. *Lord, God, how wonderful You are! You have spoken to me through this man's words. Thank You for reminding me that Your Church will remain.*

"Jesus told Peter, 'I will entrust to you the keys of the kingdom of heaven.' Peter the rock was made head of the Apostles and of the universal Church. He was entrusted with the power to bind and to loose. What is this power? It is the ability to distinguish the worthy from the unworthy and the power to admit the former and to exclude the latter from the kingdom of God."

Ugo, the Successor to Peter, felt a thrill of faith running through his blood. He knew what Anthony preached. He had heard it all his life. But now God was speaking it to his heart. The words had been directly addressed to less than two hundred men throughout history. Ugo was one.

Anthony turned toward Ugo and took his hand. Drawing Ugo forward, he raised Ugo's hand high. "Although the whole Church has power in its priests and bishops, although all the priests and bishops must feed the flock, God gave power and mission to Peter in a special manner. 'Peter, do you love Me more than these?' In his submission to God's will in leading all the faithful to eternal life, Peter has given his answer."

Still holding Ugo's hand heavenward, Anthony lifted his other hand to heaven and gazed skyward. "May we all pray for and obey Peter as he guides the flock of our Church. May the Holy Spirit grant him the words to 'feed' the 'lambs' of the fold. May the Son, the Good Shepherd, enable Peter also to 'lay down his life for the sheep.' May the Father increase in Peter the wisdom and holiness to direct the Church." His voice rose as his upheld arms trembled. "Oh, Lord, in unity of faith and communion with the Church, may we be absolved from sin and enter into heaven. Amen."

Anthony's grip tightened on Ugo's hand before he released it and dropped his arms. Ugo was left standing with his hand raised over the crowd.

A cheer rose from the listeners. The name Ugo heard was not Anthony's but his own. "Holy Father, pray for us."

Anthony stepped back as Ugo moved forward and raised his other hand to quiet the crowd. Suddenly Ugo realized that everyone within listening distance of Anthony had understood every word that the friar had preached. How could that be?

"Do not resist the will of heaven" he again heard in his heart. "I have chosen Anthony to speak mightily to My people. I have chosen you to lead My flock. Lead them well in My name until I take you home."

A profound peace penetrated Ugo's soul. Anthony's mission was to preach, and God would bless that preaching. Ugo's mission was to guide, and God would bless that guidance. Each man was where God had placed him. In that place lay each man's ultimate submission to God and ultimate salvation. In that place, each would be effective for Christ.

Bowing his head, his arms extended over his flock, Ugo called out to the silent crowd in a clear, deep voice. "May the Lord of all creation bless you. May His Holy Spirit guide you. May His Son save you and bring you to eternal life. I now bless you all in the name of the Father, and of the Son, and of the Holy Spirit. Amen."

# ∂ 20 ∞

## *Lady Delora*

**Castle Courtyard, Rimini, Italy (Late 1220s)** ∞ Twenty-two-year old Lady Delora made her way through the courtyard of Count Silvestro. Dogs yapped at her heels and chickens fluttered out of her way. This was the first time that she had walked through Silvestro's courtyard. Other times she had ridden through on horseback, preceded by banners and followed by ladies in waiting. Her gown then had been of shimmering silk, its long, pointed sleeves rubbing the flanks of her steed, and her chestnut hair plaited in the center and wreathed with flowers. Those times she had come as a noblewoman and a wife. Today she returned as a black-robed, widowed *perfecti*.

The pain of her young husband's death came back to her swiftly and unexpectedly. Curses on these feudal wars, one of which claimed her spouse. Even as she walked, she pictured him in this courtyard as he had been three years ago, proudly astride his brown stallion while she followed behind. That same horse had carried home his broken and bloodied body. Lady Delora sucked in a huge gulp of air. It chased her faintness and, she knew, brought color to her cheeks. She had promised herself that she would not cry, that she would show, like all *perfecti*, that she knew that suffering in this world was the lot of humans.

Her husband's death had opened her to *Catharist* doctrine. Her wobbly Roman Catholic faith had not sustained her in her loss. Nor had her priest been any consolation. He had been quick to take the funeral offering but made no move to comfort her.

*190*

She had to know some answers, so she sought one of the "Good Men" who had been preaching around Rimini. He had told her that her husband would not enter eternal life since he did not know the good God. Instead, his spirit would be reborn in another body. Only when he became a *Cathar* would he be guaranteed heaven.

Then he had asked, "And what of you?" Lady Delora admitted that she knew very little of her Roman faith and nothing of *Catharist* doctrine. "Our canon told us to avoid listening to the *Cathari*, so we did," she had confessed.

The elder had counseled her, assuring her that her destiny was certain if she, too, became a *Cathar*. He used Scripture as he instructed her. Certainly he must be right. So she had fasted and studied for a year and taken the *consolamentum*. Then she had gone to live at a hospice where she prayed and fasted and instructed other women who visited there. Some of them were now on their way to becoming "Good Christians."

Lord Silvestro had invited Lady Delora to his castle feasts several times since her husband's death. Today was the first time she had felt strong enough to come. A few "Good Men" were invited, too, Lord Silvestro had told her. The rest, including the lord, were *Catharist* believers.

"Lady Delora!"

She turned to her right at the call and broke into a smile.

Lord Silvestro bounded out of the stable area and hurried to the woman. She smiled at the muscular, red and black silk-clad figure who immediately dropped to one knee before her and placed his hands on the ground. "Praise the Lord," he said, turning his head to one shoulder and bowing.

How strange it felt for a good friend to greet her in this typical *Catharist* fashion! Yet she was a *Cathar* now, she reminded herself. She turned her head to one shoulder and replied, "Praise the Lord. May God bring you to a good end."

The lord rose to his feet. Lady Delora wanted him to embrace her chastely as he used to do, but he refrained. She felt a rush of pain at the loss of this touch. No man was to touch a female *perfecti*.

"So good to see you," the lord said with genuine enthusiasm. "But where is your traveling companion?"

"She grew ill of fever. I came alone."

"But the roads are not safe."

"God is with me."

"Yes, of course. Let me lead you into the banquet hall, my lady." Then the lord turned toward the stable and shouted. "And feed well the steeds of my guests."

A hooded groom peeked out the door and called, "Yes, my lord."

Lord Silvestro grinned at Lady Delora. "Tonight you shall have a surprise. Tonight you shall see the advance of the *Cathari* in the Romagna."

"You tease me," she said as they ascended a curved staircase to the castle.

"Not at all. Tonight I have invited Friar Anthony to dine with us."

She tried to hide her dismay with a smile, but Lord Silvestro had seen the swift, brief pursing of her lips.

"I know. He is dangerous."

Dangerous. An inadequate word. Anthony had created a stir when he had come to Rimini years ago before traveling to other parts of the Roman Empire and to France. More than once, he had been at the papal residence. He was now provincial of the Romagna. As such, he had jurisdiction over all the Friars Minor in the region. At his word, they were under obedience to do and say as he dictated. And he could dictate that they stir up the people against the *perfecti* as the followers of the preaching friar Dominic of Guzman had done in France. If the French wars were duplicated in the Romagna, the *Cathari* would suffer pillage and murder at the hands of Catholic crusaders.

"You fear that Friar Anthony will urge Catholics to take up arms against us," Lord Silvestro said. He did not wait for an answer. "We all fear it. It shall not happen."

Lord Silvestro led Lady Delora into the banquet hall. Already many guests were present, a few of whom were robed all in black. *Perfecti.* She saw, too, that Anthony was standing near two of these "Good Men." He was nodding as they spoke.

A tingle of fear crept up Lady Delora's spine and tightened her face. It was the same nameless but real fright that had knotted her stomach for the two days before his steed had brought her dead husband home.

—▪ ▬—

LADY DELORA WAS SEATED AT A BANQUET TABLE with other women, one of them *perfecti* and the remaining two dozen believers. Lord Silvestro had broken the custom of having the women and men dine separately. Instead, he had both genders seated in the same room, although at different tables. "We all wish to hear your words, Friar," he had told the Catholic priest.

"Or perhaps you wish to see me eat another toad," the priest had answered with a good-humored grin.

Uneasy laughter rippled through the banquet hall. Lady Delora had heard the story about the toad. A *Catharist* baron had invited the priest, plus several other *Cathari,* to dinner. They had intended to ridicule the friar by serving him a huge, plump toad, nicely roasted and lying on a bed of parsley.

As the plate had been placed before Friar Anthony, the other banqueters had burst into raucous laughter. No fastidious canon, who graced his table with the choicest foods, would dare to touch such a repulsive creature.

"We simply wish to see if you follow Scripture," the baron had said. "For St. Paul wrote, 'If any unbeliever invite you and you be willing to go, eat anything that is set before you, asking no questions, for conscience's sake.'"

Anthony had smiled gently, made the sign of the cross over the amphibian, and had dug into it with as much relish as if he were eating a fine, baked hen. After the meal, he had explained his faith at length to the guests, some of whom returned to the Catholic Church.

"No toads tonight, Friar," Lord Silvestro said.

"It was quite good," Anthony said with a smile, "although most people would prefer a trout or a hen."

Again laughter burst from the feasters. After that, the mood of the gathering relaxed. Still, Lady Delora felt that tingle of dread. Perhaps she felt uneasy because Lord Silvestro was being unusually kind to a priest whom he feared. He had seated the friar at his right where Lady Delora could clearly see him urging the priest to eat heartily of this and that delicacy.

As the banquet progressed, the women spoke quietly among themselves. The men were more spirited as they engaged in a verbal tournament with the priest. A baron would make a remark on a point of doctrine, backing it up with Scripture, and Anthony would counter with a point and Scripture quotation of his own. Terms like "Eucharist," "purgatory," and "angels" were being bandied about like balls.

Maidservants were setting small plates of cooked wheat, seasoned with herbs, olive oil, and vegetables before each guest. Lady Delora and the others would eat only after Lord Silvestro took the first bite. Discreetly watching her host spoon a few grains into his mouth, Lady Delora saw Anthony reach for his plate and then draw back his hand.

He spoke quietly. "So, my friends, you have invited me here to poison me." Swift denials rose throughout the room.

"This does not please our good God Who, all here agree, condemns murder."

Lady Delora stared in horror at Anthony's food. She could see absolutely nothing to distinguish it from anyone else's. And why should it look different? If someone wanted to poison the priest, the criminal would have chosen a substance that would be tasteless, invisible, and potent.

"Why do you want to kill me?"

"We do not wish to kill you," Lord Silvestro said. "We only wish to test this text from the Bible. Is it not written of Christ's Apostles, 'If they shall drink any deadly thing, it shall not hurt them'? Either you believe the words of the Gospel or you do not. If you believe them, why hesitate to eat? Eat then."

Anthony looked squarely at Silvestro. "It is unnecessary that the truth of this text always be shown to everyone who tests it. God works this miracle only when it is necessary to His plan."

"You claim that God wills us to return to the Catholic Church. Is this not, in your opinion, God's plan?" one of the "Good Men" asked.

"We should never tempt God's infinite power with these trials, as you well know. Even your own faith does not depend on tests."

"True. God's truth is verified by divine revelation. We have never taught that this text should be taken as written. The deadly drink refers not to drinks or foods, which, being material, are products of the evil god. Rather, it refers to the drink of doctrines of false faiths which 'Good Christians' confront and confound."

"You are wrong," Anthony countered. "This passage must be taken literally. In the beginning of the Church, this and other miracles nourished the faith that, like a tender plant, needed roots to grow.

Faith, now well planted and grown up, has no need of special miracles in order to flourish."

"You misunderstand," said Lord Silvestro. "We mean that, if we see you eating this poisoned food without harm, then we will believe what you preach. We will become Catholics because you will have proved that the Roman Church holds the truth."

Anthony nodded and bowed his head, then raised his eyes to heaven. When his gaze returned to Lord Silvestro, he said, "I will eat this food, not to tempt God, but purely to honor His Gospel. If I live, may you hold to your pledge. If I die, it will be due to my sin, not to the error of God's words or the powerlessness of our Creator."

Then, holding his right hand over the poisoned wheat, he made the sign of the cross. He picked up his spoon and dipped it into the food, then raised the spoonful to his mouth. Time seemed to halt. No one spoke. Even the dogs who roamed beneath the tables looking for scraps ceased to move.

The priest ate one bite and then another. He lifted the water glass to his lips, took a generous drink, and then finished the plate of herbed grain.

"You must tell your chef to poison your food more often, Lord Silvestro. I have never tasted anything quite this good."

Lady Delora stared at the priest. It was not so much that he had not been harmed but that he had eaten. She had never seen anyone with that much trust in God.

The guests returned to their meal. Discussion resumed at the men's table. Maids brought in more foods. The feast went on for another hour. At its end, Lord Silvestro and several other believers had pledged to return to the Catholic Church. Lady Delora was not one of them.

*He may be a good and holy priest,* she thought, *and certainly God is with him.* But she could not erase from her memory the coarse way in which she had been treated upon her husband's death. Anthony, she knew, would have treated her with kindness and understanding. *But he is a traveling friar,* she told herself. *He is not the whole Church.* For now she would remain with the charitable, compassionate *Cathari.* Miracles and theology would not make her a Catholic. Only love would do that.

# ৶ 21 ৫

## *Robber*

**Highway, Padua, Italy (Lent 1228)** ৹ Along with eleven other men, half on one side of the highway and half on the other, the robber waited in the underbrush. He had tucked his brown curls beneath his olive green snood and tied a gray rag around his nose and mouth so that only his black eyes showed. His thick knees were tightly clamped to the belly of his chestnut steed and his big, pudgy hands securely grasped the reins. He had thought that he heard a tinkling of little bells. If he had, it meant that a wealthy band of Paduans would soon be along.

Padua was a treasure trove for the robber and his band, a sensual place where wealth flowed like water. Rich silks, gaudy jewels, and luxuriant furs clothed those many citizens who lived in the extravagant palaces of the area. Money was in ample supply, and those who had too little found plenty of moneylenders from whom to borrow if they were willing to pay exorbitant interest.

Yes, he had heard the chime. A gentle jingling filled the air. The bells, the robber knew, were attached to the breast straps of mounted horses. The robber's heart began to pound with excitement, anticipation, and dread. He hated these robberies, but how could he live without them?

Five years ago when he was sixteen, the robber had been a serf, working with his father, grandfather, and brothers for one of the barons of Padua. How he hated the sowing and hoeing and mowing! His eyes smarted from the work. His plump body sweated like an animal's. The chaff from the wheat and dust from the furrows caught in his knee and elbow joints and irritated him. How many times had he wished to be done with toil forever? Yet he had been born a serf and he would die a serf.

Then muscular, intelligent Egidio, who was three years older than himself and the son of another serf, proposed a plan. They would run away and become thieves. At least they would be free from grinding labor and merciless sun. One night, according to plan, the two young men met and stole away from the estate. In the woods of Padua, they lived for a few days before meeting up with a band of eight other youthful thieves. Joining with them, Egidio soon became the leader. Now the band had grown to twelve men and their corresponding stolen steeds. The men were those who, besides the robber, waited in the underbrush as the tinkling of the bells grew stronger.

As happened every time that the band gathered to ambush a group, the robber fought an urge to wheel his horse around and streak off into the forest. He wished he could live alone, hermit-like, among the glades. He loved to wander among the thick, massive trees, the soft green feather of ferns parting before his feet. More precious to him than the jewels he stole were the clear streams whose waters danced and sang over beds of smooth pebbles. The scent of autumn compost was, to him, more heady than a woman's perfume, and the wild almonds and walnuts that he gathered in the woods tasted better to him than choice cakes. In the forest, life was free and he was at peace.

At camp, he felt differently. At camp, the coarse jokes of the other men often erupted into fights, frequently with drawn weapons. Wine, drunk too freely, intensified quarrels, and he had several times backed away from the protection of a night fire, preferring to take his chances with bears or wolves than being part of escalating and dangerous arguments among beastly humans.

The robberies themselves were not to his liking. Even now, as he prepared to commit another crime, he regretted the fear in the eyes of those he robbed, as if he, no more dangerous than a kitten, would rape or murder or beat another human being. He was horrified at the thought that maybe he would actually do those things some day and turn into the beasts with whom he lived. Finally, he hated the sickening reality that he could make a mistake and turn his back on a knife. He would feel it plunge into his side and he would topple from his horse to die in the dust of the road.

Worse than all these thoughts was the one that lurked deep inside his soul. Continuously he harbored a persistent accusation that what he did was wrong, so wrong in the eyes of God that his thievery in this life would earn him damnation in the next. The thought of his final and eternal fate terrified him.

But how could he abandon the life that he led? He could not return to the fields to work. If he ever went back to being a serf, his spirit would shrivel like a fig in the sun.

The sound of the bells grew stronger. From it, the robber could tell that this cortege had about half a dozen members. The robber tightened his grip on the reins and beat his wavering spirit into submission. Thievery was his life. It was do this or die.

As the richly blanketed horses came into view directly in front of the robber, Egidio, followed by five other robbers, burst through the bushes on the opposite side of the road. The young thief spurred his horse as did the other robbers on his side of the road. Instantly the cortege was surrounded.

Immediately in his path rode a silver-haired matron in a maroon gown and blue cape. Sharply reining his horse in front of her dappled steed, the robber pulled his thin bladed knife from its hilt and wordlessly pointed to two gold rings on the woman's hand.

As the woman's horse jerked to a halt, she gaped at the robber. The robber looked into the woman's eyes, eyes that were as huge as a cornered rabbit's, and he longed to tell her that he would not hurt her. But he said nothing. Instead, he again pointed to the rings.

With wildly trembling fingers, the woman tugged at the rings that, the robber knew, were sticking to her sweaty fingers. Patiently he waited for her as he had waited for many other frightened women. Finally, the matron managed to twist off the jewelry. The robber held out his steady palm and she dropped the rings into it.

Then, with the blade of his knife, the robber pointed to a big, golden brooch that fastened the woman's cape. As the robber paced his steed up and down before her to block any escape, the woman fumbled with the clasp. Finally, the brooch came loose. The robber thrust his dagger toward the woman who, despite her violently shaking wrist, managed to slip the valuable piece over the tip of the blade. Flicking the blade upward so that the brooch dropped securely onto it, the robber made a deep bow and then deftly dropped the brooch into his palm. As he tucked all the jewelry into a leather pouch that he had attached to his waist, the other robbers pulled back from the cortege, and Egidio swept his arm toward the woods. In an instant, the robber had wheeled his horse into the forest and was bolting back toward the thieves' campsite.

The robber reined his panting horse before the thieves' cave deep in the forest. Dismounting, he pulled the saddle from the horse's back and began to rub down his animal with a cloth that was hanging from a nearby pine.

Swiftly the glade filled with other robbers. Gray-robed Egidio rode into the clearing last of all and slid from his golden horse. With a flourish, he pulled a frayed basket from a peg pounded into a maple and tossed the container to the ground.

One by one, the robbers pitched their loot into the basket. The young robber was glad to drop in the rings and brooch whose luster mocked his own filth. He who had been born to spread dung in a field had robbed a baroness of her goods.

Shaggy haired Egidio picked up the basket and jingled its contents. "Well done, men. This will last us a while."

As the robbers rubbed the lather from their tired horses, they began their familiar banter.

"So, Egidio, today you rob the rich. Tomorrow you go to hear the saint, eh?" one man called out as he massaged his horse's flank.

"They say he preaches like the prophet Elijah," another remarked.

"I will believe that when I hear it," exclaimed a third.

"Who isn't curious about him?" Egidio said, heaving the saddle from his own mount.

"We will all go to hear him preach."

The robber rubbed white foam from the chestnut haunches of his panting horse and thought about hearing a saint preach tomorrow. Would God strike him dead before letting him sully the presence of a holy man?

◆ ━

THE FOLLOWING DAY, THE ROBBERS walked into Padua in clusters of two or three. Each had shaved and put on fresh, clean tunics and stockings. Each tried to appear confident and non-threatening. No one wanted to be recognized, so they left their stolen horses at the cave. Since the steeds belonged to the residents of Padua, they were likely to be recognized.

As they neared the main square of the city, the robber broke away from his partner. Each had agreed to separate so as to look even less conspicuous. The robber chose a spot a good distance from the platform near the edge of the massive crowd. Here he could listen to the saint, yet be able to sprint away quickly if recognized. He fished in his pouch for an almond, chosen from four baskets full that he had gathered in the forest the previous fall.

As he cracked the hard shell between his teeth, he studied the crowd. Judging by its immense size, Friar Anthony's reputation had preceded him. Having preached in Treviso and Venice, the priest had come to Padua on Ash Wednesday to preach the Lenten sermons. It was one of those daily sermons that the robber was about to hear.

The friar stood on the platform a good distance from the thief. His head, which had been lifted to heaven in prayer, now lowered. The priest gazed at the vast crowd from one end of it to the other and then called out in a resounding voice, "'Peter found at Lydda a man named Aeneas, a paralytic who had been bedridden for eight years. And Peter said to him, "Aeneas, may Jesus Christ heal you; arise and set your bed in order." Aeneas got up immediately.' The Book of Acts, chapter 9, verses 33 and 34." Anthony bowed his head and crossed himself, "In the name of the Father, and of the Son, and of the Holy Spirit."

The robber signed himself as well.

"Aeneas means poor and miserable. Aeneas is the sinner in mortal sin; he is poor in virtue and miserable because he is a slave of the devil. This sinner is a paralytic for he lies in a bed of carnal concupiscence with all his members dissolute." Anthony lifted his left hand over the crowd. "And what will be the result of this paralysis?"

He paused while the robber's mind, and probably every other listener's as well, fished for an answer to the question.

"Death! 'For the wages of sin is death,' Paul tells us in Romans 6. All of us shall die."

Anthony paused. His words penetrated the crowd that waited as still as corpses. The robber saw himself lying in the road, a dagger in his back.

"Genesis says, 'You are dust and unto dust you shall return.' How fragile we are! Psalm 90 tells us, 'Our years shall be considered like those of a spider.'"

Like those of a spider whose web often hung, dew dropped, across the upper corner of the robber's cave.

"What is more fragile than a spider's web? The flick of a hand can sweep it away at once. As easily broken is a person's life. A small injury or the slightest fever can destroy a life. When a miserable person considers how fragile he is, that person begins to think about eternity."

The robber would not always be twenty-one. Someday he would die. He might die of illness, or injury, or plague, or accident, or old age. He might be hung as a thief or killed by someone he had attempted to rob. Someday he would die. That was certain.

"'The wages of sin is death.' Those who sin mortally have already established a place for themselves," Anthony paused again, "in hell."

Hell? Was there not a commandment somewhere that said, "Thou shalt not steal"? How much had he stolen in the past five years? Jewels? Coins? Gold? The peace of mind of his victims? Perhaps they awoke at night shrieking as they dreamed again of being ambushed on a highway.

"Sinners are bound by a yoke of eternal death. For the demons that beset a person and hold him captive impose a heavy yoke on his neck. They tug the sinner along with a rope, driving him like an ox or an ass and giving the wearied one no rest as they drive him from one sin to another."

He had started out hating the fields. He had abandoned his father and run away. He had turned to thievery. He had laughed at coarse jokes and, although he had not yet assaulted a woman, he had not tried to stop Egidio or some of the others from doing so. In only a matter of time, he would become like those with whom he lived. The yoke of sin was heavy on his neck. He would move from one sin to the next as surely as a rock kicked downhill would bounce along until hitting bottom.

"Yet we are not beasts as oxen and asses are. We can command the demons that beset us to halt. Does the sinner do this? How crazy can one be, being worn out on a road and being unwilling to halt? Only when the sinner says, 'Enough. No more,' does he form a will to repent. And this will is not of the sinner's own creation. God beckons us wretches to a new life. By the inspiration of His grace and the preaching of the Church, the Lord calls the sinful soul to repentance."

The robber lowered his head. If only he could repent. But repent meant to give up. How could he give up his way of life? He had no other talents. He could not return to the fields.

"Peter's vicar says to the sinner, 'Aeneas, poor and miserable, let Jesus Christ heal you. Arise through contrition and set your things in order through confession. You yourself, not another, must get yourself in order.'"

How? How could he possibly do this? The priest had no idea how difficult it was to change a way of life when no alternative existed.

"Surely when the sinner is truly sorry, God will forgive him. For the truly sorry person proposes to confess. When this happens, immediately, the Lord absolves that person from the fault and from eternal death. Because of the sinner's remorse over his sin, his eternal death is changed into a purgatorial debt of punishment. The contrite person then goes to the priest and confesses."

Goes to the priest and confesses? The robber shuddered. Tell a priest about years of stealing? How could he do such a thing? The very idea of baring his soul made his stomach flutter.

"As soon as the soul confesses, a wondrous thing occurs. The soul is forsaken by the devil and then lifted up to God. The devil cannot abide in a repentant soul. And the one whom the devil thus forsakes, Christ takes up." Anthony lifted his hands together as if lifting a child. "You see, God has greater care for the salvation of human beings than the devil has for their perdition. Come, therefore. Admit your sin and the devil will abandon you into the arms of your Father."

Could it be true? Could God truly want him, a sinner?

"'And immediately Aeneas arose.' He left his bed of carnality and with it the paralysis of sin. He arose because Christ, in His forgiveness, healed him and absolved him from every bond of wickedness."

How the robber wished to arise as well, to walk again in freshness and goodness, to know the power of grace!

"And, to show that forgiveness must be genuine, the priest imposes on the repentant soul a temporal penance. This temporal penance replaces or lessens the purgatorial punishment. If the temporal expiation is authentically completed, the person is ready to enter into glory. Thus God and the priest together forgive and absolve."

What penance could he possibly have for all his crimes? How many lashes would it take to beat the sin out of him? How many hangings from the gibbet to repay society for all he had unlawfully taken?

"And now the sinner, having confessed and been forgiven, having entered on a path of penance, is not alone. For Jesus, Whose hand is strong, leads the soul forward from virtue to virtue. Isaiah proclaims, 'I am the Lord your God, Who take you by the hand and say to you, do not be afraid for I have helped you.' You have all seen a loving mother holding the hand of her child trying to climb the stairs behind her. She supports and encourages the toddler to take the next step and the next, never once abandoning the child who is just learning to walk."

The robber imagined his mother teaching him to walk, leading him from one step to the next. As he took those first faltering steps, he must have been a clumsy child, one whose feet frequently tangled together. Yet his mother had helped him, tugged him along, caught him when he fell, and kissed away his bruises.

"As a mother guides her child, even so, with an equally loving hand the Lord takes the hand of the humble penitent to enable him to climb the steps to the cross. The Lord supports and encourages the penitent as he moves ever higher, never once abandoning the repentant soul. In fact, God helps that soul to reach the level of the perfect wherein he may merit to behold the One so desirable to see, the King in His splendor upon Whom the angels desire to look."

Was God as supportive as that? Would God lead him all the way to eternal life?

"So come, you who are paralyzed with sin and you whom the devil goads from one blunder to the next. Come, you who are weary of life and whose bed of carnality is full of all unpleasantness. Come to Christ in total trust, for the Son Himself says in Isaiah, 'I have made and I will bear; I will carry and I will save.' I have made you and I will bear you on My shoulders like an errant and weary sheep. I will carry you as a nurse carries a child in her arms. How can the Father reply to all this but to say, 'I will save you'?"

Would God be willing to save him, even him, a thief?

"But, you say, 'I have no faith that God will save me.' Jesus spoke in no uncertain terms about this. 'Ask and you shall receive,' He promised. 'Seek and you shall find. Knock and it shall be opened. For the one who asks, receives. The one who seeks, finds. The one who knocks shall be admitted.' Ask for faith. Before all else, 'seek God's Kingdom and His righteousness.' Begin by asking for the things of heaven where our treasure, that is our salvation, is and where our heart should be. For in the treasure of our salvation is perfect joy. 'Ask,' therefore, for forgiveness and for faith, 'and you will receive both, that your joy may be full. And that joy no one shall take from you.'"

Joy? What was joy? If only he could feel that, if ever he had.

"Be slaves of sin no more, 'for the wages of sin is death. But the free gift of God is eternal life in Christ Jesus our Lord.' The law of perfect freedom is the love of God which is perfect in every way and makes us free of slavery. On the miry vastness of worldly pleasures, the works of sinners slip, so that they fall from sin into sin and finally tumble into hell. But the just man's steps do not falter because the law of love is in his heart. The one who continues in that law of love will be blessed in what he does. For love of God confers grace in this present life and happiness in future life. 'The gift of God is eternal life in Christ Jesus our Lord.' May He lead us to this Who is blessed forever. Amen."

As Anthony finished speaking, the crowd broke into wild applause punctuated with weeping. The robber stood with his eyes fixed on the friar. He did not know what to do with his life, but he had to lay it before the priest.

Spread around the platform and out into the square were clusters of people, each gathering around a priest. Some of the priests were dressed in the gray or black tunics of the mendicant or preaching friars. Others wore the black garb of parish clergy. Many of the priests were standing. Here and there, one sat on the seat of a cart or on an upturned barrel or a stool. The citizens of Padua and its surrounding towns stood patiently, waiting to confess.

The robber hung back, waiting for the crowds to disperse. Then, off to his right, he caught sight of the thief who had accompanied him to hear the saint. The fellow was kneeling, his face in his hands. The robber went over to him and touched his shoulder.

"I, too, am going to confess," the robber said. His friend, his eyes moist and red, nodded and rose.

The two men worked their way closer to Anthony. From their left came three more of their group. Clustered around the priest were Egidio and the others. The men looked at each other in wonder and embarrassment. The entire band was here.

Comments flew back and forth.

"He has shown us a better way."

"I'm done with thievery from now on."

"An honest life for me."

"Poverty is better than hell."

The men waited their turns. Hours passed as penitents filed up to Anthony, sat beside him on the platform steps, and often wept. Then it was their turn. Egidio, being leader, went first. Then another of his band. And another. The sun began to slip close to the horizon and the robber realized that the day was nearly gone. Anthony had begun speaking in the morning, ended after noon, and had been hearing confessions ever since.

It was the robber's turn. He felt his pouch. He still had a few almonds left. As he sat beside the priest, he pulled out the nuts and held them out to the friar.

"You've not had anything to eat all day, Father."

Anthony smiled. "I am used to it." He picked up a nut and looked at it. "You are also a thief, are you not?" The voice was mild.

The robber hung his head. "Yes, Father."

"And have you stolen these?"

"No, Father. I picked them in the woods."

Anthony smiled. "Very well then." He stuck the nut in his mouth and clamped down hard. The shell crackled open. Anthony picked the nut from his lips and held it in one hand and the shell in the other.

"You can learn a lesson from the almond, my brother. In Genesis, Jacob says, 'The Lord, the Almighty, appeared to me at Luz in the land of Canaan.' Luz means almond," Anthony said, holding the nut meat up to the sun. "The almond is a fitting symbol of penance for, like penance, the almond has three parts to it."

Startled by the comparison, the robber gawked at the nut suspended in the long, slender fingers of the friar who sat beside him.

"An almond has a bitter skin, a hard shell, and a sweet kernel. The almonds that you have brought today are missing the bitter, leathery hull. Why?"

"Well, Father, when the nut is ripe, the hull splits open and the nut inside falls to the ground. I gathered these from the ground, Father."

"Of course. In the bitter skin, we recognize the bitterness of penance, for penance is always bitter to begin. But you will note that you have already begun your penance by approaching the Lord. The bitter skin of admitting wrongdoing has split and fallen away, freeing you to find the joy of forgiveness."

Holding the nut meat in his fist, Anthony took the robber's hand in his own and opened his palm. Then he dropped into it from his other hand the broken shell. "In the hard shell, we identify the strength of perseverance. Penance, if sincere, always requires perseverance. With perseverance, a sinner who is sorry can perform even the most difficult penance."

Then he held the nut meat to the light. "In the sweet kernel, we rejoice in the hope of forgiveness." He placed the kernel in the robber's other palm, atop the small pile of uncracked nuts. "The Lord appears, then, in Luz in the land of Canaan. Canaan means change. My brother, you will have true peace if you change from sin to righteousness, for there, at the place of change, at the place of penance, the Lord appears." Anthony plucked another almond from the robber's hand, cracked the shell with his teeth, and popped the kernel into his mouth.

"Now, if you are willing to change, confess your sins to God."

The robber glanced at the broken shell in his one hand and the nut meat in the other. He thought of the bitter hull of penance, already split and freeing him to speak. He began his confession. He told Anthony everything that he could remember including the times that he had lied to his father before he ran away. Anthony listened, nodding.

"Are you sorry for all these offenses? And do you resolve, with God's help, never to commit them again?"

The robber's brain swirled. He wanted never to commit them again. But how could he? "Father, I cannot resolve anything. I am sick of robbery, but I can do nothing else. I cannot stand returning to the fields. I would feel trapped like...like...."

"Like a caged lark." Anthony patted the robber's knee. "I, too, love the freedom of the forest. But a greater freedom lies with God. You must reject sin if you wish to be truly free."

The robber hung his head. How badly he wanted to be truly free! But could he? What if the priest should send him back to the baron?

"You must repent and turn from sin. Trust God. He shall ask no more of you than you can bear." The priest's hand was warm on his knee, accepting, encouraging.

Within himself the robber struggled. Could he truly repent?

"Repentance is an act of the will. Will it and God will give you the grace to carry it out."

He felt his opposition weakening. He glanced again at his hand that held the broken almond shell. Turning his palm upside down, he watched the shell slide to the ground. "I will it, Father," he said in a thin voice.

The priest's voice leapt with a quiet joy. "Good. Then I absolve you from your sins." And he blessed the man. "Now I must give you a penance. Your sins were grave and deserve a grave recompense. You must make twelve trips to the tombs of the apostles in Rome. On foot. You must take nothing with you but the clothes on your back. Sleep wherever you find shelter." The robber lifted his head and looked at the priest whose eyes were twinkling.

"Even in the woods. If you need food, you may glean the forests for it or you may work for it or beg. Make your pilgrimages, trusting in God's mercy. And, when you reach the tombs, remember me there in prayer. Will you do this?"

Twelve pilgrimages? To Rome? Walking and working along the way? That would take years. How many forests lay between Padua and Rome? How many glades of ferns, wild flowers, and nut trees? He would find these beauties during his journeys. His penance would make him free.

A grin broke across the robber's face. "You are too good to me, Father."

"No. God is good to you." Anthony touched the robber's hand that held the almond lying amid a few uncracked nuts.

Curling the robber's fingers around the nuts, he took the young man's fist in his own two hands and squeezed it gently. "You have made a good beginning. Now wait here until the others confess."

Just as the sun was flinging its night purple and pink across the heavens, the last robber finished with the priest. All twelve stood about clumsily as Anthony arose. Everyone else had gone home except one friar who, all this time, had sat far off to the side of the platform, well out of earshot. He had to be waiting for Anthony.

"I shall bless you all," Anthony said. The men knelt before the friar in a cluster of colorful tunics and caps.

"But before I bless you, I have one last word to say. You are twelve, the number of Christ's Apostles, none of whom was perfect. So take heart. Christ transformed those twelve men and can transform you. You have expressed remorse for your sins and have each resolved to complete the penance which is yours. Now remember this. If you remain true to your God and follow Him faithfully, you will receive an eternal reward with those twelve who left all to follow our Lord. But if you turn back to sin, thus rejecting the One Who died to save you, you will come to a miserable end. Do you understand?"

Twelve voices called agreement.

"Now bow your heads." As the robber bowed and closed his eyes, the friar extended his arms over the cluster of kneeling men. "Dearest brothers, let us humbly entreat the mercy of Jesus Christ so that He might come and stand in our midst." Anthony's voice trembled with earnestness. "May He grant us peace, absolve us from our sins, and take away all doubt from our hearts. May He imprint faith in our minds so that, with the Apostles and the faithful of the Church, we might merit eternal life." Anthony's voice began to rise in melody as if in song. "May He grant us this, Who is blessed, laudable, and glorious through all ages. Let every faithful soul say, 'Amen. Alleluia!'"

"Amen. Alleluia!" the robbers cried out together.

## ᖳ 22 ᖰ

### *Sister Helena de Enselmini*

**Convent of Arcella Vecchia, Padua, Italy (Spring 1230)** ᖰ Sister Helena Enselmini sat on a narrow stone bench in the convent garden, her bony back propped against the trunk of a tall oak which supported one end of the seat. The other end, she knew, was supported by a second oak. Today, her thin hands mended by feel the threadbare tunic in her lap. As her fingers felt out the holes and then stitched them shut, she rejoiced at the sun's warmth and the caress of a spring breeze.

All winter she had been chilled in the convent, along with the other Poor Ladies, while the bitter north wind rattled the walls. Daily she had hobbled through the corridors on legs so wracked with pain that she could barely keep erect. Then the frosty convent walls or the warm arm of another sister had been her support.

Today spring was in the air. Helena had asked Sister Sancia to help her outdoors to sit in the welcome sunlight. She had brought her mending, for today her fingers, which had been stiff and clumsy all winter, were nimble. The sun and the spring breeze had wrought the change.

This was the season of new life in the fragrance of moist earth sprouting seeds and in mating birds calling. The season, too, of Christ's final weeks on earth, His passion and death. From His bloody agony had sprung both resurrection and salvation. Helena felt joy stirring in her heart, a joy that, for weeks, she feared had left her. *Dear Jesus, Son of God, let Your sun renew my fervor,* she begged. *Let the wind of Your Spirit blow away my discontent.*

Ever since Helena could remember, she loved no human being as much as she loved Christ. She could not remember how old she was when she tired of playthings and playmates, of fresh gowns and trinkets for her hair. Christ, Whom she had heard about in church, did not live this way. Christ was poor and Christ suffered. Surely He, Who was God, had chosen the best way. She would choose it, too.

Ten years ago, when she was twelve, Francis of Assisi came to Padua to preach and to establish a monastery here outside the walls. The nobles of the Enselmini family, all good Catholics, went to hear him preach in one of the churches. Helena sat near her mother and gazed at the friar who seemed to be Christ incarnate. Here was a humble man who had absolutely nothing but the Savior. Francis' words and manner burned with zeal for God. Helena sensed that, if she stood close to him, she would feel warmth radiating from him as from a fire.

She remembered how he, his eyes raised to heaven, had concluded his sermon with a song, beautifully sung, of his own composing.

> "Holy Queen Wisdom!
> The Lord save you,
> with your sister, pure, holy Simplicity;
> Lady Holy Poverty, God keep you,
> with your sister holy Humility;
> Lady Holy Love, God keep you,
> with your sister, holy Obedience.
> All holy virtues,
> God keep you,
> God from whom you proceed and come.
> In all the world there is not a one
> who can possess any one of you
> without first dying to self."

Desperately, Helena wanted to possess all the virtues which obviously possessed the poet who sang about them. For the next few days, Helena waited as impatiently for Francis to complete his monastery as other children her age waited for a holiday. When Arcella Vecchia was completed, she presented herself to Francis and asked to be admitted. With his own hands, he had cut off the flowing black hair that she had come to despise and handed her a patched, gray tunic. She had walked into an adjacent room where two Poor Ladies helped her remove her beads and jewels, her silks and chemise, her soft shoes and ribbons. She slipped into the tunic, kicked the heap of finery with her foot, and felt a deep peace. This was where she belonged.

Although the sisters of Arcella Vecchia sewed and embroidered for alms, the walls of their convent shut them from the world. Here, like the noble Lady Clare Schiffi of Assisi, who founded the Poor Ladies, the sisters lived in utter poverty, frequent fasts, and scheduled prayer both day and night. The friars, who lived in a small monastery right next to the convent, counseled the women and assisted them with alms. Among those friars had been one whose family in Padua was as respected as Helena's. That friar was Brother Luke Belludi, now traveling companion of Father Anthony.

When Helena entered Arcella, she never once looked back. Christ became her All. She gave Him her time, her prayers, her discipline, her love. He could take whatever He wished. And, six years after Helena entered Arcella, He did.

Pain and fever such as she had never known racked her body. She spoke to no one about it, but the sisters read the agony on her face and saw that she could take no nourishment but the Sacred Host. So they tended her and prayed. For months, the illness persisted, sometimes throwing her into convulsions and delirium.

Then she had recovered a bit, but not much. As the illness continued its hold on her, her legs grew weak and throbbed with pain. Her eyesight faded. Her voice grew faint. One day, she could not walk without support. Then her eyes no longer caught even the glimmer of a torch held in front of them. Her throat could no longer speak even the faintest whisper. Now she was painfully lame and completely blind and speechless. The illness continued to strike unexpectedly in fever and pain, then abate. Always it returned. Helena no longer cared about her sufferings. God had come to her.

Once, while at prayer, she had seen in a vision the glory of Francis and his followers in Paradise. And she was among them. How she rejoiced at it! Then a heavenly voice said, "Francis was powerful on earth, but in heaven he is far more powerful." *Oh, Father Francis,* she had prayed, *speak to Jesus about my soul. Make it burn for Him.*

On another occasion, God had thrust her into the torment of Purgatory. Ah, how the souls suffered in the fire that would purify them for their entry into eternity Yet she saw how the prayers and good works of the faithful on earth were to these souls as cups and pitchers and buckets of water on the flames, slowly drowning the fire while giving life to the souls suffering in it. Ever after that vision, she increased her prayers for the souls suffering in that place, and she knew that some of them were in heaven because she prayed.

She was praying now as she mended in the sunlight. One of the nuns at Arcella had died a short time before. That nun was the focus of Helena's prayers.

But today, as she prayed, she remembered other days, winter days, when she had shivered in the convent and her prayers had come by sheer force of will without the spontaneity that she felt today. On those days, the flame in her soul seemed to die.

She had entered Arcella radiant with joy. Her joy had increased with the newness and simplicity and holiness of her poverty. Then her illness had come and her visions, plunging her more deeply into the sufferings and the ecstasies of Christ.

But these days she sometimes felt as if she were in a tranquil spot such as that dead pool in a river above the rapids, far from either riverbank, where the waters simply lie. The pattern of convent life, the sameness of her maladies, the repetition of prayers were relaxing her, deadening her. Perhaps it was too much to expect that the joy she felt ten years ago upon her entry into Arcella would persist. Suppose her love of Christ died. She could not bear the thought.

As Helena was thinking about these things, she heard, almost imperceptibly, three pairs of footsteps approaching across the pebbled courtyard. Then, a touch of a finger on her left hand.

"Sister Helena." The voice was Sister Sancia's. "Father Anthony is here to see you."

Father Anthony! Her confessor. For the past several years, he had been preaching in Florence, Ferrara, and all the other cities and towns of the Romagna. Still he came to visit her regularly as well as some of the other nuns at Arcella. Because of her illness, she had been permitted to communicate with him inside the enclosure. The other Poor Ladies had to confess to him through the convent grate where they could hear his voice but see nothing.

Grinning, Helena thrust the needle into the cloth on her lap and raised her hands upward. Two other hands, warm and a bit pulpy-feeling, caught hers and clasped them tightly. "God's peace and all good to you, Sister." She felt the bench slightly give way as Anthony sat down beside her.

Another pair of hands, these lean and strong, caught hers and grasped them briefly. "Brother Luke, Sister. God's peace and all good to you."

Helena smiled at Brother Luke as he released her hands. Then she heard the soft smacking of the brother's feet against the courtyard stones as he made his way somewhere a bit distant and, she knew, sat down to wait. The friars always traveled in pairs as Francis wished.

She had heard Sister Sancia's footsteps, too, retreating across the courtyard and then onto the convent porch where she would wait and silently watch while Helena and Anthony met. All a precaution for chastity. Helena smiled. The nuns were not to look upon the friars unless a dispensation were given, which, of course, Sister Sancia, the protector of virtue, had earned. Nevertheless, Helena imagined that several pairs of curious eyes were having a difficult time not peeking. The nuns would want to glimpse Father Anthony whom they, like the rest of Lombardy, regarded as a saint. But the truth of the matter was that blind Helena had never seen him herself.

Helena was glad for all protectors of virtue as well as any sisters who were spying. She loved Anthony with a love that troubled her because it was so deep. She so wanted to merge her personality with his that she grew frightened. Such a love could turn from spiritual merging to physical. She did not know if he felt the same about her as she did about him—in fact, she rather doubted it—for he had many spiritual children and preached constantly on purity in thought and action. She trusted Anthony. Yet, because she did not fully trust herself, she was glad that her sisters in Christ, as well as Brother Luke, were watching.

In a familiar procedure, the somewhat puffy hands placed Helena's own hands into her lap. Then she felt a board placed on her knee. She caught the smooth plank and lifted her fingers to catch the edge of a parchment and then, with her other hand open, waited for the pen. Two fingers touched the wrist holding the parchment and Helena reached across that hand to feel for a narrow vessel of ink. There it was, held secure in Anthony's palm.

Then came the gentle voice. "Are you well, Sister?"

She smiled and nodded, lifting her hand with the pen in the direction of the friar as a way to emphasize her answer.

"Have you anything you wish to tell me?"

Oh, how she wished she could speak! But God had taken her voice and she would not ask for it back. Helena dipped the pen into the ink and began to write on the parchment. "I had another vision of heaven. Religious who live in community were more exalted than hermits. I asked our Lord why. Religious live under obedience as did He Who took our flesh and suffered and died on the cross, He said. Obedience makes their actions more meritorious." She stopped writing.

"As Gregory says, 'Obedience incorporates in itself the rest of the virtues and preserves them all.'"

She again began to write. Anthony's hand touched hers and guided it down the parchment. She knew that she must have been writing over what she had previously penned.

"This vision made me happy, but not like it once would have. I am growing dull. This frightens me."

Anthony's hand patted her own. "My sister, I know what you are thinking. Obedience is difficult. Affliction such as you suffer is burdensome. Prayer becomes routine."

Helena nodded vigorously. Anthony had read everything in her clumsy revelation.

"You ask, Sister, why is my joy not what it used to be?"

Helena held the parchment down with her pen in hand. She placed her other hand on Anthony's wrist and squeezed. Again she nodded. He must understand that he had spoken to her heart.

"When these thoughts come upon you, Sister, think of this. The Father sent us His Son, the best and the perfect Gift Who is co-eternal with the Father. Consider this needle which you are using so skillfully." Anthony lifted Helena's hand off his wrist and laid the needle in its palm.

"The eye is the gentle mercy of Christ which He displayed at His first coming; the point is the penetrating justice by which He will pierce us in the judgment. With this kind of needle, Christ, our embroiderer, will make for the faithful soul a beautiful tunic, startling by the multiple color of its virtues."

She felt the needle lifted from her hand and then, a gentle prick on her palm. The point startled her but it did not hurt.

"But justice pierces and pricks as these thoughts of yours do. Yet remain true to Christ. Let Him embroider on your soul as He sees fit.

With each pain of soul, the eye of Christ's mercy is drawing a thread of virtue through you. Sister, you remember colors, do you not?"

Helena nodded vigorously. How she remembered them! The flame of the sun. The brilliant blue of violets. The blinding white of snow.

"Try to picture the colors now, Sister."

She felt the thread being drawn across her palm as Anthony spoke.

"The purple of the Lord's passion and your own suffering." The thread tickled her palm.

"The white of chastity."

The thread was again dragged across her palm. And so it went with each color.

"The blue of contemplation. The scarlet of love of God and of neighbor. And so on. Christ, the gift of highest value, can stitch for you an everlasting tunic if you, despite these inner struggles, remain obedient to Him. And what a beautiful and colorful tunic it will be, woven of all the virtues!"

Anthony lightly laid the needle in Helena's palm.

Helena plucked the needle with her hand and rubbed it through her fingers. Oh, if only Christ would embroider for her a tunic as Anthony said! Her Savior had favored her with visions, yet her internal deadness made her feel like Judas.

She felt for the tunic which she had been mending and threaded the needle into it. Then she fumbled for the pen. Anthony slipped the piece of parchment out from under her fingertips and replaced it with what Helena knew was a clean sheet. Then he guided her pen to the ink and she wrote again.

"I feel like I betray my Lord."

"Then let us see how you are betraying. Christ wore a tunic which He Himself designed. It was a tunic of sackcloth, stretched on the cross for us, torn by nails and pierced with a lance."

Helena shuddered for, beneath the tunic that she was now wearing, unknown to anyone else, she wore a shirt of sackcloth. Did Anthony somehow know?

"Sackcloth is a sign of guilt, worn by a penitent, worn by a sinner, not by a Redeemer. Yet Christ wore this tunic, stitched of human flesh and suffering, when He assumed the burden and guilt of our sins.

"And the sackcloth of our sins, with which He had cloaked His divinity, led Him to death on the cross. Christ came to redeem us.

For 'we were dead in sin' but Christ died so that we might live in God. Wasn't Christ, then, God's most perfect Gift?"

Helena nodded. Her hands began again to write. "I know this, yet I still feel as if I betray Him. I am so lax. He has given me so much."

"My Sister, as you sew and pray, think of the poor sackcloth of His earthly Body that Christ stitched for Himself, a garment that He restored to immortality by His wisdom and power of His resurrection. Think, too, of the glorious tunic that Christ is making for you as you remain obedient to Him. Your garment, my Sister, is coming to resemble His and your reward shall be with Him.

"And when you are tempted to give up because life seems burdensome and prayer ordinary and poverty too difficult and joy gone, think of Who you are exchanging and for what."

Anthony took the pen out of Helena's hand. He took her two hands and placed them both, palm up, on the parchment in her lap. Then, with his finger, he traced a cross on her right palm.

"'What will you give me,' Judas said, 'if I hand Jesus over to you?' What price can be set in exchange for the Son of God? What can they give you? Were they to give you Jerusalem..."

Helena felt a pebble drop into her left hand.

"Galilee..."

Another pebble.

"And Samaria..."

Yet a third pebble.

"Would these be a suitable price for the Son of God?"

Again a finger traced a cross in her right palm.

"Were they to give you heaven with all its angels..."

A rain of pebbles in the left palm.

"The earth with all its peoples, the seas, and all they contain..."

A greater sprinkle of pebbles.

"Would all these suffice in exchange for Jesus..."

Again, the tracing of a cross.

"'In Whom are hidden all treasures of wisdom and knowledge'?"

Anthony closed the fingers of both her hands. The one with the pebbles felt heavy and gritty, the one with the cross light.

"Sister, God alone knows what is 'the way of the spirit.' The writer of Hebrews says, 'He is a discerner of the thoughts and intents of the heart. All things are bare and open to His eyes.' So He knows that, in these afflictions, you seek Him. And He has promised, 'The one who perseveres to the end will be saved.' As you remain obedient to Christ when fervor dies down, Christ is stitching your tunic of everlasting life with the gold thread of perseverance and the silver thread of obedience. And you will have a precious garment if you do not exchange the world..." he said, tapping the hand with the pebbles, "...for the Lord."

He patted the hand that had been traced with the cross.

"In time, the song of the bride in the Canticle will again be yours when she sings, 'Arise, north wind, and come, south wind, blow through my garden that its perfumes may flow.' The north wind which freezes the waters of the soul is the devil who, by his cold malice, removes the consolations of God. To the devil, you will say again, 'Arise and go away,' and to the south wind, the Holy Spirit, 'come.'"

She felt a warm finger on her cheek, gently angling her face directly into the breeze, then a finger under her chin lifting her face full into the sunlight.

"Come, blow through my conscience so that the perfume of my tears may flow. You will experience again the hidden things of contemplation, the joy of the spirit, the sweet experience of inner delight, which are the secrets of the Holy Spirit, for He will dwell in you and by His indwelling blow through with the soft breath of His love."

Helena sat as still as a dove at rest, the cross in one hand, the world in the other, her face bathed with the breeze and the warmth. A fire seemed to burn in her hand with the cross. She felt herself transported into the Passion of Christ, reliving it as He lived it. Mockery of Herod. Treachery of Pilate. Whipping. Thorns pounded into scalp. Jeering of the mob. Wooden beam digging into soft shoulder blade. Bare toes grappling stones in a struggle to walk. Falling. Jerking upright. Being thrust onto hard wood. The sear of iron nails driven into flesh. Cross jolting upright. Indignity of nakedness. Sticky blood running down back, arms, belly, legs. Flies and gnats, buzzing, stinging, itching. Blinding sun. Burning thirst. Abandonment of God. Death. Then tomb. Resurrection. Life.

When her meditation had ended, her hands were still cramped closed in her lap. The breeze had turned cool and the sun's warmth had faded. With her fists, she felt in her lap for the tunic but it was gone. Helena stretched and opened her cramped fingers. She threw the pebbles to the ground and clasped the imaginary cross to her heart. Then she groped at her feet and found the tunic that had fallen from her lap. As she went to pick it up, her finger caught the needle and its point pricked her. The sudden pain brought back to her Anthony's words about the needle of Christ's mercy and justice. She turned to thank the friar, feeling for his hand. But he was gone. Holding the needle in one hand and pressing the tunic to her chest where she had earlier pressed the cross, she felt her way into the convent.

There is joy in joy, she realized. And there can be joy in dryness. Where Christ is, all is joy. Compared to the perfect gift of Christ, all the world is pebbles.

## ❧ 23 ❧

## *Brother Elias*

**Paradise Hill, Assisi, Italy (May 30, 1230)** ❧ In the fading sunlight at the end of day, Brother Elias Bombarone stood facing the basilica that he had designed. His one hand stroked the drooping head of his gray ass. The other was on the saddle pommel. He hesitated a moment before mounting.

This past week, Elias had been busy finalizing plans for the ceremony involving the reburial of Father Francis' remains in this very basilica. Elias, whose weak legs and feet could not tolerate excessive standing and walking, had stood and walked far too much. Now the thin calves of his long legs were throbbing with the familiar pain of chronic affliction. His tender feet, swathed in soft leather shoes, were stinging. However, this evening the physical pains in his limbs did not match the spiritual pangs in his heart.

For the last time, he gazed at the massive, half-completed rose-and-white stone basilica that jutted skyward before him. This majestic, unfinished church of Assisi was beginning to look as solemn and holy as Elias had intended when he designed it after the fortress sepulchers that he had seen while provincial minister of Syria.

By the pope's orders and under Elias' direction, workmen had chipped and cracked out the church's deep foundation on this jagged rock promontory once called Hell Hill. Now this outcropping that sloped steeply down to the river Tescio had a new name: Paradise Hill. For here in the magnificent, grotto-like lower level of the church lay the body of the greatest saint of this age: Francis of Assisi.

This late in the day, all was quiet. The workers had gone home. The building's architect, Philip of Campello, had embraced Elias with tears and then left the site.

"When will I see you again?" Philip had choked out the words.

Elias' voice had been deep and hoarse. "I don't know."

After Philip had left, Elias had walked through the basilica alone, caressing pillar and altar and door as if touching them would hold them in his memory until he returned.

Unlike Jean Parenti, the minister general of the Friars Minor, Elias did not possess the gift of tears. But even though no droplets welled in his huge, black eyes, his heart was weeping. He must leave the basilica in Philip of Campello's hands. He must leave the remains of Francis whom he loved. And he must spend time, how much he did not know, alone and in shame, until others told him that he had been repentant.

Lifting the hem of his gray tunic, Elias swung himself onto the ass and turned the beast away from the shadowy structure and down the steep grade that led into Assisi. Using the blessing that Francis himself had taught, he whispered to the night breeze, "God's peace and all good, Father Francis."

If only he could forget today! Yet the memories stuck in his mind like cockleburs.

Six hours earlier, Elias had been sitting in his cell at the hermitage Francis loved, the Portiuncula. Before him lay an open ledger. His mind had been swirling with calculations. The provincial of Germany had sent this much money for the basilica, the provincial of Tuscany more. How much would Emperor Frederick give if Elias asked him to donate again? What materials were needed to complete the basilica's upper level and how costly were they?

Elias' feet were aching. This past week, he had walked too much. He was stretching his legs when a rapid, sharp knock sounded at his door.

Without standing, he called, "Come in."

Brother Sebastio entered with a sea of friars behind him.

"Come to the chapter meeting," Sebastio had pleaded. "We want you as minister general in place of Brother Jean."

Before Elias could respond to the unexpected plea, another friar spoke up. "Brother Jean has surrounded himself with clerics."

And another voice. "Father Francis wanted the Order to be simple."

Then more men calling out, one after the other.

"Brother Jean lets them have breviaries. Father Francis never did."

"We friars all came to Assisi for Father Francis' burial in the basilica. You were right in saying that we could attend the chapter meeting. Brother Jean has no right to keep us out."

"Before he died, Father Francis blessed you, not Brother Jean. You must be minister general."

Elias was confused yet honored. "I cannot walk. My feet"

"We will carry you," Brother Sebastio offered.

Suddenly Elias was hoisted over the heads of five friars. Should he protest? If this many men wanted him to be minister general, perhaps it was God's will that it be so. He allowed himself to be carried along, bouncing on the men's shoulders, their eager voices blowing away his doubts.

When Brother Sebastio knocked at the chapter-house door and demanded entrance, a call came from within. "You know the Rule. Only provincials and custodians may attend the chapter meeting."

Before anyone could stop him, Brother Sebastio had bashed the door. The wood cracked, the door gave way, and the friars bearing Elias burst into the room. Almost as one man, the provincials and custodians rose, anger and surprise flushing their faces.

The friars had eased Elias down next to a gaping Jean Parenti. What should Elias say? He would let Brother Sebastio and the others do the talking.

Sebastio shoved Jean aside.

"Brother Elias will be our minister general."

Several provincials and custodians objected. A few pushed forward. The friars accompanying Elias held them back. Shouts flew back and forth.

"Let us have peace."

"Everyone sit down."

"You have barred us. Father Francis never would."

"Brother Elias said we could come to the chapter."

"It is the Rule. Only custodians and provincials may attend,"

"In God's name, brothers, let us have peace,"

More shouts. More pushing.

Anthony, provincial of the Romagna, had somehow moved to the front of the assembly. With his hands and face upraised, he began to recite in a voice at once prayerful and commanding, a prayer that Father Francis had taught and had applied to himself. Anthony was applying it to the assembly.

"O most high, glorious God, enlighten the darkness of our hearts and give us a right faith, certain hope, and a perfect love, understanding, and knowledge, O Lord, that we may carry out Your holy and true command."

Sebastio pushed him aside, "You are not Father Francis. Did he not change our Rule to allow you to teach and use books? Did you not allow the brothers to possess the church and convent at Bassano when Father Francis forbade us to hold property? You have no right to speak his words."

Anthony dropped to his knees, his head bowed, praying. Elias stared at him as the shouts and pushing increased. Swiftly other provincials and custodians knelt. Some friars who had carried Elias knelt as well.

Uncertain, Elias stood, silently watching, wondering what to say or do.

Suddenly Jean Parenti tore off his robe and flung aside his breeches. The man was standing naked before the assembly. Elias turned away in embarrassment at this anguished gesture so reminiscent of the High Priest who had torn his robes while crying out that Jesus had blasphemed in claiming to be God.

The whole gathering froze at Jean's action. In the silence, five novices, who had come with Elias, spoke up, their voices trembling.

"We have been knights."

"We lay down our weapons to follow a way of peace."

"This will bring no good to our Order."

"There can be no order with disorder."

The groups backed off. The riot fizzled. One of the men who had come with Elias handed Jean his breeches and robe. Jean re-clothed himself.

Still standing on aching feet, the heat rising in his neck, his mind swirling, Elias did not move.

A provincial shouted, "What do we do with these intruders?"

A custodian answered back, "Assign them penance."

With face flushed, Jean turned to Elias. "I will assign some infractors to each provincial who will give them a penance."

Anthony stood. "Do you remember, Brother Jean, that I asked to be relieved of my post as provincial of the Romagna?"

"I had forgotten," Jean said. "You are not well enough to travel far. You are relieved. Go wherever you wish and preach." He paused, his gaze sweeping the room. "Brother Albert, you shall take Brother Anthony's place as provincial."

Albert, a gentle-faced friar, well past middle age, nodded amiably.

"Thank you, Brother Jean," Anthony said, sitting. Elias suddenly saw the man anew. Anthony's body was swollen with dropsy, and swiftly, in Elias' mind, the heavy man before him was Anthony no longer but Francis. For dropsy had swelled Francis' body, too. For long months, Elias had tended Francis. As Elias stood in that chapter meeting, an image leapt to his mind of Francis astride a mule. His swollen, bloody palms were dangling at his side and Elias walked, holding the reins. Francis' feet, swollen and bloody, were bumping the belly of the ass. The wound in his side was staining red through the tattered, dusty tunic. Francis was pierced in his hands, feet, and side with the wounds of Christ, the *stigmata*.

Suddenly Elias was reliving Francis' last days. When Francis became too weak to preach, Elias had taken him by cart to Assisi. There in bed, Francis had placed his hand on Elias' head and had spoken a blessing in his weak voice. "My blessing on you, my son. I bless in you, as much as I am able, all my friars and my dear sons."

Francis had blessed bread and passed it to his brothers, but Elias had been weeping so intensely that he could not eat it.

Francis died. In Elias' mind, he saw the eyelids flutter again and again and yet again and then become still. A grief so palpable he could squeeze it rose afresh in his heart even as, on the edge of awareness, Elias heard Jean assigning this friar and that to this and that provincial for the administration of penance.

Following Francis' death, Elias had written to the brothers: "I weep and not without reason, for sorrow like a mighty torrent has flooded my heart. He who was our stay and our consolation is no more. For ourselves, we can never weep enough, deprived as we are of the light of his presence and plunged as it were in darkness and the shadow of death."

Darkness. Elias was still in darkness ever since Francis died.

"Brother Elias."

Jean's call broke into Elias' recollection.

"Brother Elias, you have usurped your authority three times in one week. Once when you allowed those whom the pope did not appoint to handle and bury Father Francis' body. Again when you told these friars that they could attend this chapter meeting. And today by unlawfully disrupting this meeting and attempting to be made minister general by force. You will depart from here to your hermitage at Cortona where you will do penance until we determine that you are totally repentant. The work on the basilica will be under the care of Philip of Campello and Picardus Morico until you return."

Elias stared directly ahead as he heard the judgment.

"Brother Aymo, please escort Brother Elias to the door."

On the arm of a friar whom he did not even look at, Elias plodded to the doorway outside of which waited many of the friars who had carried Elias into the meeting. Now they hoisted him onto their shoulders and carried him back to his cell. Elias barely heard their angry remarks and apologies. His mind was on the basilica.

"You will do penance until we determine you are totally repentant," Jean had said. "The work on the basilica will be under the care of Philip of Campello and Picardus Morico until you return."

"Until you return." When would that be?

Tomorrow at dawn, Elias would go to Cortona, to his mud and stone cell beside a deep gorge. For six years after joining the Order, he had lived in that cell. Francis had lived, for a time, in another cell nearby. Elias would live like a rat, in solitude with rats, and neither bathe nor shave until he was recalled. When would that be?

The friars deposited Elias in his own cell at the Portiuncula. Some wanted to stay and speak with him. Having no time to speak, he dismissed them.

Elias gathered up his ledger, records, and architectural plans for the basilica. Folding them neatly into two pouches, he saddled his ass that was tethered beneath a nearby tree, then threw the pouches over its back. Climbing into the saddle, Elias turned the beast toward Assisi. With aching heels, Elias kicked the animal into a trot.

*Hurry, beast. I must find Picardus and Philip.*

Picardus was a genius with ledgers and accounts. Philip was the basilica's architect. The lower level of the church was complete. But not the convent or the upper church. In Elias' absence, work must continue. He must find Picardus and Philip and give them the paperwork that was bouncing against the ass' ribs.

Picardus was not home. He had gone to Foligno, said the servant who answered Elias' frenzied knock. Elias hurried away to Philip's house where he waited impatiently for the maid to summon the tall, flaxen-haired architect from somewhere within the dwelling.

Elias' words poured out in a rush to the dignified gentleman in a green tunic. "Philip, I must leave Assisi until I am recalled. I have brought you the ledgers and plans for the basilica. You will have to speak to Picardus. He is not home. Come with me. I must show you a few things at the basilica before I leave."

On the winding, hilly streets of Assisi, Philip's black steed pranced impatiently beside the plodding ass. Just five days ago, these same two men had ridden the same streets together, only then the lanes were clogged with people. That day, May 25, Francis' body, which had rested in a heavy sarcophagus beneath the altar in St. George's Church, had been solemnly carted from that church to its permanent home in the basilica.

Elias' troubles had started that day. No, not that day. A few days earlier.

A few days earlier, Elias, Philip, Picardus, the Podesta of Assisi, the town council, and other prominent citizens had been finalizing plans for the magnificent celebration that would accompany Francis' entry into his awe-inspiring tomb.

One of the council members had raised the question. "What if the Perugians try to steal the body?"

The city of Perugia had been a long-time enemy of Assisi. Before his conversion, Francis had journeyed as a knight to fight the Perugians. After his submission to Christ, Francis had struggled with meager success to make peace between the two cities.

"We will have a guard, as we had all these years at St. George's," Elias said. "Won't that be sufficient?"

"Perhaps. Perhaps not," the Podesta, who was the ruling official of Assisi, said. "The people themselves might get too close to the body and desecrate it."

"The grate over the sarcophagus is sturdy. The openings are narrow. No one could reach in to touch the body."

"Brother Elias, who is to say that a heavy hammer, wielded by a sturdy man, or a thick saw, could not destroy that grate?" the Podesta remarked. "Or that someone could not have devised some sort of narrow knife or tongs to extend through the grate?"

"If we let them up close, they might cut off pieces of Francis' tunic," one council member reasoned.

"Or pluck his hair."

"Cut off a finger."

Elias winced. The people were crazy for holy relics. If the Perugians did not steal the whole body, the citizens of Assisi might well steal parts of it.

"I know what we'll do," the Podesta said. "Brother Elias, you ride with Francis' body on the cart. The rest of us will ride before and after and on either side of it. We will post soldiers all around as well as along the route." The Podesta had paused a moment before adding, "And if the crowd begins to threaten the body, we will fight them off and rush it into the basilica. If we bolt the doors, no one will be able to enter and we can have Francis in the tomb before anyone can do him harm."

"Only the friars appointed by the pope have permission to touch the sarcophagus and the body," Elias pointed out. "Father Francis is a saint. His body is sacred."

"Brother Elias," Picardus had said, "if Francis' body is in danger, the pope is not going to care who touches it to keep it safe."

So Francis, who had been baptized at St. George's as an infant in 1181, and canonized there in 1228, was taken from that church to the basilica. Barefoot Jean Parenti, the pope's official delegate, and Elias directed the removal of the massive stone sarcophagus containing Francis' shriveled body. After carefully raising the casket from its vault below the altar, a contingent of sturdy friars, duly appointed by the pope, hoisted the casket into a massive wooden box and then onto an open-bed cart pulled by two oxen draped in purple silk. Jean had stroked the wooden box tenderly, weeping openly, then draped it with sumptuous purple banners.

Elias swallowed the lump in his throat and climbed up onto the cart beside the driver. Jean and other friars and cardinals appointed by the pope to be his representatives took their places behind the armed guard. The cart driver clicked the reins, and the oxen had begun their slow journey surrounded by all the governing officials of Assisi and a well-armed escort.

The air rang with shouts of joy and the music of countless pipes and tambourines. Behind the cart and the papal representatives paraded countless brightly dressed archers, a whole army of mounted knights in full armor, and all the guilds of Assisi, bearing a hundred banners. Clogging the streets around all of these, as well as preceding the procession and surging along behind it, were nearly all the citizens of Assisi. There was a flood of visitors as well. They had been sleeping in the streets and fields. Many were dancing and leaping with happiness. Mingled with them, singing and dancing as well, were two thousand friars who had come to Assisi to see Francis buried.

Elias felt like singing, too, but inside his breast nagged a persistent fear. *Lord, let the guards keep the revelers at bay.* But try as they might, the guards could not hold back the mob. Bodies pushed between the mounted soldiers, hands reached out reverently, fingers clawed at the fluttering purple banners, hands stroked the casket.

"Father Francis, pray for me."

"Father Francis, bless me."

The procession was a stop-and-go march, the cart forced to pause periodically as the people in front of it clogged the streets or those to the sides pressed too close to allow easy movement. During these lags, fingers tugged at Elias' robe.

"Bless me, Brother," voices rang out.

Agitated at the disorderly joy, Elias raised his hand again and again in blessing while alert to any suspicious movement that meant desecration rather than devotion.

As the procession approached Paradise Hill, Elias saw the basilica before him, rising in the sunlight like a giant altar. As the massive oak doors of the lower church came into view, the crowd to the right of the wagon pushed against the guards. With a start, Elias saw that the guards were having difficulty holding them back. More pushing. Shoving. Shouting. A crowd of peasants, nobles, friars, and unfamiliar knights was hemming in the cart, surrounding it, reaching toward the wooden coffin, touching it. Hands were stretching toward the soldiers, grappling with them, trying to tug them from their saddles.

Suddenly Elias heard a shout. The Podesta. "Get the cart into the basilica. At once!"

The cart driver lashed the oxen, hurrying them forward. The crowd scattered before the trotting beasts. The mounted guards fought off the hands that grappled with them and the wagon.

Elias grabbed the cart driver's arm. "Hurry!" he ordered.

The calls of the people pelted Elias' ears like hailstones.

"Let me touch him."

"Let me kiss him."

"Our dear saint."

"Spare us, St. Francis."

Before the oaken doors, guards forced the crowds back. The wagon, in its protective cluster of Assisian officials and soldiers, rushed into the church made brilliant with already lit torches.

"Bar the door!" the Podesta shouted.

Wood slammed into place. Bolts thumped. Outside, demonic, angry shrieks rose. A frightening pounding echoed at the doors.

"Over here," the Podesta called to the cart driver. The driver followed the Podesta's horse to the twelve-foot-deep burial vault cut down into the floor of the basilica.

"Remove the coffin," the Podesta commanded.

Behind Elias, a thick cluster of muscular soldiers grabbed the massive casket and dragged it off the cart. The purple banners caught beneath the casket. Elias heard one rip as the banners were pulled off, the wooden box opened, and what had once been an animal's stone drinking trough removed. For the briefest moment, the men gazed through the sturdy iron grate bound over the trough and around it by thick pipes. Beneath the grill lay a shriveled body in a patched gray habit.

"Hurry," the Podesta commanded.

*Father Francis, help us,* Elias prayed.

Following the frenzied directions of Elias and Philip, the soldiers grabbed a series of ropes and pulleys. These they fastened to the ponderous casket and the grate that covered it, both top and bottom. The heaving against the basilica doors increased. Suddenly a pounding sounded from the narrow windows on the sides of the chapel. Elias' heart leaped. *God, don't let them break the glass.* Elias and Philip scrambled among the men, securing ropes, certifying that the pulleys were working and sturdy.

"She's ready," Philip said.

Elias agreed. "Lower the casket," he ordered.

With the men straining against the ropes, the casket eased down into the rectangular hole readied for it. Elias watched it descend into the vault that was lined with finely chiseled slabs of travertine stone, shimmering white in the torch light.

The taut ropes went slack as the coffin came to rest on the travertine-lined floor of the hole.

Suddenly, the doors to the church burst open. With savage voices, the populace surged forward. The mounted soldiers inside the building surrounded the casket, blocking its view with the bodies of nervous, sweating steeds.

"Release the ropes," Elias ordered. "Pull back the pulleys." In a matter of seconds, the apparatus which had lowered Francis twelve feet into the rock was rendered useless to lift him out again.

The angry crowd pressed the guards as the Podesta of Assisi rode forward. "We will have order or we will arrest the rioters," he warned.

The pushing stopped. Guards shoved the people into a semblance of order. Soldiers rode up and down among the crowd to maintain peace. The people began to file past the hole, kneeling among the pulleys and ropes to peer down at the saint. Some lay on the floor and reached down, attempting unsuccessfully to touch the grill over Francis' body. Others leaned against the empty wooden coffin and wept. Some rubbed the discarded purple drapes against their cheeks. A few flung a coin or two onto Francis' body below them.

"Brother Elias." The voice was trembling and choked, as if with tears. Elias turned from watching those venerating the corpse to the source of the sorrow. A young friar, his cheeks wet with tears, stood at Elias' shoulder.

His words quivering with emotion, the friar spoke. "Brother Elias, I am Brother James of Iseo. I....I touched his coffin. Out there by the door. I...I just wanted to pray. And the hernia. I had a hernia since I was a boy. The hernia." The friar rubbed his hand over his belly. "It's gone, Brother." The friar looked down and bit his lip. "Why did you bury him like that? Before we friars could see him? Before anyone could touch him?" The brown eyes lifted and glistened. "Father Francis might have healed them. Like...he healed me."

Before Elias could reply, another voice broke in, this one harsh and from the right. Elias turned toward it. Brother Jean. "How could you plan such a travesty, Brother? The pope strictly ordered that none but his official delegates should handle the holy remains. You have made this sacred ceremony into a mockery."

A mockery? The words stung. Elias mock Francis? He would rather die first.

And that was how Elias felt now as he made his way back through the woods to the Portiuncula. He felt like dying. First the confusion five days ago at the basilica. Then today's savage chapter meeting. An hour ago, his conference with Philip and his tearful farewell to the church into which he had poured his heart. He was to go away to do penance. Until when? How could he live apart from the church which held the body of the man who had been life for Elias? If only Elias could die. Then he would be at peace. Peace. Peace like the peace that surrounded him now.

Peace.

For the day was done. Now soft sounds of evening were rising in the woods. Soothing sounds. Crickets chirping. Frogs croaking. Breezes, tenderly sighing, lulling the world to sleep. Elias passed the still, dark cells of the other friars. The soft plod of the ass wakened no one if indeed anyone heard. Or cared.

Peace.

Oh, familiar, gentle dusk! What precious balm! What wondrous drug! The gray shadows sucking the green from the foliage, sipped the anguish from Elias' soul. All here was as it had always been. The violence and disorder of this day, of this past week, had nothing in common with the evening's peace. Could his banishment today have been a nightmare? In the womb of eventide, Elias could persuade himself that nothing had changed. He would rub down the lathered hair of his beast and then he would fall onto his pallet and sleep. Sleep and forget. Tomorrow he would wake and return to the basilica to supervise the workers.

For nothing could really have happened. He was twenty years in the Order, clothed by Francis himself. Provincial minister of Syria. Minister General under Francis, his vicar for six years. Designer of the greatest church in the world. Friends with pope, emperor, kings. No one would possibly send him off to do penance. Not Elias.

As he tied the ass to a tree, his eyes caught a movement beside his cell. His heart leaped. Bear? Thief?

"Brother Elias." The voice was gentle, the corpulent figure several inches shorter than Elias. Brother Anthony. "I hope I did not startle you. I've been waiting here since the end of the chapter meeting, hoping you'd return. You've been to the basilica, haven't you?"

Anthony was beside Elias now, the dark lines in his forehead and under his eyes looking even darker in the meager light.

Elias tugged the light saddle off the ass and flung it over a stump. "How did you know I would be at the basilica?"

"Because if I were you, I would have gone there. To set things in order before I left."

Elias' denial that today's events had actually happened splintered like spring ice. Frozen shards of truth jabbed his soul. The chapter meeting was no nightmare. Banishment was reality.

As he grappled among the tree roots for rags that he had tossed there, he suddenly realized, *this is my last night in this place. Tomorrow I will be on the way to Cortona.*

Elias found the rags and began to rub the animal's neck with one.

"Give me a rag, Brother, and I will help you."

Elias fished between the tree roots for more cloth and handed a swath to Anthony. Anthony walked around the animal and, on the side of the beast opposite Elias, began to rub down the beast's neck.

From the corner of his eye, Elias scrutinized Anthony. He had seen him last at Francis' canonization. Now he noticed the man's swollen fingers and feet and pregnant-looking belly. What disease had so changed Anthony's body in two years time?

Elias knew this man. While Francis was still alive, Elias had sent both Anthony and Francis to the pope to discuss the Rule. Elias knew then that Anthony was forceful. Time had proved just how forceful. Anthony could be scathing in his preaching.

Certainly Anthony had come today to castigate him. And he had thought that his penance would begin tomorrow as he left for Cortona. Oh, not so. Anthony would begin it today. Here. Now.

Elias grit his teeth. He would say nothing. He would rub down his lathered beast and allow the rebukes to fall like sleet on his frozen heart.

As he wiped down the beast's neck, Anthony spoke. "Brother Elias, I need your help. Brother Jean is sending a delegation of seven to Rome to confer with the pope. I am to head the group. We are to discuss Father Francis' last testament. The brothers want to know what is binding and what is not. You were with Father Francis when he dictated the testament, were you not?"

Elias rubbed and muttered his assent.

"Perhaps you can tell me about it."

Was this a trick, a way to catch him off guard? Talk about the testament, then counter with a comment about sin. Elias spoke truthfully but guardedly. "Father Francis was dying when he dictated the testament. It expresses his firm wishes for the Order. He wanted the Rule followed as he had written it. Whatever is written in the testament is as he wished."

"That does seem to be clear. 'Rather, as the Lord has granted me simply and plainly to speak and write the Rule and these words, so simply and without gloss are you to understand them, and by holy deeds carry them out until the very end.' That was how Father Francis ended the testament before his blessing, is it not?"

"You remember it well."

Anthony wiped the beast's chest. "Did Father Francis consult anyone while composing the testament?"

"No. As you yourself just recited, he said that the message was granted him by the Lord."

Anthony whistled softly. "Do you think Pope Gregory will accept that?"

Elias was swabbing the ass' throat. "When Pope Gregory was still cardinal of Ostia, he did not accept Francis' Rule. That was 1221. Francis said that was given by Christ, too."

Anthony sighed. "Brother Elias, whatever the pope decrees concerning the Rule, we must accept whether or not we agree. He is the head of the Church. He speaks in the name of Christ. But, Brother, will you pray for us? For our Order? For me? As we go over this for the future and the good of the brothers, will you pray?"

Elias bent down to rub the ass' front leg. Anthony was still standing, drying the withers. What should Elias say? He would open himself for Anthony's attack. He would tell the truth. "Brother, I am not good at prayer."

"Would you like to be?"

Elias was stooping, rubbing the ass' fetlock and trying to maneuver his own painful feet into a comfortable squat. "With Father Francis, I could pray. But when he died, that seemed to die, too."

Warm fingers touched Elias' wrist. Anthony was stooping, reaching under the ass. "My brother, we have joined the Order to follow Christ, not to follow Francis. That is what Father Francis wanted."

Elias' words came too quick, too sharp, too pointedly truthful. "I have not been able to find Christ without Francis."

Anthony's long, swollen fingers tightened on Elias' wrist "My Brother, prayer brings us to the Peace Who is." Then the grip loosened, and Elias saw the bulky form of Anthony stand to rub the ass' shoulder.

*Here comes the rebuke,* Elias thought.

"My Brother, I have a riddle for you. Are you this ass' servant? Or is he yours?"

Elias grunted as he stood. "He is mine, of course."

"You are only half correct. Brother Elias, you care for your beast. You feed and shelter him and tend to his needs. Thus, you are his servant."

As he swabbed the ass' shoulder, Elias protested. "Ah, he is also my servant for he bears me places."

"True. Now listen. Did not God become our servant for thirty-three years on this earth, even to dying for us to free us from slavery to the devil? Did you ever think that God became our servant so that we might become His?"

"I had not thought about it."

"Think of it this way. Are you going to leave the basilica forever as it stands today?"

"Of course not. It is only partly finished."

"You wish then to give the entire, completed structure as a monument to Father Francis. Just so, God gave Himself totally to us so that we might give ourselves totally to Him. God does not only want a part of us. If we reserve a part of us for ourselves, then we are ours and not His."

Anthony raised an arm skyward, the cloth in his hand waving like a banner against the deep gray sky. "Oh Father, to give You everything is to prove our love for You! All our faculties, all our thoughts, our entire consciousness and our whole life we must return to You Who first gave them to us. Everything that we are, everything that we have, we must give to You, Lord, for You are the object of our love."

With his hand still thrust toward the sky, Anthony paused for a long moment. Then he reached across the ass' back and grasped Elias' hand. "We must give everything to God. Everything. All our works, all our actions. Everything. Whatever we do for the sake of our own glory, we totally lose. When our actions are to glorify ourselves, we cannot persevere to the end and we thus lose heavenly glory. Only wholly in God do we become wholly who God intends us to be."

Anthony bent to wipe the ass' front leg. "Listen, my brother, to the sounds of night. Do you hear the melody of the wind in the leaves?"

Elias heard it, the sweet, lilting tune of night.

"Do the leaves make a melody by themselves or is the wind in them creating the music?"

"Leaves only rustle when the wind blows them. Therefore, the wind creates the sound."

"Suppose each leaf moved on its own. Or did not move, depending upon its own desire. Suppose some bobbed furiously while others simply fluttered or just lay still. Would we hear the melody that we hear tonight?"

"We would hear something. But not as rich or beautiful."

"Correct. If each leaf acted on its own will instead of acting as the wind blows it, the forest would hum with far poorer music. Just as the leaves vibrate to the caress of the wind, so must our souls vibrate to the touch of the Divine Spirit. We, like leaves, must act not on our own will but only as the breath of the Spirit directs. Then our actions will be as God wishes and not as we wish. Our life will become like a melody fit for angels to hear. The secret of success is to act in the name of Christ, in the inspiration of Christ, and to attribute all to Him and nothing to oneself."

Anthony stood and began to rub the ass' back. "Listen. Do you hear the croaking of the frogs disturbing the harmony of dusk?"

Elias heard them, their discordant croaks interrupting the peace.

"Have you ever eaten a frog, my brother?"

Elias grunted. "I can think of nothing more disgusting."

Anthony laughed. "I ate a toad once. It was not too bad tasting, but a fish is much tastier. That is why, when fishers cast their nets, they gather in the fish to eat but throw away the frogs."

Suddenly Anthony flung back his head and threw open his arms, his face arched upward, his voice tremulous with a contained grief. "Oh, Lord, only in Your name will I cast my net, because each time that I have done so in my own name, attributing the merit to me, and not to You, I have preached Anthony and not Christ, my things, not Your things. Therefore, I took nothing except perhaps some croaking frog who sang my praises, but, indeed, no fish. Truly, I took nothing."

Slowly he lowered his arms and gazed intently at Elias.

"In our own power, my Brother, we do nothing of value. How vital it is to submit one's whole will entirely to God!"

Anthony stooped to swab the ass' belly. "And it is easy to give ourselves completely to our Lord when we remember who we are. Look at your beast here. He reminds me of the types of people in the world. There are wild asses which, like haughty and vain people, grow proud in the outward signs of their exalted rank or in the inner vanity of their own hearts. But they are, after all, only asses."

The calm, conversational voice receded into the sluff of cloth over hair.

"And then there are other people who, like the ass on Palm Sunday, humbly bear Christ the King into the marketplace."

Silence. A hollow patting sound. Anthony patting the beast's side.

"Both are asses. One realizes that he is an ass. The other thinks he is much more. One lives in truth, the other in deception. Christ said that He is the Truth. We can never know the truth about Christ unless we know the truth about ourselves. Our value comes, not from ourselves, for we are only humble beasts, but from the fact that, like the little Palm Sunday ass, we are bearing Christ. If we see ourselves this way, one day Christ, our Truth, will call to us in His eternal banquet, 'My honest and humble friend, come up higher.'"

Anthony stretched to rub the animal's croup. Elias was doing the same. "Just as all vices depend on pride, for it is the beginning of all sin, so humility is the mother and root of all virtues. God resists the proud but shows Himself to and uses the humble."

As he shifted his weight from one throbbing foot to the other, Elias rubbed from the animal's tail down to its thigh. Anthony, on his side of the beast, followed the same drying pattern.

"My brother, do you know that I can not even build a sand castle while you build a basilica?"

Elias guffawed. As a boy, he had built marvelous sand castles, complete with moats and bridges and towers, all supported with inner grid work of stone and branch.

Anthony whooped. "You are laughing at me, my brother."

"So I am," Elias chuckled.

"The basilica is magnificent. Never have I seen such an edifice. It will someday rise high because you sank the foundation deep into rock. So you can understand the truth of what Blessed Bernard says, 'The deeper you lay the foundation of humility, the higher the building is able to rise.'"

Anthony stooped to swath the animal's rear leg. "True humility cannot be made to suffer either pain because of some injustice or ill feeling because of another's good fortune. This is as it should be, because if humility fails, the entire structure of the virtues collapses like a castle in the sand. Only the truly humble person can love God who humbled Himself to become a man. And only love of God leads to prayer."

Anthony straightened and handed his sopping rag across the ass' back to Elias. "Your beast is dry on this side. Have you any water here for him?"

"There's a full bucket to the right of the cell."

Elias swabbed the ass' rear leg on his side. Now the beast was dry on this side as well. Elias draped the wet rags over a nearby shrub as Anthony set the sloshing pail of water before the animal. The ass drank eagerly and noisily as Elias felt in the darkness for a familiar clump of root. As he sat, the pulsing in his feet seemed to ease out at his toes like a giant breath.

Anthony walked around the ass and sat beside Elias. "Have you ever been thirsty, Brother? As thirsty as this ass?" Anthony asked.

"Many times. Sometimes thirstier."

"So you know how good it feels to have your thirst quenched. As your beast thirsts for water, so must we thirst for the living water of Christ. For Christ tells us that if we drink of Him we will never thirst again. And we will drink of Him if we seek, first of all, the kingdom of God. The kingdom of God is the highest good, the most important thing in our life. Everything else must be sought in view of this kingdom; nothing should be asked beyond it. Whatever we ask must serve that end."

Elias felt a firm hand on his shoulder. He turned to look at Anthony whose form was now a dark shadow nearly lost in the soft, black cape of night.

"We ask all in prayer, my Brother. Prayer gives us the grace to act for God. Only from the heights of contemplation can we descend to instruct and work among the faithful, to show forth in our own lives the way of salvation to the people. My Brother, the Holy Spirit will teach you to pray."

While the still standing ass wheezed softly into sleep, Elias felt the hand slip from his shoulder as Anthony shifted before him and knelt. Elias attempted to push himself into a kneeling position, but a firm hand pressed against his chest and held him back.

"Sit, Brother. Your feet are sore."

With a sigh of relief, Elias settled back onto the root. Anthony's swollen, warm fingers curled around Elias' hands. Although Anthony was directly facing Elias, the darkness was now so deep that his eyes were shadows.

"The Apostle Paul in his letter to Timothy shows how we must proceed in prayer. 'I urge first of all that supplication, prayers, petitions, and thanksgivings be made.' First, supplication. Supplication is an urgent pleading to God. In supplication, we must never set knowledge before grace or we will only find frustration. We must, therefore, ask for grace first if we wish to obtain anything else. With God's grace, we will know how to act."

Anthony pressed Elias' hands against his own chest. The gauntness over the man's heart, contrasted with his bloated belly, startled and dismayed Elias. Francis had suffered the same strange combination of emaciation and swelling before he died.

Anthony's voice was a gentle plea. "Oh, Lord, give us the grace to follow You as You would have us do and to know You as You would have Yourself be known."

He lowered the hands while still holding them. "Prayer is the expressly affectionate state of a person united to God. During prayer, we speak to God in a familiar and respectful manner and enjoy God's presence as long as His grace allows."

Elias felt his hands being lifted skyward. "Blessed be You, O Lord, our God, the Son of God. We, the children of Zion, exult in our heart and rejoice in our work because You have given us the Spirit of Grace Who teaches us to show forth His justice to each and every person. May You, the Holy Spirit, You Who are the Love of the Father and the Son, cover the multitude of our sins by Your charity. Oh, to You, Lord, be honor and glory forever."

Anthony's words faded but his hands did not lower. For long moments, in the silence of the night, the men paused, their hands and faces lifted to the sky, the leaves far above them receding into blackness.

Finally Anthony lowered his hands. "Petition is any prayerful attempt at obtaining some of life's temporal needs. In petition, God approves the good will of the petitioner but still does what He judges better. When we ask in faith for anything in particular, we must always submit our own will to the will of God. We must pray with childlike faith and never cling stubbornly to our demands, for we do not know what is truly necessary or good for us in temporal matters, but our Heavenly Father does know."

Anthony placed Elias' hands into the weary friar's lap. Then Elias felt a firm press of fingers against his soft, leather shoes, fingers pressing into, curling around, his feet.

"Oh, Father, my Brother Elias suffers from pains in his feet and legs. If it be Your will, Lord, relieve him of his pain. Your will for him be done, Oh Lord."

The pressure increased, then was lifted. Elias felt his hands again taken up. "Thanksgiving is an unfailing and steadfast turning of a good will to God, even if at times there is no external giving of thanks, nor any inner affection, or even if given in a sluggish way. This is the charity which never fails; it is praying without ceasing and giving thanks always."

Again Anthony raised his hands and Elias' in them. His voice cried out, "Dearest Father, how can we ever thank You enough for the gift of Yourself? Lord Jesus, You will send Your Spirit to be with Brother Elias on his journey tomorrow; You will ever call him as he prays in his cell. O Divine Father, You turn humiliation and pain to Your purpose. You heal the wounded soul and forgive. Help us conceive the spirit of salvation and bring to birth through a sorrowful heart ourselves as heirs to eternal life. May we merit to drink from You, Lord, the River of Living Water, so that we may rejoice together with You in heavenly Jerusalem. Grant us this, You Who are blessed, glorious, laudable, lovable, sweet, and immortal through all centuries. And let us shout, Amen. Alleluia!"

As Anthony dropped his hands, his grip tightened on Elias' fingers. "My Brother, can you pray like that? Supplication. Prayer. Petition. Thanksgiving. Will you try? Will you pray for me, my Brother?"

"I will try."

Anthony shook Elias' hands heartily. "Good. Then come. I will help you to your cell. I brought some bread. You must eat or you will not have the strength for your journey."

▬ ▬

FIVE MONTHS LATER, as the leaves showed tints of red and yellow and the air around Elias' cell at Cortona grew nippy with autumn, a letter arrived.

"My dear Brother Elias, Pope Gregory has spoken. Francis' testament is not binding as he did not consult the ministers before writing it, and one minister may not bind another. We may have the use of houses to live in as well as furniture and books, as long as these are owned by another. Money may be accepted through an intermediary for future necessities.

"My brother, you see that our Order is changing. But Father Francis, who lived in utter poverty, possessed as well poverty of spirit. With great effort and deep faith, it is possible to retain poverty of spirit amid any circumstances. No matter what we think of the pope's decree, we must do as Father Francis always did and humbly submit to the decision of the Vicar of Christ.

"I continue to pray for you daily. Please continue to pray for me.

"Brother Anthony"

Elias read the letter twice. If Francis' testament was not binding, then what was? The brothers whom Francis had wanted to live in utter poverty were now going to become well-housed, secure monks just like every other Order. This was not what Francis had wanted. This was not what Francis had said Christ had revealed to him.

Even in his cell, Elias felt the chill of winter stinging his face through the beard that he was growing as a penance. Now he felt a chill touch his heart. If only he had Anthony's faith and trust!

Anthony wanted Elias to submit everything to God. Elias had tried. He had prayed. But he could not give himself totally to the Lord. If he did, God might swallow him.

As it was, Elias was gone and forgotten in this out of the way cell. If he gave God his all, he might perish here in nothingness. He could not stand to be nothing. His gifts were too great, his intellect too keen. Surely God did not want him to bury himself.

But what did God want? Was it even possible to know? Francis had said that his testament was from Christ. Yet the pope, Christ's Vicar, had rejected it. Had Christ spoken to Francis? Or had Francis misunderstood? Or had the pope? Had the Rule and testament been good for their time but not good for this time? Suppose Francis were a fraud. Suppose the visions that he claimed to have were spawned by illness or imagination. Suppose the *stigmata* were self-inflicted, Francis' own unique way to experience bodily Christ's passion.

Elias shuddered with doubt that churned nauseously in his belly. How could he be certain of anything but himself? How could anyone know the mind of God?

Someday Elias' penance would end. Someday he would leave this cell and return to work on the basilica that was rising now without him, and rising well judging by reports that came to his cell. He would pray, yes, while he was here. And he would pray when he left. But he would think as well. Anthony had said to seek grace first and not knowledge. But was not knowledge a gift of the Spirit? Grace was as intangible as breath, but knowledge could be pinned down in words or positions of honor or structures of stone. Elias could trust knowledge because he could see its results. But grace? Where was that in a testament that the pope rejected?

Elias read the letter again and then tossed it onto the small ash heap just outside his cell. Tonight, for warmth, he would burn a log or two and the letter would shudder and die in the flames. Perhaps Francis and Anthony and a few others could trust a God they could not see. But Elias would trust the only one he could depend on. Himself.

PART FIVE

The Final Month

# ᘓ 24 ᘔ

## Ezzelino da Romano

**Castle Fortress, Verona, Italy (May 1231)** ᘔ Astride his broad-chested, sturdy-legged brown steed, Ezzelino da Romano led his band of six knights within sight of his castle fortress. Behind him the mournful lowing of a cow almost overpowered the snorting of the lathered horses, whom, Ezzelino knew, could now smell their stable in the air. The animals wanted to be rubbed down and fed and were pulling against their bits in impatience to hurry on.

Seeing his castle's massive stone walls made Ezzelino want to hurry, too. Now that he and his band had completed their patrol of Lombardy, and had a bit of fun as well, Ezzelino was anxious to be out of his heavy chain mail. His eleven-year-old servant, Ariana, knew how to bathe his dark, black-haired body and then massage the weariness out of his bulging muscles. She would ease the tangles from his luxuriant, sandy hair, and delicately shave his stubbled face.

Ezzelino had killed a peasant who had bumbled from his cottage, half-asleep and probably half-drunk. Why else would he threaten six knights and Ezzelino, the lord of this territory, with a scythe? The threat was a good excuse to slaughter the man.

Ezzelino himself had taken care of the serf, riding up to him and thrusting him through with his sword.

A woman, probably the man's wife, and two small boys emerged at the door of the cottage. The woman shrieked. Ezzelino motioned to two of his soldiers. At once, they swooped down upon the cottage, killing the children and the woman. Then the men had dragged the four bodies into the cottage and set it afire.

Ezzelino reined his horse to the pasture around back where he had spotted a tan cow, her udder plump with milk and her youngster. Sliding off his horse, he had ambled over to the big-eyed, trusting calf. The wobbly-legged creature had let him approach and fondle its broad head while its mother watched. With a swift stroke, Ezzelino had slit the little beast's throat and drained the blood while its curious mother looked on.

When the knights rounded the barn as they sought Ezzelino, he called, "torch the building." With smoke rising from both cottage and barn, Ezzelino had flung the calf, its tongue dripping blood, over a knight's horse and then mounted his own. The cow, he knew, would follow her infant. And she did, all the way to Ezzelino's castle where she would join his herd.

—◆—

Ezzelino lay on his belly, uncovered, his left hand folded under his left cheek, a red silk pillow under his head. His right arm dangled over the rim of the dais on which he lay, his fingers dallying with the soft, droopy ears of a large, black dog that snoozed beside him on an auburn wool rug.

Golden-haired Ariana, just on the verge of womanhood, knelt beside the dog, her slender fingers kneading the tension out of Ezzelino's well-scrubbed shoulders. She would work her way across his arms, down his back and buttocks to his heavily muscled thighs and calves. Finally she would massage the soles of his feet, rubbing sweet perfume into every muscle of his perfectly clean body as she worked. Then he would roll over and she would repeat the process.

When Ariana had completed her task, she would help him into clean silken garments, then bow to take her leave. Before dismissing her, Ezzelino would slip into her tender hands a few almond cakes as a special treat. She would smile and say, as she always did, "You are a good master, Lord Ezzelino." And she meant it. In Ezzelino's castle, every female remained a virgin until her wedding night and loyal to her husband thereafter. If not, the unchaste parties were killed.

Virginity was honorable, so Ezzelino insisted on chastity and practiced it himself. Even though he embraced no religion, he protected the *Cathars* and agreed with their emphasis on purity. If Ezzelino caught anyone, even his most capable knight, violating a woman, he would slaughter the assaulter on the spot. He followed this policy into battle and had personally cut down more than one knight whom he caught raping a captured woman. To take a woman's life, even to take it brutally, was typical in war, but to take her honor was criminal.

Ariana's fingers massaged Ezzelino's lower back. He closed his eyes and sighed. How good to be master of Lombardy! The boy who had once considered himself too short and squat to be a knight was now the terror of his region. He grinned at the thought. He, a terror? When he was a child, he had dreamed of being as powerful as his father and grandfather, both of whose names were the same as his. Now, in his late thirties, he had far surpassed his dreams, for he had retained the cities that his family had controlled and had brought others under his dominion.

Ezzelino's father disapproved of his son's lust for power. What did he know, he who had gone mad in his old age? Ezzelino well remembered the day when his father, who in his youth would fight a man to the death in revenge, announced to his family that power was empty. Only weakness before God, he told Ezzelino and his other children, was strength enough to fulfill the soul. Ezzelino understood not a word. Struggling with bitterness and anger, he bid his father farewell as the man whom he emulated left his family and his castle to become a poor, black-robed monk. The Church of St. Donatus near the bridge of Bassano was a constant reminder of his father's foolishness, for Ezzelino the monk had given that church to the followers of Francis, the now-canonized friar of Assisi.

Ezzelino would never go soft. He resumed the battles that his father had abandoned. One after the other, the towns of Lombardy fell to Ezzelino's men. With each victory, more barons and lords grew thin in his scattered dungeons. More peasants and clergy trembled at his approach. More tales of his army's bloodshed spread across the region, making the taking of successive towns easier. Nobles and religious were persuaded to align with him rather than risk imprisonment or death. Ezzelino earned nicknames: "The Tiger," "The Ferocious," "The Devil." He loved them.

Grinning, Ezzelino scratched the dog's bony head. *Ah, you serve me,* he thought, *and I serve me. How right! All-powerful people serve themselves, even if they pretend to serve others.*

He thought of Frederick II, head of the Roman Empire. Frederick was a fine example of self-interest. But he went about his dealings in ways that Ezzelino despised.

Ezzelino respected his emperor's power and military prowess, but he disdained his person. To Ezzelino, the fair, reddish-haired emperor was a lecher and a hypocrite. Frederick had two wives, both of them now dead, but whispers of his trysts with this or that maiden, even when married, filtered to Verona. Yet Frederick pretended piety, attending Mass, carrying the papal banner, fawning on the pope.

Despite his cleverly worded promises, Frederick never actually followed the pope's bidding if it conflicted with his own goals. Like Ezzelino, he regularly consulted astrologers rather than prayer. Their advice and his own insight guided Frederick's schemes.

Emperor Frederick had continuously deceived Pope Honorius III, promising help with this or that crusade or papal project without following through. After Honorius's death in 1227, crusaders thronged the ports of Apulia to set sail for the Holy Land. They found a lack of ships but an abundance of plague. Falling ill himself, Frederick, who had promised to sail in August, postponed the crusade until spring. The new pope, Gregory IX, did not accept his excuse and promptly excommunicated him.

No matter. Eager to expand his empire, Frederick sailed from Brindisi for the Holy Land in June 1228. Peacefully through treaties, he secured the Holy Land for himself and for Christianity, entering Jerusalem in March 1229. At the Savior's tomb, he placed the crown on his own head. As the self-crowned, rather than papal-crowned, king of Jerusalem, Frederick considerably increased his popularity in the empire while making the pope look foolish. The excommunicated emperor continued to expand his territory and consolidate his power while pretending to be a pious man wronged by a corrupt papacy.

Unlike Frederick, Ezzelino was too honorable to use deceit to gain power. He refused to pretend service to a legate of a Church in which he did not believe. Nor did he pretend to embrace the beliefs of the *Cathars,* although he was in sympathy with their ideals. Ezzelino's loyalty lay with living mortals, not with a crucified God.

Unlike other lords who made and broke alliances for personal gain, Ezzelino's fidelity never shifted, for he made no alliances unless he meant to keep them. Loyalty was one of the strongest traits

of the da Romano family. Two hundred years earlier, Ezzelino's an-
cestors had come to Lombardy from Germany in the suite of Emperor Conrad II. Ever since, the family had remained loyal to the
emperor. Ezzelino's father had ridden and dined with Emperor
Frederick's predecessor, Otto IV. Ezzelino had secured Lombardy
for Frederick. The victory had not been easy.

Some cities were difficult to control. Ever loyal to the pope, Padua was one. Ezzelino's grandfather, Ezzelino I, known as "the stam-
merer," had been a citizen of Padua and had built the exquisite
palace of Santa Lucia. Ezzelino's father, Ezzelino II, had been friendly to the city. But as Ezzelino III consolidated his alliance with the excommunicated emperor, Padua increasingly allied with the pope.

Ezzelino had a plan. For the time being, he would let Padua
alone. Peace would relax the city's vigilance. Friar Anthony, whom
Ezzelino had heard of but had never heard speak, made the city his
home. The friar would continue to exhort the citizens to lay down
their arms. Soon the Paduans would forget how to fight. Their
peacefulness would play into Ezzelino's hands. When the Paduans
least expected attack, Ezzelino would launch a surprise and vicious
assault and secure his control. He would, of course, succeed. No
god could hold this "devil" at bay.

＊ ＊

EZZELINO WAS SITTING AT TABLE, enjoying a hearty meal with the
dozen knights who headed his companies. Each knight used a gold-
en wine goblet and bowl, all pilfered from various barons and lords.
The wine was part of the tithe Ezzelino demanded from the citizens
of the March of Treviso.

The veal soup they ate was one of Ezzelino's favorite dishes. The
chef had boiled in its mother's milk the tan calf whose throat Ezzelino had slit three days earlier, then added some parsley, carrots, and
a bit of salt. Ezzelino was half way through eating his second bowlful
when a servant approached through the doorway to the entrance
hall. He strode up to Ezzelino and bowed low.

"Lord Ezzelino, a friar requests entrance into the castle."

Ezzelino sopped a hunk of bread into his soup. "A friar? You
mean two."

"No, my lord. One."

Ezzelino turned to his knights. "Don't the friars travel in pairs?" They all agreed.

"Only one friar, my lord," the servant repeated.

Ezzelino popped the dripping bread into his mouth. Swift visions of clergy whom he'd personally disemboweled flashed through his mind. The friar was either a fool or a saint to come to Ezzelino alone. What should he do to this one?

"Show him in," Ezzelino said.

The ruddy, obese friar who walked into the banquet hall strode directly to Ezzelino. Breathing heavily, he bowed at the waist, then spoke. "I have come to request the release of Ricciardo, Count of San Bonifacio, and the other prisoners whom you are holding." The bold request was spoken gently but firmly.

Ricciardo? Ezzelino burst into loud laughter. "You come to me requesting the release of my brother-in-law? Since when do friars involve themselves in family matters?"

"Count Ricciardo and his men have been in your prison for four years. This is a matter of justice, not a family dispute."

"It is justice only in the eyes of the nobles who ally themselves against our emperor. Which of them sent you here? My uncle Tiso perhaps? And how holy is that family of Camposampiero?" Ezzelino spat out the words. "Surely you have heard how courteously Tiso's brother treated my mother."

The friar stood blank faced.

"So you have not heard." Ezzelino thought quickly. Should he mention his father's first wife, Speronella, who ran away from home after his father had commented on the beauty of another woman whom he had seen bathing? No. He would go on to Cecilia. "Count Tiso's brother, Gerard, ravished the woman who was mother to me. This is how the nobility, so loyal to your holy Church, behave. Now I have another count in prison. I have robbed Ricciardo of his home, it is true, but not of his honor. The noble Gerard took both from the Lady Cecilia."

"Neither Count Ricciardo nor the other prisoners whom you are holding had anything to do with Gerard," the friar calmly said. "They are not responsible for the vicious crime against your mother."

"I offered them freedom. If Ricciardo deeds to me his well-armed castle, they can all go free today."

"That is an unreasonable demand. In God's name, I beg you to free those men."

Ezzelino looked directly at the friar. "In God's name," he repeated with a snigger, "no."

"I have come to ask. You have refused to grant. God will give you mercy only if you extend it to others," the friar said.

Ezzelino chuckled. "Mercy? Do you know who I am?"

"Who does not know the devil of Lombardy?"

"Is that what you call me?"

"That is what you are called throughout this region."

"And what do you call me?"

"A rebellious child of God. A sinner on his way to hell. A man for whom Christ died to save." The reprimand was given as courteously as a compliment.

Ezzelino dipped another hunk of bread into his soup and held it out to the friar. "Have some. You look like you enjoy a good meal."

The friar shook his head.

"Why not have a taste?"

"I want no food gained by bloodshed."

Ezzelino dropped the bread into his bowl. "Do you know that if I snap my fingers any one of these knights will slay you in an instant?"

"I know it."

"Perhaps you would prefer torture."

"Whatever the Lord permits, I will accept."

Ezzelino gazed into the friar's black eyes, looking for some unsteadiness that would denote fear. He found none. But he caught something else. The face was gaunt, the eyes hollow, with dark circles beneath them. He studied the man, his swollen bare feet and ankles, his long, fat fingers clutched together over a protruding belly. The friar was breathing too deeply. This was not healthy obesity. This was illness. Far advanced.

"How did you get here?" Ezzelino asked.

"I walked."

"From where?"

"From Padua."

Padua. His primary rival. He might have known. Ezzelino marveled. How had the friar come this far without collapsing? He motioned for the knight across the table from him to yield his chair. The knight rose. "Sit," Ezzelino commanded the friar. The man obeyed.

"I have heard that Friar Anthony stays at Padua."

"I am he."

Ezzelino crossed his arms on his chest and nodded. "So the saint comes to the devil."

Anthony smiled slightly. "I do not say that either of those terms are correct."

Ezzelino liked this friar's directness. He decided to humor him. "What, other than releasing the prisoners, do you want me to do?"

"Turn away from sin to life."

Of course, a friar would say that. But why did he not raise his voice in condemnation as other friars did? Ezzelino tipped backward in his chair, his hands steadying himself on the table. "Why should I?"

"Because if you do not, you will die in your sins and will be forever condemned to hell. Look at me. I am suffering from a disease called dropsy. Dropsy causes an abnormal accumulation of water in the body. One of the symptoms of this sickness is an unquenchable thirst. The more water I drink, the more thirsty I become."

Anthony placed his puffy hands on either side of Ezzelino's muscular ones. "You see how dropsy has misshapen me. Dropsy is fittingly compared to a person's addiction to power and greed." Anthony looked directly into Ezzelino's eyes. "Power for power's sake and greed for worldly possessions inflict dropsy on the soul, misshaping it and producing in it a thirst which cannot be quenched. Am I not right, Lord Ezzelino?" The tone of the question was as mild as a caress.

Ezzelino stared at the friar who had read his very soul.

"Greed and power are bottomless pits. They hold the soul imprisoned like an enemy in a besieged fortress. Solomon says, 'When a sinner enters the depth of sin, he holds everything in contempt.' Loving sin, he has no hope of future glory."

Anthony leaned toward Ezzelino. "Today I came to ask you to release prisoners who have given up hope of freedom. Suppose that you and not they were in prison. And suppose that you heard that the man who would release you had finally come. Would you not leap for joy? Most certainly you would."

Anthony placed his puffy hands on Ezzelino's. The friar's touch was gentle and warm, the voice earnest with concern. "Well, Lord Ezzelino, you are in prison. You are in the prison of sin and there is only one who will release you. The Lord Jesus has come to release you from the devil's power and from unending imprisonment in hell."

Ezzelino had heard enough. He would see just how peaceful this priest would remain.

Impetuously, he threw off Anthony's hands. Leaping to his feet, Ezzelino rounded the table and approached the friar from the side. Anthony rose to face him. Ezzelino's hand flew to his waist where it gripped the hilt of his sword. He scrutinized the friar as a wolf stares down a cornered doe, waiting for some sign of fear before lunging to attack.

The friar stood unflinching, his gaze locked on Ezzelino, his face calm. Ezzelino could not bluff this man.

Ezzelino let out a low whistle of defeat. The game had gone on long enough. Suddenly he ripped his belt from his waist and spun it around his neck like a noose. With exaggerated gestures, he bowed to the floor as he thrust the belt toward Anthony with a grand flourish. Then he raised his head to the friar, black eyes fixing coldly on black eyes. "You want me to put my head in a noose, to bow to your God, and to become His slave?" Ezzelino paused and furrowed his brow. "Never. You are right. I am a prisoner of greed and power. And I love it. The only god I know is me."

Ezzelino whipped the belt from his neck and threw it to the floor. He jumped to his feet as his anger gave way to gratitude. By some act of grace, he had not killed the friar. Had he murdered him, all of Lombardy would have risen against the man who slaughtered their saint.

"Show him safely out," Ezzelino commanded the nearest knight. Then, impulsively, he grabbed one of the golden wine goblets and held it toward Anthony. "For you."

Anthony shook his head. "No, Lord Ezzelino." His voice approached a whispered sob. "The only thing gained by bloodshed that I want is your soul. Christ shed His Blood for that. I will pray for you."

As he watched Anthony follow the knight through the doorway, Ezzelino thought of his own father. "Only in weakness before God is there strength," he had said. Today Ezzelino understood what his father had meant.

## ❧ 25 ❧

## *Count Tiso da Camposampiero*

**Camposampiero, Twelve Miles Outside Padua, Italy (May 1231)** ❧
As he mounted a gray-speckled horse at his estate's stable, Count
Tiso da Camposampiero resembled a stablehand himself. Nearly as
good looking now as he was fifty years ago, the white-haired gentleman was comfortably dressed in a dull ivory-colored tunic, coarse
workman's breeches, and gray stockings bandaged about his legs
with lengths of rag. He did not care how common he looked. He
was off to work, and he was eager to begin.

The count's old heart was singing with joy as he turned his horse
down one of the narrow, rutted roads that led to the hermitage of the
Friars Minor on the edge of Tiso's estate, Camposampiero. The saint
was coming to Camposampiero! Coming to stay at the hermitage.

Anthony had preached daily in Padua until May 11, Pentecost,
and then for a short time thereafter. As the grain ripened in the
fields, he ceased preaching and dismissed his hearers to begin the
harvest. He had retired to St. Mary's convent in the heart of the city
to work solely on his "Sermons on the Saints," which Cardinal Ri-
naldo dei Conti, bishop of Velletri and Ostia, had commissioned. A
few days ago, in a moment of inspiration, Tiso conceived a plan. He
rode into Padua to invite Anthony to leave St. Mary's and stay at
Camposampiero.

Anthony had been to the Camposampiero hermitage a few
times. Here, twelve miles outside of Padua, he was left in relative
peace, whereas at St. Mary's he was constantly swamped by visitors
and by requests, which he never denied, to visit the ill and the

dying. If he came to Camposampiero, he could tranquilly work on his sermons. Anthony needed a respite.

At the not so subtle hinting of Tiso and other nobles of Padua, Anthony had just returned from a failed mission to the tyrant Ezzelino. Anthony's journey was an effort of last resort, for the Paduan nobles who had employed force of arms against the "devil of Lombardy" had been rebuffed. Ezzelino had denied Anthony's request to release the Paduan supporter, Count Ricciardo, and the others whom Ezzelino had imprisoned. If Ezzelino's heartlessness depressed Tiso, it must have devastated Anthony. Only God knew what the prisoners suffered in Ezzelino's chains. Neglect? Filth? Starvation? Torture? Because of Anthony's failure, the prisoners might die.

In addition to dealing with this disappointment, Anthony was suffering in body. Since his first arrival in Padua in 1227, the friar's body had bloated and weakened. For recovery of mind and body, Anthony needed to rest.

So Tiso had gone to Padua. He found Anthony in his cell at St. Mary's, papers and books strewn about, a parchment before him, pen in hand.

Anthony was receptive to Tiso's invitation. "But I must first ask permission of my minister provincial," he said.

"Of course, he will give it," Tiso said.

Anthony nodded. "Most likely he will." Then he had paused. "And I must also ask permission of you for something, Brother Tiso. Do you remember the giant walnut tree I once showed you near the hermitage? I shall have to build a cell for myself if I am allowed to stay at Camposampiero for any length of time. Would you mind if I built it in that tree?"

Mind? Tiso would have permitted Anthony to build twenty cells in twenty trees.

The walnut tree that Anthony had in mind was a beauty. Tiso himself had always admired the giant tree from whose three massive trunks spread six great branches that lifted upward like a crown. One day, not two months ago when he and Anthony were walking in the forest, Anthony had paused beneath the walnut.

"Ah, Count Tiso, what magnificent trees God has grown on your estate!" Anthony had thrown his arms open wide as if to embrace the entire glen. "Every time I visit here, the voices of the trees beckon me. But this one calls the loudest. See how Brother Walnut lifts his hands to the Father in praise. 'Come,' he says, 'come and sit within my palm and cry out with me, Glory to you, Mighty Lord!' And then I must say to Brother Walnut, 'My brother, I may be as drab as the birds who sit within your boughs, but, alas, I am not one. So I shall sing to my Lord from the ground.'"

Anthony had turned to Tiso with a grin. "My Brother, don't you sometimes wish that you were but a poor sparrow, so dull and small that no one took the least notice of you? You would be free of all clamor and bother, and you could fly to a tree such as this one and hide away in its branches and sing forever of God." For long moments, Anthony had gazed at the tree, then, sighing and lovingly patting the bark, he had resumed his walk in the forest with Tiso.

Yes, Anthony would be glad to come to Camposampiero and build himself a cell in that tree. Anthony had written to his minister provincial, asking permission to accept Tiso's invitation. Surely an angel must have carried his letter to the provincial's office, so swiftly did the positive reply return.

Three days from now, Brother Roger, a friar from St. Mary's, would arrive in advance of Anthony to see that all was in readiness for his arrival. Two days later, Anthony and his companion, Brother Luke, would come.

Oh, Tiso would surprise all three of them! As he reined his horse down a trail that led deep into the forest, he felt as giddy as a schoolboy who secretly planned to send violets to his sweetheart.

Anthony's words had given Tiso so much peace and joy that the count deeply loved the man who had taught him Who Love is. Now he would do an act of love. He himself would build Anthony his tree house, a much sturdier and larger house than Anthony would ever build for himself.

When Anthony first came to Padua on Ash Wednesday in 1227, Tiso was a different man than he was today. At that time, he and his supporters took part in the fierce wars that raged in Lombardy. Cities were divided between their loyalty to the pope and to Emperor Frederick, who was on a collision course with the Church. In 1227, Tiso's nephew, Ezzelino, had swept into nearby Verona in a surprise attack, securing the city for Frederick and setting up his headquarters there. Those nobles loyal to the pope who did not flee in time were imprisoned. Among them were Count Ricciardo of San Bonifacio, Ezzelino's brother-in-law, whom Tiso held in high esteem.

Shortly after Ricciardo's imprisonment, Ezzelino stormed the Camposampiero family's Castle Fonde and took away in chains Tiso's young grandson, William. Tiso responded. Gathering his followers and other nobles of Padua, he struck at Ezzelino, forcing him to relinquish first the child and then the castle. With Ezzelino's help, the people of Treviso returned to seize the archbishop's property. Again, Tiso and the other nobles of Padua marched against them and forced the return of the possessions. Thus, the battles went back and forth. Such was Tiso's life in those days when he believed that God often advanced His cause through weapons and war. He no longer believed that. Anthony, the man of peace, had taught him, and much of Padua, otherwise.

For, beginning in 1227, Anthony preached in Padua and the other towns in the Marches of Treviso. People crowded to hear him. So many men wanted to join the Friars Minor that Anthony founded St. Mary's monastery for them within the center of Padua. From Padua, Anthony moved to the surrounding towns and then south to Florence. By the end of 1229, he was back in Padua, living at St. Mary's.

By 1229, Padua and other nearby towns in which Anthony preached began to change. More and more citizens flocked to hear the friar whom they openly called a saint. Following his sermons, other friars, some of them burly, would surround Anthony to keep the crowd from crushing him. The friars would assemble the mob in a sort of order so that only one or two had access to the man at a time. Sometimes a person, almost always a woman, would slip a scissors from her gown to snip off a portion of Anthony's habit as a relic. These were the only people whom he sent briskly away.

Notorious sinners and well-known heretics repented and returned to the faith. Conceding to their request to live together in community as they expiated their sins, Anthony bid them purchase a home in the town. Here they built a chapel to the Virgin of the Dove. Occasionally, Tiso saw one of these penitents, dressed in a long, rough, ash-colored tunic with a cord about the waist.

Others converted, too. By the hundreds, people threw their weapons at the friar's feet.

Some gave up everything and joined the Friars Minor or the Poor Ladies, the second Order which Francis of Assisi had founded. Many more continued to live in their homes while embracing the Rule of the Continent Brothers and Sisters, a Rule given by

Francis in 1221 to lay men and women. Being received into this Order of penitents entailed a permanent commitment and a religious vow. Part of the obligation was the refusal to bear or possess weapons and to refrain from oaths of loyalty to any human party. Thus, these penitential followers of Francis of Assisi, their faith renewed through Anthony's preaching, deprived the warring nobles of support.

As a result of the men and women penitents of the region, peace came to reign in the Marches of Treviso.

With peace came tolerance for the poor. Prior to Anthony's arrival, moneylenders in Padua resorted to usury to gain easy riches. With interest on borrowed money at twenty percent to thirty percent and some usurers charging as high as seventy-five-percent interest, debtors abounded. Those unable to pay were stripped of their property, condemned to punishment, or jailed. Anthony spoke forcefully and frequently against usury, pride, and avarice. The story was proclaimed that in Florence he had preached at the funeral of a usurer on the text, "Where your treasure is, there shall your heart be." His listeners were so moved that they visited the dead man's treasure trove and discovered a human heart, still warm, among the coins.

The rumor and the sermons changed the city. Those who had borrowed money sold their property to repay their debts. Others who had acquired ill-gotten goods threw them, weeping, at the saint's feet. Many more made two- and three-fold restitution to those whom they had cheated. On March 15 of this very year, Padua enacted a statute stating that "no one, henceforth, should be held in prison for money debts, past, present, or future, if he forfeited his goods. And this applies to both debtors and their bondsmen. This statute has been enacted at the instance of the venerable brother and blessed Anthony, confessor of the Order of Friars Minor."

Within the past few months, scores of debtors, clad only in shirt and hose, had each three times sat tearfully on the blaming stone in the Piazza delle Erbe. Before a hundred witnesses, each had proclaimed, "I give up my goods," invoking the statute that bore Anthony's name.

Anthony, who had wrought the conversion of a city, had also wrought the conversion of a count. When Anthony first arrived in Padua, Tiso paid him little attention. Other friars had preached in the city, among them the Friar Preacher Albert, son of a German count. Albert had been educated at the University of Padua and his uncle, whom Tiso knew well, lived in the city. The young Friar Albert's preaching converted many, but Tiso heard only two of his sermons.

Tiso was a busy man. Certainly God knew that he had little time to spare for spiritual matters. Tiso was embroiled in all the duties that naturally go with being the head of one of the wealthiest and most powerful families of the region. Affairs of his family, estate, city, and territory consumed his days. Sometimes he felt like a rabbit who, in a futile attempt to sample the entire garden, skips from beets to cabbages to carrots without ever fully finishing off any particular plant.

Judging by the world's standards, Tiso was a good man. He treated his servants fairly. He attended Sunday Mass and gave alms generously. He confessed and received the Eucharist yearly as was required. He had even given the followers of Francis of Assisi a corner of his vast estate on which to build a hermitage, a quiet place for them to rest after their busy affairs in Padua.

Tiso not only supported his Church, but he also supported his city. He lent its governing commune money and saw that the nobility were suitably protected by the statutes. He also loaned money to individuals at a reasonable interest and was patient in waiting to be repaid. Unlike some of the other nobility, Tiso had only a few debtors in prison, and they were irresponsible, lazy wretches who had incurred immense debts.

When Anthony had come to Padua, Tiso had wanted to hear him preach, yet could not seem to find the time. But Tiso's friends spoke so highly of Anthony's sermons that curiosity got the better of the count. Time or no time, he had to go to listen for himself.

Anthony's sermons troubled Tiso. They pointed out to him his spiritual emptiness. So Tiso increased his prayers. Beneath his silks, he wore a hair shirt. He began to attend Mass a few times during the week. He invited the friar to lodge at his home either in Padua or at the hermitage at Camposampiero, and Anthony frequently took advantage of the invitation.

But no matter what he did, Tiso could not name or suppress the growing uneasiness in his soul. He was not a great sinner. Why were the friar's words making him so uncomfortable? Until two months ago, Tiso had struggled with these feelings that sometimes, for weeks on end, died down like wilting flowers. But then, just when Tiso had convinced himself that he really was a good man who had given God so much, a flash of insight at Mass or during his prayers would flood him with a cloudburst of grace. Then the dying questions in his soul would revive and spring up, sturdier than ever.

Tiso was a good man. A busy man. An important man. Surely God did not want more of him than he was already doing.

This year for Lent, Anthony proposed to preach daily. On Ash Wednesday, Tiso had gone to hear him. With countless others clustered at Mass, Tiso had slowly moved his way toward the friar to receive the ashes. As he did so, God's words burned into his brain: "Remember, man, that you are dust and unto dust you shall return."

Tiso began to tremble with expectancy. Something about the average-sized, corpulent friar in the drab, gray robe, about the motley crowd, about Tiso's own inner unease, whispered to his soul, "Tiso, after this Lent, you will never be the same."

As Tiso knelt before Anthony, his head bowed to receive a cross of ashes on its crown, he felt the friar's sleeve brush his cheek. It thrilled him as would the touch of an angel's wing.

Thereafter, Tiso went to hear Anthony preach as often as his business allowed. The words that he heard were like a continual, gentle spring drizzle. Day after day, it watered the blossoms of grace in his soul, coaxing new, green life from the barren landscape.

Even now, as he rode at an easy canter toward the hermitage, he remembered Anthony's renewing words.

"If the spirit does not put aside anxious care about temporal things, it never comes near to God. Those who are trapped in endless temporal concerns cause the burdens of sin and the weight of secular care to reach their souls. Temporal things are like a morning cloud. They are like nothing at all, but yet, like a cloud, they appear to be something. The morning cloud hinders our view of the sun, and the excess of temporal goods diverts the soul from thoughts of God."

Tiso, who daily was up early riding about the fields of his estate, had often seen the morning clouds that obscured the sun.

On another occasion, Tiso heard: "The unfruitful soul is suffocated by an abundance of temporal goods. It is then buried and pressed down by the great weight of its own evil ways. The rich man whom the evangelist Luke tells us was 'clothed in purple' was buried in the pains of the nether world because during his earthly life he buried himself in pleasures. Solomon says in Proverbs, Chapter 20, verse 17."

Tiso had gone home and looked up that verse and read it again: "'A man finds bread sweet when it is got by fraud, but later his mouth is full of grit.' The bread got by fraud is all worldly pomp and glory which deceptively asserts that it is something whereas it is nothing. This world's glory, because it is sweet to man's taste, will fill his mouth with the grit of fiery ash in eternal punishment where he will be unable to swallow."

For days after, Tiso could not eat sweet raisin bread without remembering Anthony's words.

And then, a third day, Christ Himself had called to Tiso in the holy friar's words. "The Lord said in Matthew, Chapter 19, verse 21, 'If you wish to be perfect, go and sell all that you have and give your proceeds to the poor. And come and follow Me.' To a person with charity and with a desire to share in the poverty of Christ, the Lord appears.

"For Christ says 'Follow Me.' You who have nothing, who have never possessed anything, follow Me. You who are weighed down with the troubles of life, follow Me. To follow Me, you must cast aside anything that will weigh you down or hold you back, for you will not be able to keep up with Me if you are burdened with extra weight. 'Whoever wishes to be My follower must deny himself,' renounce his own will, 'take up his cross' of denial and mortification 'each day' without ceasing, 'and follow in My steps.' That is what Christ meant when He said, 'Follow Me.'

"Since Christ alone knows the way, how reassuring are His words when He invites us to follow Him! When we follow Christ, we walk a very narrow path. It is the path of justice, poverty, and obedience, a path that Christ followed throughout His life. Although it is a narrow path of moral courage, one can walk along this path with great freedom. Although obedience and poverty appear to confine and restrict one's freedom, they actually liberate us from our chains and set us free. Whoever follows Jesus along the straight and narrow path will not be hampered by attachment to material things or by selfish dependence on His own will, both of which hinder and restrict spiritual progress.

"Follow Me and I will show you what 'eye has not seen, ear has not heard, nor heart of man conceived.' Follow Me and 'I will give you treasures out of darkness and riches that have been hidden away' and 'then you shall be radiant at what you see and your heart will throb and rejoice.' You will see 'God face to face, as He really is.' You will become radiant in body and soul; your heart will throb and overflow with wonder at the choirs of angels and the celestial kingdom of saints."

Tiso was old enough to see, only too clearly, the transitoriness of temporal goods and the approaching end of his earthly life. He realized that Anthony's clear call to follow Christ could possibly be the very last invitation that the count might receive. The total, evident joy and peace that radiated from Anthony and permeated his sermons filled Tiso with a desperate longing for Christ. But how could he, an old man, dispense with his riches and follow the call that each day burned more intensely in his soul? Finally, after three weeks of sermons, Tiso could no longer stand the relentless pain of a life grown burdensome and pointless. He invited Anthony to spend the night at his home within the city walls.

The night before that Tuesday on which Anthony was due to arrive, Tiso calmed his fluttering soul and slept nearly as soundly as the hound at the foot of his bed. But then, while the night was still and dark, he had awakened as suddenly as if someone had poked him with a stick. Eyes wide open, he stared into the darkness as all his fears and questions rose up in his soul like moths. They flew about his brain, alighting here and there, leaving him in agony. What did God want of him? What if it was too much to give? Should he change? How? What if he never reformed at all? Could he then live with himself in peace? If he did change, could he live with himself? Would the priest ask him to renounce all his comforts? Could he?

Each question seemed to spawn another and no answers came to swallow any of his wonderings. Finally, in desperation, he threw back his soft blankets and groped in the dark for his breeches that hung on the peg above his bed. He dressed quickly, as if pursued by demons, pulling on the silken garments that he had worn yesterday to a meeting with one of his notaries. He groped his way out of the room to the hallway and, taking one of the lamps with him, hurried through the hushed house, and slipped outdoors.

As Tiso knew they would, his thoughts seemed to scatter a bit in the vastness of the sleeping city. In his many years of business deals and legal wranglings, he had learned that problems that squeezed the life out of him in his bedroom always seemed smaller outdoors.

That Tuesday morning, the heavens were still black, but, just beyond the outlines of the houses, the most subtle shade of pink tinted the sky. Nothing stirred. Not a dog yelped. Not a rooster crowed. Not a maid scurried to market or tossed wastewater into the street. Using the lamp to guide him, Tiso walked through the dozing city.

*Oh, God,* he prayed, *I want Father Anthony to come, but I am afraid of what he will demand. Help me, Lord. What do You want of me?*

Heavy dew clung like glass droplets on the flowers and vines that fronted the wooden and stone houses. Even the garbage piled up here and there twinkled with radiance.

In a flash of insight, Tiso recalled Anthony's message of the previous day.

"Dew is like the Paraclete, the Spirit of Truth, that comes gently into the sinner's heart and cools the desires of the flesh."

Could the turmoil within him be the stirrings of God's Spirit?

Lost in thought, he stood still in the street, the light of his lamp playing over a scattering of discarded root tips and wilted greens tossed beside the curb. The dew sparkled on them, making them look almost like gems, but underneath the luster they were still rotting refuse. He saw within himself the Spirit of God, drenching and transforming his indifference, neglect of God, and immersion in the world. Beneath the glitter, in the lamp of a soul being renewed, he now could sense the rot.

From the house that fronted the decaying pile came a shriek that startled Tiso out of his pondering. Then another scream, a panting that ended in a cry and a low whimper. Then stillness. For a moment, he thought that an irate husband was beating his wife. But then he heard the voice again, a woman's voice, sharp with sudden pain. Rapid, agonized breathing. A squeal of surprise. A prolonged moan. And then a man's voice, gruff. "Hold on. A few more pushes, and you'll have him."

Tiso smiled. In the room above his head, a child was being born.

Anthony's words fell like dew upon his thoughts.

"Isaiah says, 'In Your presence, O Lord, we have conceived and have brought forth the spirit of salvation.'"

Was Tiso, too, in the process of giving birth?

"After it becomes pregnant with the Holy Spirit's grace, your soul feels distress because it is conscious of its sins. 'A woman, when she is in labor, has sorrow, because her hour has come.'"

Yes, his soul was straining to give birth, to bring the new man out of the old. There was only one way to do this, and it involved Father Anthony.

"The hour of birth is your hour of confession. Now your soul is sorrowful, expressing bitter groans, so that shamed for your sin, your soul might acknowledge it, weep over it, and in tears receive grace. There you will be delivered."

From the room above Tiso's head erupted a horrifying shriek, a long moan, and then a squeal of laughter. "Oh, my precious daughter. I wanted a daughter, doctor. We have all sons."

Tiso grinned as he imagined the woman holding to her breast her newborn.

"If the soul would endure the pain of labor, beyond a doubt it would rejoice at the birth. About this spiritual birth, the Lord says, 'There is joy in heaven over one sinner repenting.' For, as Isaiah says, 'The troubles of the past will be forgotten. Instead you will be glad and rejoice forever.'"

The woman in the room above him, the woman who had brought forth new life just beyond the dew-covered rot at Tiso's feet, rejoiced in her child. What her child would become she did not know. Yet God knew. Enough to have brought the babe forth and to leave the future of the child up to the Lord Who created her. Tiso had been struggling over the birth of his own new man and worrying over what the new man might be. It was enough for him to bring the babe forth and to let God determine his future.

That evening, Tiso, who had worried about whether he could confront the priest with his sins, told him all of them in great peace. By the dying embers of a fire in an ornately carved marble fireplace, Anthony had pronounced absolution and blessing. He had administered penance—twofold restitution of any ill-gotten gains, release of those whom he had imprisoned for debt, and daily attendance at Mass for the remainder of his life. And Tiso had invited him to spend more time at his house, both in Padua and at Camposampiero. The friar had agreed.

As the weeks of Tiso's conversion increased, so did the inspirations of the Holy Spirit. He began to think more and more about those known as penitents. In simplicity, charity, and holiness, these people gave God their life. The desire to surrender himself completely to God swelled in Tiso's heart. One day when Anthony visited the hermitage at Camposampiero, Tiso asked to speak to him about the matter. Together, the two of them had walked into the woods.

"Father, do you think I could become a penitent? I am old, much attached to the world, and feeble in resolve. I want to do this, but I wonder if I can."

"Ah, Count Tiso, you remind me of the women who went to the tomb of our Lord to anoint His body. The Holy Spirit drew them there, and they so wanted to do our Lord this service. But on the way, 'they were saying to one another, "Who will roll back the stone for us?" for it was a large stone, probably much larger than this one.'" Anthony put his bare foot on a lump of gray granite that protruded from the forest floor and rose about half the height of a man. "When they got to the tomb, Count Tiso, what did they find?"

"That the stone had already been rolled back."

"Yes. Now it would be difficult, in fact, I would say impossible, for you and I together to dislodge this boulder at our feet. Do you agree?"

"I have no idea how deep this goes into the ground. It is possible that not even a team of oxen could remove it."

Anthony nodded. "But a stone, probably larger than this one, was already removed when the women reached the tomb. The Holy Spirit did that." Anthony touched Tiso's arm. "My Count, you have proposed to become a penitent. This idea has not come from you but from the Spirit of God. Yet you say, 'Who will roll back the stone for me? Can I stand the severity of the religious life? Can I tolerate the frequent fasts, the simple dress, the voluntary poverty, the required daily prayers?' Do not be fearful, Count Tiso. The stone has already been rolled back. Like the angel who removed the stone for the holy women, the Holy Spirit has already removed the stone for you. The Spirit says to you, 'I will strengthen your weakness, make severity easy, and sweeten every bitterness with the balm of My love. See, the stone is rolled back. Come and enter the tomb where you will see the place in which your Savior was resurrected.'"

Tiso had looked at the boulder beneath Anthony's foot. He had looked at his own fearful heart. And he had leapt into the arms of God.

Now, as he approached the hermitage, Tiso did so as a penitent. He had exchanged his silks for humble, undyed, and inex-
pensive cloth, and his luxuriant fur capes for garments of lamb's
wool. All other adornments he had forsaken. He abstained from
meat three days each week, feast days excepted, and would fast
several times during the year. He prayed daily the seven Canoni-
cal Hours. Monthly he would confess and receive the Eucharist
thereafter. He engaged in several works of charity that included
visiting the sick weekly, giving alms freely, and assisting at the fu-
nerals of other members of his brotherhood. Moreover, he refused to bear weapons or to take oaths and, each day at evening,
he rethought his sins of the day and prayed for God's forgiveness.
Every month he met for divine services with other penitents
where words exchanged between them strengthened them in
their life of reform. And next year, he would be permanently received into their Order.

Tiso had never been happier. As the walnut tree came into view,
he laughed with delight. Now he would make Anthony happy.

Tiso had told two of his serfs to meet him at the tree. Both, four
decades younger than Tiso and muscular as oxen, were waiting beneath the walnut. Tiso knew exactly what he wanted. He reined in
his horse and tied him to a tree. Sliding off the saddle, he called
out, "A cell woven of reeds, with a sturdy floor and a gabled roof.
Spacious and water tight. And as high in the tree as we can make it.
Father Anthony will be writing his sermons there. He must be comfortable and protected."

The young men nodded. "We have brought the tools, my lord."

"He will have two friars to attend him," Tiso continued, "so I
want two additional cells, lower down in the tree and smaller, for
those two friars. They must be close enough to Father Anthony to
hear him call, but far enough away so as not to disturb him."

"It will not be difficult, my lord. The tree is large enough for
three cells."

So Tiso and the young men began to build. How Tiso worked!
He felt years younger as his hands cut and wove the reeds. The cells
must be just right. And, by the end of the day, they were. Tiso
walked around the finished cells, their floors level and smooth,
their little windows open to the breezes and the birds. Then he shut
the cells up tightly and hoped for rain.

Nature did not disappoint him. The following day, a storm blew up. Tiso, covered with a thick cape, rode up to the tree whose branches were tossing wildly in the wind. Tethering his horse, he climbed the sturdy ladder nailed into the trunk and visited the two smaller cells first. Their doors and shudders were securely shut, and inside, the floor was dry. Then, buffeted by the wind, Tiso pulled himself higher to Anthony's cell. He unfastened the door and went inside. The oratory shivered in the wind but held firm. Tiso felt every inch of wall and floor. Dry. Satisfied, he knelt on the floor and thanked God. He would not come up here again. From now on, the cell belonged to the saint.

# ✑ 26 ✑

## *Brother Luke Belludi*

**Road Outside the City, Padua, Italy (About May 30, 1231)** ✑
Through the smattering of trees that lined this narrow road out of
Padua, Brother Luke Belludi gazed at the slope of the grassy hill
that rose on his right. Halfway up the hill, a cluster of sheep grazed
in a lush, flower-dotted meadow. The slope was not especially steep
for someone in good health. But for Anthony?

"I want to see Padua for one last time," he had told Luke. But
should he climb this hill to view it? Just after Lauds, as dawn was
breaking, the two friars had left St. Mary's to begin their twelve-mile
journey to Camposampiero. Already, as the sun was climbing to its
zenith, Anthony's deep, labored breaths strained his lungs. They
still had miles to go.

Luke looked at his companion's haggard face, its skin dry and pale
as parchment. "Are you sure you want to climb, Brother?" Luke asked.

"I'll rest under this tree for a while," Anthony said, easing himself down. With the tree propping up his back, he sat with his legs
splayed out before him. "If I rest, I'll be able to make it."

Luke slipped from his own shoulder the wool pouch that held
Anthony's sermon manuscripts and breviary as well as his *Moral
Concordances* and *Commentary on the Psalms* that Anthony had written
for his own use. Today was the first day that Luke had ever carried
these precious burdens. Previously, Anthony had always insisted on
carrying them himself, flung over his left shoulder, as the two friars
had tramped from place to place to preach. It was not that Anthony
did not trust Luke to carry them; it was simply that he felt responsi-

ble for bearing his own burdens. But today Anthony's swollen legs could barely carry his body.

"I will carry the writings," Luke had told Anthony that morning. "It is difficult enough for you to walk without having to carry around more weight."

Anthony had conceded to the favor.

Luke placed the precious sermons next to him on the grass, then pulled his long legs up to his chin and tucked his habit around them. After wrapping his gangly arms around his legs, he rested his bony chin on his knees as he used to do when he was a boy.

Out of the corner of his eye, he glanced at Anthony. From beneath the friar's habit thrust bloated feet that joined legs as thick as logs beneath a tattered, gray drape. Anthony's hands were clasped over his distended abdomen and his head was tilting toward his bony right shoulder. Eyelids the color of a rain-battered sea drew closed. A charcoal blush encircled his deep brown eye sockets.

Anthony was snoring.

Luke felt a sense of relief. If Anthony slept, his heaving breaths might ease and the friar could possibly make the climb.

When the minister general had first assigned Luke to accompany the priest, Anthony had already been ill. The dropsy that had been swelling his abdomen now so inflated the man that, despite Anthony's continual fasting, his belly was as stretched as a glutton's and his ability to hurry was gone.

Luke reached over and gently tugged the hood of Anthony's tunic from behind the man's back. Pulling the hood over Anthony's brown neck, he carefully tucked its point over the tonsured head, pressing the fabric around Anthony's ears. Then, in a swift motion, he pulled up his own hood. Now the gnats would annoy neither man. Luke closed his eyes to rest.

Born near the dawning of the century, Luke had left behind the opulence of the Belludi family, who lived just outside Padua, to join the followers of Francis. Luke had been twenty years old at the time. Blessed Francis himself, whom Luke admired deeply, had clothed the young man. Now he accompanied another man whom he also held in high esteem.

As Anthony fulfilled his duties as provincial, Luke had traveled with him through the towns of the Romagna: Milan, Vercelli, Varese, Brescia, Breno, Lake Garda, and Mantua. On the roads, they had seen the common parade of clergy, friars, nobility, knights, farmers, and peasants, but also exquisite and strange creatures brought from Asia and Africa by the emperor. Elephants. Lions. Apes. Anthony noted these exotic beasts and sometimes used them to illustrate his sermons. If he but mentioned a leopard, wild cow, or rhinoceros, his curious audience was immediately attentive.

On their journeys, Anthony had pushed both men to their limits and sometimes beyond them. The priest had preached, prayed, established convents, welcomed novices, forgiven sins, shared alms with cripples and beggars, healed the ill, and raised the dead. In him, Luke had seen the intimate union of both the divine and the human.

In one town a woman approached the two friars. In her arms lay a pale, limp child whose legs were curled tightly to his chest as if in a death agony. The pallid, twisted body filled Luke with grief.

"Can you heal him, Brother?" Luke begged.

"I will bless him," Anthony said.

Making the sign of the cross over the child and his mother, Anthony sent the two away. The following morning, the woman approached the platform on which Anthony was preparing to preach. With quick, short steps, the child walked along beside her.

"Father!" the woman called out.

Anthony had raised his hand to silence her. Again making the sign of the cross over the twosome, he sent them off into the crowd with the words, "Give glory to God for His mercy."

Another time, a young man named Leonardo had come to Anthony for confession. As he did with all penitents, Anthony had listened patiently, given counsel and absolution, and sent the youth home. Not long afterward, word came to Anthony that Leonardo had cut off his foot. Anthony's face grew wan. "Precious Jesus, no!" he had whispered.

He and Luke had hurried to the young man's house where they found his weeping mother and the young man bleeding profusely from his stump.

Cradling Leonardo's face in his hands, Anthony had asked in a voice full of agony, "Leonardo, why did you do this?"

"Father," the trembling boy cried, "when I told you that I had kicked my mother, you said that the foot of him who does such a thing deserves to be cut off."

With bowed head, Anthony had moaned, in a voice so full of anguish that it startled even Luke, "Oh, Leonardo, my sincere penitent. Where is the foot?"

Leonardo pointed to a basket. Anthony lifted by its big toe the blue, bloody foot. With his eyes raised to heaven, he had knelt at Leonardo's side while pressing the foot to the stump. Then he closed his eyes and shuddered.

"My lady, quick, a rag," he had said.

The boy's sobbing mother grabbed a cloth from a peg on the wall and handed it to Anthony. "Tear it in strips, Luke," he had ordered.

Using a kitchen knife to help him, Luke had made some ragged bandages with which Anthony wrapped the foot and stump. When Anthony's bloody fingers slowly uncurled from the heel, the foot remained attached.

"Stay in bed, Leonardo. May God have mercy on you." Anthony blessed the young man, then took his hands in his own. "Leonardo, the body is God's temple. Never, never mutilate it. How I repent for having said what I did to you! Please forgive me."

Anthony bowed his head to the boy's hands. "Please forgive me."

The boy arched his eyebrows and glanced from Luke to his mother and back again to Luke. Timidly he slid one hand out from underneath Anthony's face and, with a quick, light movement, touched the priest's shoulder. Then he drew back his hand and held it to his chest as if unsure what to do with it.

His voice came in hesitant syllables. "That's all right, Father. I guess you didn't mean for me to really cut it off."

Anthony raised his head, his closed eyes fluttering open, a deep sigh escaping from his chest. "Let us pray, Leonardo." For long moments, the four in the house prayed together. Then Anthony rose to leave. "Do not remove that bandage for many weeks. I will continue to pray for your healing."

Many weeks later, when Leonardo undid the bandage, the foot remained attached. He had shown Anthony and Luke the huge, jagged scar that indicated where the foot had once been cut off.

On another occasion, Luke and Anthony had been part of a crowd gathered to hear an abbot of the Order of Black Friars. In his preaching, the abbot had quoted the speech of St. Paul to Dionysius and the other citizens of Athens.

"The God who made the world and everything in it, He Who is Lord of heaven and earth, does not live in shrines made by human hands, nor is He served by human hands, as though He needed anything, since He Himself gives to all mortals life and breath and all things. From one ancestor He made all nations to inhabit the whole earth, and He allotted the times of their existence and the boundaries of the places where they would live, so that they would search for God and perhaps grope for Him and find Him—though indeed He is not far from each one of us. For 'in Him we live and move and have our being': as even some of your own poets have said, 'For we too are His offspring.'"

As Anthony listened to these words, a great smile spread across his lips and his entire face seemed radiant with joy. He sank to his left knee, his right knee bent, his clasped hands resting on his right thigh, his face lifted to the sky. For the remainder of the sermon, he remained in this position, unmoving even when the preacher stopped speaking and the crowd dispersed. Luke held the curious back. "He is in ecstasy," Luke told them. Luke waited, standing guard, until Anthony lowered his gaze and stood.

"What did you see, Brother?" Luke had asked.

Anthony had raised his hand to his lips and had shaken his head. Luke did not ask again. Nor did he question subsequent ecstasies which were now becoming more frequent. Truly, sometimes Anthony seemed already to be living in heaven, but other times, like today, when Anthony's labored snoring indicated the progression of his disease, the man seemed very much mired in earth.

Anthony had pressed a rigorous schedule, finally coming to Padua where he had worked diligently on his sermons. He was still working on them; that's why Luke was carrying them to Camposampiero.

Luke had read parts of the sermons. "I have tried, insofar as divine grace imparted it to me and my poor little supply of knowledge responded, to establish a concordance," Anthony had written in the introduction. "While quite aware of my own insufficiency for accomplishing such a great and difficult labor, yet I let my fear and awe of the task be overcome by the prayers and the charity of the brothers who urged me on." Luke had smiled when he read that. He had been one of the encouraging brothers.

Later Anthony had added, "Oh, dear Brothers, I am the least among you, your brother and servant Anthony. For your consolation, for the edification of the faithful, and for the remission of my sins, I have written to the best of my ability this work on the Gospel. Thus I ask that when you read these pages, you offer up to God the memory of me, your brother."

Luke swallowed a lump that rose suddenly in his throat. Would only Anthony's writings soon be all that was left of him? Oh, Luke would read them and pray for the man who was napping at his side.

Anthony had worked on those sermons until Lent and then had preached daily throughout the forty days. When Luke had tried to dissuade him from this brutal schedule, Anthony had been inflexible. "No, I must preach," he said. "The harvest is great, and I must work while there is still time. For me, night is coming, but while it is still day, I will labor in the vineyard of my Lord."

Every day Anthony had preached, not in the churches that he had scheduled, for they were too small to hold the crowds who came, but in the meadows. At night, the streets of Padua were alight with torches and lanterns. Nobility and knights, peasants and beggars made their way to the place where Anthony was to preach. Every morning, the grass was crowded with listeners who had camped overnight to hear their saint. Sometimes the crowds swelled to thirty thousand, all voices, including those of vendors who had come to sell their wares, falling silent when Anthony began to speak.

Luke and several other friars who accompanied Anthony would line the people up for confession while Anthony, who daily ate nothing until sunset, became so absorbed in hearing confessions that even rain showers did not slacken his zeal. So many came to confess to Anthony and to the other priests of Padua that clergy from neighboring towns were called in to help. Padua was entering God's kingdom in a wave.

Like clouds of mosquitoes, the crowds sucked from Anthony his ebbing strength and went away strong, faith-filled, and encouraged. At the day's end, Anthony pushed his body to the little monastery of St. Mary's in the heart of the city where sleep, interrupted by prayer, never quite replaced the energy that he had lost.

Sometimes disturbances other than prayer interrupted that precious rest. One night around the beginning of Lent, Luke awoke to what he thought was an anguished choke. Throwing his tunic over his body, he had rushed out of his tiny, candle-lit cell into the adjoining one. Anthony was sitting bolt upright on his pallet, staring at the wall.

Luke stood helplessly in the doorway. In the weak candlelight, he could see by the radiance of the friar's face that he was experiencing another ecstasy. In a moment, Anthony closed his eyes and sighed deeply.

Luke took one step into the room and knelt by the friar. Swiftly he took the blanket that lay across Anthony's loins and wiped beads of sweat from the man's bony chest and neck.

Anthony reached up and took Luke's hands in his own. His voice was gentle but shaky. "You are the father coming in to console his child who is troubled by terrors of the night."

"Did you have a dream, Brother?"

"It seemed to me as if the devil tried to choke me. I could scarcely breathe."

Luke felt horror rising in himself. "Brother, no!"

Anthony smiled. He patted Luke's hand. "I'm all right, Brother. I begged the Blessed Mother to help me and I sang her hymn, 'O Glorious Lady.' When I made the sign of the cross on my forehead, I was freed from the demon's power."

"Did you see him, Brother?"

Anthony shook his head. "No. I thought I would when I awoke. But, instead, my room was lit with a heavenly brilliance. I saw Our Lady."

Luke feared for Anthony's safety. "Perhaps Satan will return. I will stay with you tonight"

Anthony smiled. "No, Brother. I have nothing to fear from the devil. In the light of God's love that flooded my cell, the angel of darkness could not possibly remain. You return to bed now. I shall be fine."

Lent continued, ended, and Easter came and went. If Anthony confronted the devil again, he did not mention it. The only confrontation that came close occurred when Anthony had visited Ezzelino da Romano. Refusing to take Luke along on the dangerous mission, Anthony had pleaded for Count Tiso's relatives whom the tyrant had imprisoned. Luke had prayed fervently for their release and for Anthony's safe return, but God had answered only one of his prayers.

After Lent, and up until now, Anthony had continued to preach on Sundays and on many weekdays. Daily he wrote, consoled, forgave, visited the sick and the poor. Then, as the grain ripened in the fields, Anthony ceased preaching during the week. "Your duty, my people, is to the grain," he called out in his final daily sermon. "As you glean it, remember that Christ came to you as a humble grain of wheat. Crushed and broken for your sins, He feeds you with the Bread of His life and thus gives to you life eternal."

Today before dawn the two friars had left St. Mary's to go to Camposampiero. There Anthony could rest and work on his sermons in peace. And he desperately wanted to finish them. The sermons were intended as very detailed notes for itinerant preachers and clergy who had difficulty composing their own sermons. These men would gain inspiration, knowledge, and guidance from Anthony's words and be able then to pen their own homilies. When Anthony finished these intensive writings, filled with Scripture, examples from nature, and analogies, he wanted to write a book for all Christians to read. He wanted God's Spirit to bathe with light the people who would read his words.

At Camposampiero, Anthony had the chance to finish his sermons and begin his next work without too many interruptions from his devotees. Only those Paduans who needed to see him personally would make the long trek out to Lord Tiso's estate, especially during the stifling heat of summer. Of course, Anthony would continue to receive all visitors graciously as he always did. Devotees in Padua who simply wanted to see and speak to the man whom they venerated as a saint would have to content themselves with the other friars at St. Mary's.

Luke was nearly asleep. Suddenly a flutter of wings swept his face. Startled awake, he caught a turtle dove winging upward. At the same moment, Anthony's eyes fluttered open. The priest laughed. "For a moment, I thought I was again singing the responsory in St. Mary's Church."

Luke grinned. On February 2, the Feast of the Purification of Mary, Anthony had been singing in his sweet voice, "They offered to the Lord for the return of Jesus two turtle doves or two young pigeons."

Suddenly two turtle doves flew over the pulpit. Anthony's song had risen with joy. In his sermon he asked in astonished glee, "Have you ever wondered which gift the Holy Family offered? I had just been wondering myself. 'My Lady, was it two turtle doves or two young pigeons?'" Anthony's hand had swept upward to where the two turtledoves were perched in the rafters. "Today the Blessed Mother has revealed the gift to us."

Today the turtledove winged into the sky and disappeared.

"I am no agile turtledove, my Brother. I am an old mare that dozes in the harness," Anthony said. "But she is ready to press on, if you are."

Luke pushed to his feet and stretched his sleep away. He shook the cramps out of his legs. "I was napping, too, Brother." He held out his hand to Anthony who, with a struggle, pulled himself to his feet. Luke picked up the pouch of Anthony's writings and hoisted it over his shoulder.

The two men climbed the hill, brushing through soft grass and trampling pink and purple blossoms whose fragrance wafted upward in fragile waves. Sheep bleated and parted as the men passed through. The two climbed silently. At times, Anthony paused to catch his breath while Luke waited. Other times, when they came to a particularly steep incline or to a heap of rocks, Luke helped pull and push up the friar's thick, clumsy body.

"I am a bother," Anthony said.

"No. You are my brother," Luke replied. And they both laughed.

At the crest of the hill, Anthony paused. Far beyond them to the north rose the Tyrolean Mountains, their snow-capped peaks jutting into the pale sky. Nuzzling up to them like suckling lambs lay the hills of Vicenza. Closer to the east wound the serpentine mountains of Este thrusting through a vast green plain of grass and trees. Before them in the valley lay Padua, a city resting between the hills as naturally as a child sleeps between its mother's breasts. In the sunlight, marble palaces glittered. Domes and bell towers thrust gloriously toward the heavens. Dotted with moving workers and beasts, a vast array of brown and green fields and vineyards surrounded Padua's red roofs, gray stone walls, and open market spaces. From this height, even the hovels of the poor looked quaint and inviting.

Luke felt a warm hand on his own. "Look at Padua, Brother," Anthony said. "Is there a more beautiful location in all the world? Its beauty is a testament to God."

Anthony threw his arms open wide as if to embrace the entire scene. "Blessed are you, O Padua, for the beauty of your site!" His voice, firm and powerful and full, rang across the hills. "Blessed are you for the harvest of your fields! Blessed are you in your people who follow the Lord." Then, lifting his hands heavenward, he cried out, "Blessed also shall you be for the honor with which heaven is about to crown you!"

For long moments, he remained with his hands stretched heavenward, his eyes fixed on the skies, his whole body straining toward heaven as if it could fly there just by willing it. Luke bowed his head and clasped his hands. Wetness trickled down his cheeks, but he did not know if his tears were of joy or of sorrow. *Oh, Lord,* he prayed, *is he telling me that he will die? Does he know how people will flock here if he does?*

Until the sun began to cast long shadows over Padua, the two men remained, Anthony reaching upward, Luke kneeling with head bowed. With the rise of an early evening breeze, the intensity of the Spirit blew aside and the friars gazed again at Padua that now appeared grayer and more drab in the dusk.

Anthony was the first to speak. "Good-bye, beloved city," he said in a trembling whisper. "I shall not preach in you again."

Through the twilight, the two friars made their way down the hill to Camposampiero. By the time they arrived, dusk had deepened to dark.

# ஃ 27 ௸

## *Brother Roger*

**Convent of the Friars Minor, Camposampiero, Italy ( June 13, 1231)** ௸
On his wooden platform in the boughs of a great walnut tree, a huge,
round-cheeked friar squirmed in his slumber. Although it was nearly
dawn, Brother Roger was not quite asleep. These nights, he never
seemed to be quite asleep. Not that he minded squeezing his lumber-
ing body onto this tiny platform, nor did he bother about sleeping
with his oversized hands and feet thrust against the willow-woven
walls of his cell. Discomfort was not keeping him awake. Anthony was.

Anthony, who slept on a larger, gabled platform above him,
breathed laboriously all night long and occasionally snored. Brother Luke, who also lived in the tree, in a little hut built slightly above
Roger's and to the right of the trunk, mumbled in his sleep. Those
noises, however, did not bother Roger, who had learned to sleep
well in the company of friars who snorted and coughed the whole
night through. What bothered him was Anthony's illness and the
fact that, at any time, it might claim his life.

When the men had first begun to live in the tree together, Luke
told Anthony, "If you need help during the night, you must call for us."

Anthony had shrugged and looked from Luke to Roger. "You
brothers will need your rest for whatever you might find in the
morning. I will be all right."

Would Anthony cry out if he encountered a crisis? Roger sickened at the thought of finding the priest's stiffening body in the
morning, and he cringed at the possibility of tending him in his final death throes during the night. When dark descended and the

men lay down to sleep, Roger could not relax. All night he listened for a scream, a choke, a gurgle, or absolute silence that would mean that death had entered the covered cell above his own.

Every night as he listened, the memories of his grandfather's death returned. When Roger was eight, he and the sixty-year-old man had been weeding the family carrot patch when pain's demon-talons had plunged into the elder's chest. His grandfather had buckled, grabbing his breast, his brown eyes wide with fear and agony. As he had crumpled over the feathery green shoots, he had clawed at Roger and hissed, "Get your father."

Terrified, Roger had run to the meadow where his father was plowing under the stubble left from the wheat harvest. "Grandpa fell down and screamed in the garden," Roger had shouted. He had seen his father's eyes widen with fright, seen the panic as he threw down the reins and thrust the plow deeply into the ground to anchor it. Leaving the oxen standing stupidly in the furrows, he had outraced his son home. By the time pudgy Roger arrived, breathless with running and fear, the old man was lying indoors on his bed, squeezing his son's hand and screaming in anguish.

For ten minutes the man whom Roger loved even more than he loved his own father shrieked and trembled. Then, convulsing terribly, his entire body went limp. As his grandfather's eyes rolled backward in his head, the town canon had rushed breathlessly into the cottage. Over the still body he recited the prayers and performed the anointing that would escort the old man's soul into heaven.

The incident left one impression on Roger. Death was horrible. He never, ever again wanted to see anyone die. And he never did. Even though he had knelt beside dying friars in St. Mary's convent in Padua and recited with other friars the Penitential Psalms, he had not seen anyone die. In what must have looked like piety to others, he had kept his eyes tightly closed, his body unmoving, his mind focusing on the words of the prayers. He would pray this way until someone else announced the death, and then, taking a deep breath and averting his eyes from the corpse, he would rise and file out of the body's presence, his gaze on the floor.

Roger hated his childish, secret aversion. Even though he believed with all his heart in God's saving mercy, even though he had joined the Friars Minor to die to the world, even though he knew that he must think of his current life as nothing but a preparation for death, even despite all his faith, he still feared seeing anyone die. Who could he speak with about this unchristian terror? Who would understand?

Roger had sometimes thought of speaking to Brother Anthony about his trepidation, for Brother Anthony was gentle and good. But Brother Anthony was ill himself, weakened even more by the continuous stream of visitors who kept coming to St. Mary's seeking his counsel. Roger thought too highly of the man to bother him with a fear that should have no hold on a follower of Christ. And, deep inside, he dreaded being alone with a man whose swollen body was obviously nurturing death. Suppose Anthony should be stricken in Roger's presence? So he preferred to smile at the priest, greet him, listen to him teach, and then leave him alone.

Now all had changed. Two and a half weeks ago, the guardian of the friars at St. Mary's had summoned Roger.

"We all realize that Brother Anthony is not well," the guardian had begun. "Now he has not the strength to greet the many people who flock here to see him. Count Tiso has invited him to Camposampiero and Provincial Brother Albert has given him permission to go."

Roger nodded. He had been to Camposampiero himself a few times. It was a restful spot indeed.

"Someone must be with Brother Anthony at all times. That will be Brother Luke," the guardian continued. "But you are to tend him as well."

The assignment came like a punch to Roger's groin.

"Should he require pen or parchment or a drink of water, you are to get it. He may send you back here or to Arcella on business. He may need help walking. As he grows weaker, he may be unable to rise from bed. You are strong and can assist him in his bodily needs. You will go out to Camposampiero two days in advance of Brother Luke and Brother Anthony to make sure that all is in preparation for their arrival. With Brother Luke, you will remain at Camposampiero to tend Brother Anthony until the end, if necessary."

As the full import of the assignment sank into Roger's brain like a stone into muck, nausea overwhelmed him and he nearly gagged. The guardian seemed not to notice. On jellied legs, he left the guardian's cell and, just outside the door, he retched. The guardian had assigned him to watch Anthony die.

For days, Roger secretly hoped for the unspeakable—that the priest would die at St. Mary's or on his way to Camposampiero. But he did not. Two weeks ago after dark, Anthony and Luke had arrived at Count Tiso's estate.

It was obvious that Anthony was failing. While he loved to sit in the tree house that Count Tiso had built for him, he had great difficulty climbing into it. Roger knew that the priest tried his best, but it took both him and Luke, one tugging the friar's hands and the other guiding his grotesquely swollen feet, to get the man up the ladder. Anthony would remain in the house all day except for the times of Office and the two small daily meals which he ate with the other brothers in the little, rustic refectory.

Frequently Anthony called out notes or comments to Luke who wrote them down on papers he had with him in his own leafy cell. Roger was the errand boy. He supplied quill pens and parchment and, on breezy days, stones to hold down the pages. On warm days, he passed cups of water through the clouds of leaves that hid the brothers from sight.

To those visitors who came all the way from Padua seeking the priest, Roger, towering over most of them, always made one authoritative comment. "Brother Anthony is not well. He is writing his sermons in the tree and must come down with great difficulty. You may speak to him from down here or, if you wish, you may climb up to him."

Roger had listened to a dozen sermons preached from the leafy heights to eager ears below. Once a crowd of careless listeners had trampled underfoot one of Count Tiso's wheat fields in their eagerness to cross the estate and surprise Anthony in his tree. When Anthony heard about the destruction, he asked Roger and Luke to join him in prayer. The following day, Roger had to skirt the field on his way to Count Tiso's manor house to request some additional parchment for Anthony. The wheat stood erect in the field.

Frequently individual pilgrims came to see the priest. Roger had helped about two dozen people climb the tree including a few well-endowed noble women who unsuccessfully attempted to hold their billowing skirts around their ankles while making the ascent. Roger was patient with these penitents. He knew that they came seeking God's forgiveness and guidance reflected in the words of the priest.

Whether Anthony was alone or with a visitor, Roger always subconsciously listened for those deep, labored breaths. He had become used to them and often entertained a fantasy. Perhaps Anthony was not as ill as everyone thought. Perhaps, in the summer air, he would recover and move back to St. Mary's. But at night Roger's fairy tales fled. Even above the distant howling of wolves, Roger listened to sounds above him.

This Friday, as a tint of light began to whiten the darkness, Roger stirred awake. He heard a rustling above him and to his right. Rising, he brushed the straw from his tunic and pushed it into a pile in one corner of his cell. This evening he would fluff it out again across the floor to create a bed. As he pushed aside the supple branch that he had come to regard as his door, he saw Luke ascending the ladder to Anthony's cell. Roger climbed up after him.

After helping Anthony down the ladder, the three men proceeded a short distance through the forest to the tiny chapel that Count Tiso had built for them. There, before a wooden altar and a tiny tabernacle lit by a single candle, the three brothers joined a half-dozen other friars as they stood to chant the Morning Office.

After the Office, Luke and Roger helped Anthony climb back up to his leafy oratory. Roger and Luke took their places on their own platforms. Although the day was already warm, Anthony was busy completing the sermons that the Cardinal Bishop of Ostia had commissioned. The rustle of parchment and the scratch of a pen lulled Roger into a kind of torpor.

The sky brightened. Morning bird-songs swelled. Tiny black ants that perpetually climbed up and down this tree scurried along the bark. Hours passed with Roger at prayer and Luke taking notes that Anthony called out to him. When the sun was high in the heavens, a bell rang from the convent. Roger and Luke climbed the ladder to help Anthony descend for the first meal of the day.

As usual, several friars were missing from this noon meal for they had gone into Padua or neighboring towns to preach, work, or beg. The two left at Camposampiero, one of whom was the guardian, were standing at the table in the refectory. When Anthony took his place, with Luke and Roger on either side of him, the brothers bowed their heads while the guardian recited the blessing. Then the friars sat as the guardian broke the bread that Count Tiso's servants had brought and passed the loaf around the table. As Anthony attempted to pick up his portion, his hand trembled and fell. His heavy body sagged as his thick fingers clutched at the table. Had Roger and Luke not caught him, he might have toppled to the floor.

The guardian of the convent leaped to his feet. "Is he in ecstasy?" he demanded.

Anthony shook his head.

"Brother, perhaps you should lie down," Luke suggested.

Anthony nodded, then attempted to stand. As he did so, his legs collapsed beneath him. Luke and Roger caught his arms. The other friars grabbed at the body. In a cluster of gray and tan tunics, Anthony was half-carried, half-escorted to the nearest little straw hut. Once inside, he seemed to lose all strength as his body bent headlong on the mattress of vine branches. With great difficulty, the brothers turned him so that he was lying on his back. The hut was barely large enough for Anthony. Roger's back pressed against one wall, Luke's back at the other. The other two friars stood helplessly at the door.

"Brother Luke, do not leave my sermons in the tree," Anthony said weakly.

As Luke left, Anthony turned to Roger. His dark eyes held Roger in a gentle grasp. "Brother Roger, I am dying."

The whispered words screamed in Roger's brain. He stared at those eyes, looking especially huge and deep-set in the gaunt face, and saw again his grandfather's eyes roll backward in their sockets. As a huge wave of terror swept over him, he began to tremble uncontrollably.

Anthony's left hand slowly, slowly lifted until his fingers touched Roger's wrist. "Do not be afraid, Brother. Now comes the end of night which is life darkened by sin. Dawn is breaking for me, Brother. There is no need for anymore struggle." The smile on his face was faint. "Life's misery is at an end and glory is beginning." Anthony's hand felt heavy on Roger's wrist, heavy and warm and calm. Warmth and peace flowed from the touch.

"Brother, I am going home."

Roger nodded, pushing away the fear that dizzied him.

Anthony continued to speak. "My Brother, can you do a little job for me? These hermits have been kind to us. But they have come to Count Tiso's to live in peaceful solitude. For these past two weeks, they have patiently endured visits of penitents coming to see me."

Roger nodded. "I know, Brother."

"I don't wish to put these friars to the expense and trouble of my funeral. If I die here, they and Count Tiso will have to suffer endless lines of pilgrims to this lovely estate."

"The whole world calls you a saint, Brother," Roger managed to choke out.

Anthony nodded weakly. "A great burden to everyone concerned. If you approve, we will go home to St. Mary's at once. Oh, that I might die and be buried there! There at the church dedicated to the Mother of God! Will you get a cart ready, Brother?"

As Luke entered the hut with Anthony's manuscripts, a surge of relief came over Roger. He would leave quickly. Perhaps Anthony would die in his absence. Carefully, he picked up Anthony's warm, puffy hand and placed it on his chest. "I will get a carriage," he said in a voice that rasped.

Roger flew through the woods to Count Tiso's stable. His mind raced. *Lord, let him die before I return.*

In a quavering voice, Roger told a stable hand, "Father Anthony needs a carriage to go to St. Mary's."

The gray-bearded man shook his head. "Count Tiso is out with the carriage. Got a cart left."

Roger nodded ascent as the stablehand harnessed a pair of oxen. Together he and Roger threw huge armloads of hay into the cart and then the servant hitched the beasts to it. Roger climbed into the seat and took the reins in his hands.

As he approached the convent, the guardian ran up to him. "You will have to take him. He refuses to stay here."

Roger's heart pumped wildly. Anthony was still alive.

Luke and Roger and the two other friars carried the bloated body out of the hut and placed it on the cart's bed of hay. Then, with Roger driving and Luke sitting in the back holding Anthony's hand, the cart jerked away from Camposampiero.

If only Roger could make the ride smoother! He was striking every rut and rock in the road. Any moment he would hear an anguished moan or a shriek of pain. None came. The cart jolted along. One mile. Two. Three. Whenever the cart traveled on a smooth length of road, which was not often, Roger could hear Anthony's gasping over the creaking of the wood. He was still alive.

Ten miles. In the distance Roger could see the peaceful suburb of Capo di Ponte. But who was this coming toward them? Another friar?

As the tan habit drew closer, Roger recognized Brother Ignoto, the chaplain at Arcella.

Ignoto waved. "How is Brother Anthony? I'm on my way to visit him."

Roger shook his head and waved to the back of the cart. Ignoto gave a little shriek as Roger reined the oxen to a halt.

"He wants to go to St. Mary's." The voice was Luke's.

Roger felt a tug at his sleeve. Ignoto. "He won't make it to St. Mary's," he whispered in Roger's ear. Then in a louder voice, Ignoto said, "Brother Anthony, if you go to St. Mary's, so many people will be coming and going that the friars will be unable to keep them out of your cell. No one there will have a moment's peace. Why don't you come to Arcella? It is but a stone's throw away from here and you can stay in my cell."

"That is a good idea, Brother," Anthony said in a husky voice. "But I beg you, please give me your command of obedience. When I die, if it is in any way possible, bring my body for burial to the Church of St. Mary, the house of the Mother of God."

"I promise, Brother," Ignoto said. Then Ignoto hopped onto the seat beside Roger who directed the wagon toward the abbey.

At Arcella, at the chaplain's door, Ignoto helped the two others lead Anthony into a small room and lay him on a straw mattress. They had no sooner got indoors than the other friars at Arcella began to gather. Soon the thin, sweet songs of the nuns filtered through the walls. They were singing the Psalms for the dying, praying that the gates of heaven would open for their beloved confessor, Anthony.

Roger went outdoors to see about the oxen, but one of the friars at Arcella was already unstrapping them from harness. Another was rubbing down their sweaty ribs with the skirt of his tunic.

"Go inside, Brother. He may need you," the rubbing friar said.

It was the last thing that Roger wanted to do.

As he entered the room, he saw at once that Anthony could scarcely breathe. His chest was heaving in great waves and his brown face was smeared with sweat. His eyes were wide, his mouth open with fright.

"Brother Roger, quick!" Luke shouted. "Hold up his head."

Roger felt as if he would vomit. His breaths rolled over each other in swift, shallow waves.

"His head, Brother. He needs to sit."

Roger shoved his hands behind the priest's head and neck. With Luke's hands behind his back, the friars lifted Anthony to a sitting position. Ignoto pulled a chair next to the bed. Together, the three friars lifted Anthony into it. Kneeling at his side, Roger continued to hold the friar's head erect for Anthony had not the strength to hold it up himself. As the three brothers tended to Anthony, the other friars of Arcella crowded into the small room and knelt along the walls, their heads bowed.

Anthony's breaths continued to burst out in gasps. His wide-open eyes focused on a spot near the door and his body shuddered like a leaf in a November breeze.

"The water is rising in his chest," Ignoto said. "He is choking."

"Perhaps a demon has appeared to torment him," Luke offered.

*He is afraid to die,* Roger thought.

Roger stared at the spot near the door as the moist neck beneath his hand trembled. Roger saw nothing.

Suddenly Anthony sighed deeply and the trembling ceased. His eyes closed and he sank back in the chair, the tension gone from his body as surely as it leaves a goat that has jumped a chasm and left the pursuing wolf on the other side.

"Brother Ignoto, I must make my confession." The voice came in a husky whisper.

Roger and Luke exchanged glances. Anthony seemed to read their thoughts. "It matters not if you hear my sins. You shall hear them all anyway at the final judgment."

In an attempt to drown out Anthony's whispered words, Roger shut his eyes tightly and prayed the Our Father over and over in rapid succession. Nevertheless, he could not help overhearing. "Illicit thoughts. Distraction in prayer. Desire for comfort. Pride in my preaching. Attraction to popularity. Failure to trust fully in the mercy of God." Then, with a shaky voice, "Doubt over my salvation." Finally his voice was silent.

*But deliver us from evil. Amen,* Roger prayed, concluding the prayer. He opened his eyes.

"I absolve you of all your sins," Ignoto was saying, "including those confessed and those forgotten." Then Ignoto took Anthony's right hand in his own and traced the sign of the cross over the man as Ignoto blessed him. "And I bless you in the name of the Father, and of the Son, and of the Holy Spirit. Amen."

"Amen," said Anthony with a sigh. Then a great smile spread across his face and in a clear but faint voice, Anthony begin to sing.

> "O Glorious Lady,
> Raised above the stars,
> He who created you with foresight
> You fed with milk from your holy breast."

Anthony's voice grew stronger, louder. His head pressed against Roger's hands as he lifted his gaze heavenward.

> "What sad Eve took away
> You give back through your beloved Son.
> So that we poor wretches might ascend the skies,
> You become the window of heaven."

Was this how someone ought to die? Roger felt fear begin to crack inside him as Luke, Ignoto, and the other friars joined in singing the third verse.

> "You are the door of the High King.
> You are the gleaming gate of light.
> O redeemed nations,
> Acclaim life given you through the Virgin."

The clear, strong voices, and the meaning of the familiar words sung during the Morning Office, sank into Roger's soul as water into bread. Anthony had faced the terror of death and banished it. As Anthony sang his way into eternity, God's eternal light bathed Roger's own soul with a similar peace. In a deep, strong voice, he sang the final verse with the others.

> "Glory to you, O Lord,
> Who were born of the Virgin,
> With the Father and Holy Spirit
> Unto endless ages."

As their voices faded, Anthony raised his head even more. His eyes focused on the upper corner of the room and widened with wonder and joy. A gasp of surprise squeezed from his lips as his smile grew in radiance.

"What do you see, Brother?" Roger asked.

"I see my Savior."

Roger stared at the corner. *My Jesus, what am I to do in Your presence? Thank You for coming to him. For coming to me. My Jesus, I am a sinner. I do not deserve to be here in Your holy presence.*

"Brother Anthony," Ignoto interrupted Roger's prayer. "I have brought the sacred oil to anoint you."

Anthony's gaze left the corner and turned to Ignoto.

"Brother, there is no need for you to do me this service," he said gently. "I have this unction within me. Nevertheless, it is good and gives me happiness." He stretched out the palms of his hands for the anointing while, through the walls, the songs of the nuns continued to drift.

Ignoto anointed Anthony's eyes. "By the strength of this holy unction and its most pious mercy, may the Lord pardon the sins you have committed with your sight." His voice a fervent plea, Anthony whispered the words along with Ignoto.

The priest anointed Anthony's ears, nose, mouth, hands, sides, and feet, praying that God would forgive any sin committed through each body-member in turn while Anthony continued to pray with him.

As the priest put away his holy oils, the kneeling friars began to recite the seven Penitential Psalms. With his hands clasped, Anthony joined his tremulous voice to theirs.

With his hands supporting the head of a dying man, Roger began to recite Psalm 6. He watched Anthony's face as he prayed, searching for any sign of breathing difficulty, adjusting the angle of the head to help him breathe better.

"Be gracious to me, O Lord, for I am languishing."

As he prayed, Roger realized that he was supporting a saint. Yet he who had forgiven the sins of so many prayed with passion the words of Psalm 32: "I said, 'I will confess my transgressions to the Lord' and You forgave the guilt of my sin."

Anthony's voice deepened in fervor with Psalm 38. "But it is for You, O Lord, that I wait; it is You, O Lord my God, Who will answer." Roger felt a shiver run through the friar. Was it a thrill of anticipation, delight, awe?

Anthony's neck trembled. The friars were praying their way through Psalm 51. "The sacrifice acceptable to God is a broken spirit; a broken and contrite heart, O God, You will not despise."

By Psalm 102, tears were welling in Roger's eyes. He and the man whose head he supported were both close in age. Why was the Lord taking the one who knew so much, who loved so deeply, who forgave so readily, and leaving the other, a clumsy ox?

"He has broken my strength in midcourse; He has shortened my days. 'O my God,' I say, 'do not take me away at the midpoint of my life, You Whose years endure throughout all generations.'"

The tears were dripping swiftly from Roger's cheeks, tickling him and dampening the chest of his tunic. He could not wipe them away without dropping his grip on Anthony. The words of Psalm 130 penetrated his sorrow. "I wait for the Lord, my soul waits, and in His word I hope; my soul waits for the Lord more than those who watch for the morning."

Then the final Psalm. Roger's voice was no more than a whisper while Anthony's was quivering with emotions: "In You I put my trust. Teach me the way I should go, for to You I lift up my soul...for I am Your servant."

As Psalm 143 ended, Anthony sank back into Roger's arms. The friars remained on their knees, their quiet prayers rippling throughout the room, droning over the high-pitched lull of the nuns' voices. Keeping his eyes on Anthony's face, Roger prayed over and over the Psalms, the Lord's Prayer, his own anguished pleas and his glorious praises. Anthony lay quietly, his eyes closed. The priest's breaths came deeply, measuredly, gradually growing farther apart until, after about half an hour, they came no more. The head felt heavy in Roger's hands, like a melon fully ripe and sweet.

Ignoto, who had remained kneeling by Anthony's side, was the first to speak. "He has gone home. Amen. Alleluia."

"Amen. Alleluia," the friars echoed.

Roger and Luke eased the heavy body down. Through his tears, Roger could see that already the color was draining from the skin. The brown tint was fading and, at its disappearance, Anthony's skin was whitening.

"He looks like a child," one of the friars remarked. "This is no child," Ignoto said abruptly. "This is a saint and when Padua finds out that he has died here, they will swarm this place."

"What should we do?" another friar asked.

"We must not let anyone know that he is dead. Not yet. Perhaps if we take the body secretly to St. Mary's, the friars there will know what to do."

Roger nodded. He would go to prepare the cart.

A knocking sounded at the chaplain's door. Roger, who was on his way out, brushed the tears from his eyes and opened the door. A little girl stood there.

The child cocked her head curiously. "Are you sad?" she asked.

Roger tried unsuccessfully to ease the huskiness out of his voice. "What do you want?"

"I want to see Father Anthony."

## ∞ 28 ∞

## *Paduana*

**City Street, Padua, Italy (June 13, 1231)** ∞ Six-year-old Paduana squatted in the shade of her parents' modest house, playing with the stubs of wood that she used for dolls. Her curly, brown hair was frizzing out of the two short braids that Mama had twisted three days ago. Her bare feet and legs were gray with the dust of a dry street, and her plain, white frock was dingy. As her toes scrabbled in the dirt, they kicked up tiny clouds of dust that settled over her fingers and over the little scene that she was imagining.

She had not played "Being Cured" for several weeks, but today she felt like playing it again. That was because today she was going with Papa to take some fig cakes to Father Anthony. Father Anthony and Papa and she were the main characters in "Being Cured."

At breakfast this morning, Papa had been dressed in his deep-brown tunic and matching stockings. His drooping mustache and pointed beard were neatly combed and Paduana caught a whiff of seldom used and costly perfume. All these things meant that Papa was traveling somewhere important today. But before Paduana could question where, Papa bit into a huge hunk of bread and, with his big mouth full, had commented, "I wonder how Father Anthony is."

Paduana had been eating her bread, too. "Is he all right?" she had asked.

"Bambina, you know that he is very sick," Papa had said, tickling her chin. "That is why he left St. Mary's."

Paduana thought of Grandma who had been very sick before her death. She looked at her gentle, round-faced father. "Will he die, Papa?"

"We will all die sometime, Bambina."

"But not Father Anthony. He is too good to die."

"Even Jesus died, Paduana," Mama had said. Mama was dressed in her everyday cream-colored tunic, so she was not going with Papa or she would have put on her single gown, the one with fine, soft pleats, the one that Paduana coveted.

Mama poured Paduana a cup of goat's milk. "I baked Father Anthony some fig cakes. He likes those. Maybe they will make him feel a little better. Today Papa has to take Count Tiso ten bolts of cloth. He will take Father Anthony the cakes."

Paduana became so excited that she almost tipped her cup. "Can I go, too, Papa? In the carriage? Please? Please?"

"If you promise not to eat the cakes on the way, Bambina," Papa said.

"Papa!" Paduana protested.

"Promise," said Mama.

Paduana twisted her smile into a grimace. "I promise."

"I baked a few extra for you," Mama said with a smile.

So Paduana drank her goat's milk and then wandered outside to pass the time until Papa was ready to leave. Spying the wooden stubs at the edge of the family's garden patch made Paduana think of playing "Market." Three days ago, she had gathered stray lentils from the lentil patch for her dolls to buy and sell. But she was tired of "Market." What could she play today?

Today she was going to see Father Anthony. Maybe she would play "Being Cured." She had made Papa tell her the story so often that she had memorized it.

Paduana gathered up the stubs and, piling them in the skirt of her frock, had carried them into the shade of the house.

"This one is Father Anthony," she said, taking the stubbiest, fattest stick. "And this one is Papa." Papa's stick was longer and a bit knotty. "And this one is Mama." Mama's stick was smooth and slender, just like Mama. "And this one is me." Paduana chose the tiniest stick to represent herself. She still had a fist full of sticks left. She pushed them to one side. "And these are everybody else."

Then she put herself and Papa and Mama into the pile of "everybody else." She put Father Anthony a little distance from the pile. "Now believe in God and do what is right," she said in a deep voice. "Or else you'll go to hell." That was Father Anthony preaching to the citizens of Padua. "Amen."

"Hurrah! Hurrah!" she called out. That was the citizens cheering the priest.

Now she made Papa carry herself up to Father Anthony. Mama went along, too.

"Father Anthony," Papa said. "This is my little daughter Paduana. When she was four years old, a disease struck her and she could no longer walk. She crawls, Father, like a lizard. Many times she has fits like epilepsy." Paduana smiled. See, she had remembered the big word and said it correctly, too. Epp—ill-lep—see. Epilepsy. Now she made Papa continue to speak. "Epilepsy makes her fall to the ground and roll about senselessly. She is a good girl, Father. Will you bless her?"

Paduana made Father Anthony nod. "Of course I will bless her," she said in a deep voice. "In the name of the Father, and of the Son, and of the Holy Spirit."

Papa made a deep bow. "Thank you, Father."

Paduana made Papa and Mama walk home, taking turns carrying her. She decided that home, today, would be the broken piece of crockery that Papa kept by the door. He used the pottery shard to scrape mud off his boots before coming indoors. She leaned the crockery against the house, then searched in the dust for a pebble to represent a chair. Here was a smooth one that would do just fine.

Now Paduana walked the little family home. Papa stood Paduana on her feet and placed her hands on the chair.

Humming to herself, Paduana made her stick teeter and totter as it remained erect.

"Look!" Papa called to Mama. "Paduana is standing."

Paduana hummed a lullaby as she put the sticks to bed, then whistled like a morning birdsong. Again Papa placed Paduana next to the chair. Again she stood. Bed again. Birdsong. Today Paduana pushed the chair around the house.

"Look!" Papa called. "Paduana is walking."

Bed. Birdsong. As the days and nights sped by, Paduana was walking about the house unaided. Then she was running. And then the little family was walking all together to see Father Anthony to tell him what his blessing had done. For Paduana, who truly had been a crippled victim of epilepsy, now walked and ran as normally as other children. And never, since being blessed by Father Anthony, had she had another epileptic fit.

"Paduana!" Papa called from the tiny stable. "The mule is hitched and the carriage is ready. Get in!"

Paduana leaped up, leaving her sticks in the dust.

GLUMLY PADUANA SAT IN THE CARRIAGE as it headed back to Padua. She had gone all the way out to Count Tiso's with Papa, but Father Anthony was not there. "He left this morning in a cart for St. Mary's," a friar had told them. St. Mary's! St. Mary's wasn't even far from home. And it didn't have a big tree near it that Father Anthony lived in. Paduana had wanted to visit Father Anthony in his tree. Maybe if she climbed way, way up there, she would know how the larks felt and maybe even be able to sing like them. Or maybe fly. But probably not. Still it would have been nice to imagine. And now she did not get to go in the tree at all. They were going back to St. Mary's.

Papa drove up to the familiar convent. He and Paduana got out of the carriage. He allowed Paduana to hold the basket with the fig cakes while he rapped at the door. A wrinkled-faced friar opened the door. His hair was so white that Paduana thought that he must be at least a hundred years old.

"We've come to see Father Anthony," Papa said. "My wife baked these cakes for him."

"Father Anthony isn't here. He went to Camposampiero over two weeks ago."

"The friars there said he returned here today."

"Did you pass him on the road?"

"No."

"He is not here. Maybe he went to Arcella first."

Papa groaned. The friar closed the door gently. "Honey," Papa said, leaning down toward Paduana. "The mule is tired. I must get him home and rub him down and feed him. We will take the fig cakes to Father Anthony tomorrow."

Paduana's lip trembled. She wanted to see Father Anthony today. He would bless her and tell her a story and share a fig cake with her.

"Papa, I can walk to Arcella. I went there before all by myself with some bread for the nuns. I went often. Let me go today, Papa. Please."

Papa smiled. "All right, Paduana. But be sure to start back early enough so that you get into the city before the gates close."

Paduana grinned. "I promise, Papa!"

At Arcella, Paduana never saw the nuns, for they remained within the convent. But sometimes she heard them singing the Psalms, their voices joyful with prayer and praise. Today she heard the singing, too, but the songs were different. Today the nuns seemed to be sobbing the words.

*Are they sad?* Paduana wondered.

Paduana knew that Father Anthony would not be at the convent. He would be at the friary off to the side. Usually Paduana saw a friar or two in the garden. Today the place seemed deserted. Where was everyone? At prayer?

Paduana went around to the chaplain's cell. Under a tree, she spied a cart of straw near which two oxen were tied and grazing peacefully. She would have liked to pet the beasts but Papa told her never to do so. Too many people had been gored. So Paduana just looked at the reddish creatures as she knocked at the monastery door.

A huge, wide shouldered friar who looked a lot like Paduana's red-faced Uncle Rocco answered her knock. The friar's eyes looked puffy. People had puffy eyes when they cried. Mama's eyes had been puffy when Grandma died. And the nuns were singing sad songs today.

Paduana was curious. "Are you sad?" she asked.

"What do you want?" the friar asked. Paduana smarted at the gruff tone.

"I want to see Father Anthony. Mama baked him these cakes." Paduana held up the basket.

The friar took the basket. "Tell your Mama thank you."

"But I want to see him," Paduana insisted.

"You can't see him," the friar said, about to close the door.

"He likes to see me. Isn't he here?"

"He's here."

"Then let me see him. I want to see him. He tells me stories."

The friar bit his lip and closed his eyes. Hard.

"Why are you making a face at me?"

The friar took a deep breath and spoke slowly, accentuating each word. "Father Anthony can't see you."

"But why not? He always sees me."

The friar gulped a big gulp of air. "Little girl, please go home." He began to close the door again.

Suddenly a realization struck Paduana with as much force as if someone had smacked her cheek. When Grandma had died, no one let Paduana see her. Her father had closed the door to Grandma's room to keep Paduana out. Grandma had been very sick when she died. Papa had said that Father Anthony was very sick. Mama said that everyone died sometime, even Jesus.

"He's dead," Paduana shrieked. "You won't let me see him because he's dead."

"Shhh! Little girl, be quiet"

"Father Anthony is dead!" Paduana screamed. She thought she would burst with pain. Dead like Grandma who never came to life again to sing to her. Dead like her dog who never got up after being kicked by a horse. Dead meant still, and dead meant gone. "Father Anthony is dead!"

"Little girl. Please. Don't tell anyone."

She had to tell. She would explode if she did not tell. Leaving her basket in the sad friar's hands, Paduana ran from the monastery, weeping, stumbling in ruts that she could not see through her tears. As she raced through the streets of Padua, children that she had seen at market and at church looked up from their play at the sobbing little girl. "Father Anthony is dead!" she cried. "The holy priest is dead."

Soon the streets of Padua were overrun with children, crying out to one another and to everyone else, "The holy father is dead! Saint Anthony is dead!"

## ✂ 29 ✂

### *Abbot Thomas of Gaul*

**St. Andrew's Monastery, Vercelli, Italy (June 13, 1231)** ✂ Abbot Thomas of Gaul sat at his desk in his small cell, his forehead pressed against his fingertips. As he massaged his temples in a vain effort to stimulate his brain, his black tonsure flecked with a great deal of gray bobbed up and down like a narrow halo. Try as he might, he could not concentrate on the manuscript that lay before him. He was in the midst of writing a treatise on heaven, but his words had stopped flowing.

A few weeks ago, Thomas had developed a sore throat which, despite his best doctoring with herbs and olive oil, had only grown more severe. When he swallowed, he felt as if he were forcing down a chestnut burr. How unfair that one small part of his body should make all the rest of him miserable! His painful throat had robbed him of sleep, and lack of sleep always hindered his logic and creativity. Today he might as well have been just an average, middle-aged canon instead of, as many theologians declared, the greatest living doctor of theology in all the world. Being a doctor meant nothing to Thomas today. Today he wished he had seen a doctor.

Thomas leaned back in his chair and closed his eyes. The thoughts just weren't coming. Instead of thinking about heaven, he began thinking of Brother Anthony. Pain didn't seem to impede Anthony. Thomas knew that Anthony was ill in Padua, but he was under obedience to write his sermons and he was doing it there. He was writing in a tree, nonetheless! Maybe if Thomas climbed a tree, the breezes would clear his brain and he'd write better. He shook his head. No, the way he was feeling today, he'd probably topple out.

If only he had a quick mind like Brother Anthony. When Anthony had begun his preaching mission, Francis had sent him to Vercelli to lodge with the Friars Minor in their convent near St. Matthew's Church. Anthony was to preach in Vercelli and Milan and to confer with Abbot Thomas to make certain that his theology was sound.

Thomas moaned. Sound? Anthony's theology was so sound, deep, and broad that he had enlightened Thomas. The two men had sat up well past sunset several nights, discussing this and that matter, before Anthony would depart for the night. After hearing a few of Anthony's sermons and spending hours in discussion with him, Thomas had insisted that Anthony teach some of the abbot's theology classes here at St. Andrew's monastery.

At the same time, Thomas had spoken fervently and frequently with Anthony about one of his deepest convictions, namely that the Church should be stressing individual confession to a priest as Pope Innocent III had declared in 1213. Unfortunately, not every Catholic followed the pope's directive to confess yearly. Many misunderstood the directive and still believed that the rigor and embarrassment of public confession was the only type of repentance acceptable to God. Many of the faithful waited until death approached to confess. Others felt that true contrition could be effective without the absolution of a priest. Nothing fed these attitudes more than one alarming fact: the Church had a shortage of ordained clergy who were themselves morally pure. No wonder conversion progressed slowly, if at all! The faithful should be urged to confess and return to God at once, Thomas argued. Every priest should promote this return and, if in sin, should himself repent. Anthony had agreed wholeheartedly.

Thomas had sent Anthony back to Francis with the words, "Many men have penetrated the mysteries of the Holy Trinity, as I have found had been done by Anthony during the course of the familiar relations which I had with him. Knowing little of profane science, he yet so quickly acquired a knowledge of mystic theology, that within he was on fire with heavenly ardor, and to men he seemed lit up with divine knowledge."

Thomas had seen Anthony periodically over the years when Anthony had passed through Vercelli or preached there. When

Anthony had come through Vercelli in 1229 on his way to build a convent in Varese, Thomas had noticed the friar's unhealthy corpulence and apparent weakness. Anthony had said nothing about his condition, and the two men had discussed spiritual matters as they had done several times before. Thomas had heard that Anthony had blessed a well in Varese whose waters had healing powers. Thomas hadn't tried the water, but today he felt tempted. Still, the waters had not healed Anthony. Thomas, and all of Lombardy, knew that Anthony was very ill in Padua. Yet Anthony was still writing his sermons. Anthony could write of heaven even if he felt that his throat were aflame with the fires of hell.

Heaven. Heaven. Thomas rubbed his temples. *Lord, can't You give me a little insight the way You give it to Brother Anthony?*

Tap. Tap. Someone was knocking at Thomas's door.

"Come in." The hoarse words scratched Thomas's throat.

The door opened. Brother Anthony.

Before Thomas could force out a greeting of joy, Anthony spoke. "See, Father Abbot, I have left the ass near the gates of Padua and am hastening to my homeland."

Anthony was stocky but not swollen, his carriage straight, just as he had been on his first visit to Thomas.

"You are well again!" Thomas managed to choke out.

Anthony smiled as he bent over the desk. "And you are not," he said, gently touching Thomas's throat.

"Can you stay a bit before returning to Lisbon?"

Anthony straightened and shook his head as he turned toward the door. "No, Father Abbot. I am going home."

With that, he walked out the door, leaving it ajar.

Thomas leaped up from his desk. The manuscript could wait while he walked Anthony to the gates of the monastery.

The hallway was empty except for a canon with a breviary in his hand. How could Anthony have walked the corridor's length so swiftly?

"Which way did Father Anthony go?" Thomas asked.

"I didn't see him," the canon replied.

Thomas decided to go in the direction of the courtyard that led to the street. Here a group of canons sat on a bench.

"Did Father Anthony come through here?"

"No."

Thomas was puzzled. He began to methodically search the monastery, asking everyone he met, canon and servant alike, if Anthony had passed that way. No one had seen the priest.

Finally, Thomas went to the monastery gates. He asked the canon who was acting as porter. "Did you let Father Anthony in to visit me?"

"I let no one in to visit anyone," the porter said.

Thomas heaved a great breath of disbelief. He gazed down the road. Of course, Anthony was not walking it. Thomas looked upward. Heaven.

Suddenly he knew. Anthony had left the ass, the friars' word for their body, in Padua.

He was going home to heaven.

A lump of wonder, joy, and grief pushed up in Thomas's throat. As he swallowed hard to keep from bursting into tears, he was astonished that the fire in his throat was gone.

# Chapter Notes

*These notes will help the reader discern fact from fiction in this biography of St. Anthony.*

## Prologue

### Bedchamber, Rome, Italy (Spring 1232)

Upon Anthony's death, the convent at Arcella and St. Mary's Monastery at Padua contested for his remains. The bishop of Padua declared that the remains should be interred in St. Mary's.

Thousands of pilgrims flocked to his tomb. Following custom, many brought votive candles—some so huge that sixteen men had to carry one candle into the church. One candle that had to be lopped off to fit into the church was donated by university students.

Miracles due to Anthony's intercession were reported in abundance. His cause for canonization was introduced and the pope appointed a learned committee to study the matter. The committee approved forty-seven miracles, some of which are recorded in this book's prologue. One cardinal opposed the canonization, but changed his mind following the dream described in the prologue. The cardinal's words to the Paduan ambassadors are recorded by Anthony's biographers.

Anthony was canonized on Pentecost Sunday, May 30, 1232, by Pope Gregory IX. Some of the pope's actual words are recorded in the prologue.

That day, the bells in Lisbon began to ring of their own accord, and the people danced with joy.

Anthony's tongue and larynx, which remain incorrupt to this day, can be seen in his basilica at Padua. The aromas of incense, myrrh, and aloes exuding from his corpse, were again noticed when Anthony's remains were studied in 1981.

Lack of reliable information about Anthony begins with the year of his birth. Traditionally, this has been given as the feast of the Assumption, August 15, 1195. This would make Anthony nearly thirty-six when he died. However, recent scientific dating of Anthony's remains indicate that he was thirty-nine years and nine months old at the time of his death, which would put his birth in 1191. Because the day and year of his birth are contested, I have purposely been vague about Anthony's age in this manuscript.

## PART ONE
— • —
## The Beginning of Ministry

### 1. Master John, Holy Cross Monastery, Coimbra, Portugal (1220)

Anthony was baptized Fernando. His family, educational, and religious history as recorded in this chapter follow the historical record.

At Holy Cross, Fernando was guest master, receiving visitors from all walks of life and giving out alms. His dealings with the Friars Minor, including Brother Questor and the five martyrs, are accurate.

Scholars disagree on when Fernando/Anthony was ordained a priest. Some believe that he was ordained following his admission into the Friars Minor. They place this ordination at the Forli ordination in 1222. I believe that Fernando had been ordained while an Augustinian due to the historical account of the Mass he said for Brother Questor, and his assignment to Monte Paolo in 1221 specifically because he could celebrate Mass. The Church rule that men could not be ordained prior to the age of thirty had been disregarded in Portugal as shown by other ordinations of younger men. As a priest, Fernando almost certainly preached.

Fernando's teacher, Master John, accused Prior John of the charges listed in this chapter. In 1222, Pope Honorius III ordered three of Lisbon's priors to conduct an inquest into these charges since Prior John had ignored several excommunications. The prior was relieved of his post and died in 1226, the same year that Francis of Assisi entered eternal glory.

Fernando received permission of all the monks at Coimbra to join the Friars Minor. "Go then, and become a saint," one monk, whose name is not given in the histories, told him. "When you hear of that, then you will praise God," was Fernando's reply. Shortly after being vested with the Franciscan habit at Holy Cross, he was renamed Anthony after the patron saint of Olivares.

In this chapter, Fernando's words about sham sanctity and false religious and his hopeful words on repentance of the corrupt clergy are taken from Anthony's *Sermons for the Easter Cycle* (pp. 63, 148, 173). Anthony wrote about preaching and God's anointing in his *Sermons for the Easter Cycle* (p. 186). His words, written to preachers in general, I have personalized as applying to himself.

## 2. Maria, Lisbon Cathedral, Lisbon, Portugal (1220)

Contemporaries of St. Anthony disagree on his background. The younger son of the king of Portugal who knew Anthony as a young religious in Coimbra stated that "he was the son of ordinary citizens of Lisbon." Rolandino, notary of Padua during Anthony's stay there, stated that Anthony was "born in Lisbon of noble and powerful parents." Another early biography states that he was the son of a knight in King Alphonsus' service.

In Anthony's day, several classes of nobility lived in Portugal. The lowest class was the villein-knights who were able to own a horse and arms of their own. These knights frequently settled in border towns such as Lisbon where they could acquire small (for the time) territories and protect the castles and towns of the realm. If Anthony's father were a member of this class, as seems likely, his parentage would have coincided equally well with that assigned to him by both the Infante and Rolandino. As a member of the royal family of Portugal, the king's younger son would have considered Anthony's lowest rank on the scale of nobility as the rank of a commoner. But a notary, who did not have the privileges or power of a knight, would have seen Anthony as nobly born.

Thus, it seems likely that Anthony's father, Martino, was a knight and that his mother, Maria Theresa, a noble woman, although their class is disputed. Anthony had two sisters, Maria and Feliciana, and a brother Pedro. Maria became a member of the community of nuns of St. Augustine, which was attached to St. Vincent Monastery, the very monastery that Anthony entered. Pedro became a fairly wealthy man who bequeathed some houses he owned to the cathedral canons. Feliciana married. Some writers claim that Anthony raised to life her dead son.

As a child, Anthony, then called Fernando, was educated well. He apparently had a prodigious memory. Fernando had a great devotion to the Blessed Mother, which he learned from his own mother. He assisted at daily Mass and would go into any church that he passed to pray. Once, while at prayer, a demon appeared to him and he repulsed the creature by tracing the sign of the cross on the marble step.

When Fernando entered the Augustinians, he excelled at languages, preaching, and study. Once he cured a monk of an obsession by praying with him and covering him with his mantle.

When Fernando entered the Franciscans, he became Anthony, a beggar. The monastery at Olivares consisted of rude huts thrust against the walls of the abbey. The friars slept on straw with stones for pillows. They worked their land and begged alms. Anthony was a Franciscan for a short time—most historians say two weeks, but at least one says six months—when he was sent to Morocco.

### 3. Emilio, Ship Bound for Portugal, Mediterranean Sea (Early Spring 1221)

Anthony and Brother Philip of Castile, also a Franciscan, sailed for Morocco probably around December 1220. Some sources say that a Brother Leo of Lisbon was martyred in Morocco at the time of St. Anthony. Purcell believes that Leo was Anthony's traveling companion rather than Philip, but it is very possible that the three friars, Leo, Anthony, and Philip, all traveled to Morocco on the same boat.

Either on board or immediately after disembarking, Anthony fell ill with a violent fever. Apparently this illness was so extreme that Anthony was bedridden for months at the port of Ceuta and would likely have died had not someone tended him. It seems unlikely that Leo could have been tending Anthony and preaching. If Leo were martyred, how did Anthony survive on his own? It seems reasonable that a friar must have tended Anthony, and that friar would have been Philip. Therefore, if Leo did travel with Anthony, he was the one who preached and thus who was martyred.

Anthony's extreme illness was so persistent that he either decided to return to Portugal or was recalled there. Philip went with him.

In this chapter, the return voyage to Portugal is seen through the eyes of a fictitious crewmember, Emilio. Shortly after setting sail from Ceuta, Anthony's ship was caught in a storm so violent that it blew the vessel 1,500 miles off course, across the Mediterranean to Sicily where it ran aground near Messina. Anthony and Philip were taken to a Franciscan convent at Messina.

### 4. Brother Philip, Portiuncula, Assisi, Italy (1221)

The nature, goals, festivities, and prayers of this chapter meeting, as well as the words of Francis to his followers, are accurately described in this section. The game of the palm, or *jeu de paume,* played by the friars, originated in France in the 1100s or 1200s, and eventually evolved into tennis. No record exists of Franciscans playing this game, but it is entirely possible that they did since Francis encouraged joy among his followers. Philip and Anthony's discussion about sexual temptation is based on a thirteenth-century biography of Anthony that says a servant girl tempted Anthony before he entered religious life. Whether or not Philip had a similar temptation is pure speculation.

The assignment of Brother Philip and the progression by which Anthony was sent to Monte Paolo follow the historical record, although some historians have Anthony being assigned to Monte Paolo when he, not Philip, spoke to Father Gratian.

Brother Philip refers to Francis of Assisi as Father Francis, a term used by the Friars Minor throughout this book when referring to their founder. Although Francis was not ordained a priest, the brothers called him Father out of love and respect. Ordained friars usually referred to themselves and other priests of their Order as brothers, reserving the title of Father for Francis himself.

In this text, certain characters call Anthony father and others call him brother or friar. Depending on their relationship with the saint, the characters themselves choose the title. Anthony always referred to himself as brother, the term Francis applied to him.

### 5. Superior, Monte Paolo Monastery, Between Arezzo and Forli, Italy (1222)

Historians disagree on the exact location of Monte Paolo. Some place it near Forli, others near Arezzo, others near Bologna. A location between Forli and Arezzo seemed more sensible to me, so that is the location I chose. Purcell has placed Monte Paolo four miles from Forli. This text reflects that opinion.

At Monte Paolo, Anthony asked for a small cave hewn out of rock which had been used by a brother to store tools. Here he prayed, fasted, used the discipline, and worked on a commentary on the Psalms. He always left his cell for meals and prayers even though, at times, he was so weak that he had to be assisted in walking. He also celebrated daily Mass for the brothers and asked to clean the kitchen to earn his keep. When an ordination of Franciscans and Dominicans was to be held at Forli, he accompanied the superior as a traveling companion.

In this chapter, Anthony's comments on Psalm 127 come from his sermon, "The Children of God," in *Seek First His Kingdom*. His reference to the Gospels as the kiss of God comes from page 223 of Purcell's book.

### 6. Father Gratian, Convent of the Friars Minor, Forli, Italy (March 19, 1222)

The commonly accepted, but not uncontested, date for the ordination at Forli is March 19, 1222. By some oversight, no one had been asked to preach, so Anthony was ordered to do so by Father Gratian and Bishop Albert. The text he was given is the one stated in this chapter, and he was to speak as the Holy Spirit directed him. No words of his sermon were recorded. The words which he speaks in this chapter come from his sermon, "Humility, the Font of All Virtues," in the book, *Seek First His Kingdom,* and from his *Sermons for the Easter Cycle* (pp. 107–108, 194–196, 204). Anthony's sermon amazed the friars, none of whom knew that Anthony could preach. Father Gratian immediately sent Anthony to preach throughout his province, beginning with Rimini.

## PART TWO
— —
## Mission to Italy

### 7. Benedetto, Shore of the Marecchia River, Rimini, Italy (1222)

Benedetto, his family, his fishing companions, and Canon Alonzo are fictitious characters based on personalities of the time.

The doctrines of the *Cathari* as discussed are accurate. The *perfecti*, who had completed the *consolamentum*, were called the "Good Men" who preached in northern Italy and France during this time. Believers, who had not taken this sacrament, fell into two categories. Some lived chaste lives. Others planned to sin until they neared death when they hoped to receive the *consolamentum* and be to purged of their sins. The influence of this sect was due to the attraction of the holy "Good Men" as contrasted with the corruption of the Roman Church.

During this period of history, Catholics and heretics existed side by side in most areas in which Anthony preached. Anthony was commissioned to preach not only to enliven the faith of Catholics but also to refute and convert heretics.

Rimini is one of the principle towns of the Romagna, to which Anthony had been sent. His words to Benedetto, which compare a fish to faith, are taken from his sermon, "God's Love for His Children," in the magazine, *Messenger of St. Anthony.*

Anthony's sermon to the fish is in the historical record, as is the reaction of the crowd to it. Most historians claim that this miracle happened at Rimini, although one favors Padua. Stoddard (pp. 62–63) records the words of Anthony's sermon to the fishes. These are reproduced in this chapter. No record exists of the sermon that caused the crowd to disperse. I have chosen as a possibility Anthony's sermon on the tables of doctrine. This I expanded from one of his written sermons on "The Children of God" in the book, *Seek First His Kingdom.*

### 8. Bononillo, Saddle Shop, Rimini, Italy (1222)

The miracle of Bononillo's beast of burden and the heretic's conversion is related in the historical record. No mention of Bononillo's occupation exists. I have chosen saddler as one of the common trades of the time.

While historians agree that this miracle took place, they disagree on details. Depending on the account, the animal is called a mule, horse, or mare. Bononillo's name is spelled Bonvillo, Bonillus, and Bonello. Some claim that the miracle happened in France, most likely Toulouse or Bourges, others at Rimini. One historian says it was repeated three times, once at each location.

At this period of history, the Eucharist was kept in a small gold or silver dove or tower which could be removed from the church.

Anthony's words to Bononillo regarding the ring in the sewer are taken from his sermon, "Washing the Feet," in *Messenger of St. Anthony.*

### 9. Brother Giusto, School of Theology, Bologna, Italy (1223)

The facts concerning Anthony's teaching and various duties, including the papal audience, follow the historical record. Anthony taught the friars theology at Bologna, Montpellier, Toulouse, and Padua, as well as in other locations in Italy and France. Some historians claim that he held the office of lector of theology at universities in some of these cities, but this seems inaccurate since most of the universities had not established this position prior to Anthony's death. Most likely, he instructed the friars at their own convents, not at the universities. Some sources say that he inaugurated a school of theology in 1223 for the friars of Bologna that eventually developed into the school of theology for the university of that city. Quite likely, Anthony wrote some of his sermons as notes for teaching these classes.

Biographers of the saint record several instances in which he counseled religious of his Order and other Orders, advising them against temptations and confirming them in their faith. Brother Giusto is a fictitious character whose temptations are patterned after those of a Bavarian monk, Othloh, who took his final vows in 1032. Othloh's autobiography, some of which is quoted in *Life in the Middle Ages,* contains a vivid picture of his temptations and questions, and the torment that they caused him.

Anthony's teaching on the name of Jesus is taken from his sermon, "The Name of the Child," in the book, *Seek First His Kingdom.* His comments to Giusto are taken from the same book in his sermons, "Man's Encounter with God," "Christ, the Beginning and the End," "To Follow Christ," and "A Voice Crying in the Desert."

### 10. Father Vito, Rectory, Bologna, Italy (Early 1224)

Although all of the characters, except Anthony, in this chapter are fictitious representations of real personalities of the period, the usury in Bologna is accurately represented. Usury was excessive in many cities in Europe, and Anthony preached against it frequently. Zaccaria's reaction to the sermon is a typical reaction of usurers which biographers record in Anthony's story.

Father Vito's vision of Anthony is based on similar visions in the historical record. People reported that Anthony or others appeared to them in dreams, urging them to confess. Following Anthony's death, people claimed that Anthony appeared to them and named the friar to whom they were to confess.

Historians are unsure as to exactly when Anthony went to France. Apparently he was there by the fall of 1224. Almost certainly Anthony was sent there in response to the request of the pope for able preachers to be sent to France to respond to the heresies there. The pope sent this letter to the universities and religious houses sometime in the fall or early winter of 1223. By the time, Anthony received his orders to report to France, winter had likely arrived in Bologna. This chapter reflects that possibility.

Anthony's sermon against usury is taken from his sermons as recorded on pages 149–150 of Purcell's book and from "To See, To Speak, To Hear" in *Messenger of St. Anthony*. His illustration involving the dung beetle is based on his sermon recorded on page 108 of Gamboso's biography of Anthony.

Anthony's words to Vito are taken from his *Sermons for the Easter Cycle* (pp. 216–218), and from the following sermons as translated in *Messenger of St. Anthony*: "Knowledge, Virtue, and Faith," "The Preacher Warrior Against Sin," and "You Will Find an Infant." His praise of the Virgin Mary, the explanation of her name, and his prayer to her are from the following three sermons, all found in *Seek First His Kingdom*: "Blessed Are You, Mary," "Hail Mary, Star of the Sea," and "The Glories of Mary."

PART THREE

— —

# Mission to France

## 11. Friar Monaldo, Chapter Meeting, Arles, France (September 1224)

History tells of the priest, Friar Monaldo, but gives no description of him. Historians note the chapter meeting at Arles, but give no details as to the weather, the business under discussion, or the fruits grown at the convent. The generally accepted month and year of this meeting is September 1224, around September 14, the Feast of the Exaltation of the Holy Cross, although some historians place the meeting in 1225 or 1226. Biographical information about Francis and the response of the friars toward him is accurate.

Monaldo's vision of Francis blessing Anthony while the priest preached on the passion of Christ and the inscription on the cross is in the historical record. Since no record exists of Anthony's actual words, I have used part of his longer sermon entitled "At the Foot of the Cross" in *Seek First His Kingdom*.

### 12. Novice, Road from Montpellier to Arles, Montpellier, France (Spring 1225)

In the history of the saint, a novice at Montpellier stole Anthony's *Commentary on the Psalms*, with the likely intent of selling it and leaving the Order. Anthony prayed for the return of the book. A hideous beast appeared to the novice, threatening to kill him and throw his body in a river if he did not return the volume. The young man returned the book, was lovingly forgiven by Anthony, and returned to the Order to become a model religious. Today the Franciscan friary in Bologna claims to have preserved the stolen book.

In this chapter, Anthony's words to the novice come principally from two of his sermons in *Seek First His Kingdom*, namely, "Man's Encounter with God," and "The Practice of Virtue." His insight that, the Virgin excepted, even the saints sin, comes from his sermon, "Blessed Are You, Mary!" in the same book. Anthony's reflection on how to treat a fallen brother is from a sermon recorded in Purcell's book (p. 125).

History records the incident of Anthony silencing the frogs at Montpellier during prayer. It also tells how Anthony and another brother walked through a town without saying a word. Following their journey, Anthony remarked that they had preached well by example.

Hagiographers also record the miracle of Anthony disappearing from Mass in the manner described in this chapter, and, at the same time, singing the Office with the brothers, then reappearing to complete his homily. Some accounts claim that this miracle happened, as written here, at Easter in Montpellier. Others have it occurring on Holy Thursday in Limoges.

### 13. Lord Varden, City Square, Toulouse, France (Summer 1225)

Anthony was sent to the Languedoc "to preach against the heretics." So state his biographies. No details are given. Toulouse was a stronghold of the *Cathari*, who were called the *Albigensians* by those not adhering to the *Catharist* doctrines. The name came from the town of Albi, a *Catharist* stronghold and the source of the heresy in France.

Anthony taught theology to the friars in Toulouse and engaged in open debates with the *Cathari*. Lord Varden and the other *Cathars* in this chapter are fictional characters who most likely had real life counterparts in Toulouse. They accurately represent the lifestyles, ceremonies, and beliefs of the *Cathari* of the period.

Anthony's prayer before his sermon is recorded by Stoddard (p. 53). Anthony's preaching comes from his sermons, "Christ, the Beginning and the End," "The Church, Ark of Eternal Salvation," and "Christ Is Our Peace," in *Seek First His Kingdom*. His condemnation of corrupt clergy comes from his sermon, "Peter, Do You Love Me?" and his comparison of the incarnation to a marriage comes from his sermon, "The Lord Has Prepared a Feast for Us," in the same book. His discussion of why God may sometimes permit evil to be done in His name follows the argument later put forth by St. Thomas Aquinas.

Lord Varden's sermon against the corrupt Catholic clergy and Renault's conversion of the lord are taken from writings by Reinerius Saccho, himself a former *Catharist*. Saccho's work is translated by Jeffrey Russell in his book, *Dissent and Reform in the Early Middle Ages*. In the same book, "Sentences and Culpa from the Book of Sentences" describes the *endura* undertaken by Lady Varden. Lord Varden's sermon on the creator of the universe is taken from a *Catharist* book entitled *The Instruction of the Simple* as described in Jeffrey Russell's book, *Religious Dissent in the Middle Ages*.

## 14. Lord of Chateau-neuf-le-Foret, Chateau, Limoges, France (Early Spring 1226)

Anthony wrote his Easter sermons at Limoges, probably around April 1226. Whether the vision described here occurred at that time or not is questionable. However, the lord of Chateau-neuf-le-Foret did give Anthony a room in his castle. It seems probable that the saint, who sought out caves for privacy and discipline, would not have accepted this luxury without reason. Having a place to write these sermons seems to be a sensible motive.

While history does not physically describe the lord, it does record that he was devoted to the friars and to Anthony and was, therefore, likely a holy man. Anthony's words to him regarding the doves are taken from a sermon that Anthony gave at St. Martin's Abbey on November 3, 1226, as recorded by Stoddard (pp. 50–53). The Abbot of St. Martin's had given the friars lodging.

The vision of the Christ Child is recorded by several historians, although some modern historians question whether or not it actually happened. Biographers who agree that it did happen disagree on where the vision occurred. Some say at Chateau-neuf-le-Foret, others at Padua, and some at three other locations. The gentlemen who saw the vision variously saw it through a keyhole or window. In some versions, Anthony holds the Child. In others, the Child is floating and a heavenly fragrance and singing fill the air. In most versions, Anthony asks that the spy keep the vision secret while Anthony lived. He may have asked this either the night of the vision or the following morning. Whether Anthony had one or several visitations of the Child is unknown.

Anthony's prophecy came true. In the seventeenth century, the current Lord of Chateau-neuf-le-Foret rejected the Catholic Church and the house fell.

Anthony's cure of the Benedictine monk is in the historical record, although some biographers mention that the temptation was to sexual sin rather than to suicide. The nature of Anthony's illness is not given.

### 15. Notary, Saracen Encampment, Jerusalem, Palestine (1226?)

Historians agree that Anthony became guardian of the convent at Puy-en-Velay, although the date is variously given as 1225 or 1227. I have chosen the 1225 date as it seems that Anthony was extremely busy in Italy following the death of Francis of Assisi in 1226. It seems that he may not have had time to return to France and become guardian of a convent there. Anthony not only was administrator of the convent, but he also preached frequently in Puy and in the surrounding towns.

Anthony's reverence toward and prediction regarding the scandalous notary of Puy-en-Velay is true. The notary converted (the records do not tell how this conversion came about) and joined the bishop's crusade to Jerusalem. There he forcefully spoke about Christ and subsequently was tortured for three days and then killed. The type of torture was not detailed. Historical records give no indication that the notary ever heard Anthony preach.

The incident regarding the woman and husband converting after hearing Anthony preach at a two-mile distance is recorded in some of Anthony's biographies. The histories also record the healing during Mass of a deranged beggar, and Anthony's prediction about a yet unborn son who would become a Franciscan martyr. Occupations of the adults in these stories are not given.

History records that the infant, Philip, eventually became a Friar Minor and asked to be sent to the Holy Land. He arrived at Axoto, which was occupied by Saracens, who condemned to death all two thousand Christians in the city. Philip asked that he be the last to be beheaded. While he waited, he comforted and encouraged the other Christians to remain true to Christ. When the Saracens realized how Philip was encouraging the others, they flayed him and cut off his tongue and wrists. Nevertheless, he continued to preach by signs and example. All of the Christians maintained their faith and were martyred, with Philip being executed last of all.

### 16. Maid, Manor House, Brive, France (1226)

Anthony's foundation of the monastery at Brive and his life in the narrow cave, with its hollowed-out fountain, are accurate. The miracles mentioned in this section are all recounted by hagiographers. These include the dead infant raised to life, the child who was not scalded, the devilish apparition in the wheat field, and the maid who remained dry despite bringing vegetables to the friars during a severe rainstorm. Brother Pierre lived a long and holy life as a Friar Minor and often retold the incident mentioned in this chapter.

### 17. Minette, Brothel, Limoges, France (November 1226)

Minette is a fictitious character who represents the many prostitutes who were converted by Anthony's preaching. No record exists, however, of Anthony's personal counsel to these women. Anthony's concern for Minette and provision for her at a convent are typical for the period, but we do not know if Anthony ever sent a prostitute to live in a convent.

Roland's attitude toward women as vessels of sin was common in Anthony's time.

Roland's tale of Anthony's rebuke of the archbishop and accounting of his sermon in the cemetery are accurate.

The occurrences of the collapsing platform at St. Junien and the storm that bypassed the amphitheater are recorded in several sources. Every time Anthony preached, many penitents would relinquish to him sinfully gained money or weapons of war.

Anthony wrote the prayer used to preface his sermon and used it each time he preached, according to Stoddard (p. 53). Anthony's sermon is part of the sermon, "Christ: Our Way, Truth, and Life," found in *Seek First His Kingdom,* while his imaginative meditation on the Crucified Christ and His Mother come from "To See the Face of Christ" in *Seek First His Kingdom* and from Stoddard (p. 59). His admission of his own temptations to sexual impurity and the use of prayer to combat them effectively are in the historical record. In this chapter, Anthony's belief that he would have fallen into every vice had not God helped him is recorded by Bierbaum (p. 22).

Anthony's advice to Minette on sexual purity comes from his *Sermons for the Easter Cycle* (pp. 114, 145–146, 175). His prayer to banish sexual impurity is found in Bierbaum (p. 23).

The incident of a penitent coming to Anthony with sins too horrible to speak of and being advised by Anthony to write them down and bring them back is in the historical record. When this weeping penitent presented the paper, the sinner and Anthony went over the sins and, when Anthony handed the paper back to the repentant sinner, the paper was clean. The record does not tell who the penitent was or the nature of the sins.

### 18. Peasant Woman, Cottage, Marseilles, France (Late 1226)

When Anthony received news of Francis' death in Assisi on October 3, 1226, he was acting as custodian of the district of Limousin, France. As such, he was in a position of leadership over all friars in his province. At the time, he was living as a hermit in a cave at Brive. Brother Elias, then minister general of the Order, sent a circular letter to all the provincial ministers, calling them to a general chapter of the Order to be held in Assisi. Anthony and a companion set out to attend this meeting. On their way, either in late 1226 or early 1227, they would have walked the French roads with the King's armies and the heretics that were fleeing before them.

The two friars stayed with a peasant woman of Marseilles where Anthony worked the miracles described in this chapter. The friars may have asked the woman for shelter, as this chapter indicates, or she may have offered her home to them after seeing them in the street. History says nothing about the weather on the day of these miracles.

## Part Four

— —

# Return to Italy

### 19. Pope Gregory IX, Lateran Palace, Rome, Italy (1227)

The election of Ugolino (also spelled Hugolin or Hugolino) and his reaction to it are accurate; Ugo actually tore his garments and tried unsuccessfully to refuse the pontificate. He submitted because he felt that he should not resist the will of heaven.

I have no idea whether or not Ugo actually called himself by the shortened version of his name.

Ugo's relationship to the Friars Minor and the incidents involving Francis, the chapter meeting, and the rewriting of the Rule are detailed in biographies of Francis of Assisi.

No one is certain when Anthony's body began to swell from edema (dropsy). Whether or not Ugo spoke to Anthony about his health is unknown.

When did Anthony preach to the Curia, an incident mentioned in the very first biography of the saint? We know for certain that Anthony did go to Rome following the May chapter meeting in 1230. Some writers believe that Anthony's preaching to the cardinals and the crowds took place at that time. However, the first life of St. Anthony, the *Lectio Assidua*, places this incident after the preaching in Rimini, which took place in 1222 (and again later in the 1220s), but before the transfer of Francis' relics in 1230. The sequence of events in the *Lectio Assidua* is Rimini, Curia, transferral of Francis' relics. Since the *Lectio Assidua* appears to be written chronologically throughout (although it may not be since dates are not given), I have placed the Curia incident in the same sequence that it holds in the *Assidua*.

What year would this be? Early histories other than the *Assidua* say that Anthony not only preached to the Curia but also to the crowds assembled for the Easter indulgences. This could not have been during the summer of 1230. It could have been in 1223, before Anthony went to France, or 1227, after he returned.

Did Anthony accompany Francis as a traveling companion to Cardinal Ugolino in 1223 to rewrite the Rule? Although historians disagree, legends indicate that he did. If Anthony preached to the Curia in 1223 and was then called "the ark of the testament," Honorius III would have been the pope. However, biographers mention only Anthony's name in connection with the preaching incident. If both Francis and Anthony, the two greatest saints of the time, were in Rome together, one would think that authors would have at least mentioned Francis' name.

Some histories state that minister general Brother Elias sent Anthony to Rome in 1227 on business of the Order. This seems to me to be the most logical time that Anthony could have preached to the Curia. Anthony was already in Italy at the time, having been recalled there after Francis' death. With Francis, who highly regarded Anthony's knowledge and spirituality, Anthony had been to see Ugolino in 1223 (if we accept the legends) to discuss the Rule, so he would be a logical choice to return again with more questions. With Francis dead and the friars again questioning the Rule, Brother Elias would have wanted some matters clarified by the Order's protector, Ugolino. But Ugo would not be at the chapter meeting; he planned to be in Anagni. So Elias would have sent Anthony to Ugo prior to the pope's departure and prior to the chapter meeting. Anthony would have gone to Rome with a traveling companion, whom I have named Brother Jerome since no history mentions who he was.

While in Rome, the *Lectio Assidua* states, Anthony preached before the cardinals and was called by the pope "the ark of the testament" because, the pope said, "If the Bible were lost, Anthony could write it from memory." Later histories state that Anthony also preached to the crowds gathered for the Easter indulgences. Here accounts vary. Some say the cardinals all heard him preach in their native tongue. Others, instead, state that the crowd who assembled for Easter was granted this miracle. History does not record the content of Anthony's sermons on these occasions.

Anthony's sermon before the cardinals is taken from his written sermon, "A Voice Crying in the Desert." His homily to the crowd is part of his longer sermons, "Peter, Do You Love Me?" and, "The Church, the Ark of Eternal Salvation." All three of these are translated in *Seek First His Kingdom*. His castigation of the prelates is from his sermon, "You Will Find an Infant," published in *Messenger of St. Anthony*.

Anthony's words to Ugolino regarding Church reform as beginning with the individual are my own. They do, however, reflect what I believe was Anthony's attitude toward reform. In none of Anthony's sermons that I have read, or in any of his biographies, did Anthony ever attack institutions as a whole. He was out to convert individuals. This does not mean, however, that he did not lobby when appropriate, for merciful treatment of others. When a law regarding humane treatment of debtors was passed in 1231 in Padua, this law came after Anthony had preached a few years in Padua. His preaching so converted the city that the law was passed and Anthony's name was affixed to it. The statute stated that the law had been "enacted at the instance of...Anthony." This law was passed because Anthony had first converted the individuals who held the reins of government.

### 20. Lady Delora, Castle Courtyard, Rimini, Italy (Late 1220s)

Lady Delora and Lord Silvestro are fictitious characters through whom two miracles regarding the saint are related. The *Catharist* dress, manner of greeting, and lifestyle, as told in this chapter, are accurate.

The two feasts involving Anthony and the heretics are in the historical record. At the time, heresies other than *Catharism* existed. History does not tell us to which sect the heretics of the feasts belonged. Since the *Cathari* were the most numerous of the heretics, and since they were strong in Rimini, I have chosen them.

History states that the saint turned the toad into a capon, but this seem untypical for a Franciscan, since Franciscans frequently mortified the appetite by sprinkling ashes on their food. It seems more likely to me that Anthony would have eaten the toad with as much relish as if he were eating a hen.

Anthony's reaction to the poisoned meal is accurate. History does not tell how many dishes were poisoned or what they were. I have chosen a palatable dish of that time as the one that tested the saint.

History records that, after both these feasts, many heretics returned to the Church. Most of Anthony's converts were believers. He had little success among *perfecti* who had completed the *consolamentum*.

### 21. Robber, Highway, Padua, Italy (Lent 1228)

In one of the earliest biographies of St. Anthony, the writer records this anecdote. About the year 1292, an old man told a Friar Minor that he had known St. Anthony. One of twelve robbers who plundered travelers on the road to Padua, he, with the other disguised members of his band, had gone to hear the saint preach. Anthony's words so moved them all that they each went to confession to him in turn. He gave each a penance and exhorted them not to return to sin. If they persisted in their faith, they would gain eternal life. If they returned to a life of crime, their lives would end in torment. A few did return to the criminal life, the old man said, and their days ended horribly. But he and the rest had persisted in their reform, and those who had already died had gone peacefully.

Anthony had given to this man the penance of making twelve visits to the tomb of the apostles. At the time of his narrative, he was just completing his twelfth pilgrimage. With tears, he told the friar that he was now returning home to await his eternal reward, which Anthony had promised him.

The historical anecdote gives no personal background or description of the robber nor does it hint at the contents of Anthony's sermon. In this chapter, Anthony's sermon is compiled from the *Sermons for the Easter Cycle* (pp. 62–63, 98, 99–100, 148, 179, 194, 196–197, 208), and from the sermon, "Seek First His Kingdom" in the book of the same name. Anthony's comparison of the almond to penance is from his Easter Sunday sermon in the translated *Sermons for the Easter Cycle* (p. 87). His final blessing of the band of robbers is found in the same book's sermon for the First Sunday after Easter (p. 104).

### 22. Sister Helena de Enselmini, Convent of Arcella Vecchia, Padua, Italy (Spring 1230)

Tradition states that Anthony was the confessor of Helena Enselmini, a nun at the convent of Arcella. Helena had a great devotion to the passion of Christ, a fervor which Anthony fostered. No more about their relationship is mentioned, and some biographers question whether or not it existed.

As related in this chapter, Helena's background and illness, which most authorities agree struck her in 1226, are historically accurate. However, it is not known when she lost her sight and speech due to this illness. Gamboso says that she was ill for about thirteen months when the illness deprived her of her sight and speech. This would mean that she was most certainly in the condition that Anthony found her in this chapter.

However, Gamboso also says that Helena first became ill around the summer of 1230, and that Helena lost her sight and speech just after Anthony's death and died three months later. This information is based on an early biography that claims that Helena's illness lasted sixteen months, whereas most other sources say sixteen years. Therefore, Helena may have been blind, mute, and lame for only the last three months of her life. On the other hand, she may have suffered from these maladies for most of the sixteen years of her illness. Some sources say she had these conditions while Anthony was her confessor. Others say she suffered from them "for many years."

Helena actually had the visions described, but one or more of them may have taken place after Anthony's death. In the sources that I used, I could find no dates for these visions.

Francis himself received Helena into the Order of the Poor Ladies after he established the convent at Arcella. History does not record the words of Francis' sermon that so touched Helena. The poem in this chapter is a portion of Francis' poem, "The Praises of the Virtues," as translated in the *St. Francis of Assisi Omnibus of Sources* (pp. 132–134). Sister Sancia in this chapter is a fictional character, although any nun at Arcella could have acted in her role.

Helena had a reputation for holiness from her youth. Whether or not she was deeply attracted to Anthony or suffered from spiritual dryness, a common malady of faith-filled people, we do not know. Anthony's words to Helena are mainly taken from his *Sermons for the Easter Cycle* (pp. 156, 166–167, 200–202), and from his sermon, "The Passion of Christ," in the book, *Seek First His Kingdom.* His symbolic representation of colors is taken from his sermon for Easter in the translated *Sermons for the Easter Cycle* (p. 86).

Helena died on November 4, 1242, at the age of thirty-four. Her body remained incorrupt for centuries. In 1695, she was declared Blessed by Pope Innocent XII.

### 23. Brother Elias, Paradise Hill, Assisi, Italy (May 30, 1230)

The history of Brother Elias in the Order of the Friars Minor is accurate. The description at the 1230 chapter meeting and the confused burial of Francis' remains in the basilica actually happened, although details of both these events are unclear.

Elias seems to have had some chronic pain in his feet. This has not been proved, however. I have had him use an ass in this chapter and wear shoes to ease the pains in his feet. Later in his life, Elias was accused of using a fine steed.

The name of the ringleader of the friars who wished to make Elias minister general by force is nowhere recorded. I have called him Brother Sebastio.

The oldest records do not tell us what Anthony said as he attempted to make peace at the chapter meeting, but they do say that his words were ineffective. The chapter quieted only when Jean Parenti disrobed and the five novices spoke as recorded in this chapter. Anthony was released from his duties as provincial at this meeting and replaced by Brother Albert of Pisa.

Under the pope's direction, Brother Elias was in charge of building the basilica of St. Francis. The basilica's description is accurate for the year 1230, although it has since been enlarged. In Elias' absence, Philip of Campello and Picardus Morico continued the work.

Disagreement exists regarding the early burial of Francis' body. As evidenced by a papal letter condemning the actions of civic leaders in the matter, the body was buried in a fashion that was not in keeping with the pope's orders. The pope says that those whom he did not appoint "sacrilegiously seized the remains. By disturbing the transfer, they execrably profaned the holy rite." What this means is debated.

Some say that the body was buried three days earlier than the appointed time. Others claim that it was buried on May 25, but that the body was hurried into the basilica in the manner described in this chapter. I have accepted the latter theory which seems to correspond with the earliest records of the event. One event supporting the latter theory is the cure of Brother James of Iseo, which St. Bonaventure records in his biography of St. Francis. Bonaventure records that "Brother James took part in the celebration, paying due honor to the sacred relics. There he approached the tomb and embraced it devoutly" and was healed in the manner described in this chapter. Did Brother James embrace the tomb before or after it reached the basilica? Bonaventure's text is unclear, although elsewhere in the biography Bonaventure writes that while Francis' remains "were being borne through the town, a number of miracles were worked by the power of Christ whose image they bore."

Pope Gregory IX was so angry over the events around the translation of Francis' body that he issued a bull that threatened to excommunicate the Podesta and council of Assisi if they did not explain their conduct. The bull forbade the Franciscans to live at the basilica or to hold general chapters there, and the tomb was placed under the care of the bishop of Assisi. Only when Elias and several others involved explained the reasoning for what had happened was the bull lifted before taking effect.

Anthony headed a delegation, which included Jean Parenti, to Rome to discuss Francis' testament and other rules of the Order. The result of that meeting was the bull, *Quo elongati,* issued in September 1230, which stated that the testament was not binding. We do not know what position Anthony took with regard to the testament. He did accept the pope's word when it was issued.

History records no personal meeting of Elias and Anthony nor any letter written by Anthony to Elias at his penitential cell in Cortana. It is consistent with Anthony's personality, however, to seek out Elias and gently attempt to instruct him. Anthony's words to Elias are mainly taken from his *Sermons for the Easter Cycle* (pp. 125, 138–139, 147, 152–153, 190–192, 212), from Mary Purcell's biography (pp. 221–222), and the sermons, "Humility, the Font of All Virtues," "Love: the Principal Virtue," "Seek First His Kingdom," and "Man's Encounter with God," in the book *Seek First His Kingdom.*

Elias was reconciled to the Order in 1232 when he was elected minister general. He then resumed his work on the basilica, which was completed in 1236. Later, Elias commissioned famous artists of the day to decorate the church with frescoes.

Elias served as minister general until 1239 and was then deposed amid much complaint and conflict. He was accused of cruelty to the brothers, disregard of others' opinions, unjust visitations of provinces, and indulgent living. He was called to Rome to make his defense before the pope, and some historians have resurrected Anthony and had him accuse Elias at this encounter! Or they have transposed this incident to 1230, incorrectly substituting Anthony's name for the name of either Adam de Marsico or Aymo of Faversham, both of whom attended the 1239 meeting with Pope Gregory IX.

Against the orders of Albert of Pisa, the minister general who replaced Elias, Elias continued to visit the houses of the Poor Ladies. When the pope insisted that he obey, Elias allied himself with Emperor Frederick against the pope and was excommunicated along with the emperor in 1239. He remained excommunicated for years, while still wearing the habit of the Friars Minor, and was finally reconciled to the Church only on his deathbed in 1253.

## PART FIVE
—   —
# The Final Month

### 24. Ezzelino da Romano, Castle Fortress, Verona, Italy (May 1231)

Ezzelino (Eccelino) III da Romano's reputation for cruelty against clergy and lay people of both sexes and all ages was well known. The incident with the serf and the massage of Ariana are fictitious, but are perfectly reasonable considering Ezzelino's taste for brutality toward others and luxury toward himself.

Ezzelino considered chastity to be honorable and practiced it himself. His treatment of sexual offenders, as described in this chapter, is accurate.

Curtayne and Wiegler describe Ezzelino physically. Wiegler gives his family history.

In May 1231 (one author puts the date at 1228), Anthony visited Ezzelino at his palace to negotiate for the release of the prisoners as described in this book. No one knows if he took this visit upon himself or if he made it at Count Tiso's request. Anthony was unsuccessful. Seven months after Anthony's death, Luke Belludi and Wiffredo da Lucino, then Podesta of Padua, succeeded in having these prisoners released.

The earliest accounts of Anthony's meeting with Ezzelino simply state that he was unsuccessful. About thirty years later, embellished stories appeared. These state that Ezzelino was seated on his throne, surrounded by murderous troops, that Anthony preached a fire and brimstone sermon to Ezzelino, and that the tyrant undid his girdle, twisted it around his neck, and threw himself at Anthony's feet, confessing his sins and promising to amend his life. After Anthony left, Ezzelino told his servants that he saw lightning come from Anthony's eyes and was certain that, if he laid hands on him, the demons would take Ezzelino's soul immediately to hell. The legends then go on to state that a short time later, Ezzelino sent Anthony a costly gift which he refused with the words that he wanted no gifts gained by bloodshed. The accounts say that, for a short time, Ezzelino tempered his cruelties but relapsed into them following Anthony's death.

In my account of this incident, I have tried to follow the oldest record while incorporating a few details of the legend as they would seem to fit Ezzelino's character.

Anthony's words to Ezzelino about dropsy and about the insatiable desires of power and greed are based on his sermon, "Heal Us, O Lord." His discussion of the imprisoned soul set free is found in his sermon, "The Birth of Jesus Christ." Both sermons are translated in *Seek First His Kingdom.*

All his life, Emperor Frederick II fought against the papacy and the proclamation of Pope Innocent III that the emperor was emperor only by the good grace of the pope and that the empire existed to serve the Church. He battled papal power by deceit and false promises and, in time, actually engaged papal armies in combat for key cities. Frederick's success greatly diminished the power of the papacy. Frederick died in 1250, having made himself ruler of Germany and nearly all of Italy, including areas once held by the papacy.

Late in 1232, Frederick II, whose physical description in this chapter is accurate, made an alliance with Ezzelino. Shortly thereafter, Ezzelino and the citizens of Verona were put under papal interdict, which meant that they could not receive most of the sacraments or Christian burial. A few years later, Ezzelino married Frederick's fourteen-year-old daughter, Selvaggia. In 1238, Frederick and Ezzelino made war on Milan and neighboring cities that were loyal to the pope. When Padua revolted against Ezzelino, he entered the city and slaughtered 12,000 of its inhabitants in one day. Ezzelino continued to fight beside Frederick and was eventually excommunicated from the Church. Wounded in battle, he was captured at Cassano in 1259 and imprisoned. To the friars who came to him, urging repentance and confession, Ezzelino said, "I have no sins to confess save that I did not take sufficient revenge upon my enemies, commanded my army badly, and let myself be deceived and beguiled." After refusing food and medicine and tearing off his bandages, he died while still a prisoner.

### 25. Count Tiso da Camposampiero, Camposampiero, Twelve Miles Outside Padua, Italy (May 1231)

Because of Anthony's sermons, the elderly Tiso (Tisone) da Camposampiero (da Campo San Pietro or Camposanpiero), who died in 1234, experienced conversion and joined the Order of the Continent Brothers and Sisters. We do not know exactly how old Tiso was at the time or when he made his full conversion and joined this fraternity. His entrance into this Order was not likely in 1227, when some authors state that Anthony first came to Padua (others state that he first came to Padua in 1229). In 1227, Tiso was involved in war against Ezzelino, and bearing arms was forbidden to penitents. Although Tiso seems to have invited Anthony to Camposampiero and to a second home which he seems to have had in Padua before 1231, I have chosen to make Tiso's total conversion during Anthony's 1231 Lenten sermons. Tiso may, however, have joined the fraternity earlier than this. The requirements of the Order of the Continent Brothers and Sisters, as described in this chapter, were accurate for that time.

With his own hands, Tiso built Anthony his tree house. Sources say that Anthony either asked for the cell directly or made his request through another friar. I have chosen the first option. Varying accounts call the tree a walnut, oak, or chestnut. The first biography of St. Anthony calls it a walnut in one translation and a nut tree in another. I have chosen to call it a walnut.

The details regarding the effect of Anthony's sermons, his founding of convents, and his inspiration of the debtor's code is accurate. Sources disagree on which convent Anthony founded at Padua. Biographies of Helena Enselmini say that Francis of Assisi founded Arcella in 1220, but at least one biography of Anthony (Stoddard, p. 69) states that Anthony founded it in 1227 and lived there. However, the biographies state that Anthony wanted to return to St. Mary's within Padua to die because that was where he lived. One historian (Huber, p. 13) says that he took up his permanent residence in Padua in 1229 at the convent that he established in 1227. The truth of the matter, it seems to me, must be that Anthony founded St. Mary's in 1227, not Arcella, and this chapter reflects that deduction.

Most of Anthony's sermons and words to Tiso are taken from the translated *Sermons for the Easter Cycle* (pp. 77–78, 83, 149, 152, 157–158, 189–190, 205–206, 210–211) and from the sermon, "To Follow Christ," in *Seek First His Kingdom*.

### 26. Brother Luke Belludi, Road Outside the City, Padua, Italy (About May 30, 1231)

Luke Belludi's biographical background, his assignment to Anthony, and his request for the cure of a dying (or perhaps crippled—accounts of the malady differ) child as recorded in this chapter are in the historical record. Historians place Luke's birth sometime between 1200 and 1210. Since he joined the Friars Minor when he was twenty, the year of his entry would vary from 1220 to 1230. Therefore, no one can be certain when he was assigned to assist Anthony, although he certainly spent Anthony's final year with the saint.

Anthony's ecstasy at hearing the sermon on St. Paul's words to the Athenians, his healing of Leonardo's foot (which some accounts say was instantaneous), his encounter with the turtledoves, and his prophecy on the hill of Padua are in the historical record. The accounts, however, do not record the name of the friar (or friars) who witnessed or who heard about these events, nor do they record particulars of them such as what Anthony's ecstasy was like or how he affected the cure. The record also does not tell which words of the sermon caused Anthony to fall into ecstasy.

Anthony desired to write a book for all Christians to read. While still working on his sermons, he died, therefore never fulfilling this ambition.

Anthony's humble words at the beginning of his written sermons are taken from the translated *Sermons for the Easter Cycle* (p. 64). Those at the end are in Gamboso's book (p. 145).

Luke became a provincial minister of the Franciscan Order and was mainly responsible for erecting the basilica which enshrines Anthony's remains. Active in preaching and good works, Luke, who was always known as Luke of St. Anthony, died in 1285 and was interred in Anthony's original tomb. In 1927, Luke was declared blessed by the Church.

### 27. Brother Roger, Convent of the Friars Minor, Camposampiero, Italy (June 13, 1231)

Along with Brother Luke Belludi, Brother Roger was in attendance upon Anthony during the last weeks of his life. Roger may have been a friar at St. Mary's or Arcella when he was assigned to attend Anthony, or he may have already been at Camposampiero when Anthony arrived. He may have been Anthony's helper even earlier than this chapter suggests. At least one biographer describes Roger as being a large, strong man about the same age as Anthony. Whether or not he feared death is nowhere recorded.

The account of Anthony's last day follows the historical record. Coming down from his tree, he collapsed during the noon meal and was put to bed. He asked Brother Roger to take him to St. Mary's to die, but the cart was met enroute by Brother Ignoto (also called Brother Vinoto) who may or may not have been chaplain at Arcella. Ignoto told the brothers to go to Arcella because Anthony would never survive the journey into Padua. At Arcella, Anthony was placed in a chair, with Brother Roger supporting his head, for the water was rising in his chest. After experiencing anxiety, Anthony regained his calm, made his confession (the records do not tell us what sins he confessed), then sang (or chanted) "O Glorious Lady" in a clear, strong voice. His vision of the Savior and his words regarding his last anointing are accurate. Following this, he recited the seven Penitential Psalms with the friars, then maintained a peaceful quiet for half an hour before dying. The friars immediately decided to keep his death a secret to avoid crowds at the convent.

Anthony's words to Brother Roger about death are taken from the translated *Sermons for the Easter Cycle* (p. 214).

### 28. Paduana, City Street, Padua, Italy (June 13, 1231)

History records that Peter, a citizen of Padua (his occupation is not given), took his four-year-old daughter, Paduana, to Anthony and asked him to bless the child. The child was unable to walk and had epileptic-like fits. Following Anthony's blessing, Peter took the little girl home and stood her by a chair. Over a period of time, she learned to walk by pushing the chair about the room. The cure was attributed to Anthony and was the only miracle that Anthony worked during his lifetime that was included in the list of forty-seven miracles approved by the Roman Curia and read at Anthony's canonization.

Whether Anthony liked fig cakes and whether or not Paduana's mother prepared them for the priest is not known. Nor is it anywhere recorded that Paduana visited Anthony at any time.

The friars' attempt to keep Anthony's death a secret was thwarted by the children of Padua. History does not tell how the children learned of Anthony's death and mentions no role that Paduana may have played in relaying the news. However, almost as soon as Anthony died, the children began running through the streets shouting, in the words of the translated *Assidua,* "The holy father is dead! St. Anthony is dead!"

### 29. Abbot Thomas of Gaul, St. Andrew's Monastery, Vercelli, Italy (June 13, 1231)

The visits of Anthony, when he was still alive, to Abbot Thomas, a brilliant theologian and great advocate of yearly confession, are accurate, although Anthony's biographies do not record the physical appearance of Abbot Thomas. Thomas' words to Francis about Anthony may not ever have been addressed to Francis, but Thomas did write the accolade in one of his commentaries.

On June 13, 1231, Anthony appeared to Thomas as recorded in this chapter, speaking the words recorded here, and healing Thomas' sore throat. When Thomas could not find Anthony anywhere or locate anyone besides himself who had seen the friar, Thomas returned to his cell and carefully wrote down the date, time, and details of Anthony's appearance. He did not record what sort of work he was doing in his cell at the time of Anthony's appearance. A few weeks later, news of Anthony's death reached Vercelli. Thomas took out his notes and read them, realizing then that Anthony had appeared to him shortly after his death in Padua.

# Bibliography

## Biographies and Other Writings About St. Anthony

Beahn, John E. *A Rich Young Man: St. Anthony of Padua*. Milwaukee: The Bruce Publishing Company, 1953.

Bierbaum, Athanasius. *Saint Anthony of Padua: Life Sketches and Prayers*. Trans. Kilian J. Hennrich. Detroit: Third Order Bureau, 1931.

Butler, Alban. "St. Anthony of Padua." *Butlers' Lives of the Saints: Complete Edition*. Herbert Thurston and Donald Attwater, eds. Westminster, MD: Christian Classics, Inc., 1956.

Curtayne, Alice. *St. Anthony of Padua*. Chicago: Franciscan Herald Press, 1931.

Da Rieti, Ubaldus. *Life of St. Anthony of Padua*. Boston: Angel Guardian Press, 1895.

Gamboso, Vergilio. *Per Conoscere S. Antonio: La Vita-il Pensiero*. Padova, Italy: Edizioni Messaggero, 1990.

———. *St. Anthony of Padua: His Life and Teaching*. Trans. H. Partridge. Padua: Messaggero di S. Antonio–Editrice, 1991.

Gilliat-Smith, Ernest. *Saint Anthony of Padua According to His Contemporaries*. New York: E. P. Dutton & Co., 1926.

Hardick, Fr. Lothar. *Anthony of Padua: Proclaimer of the Gospel*. Fr. Zachary Hayes and Fr. Jason M. Miskuly, trans. Fr. Cassian A. Miles and Janet E. Gianopoulos, eds. Paterson, NJ: St. Anthony's Guild, 1993.

Huber, Raphael M. *St. Anthony of Padua: Doctor of the Church Universal*. Milwaukee: The Bruce Publishing Company, 1948.

*Lectio Assidua*. Padua, Italy: 1232 unpublished translation. Translator unknown. Franciscan Monastery of St. Clare, Jamaica Plain, MA.

LePitre, Albert. *St. Anthony of Padua (1195–1231)*. London: Burns, Oates & Washbourne Ltd., 1924.

*321*

*Life of St. Anthony: Assidua.* Padua, Italy: 1232. Trans. Bernard Przewozny. Padua: Edizioni Messaggero, 1984.

Marin, Vito Terribile Wiel. "Sulle Possibili Cause Della Morte di S. Antonio di Padova." *Ricognizione del Corpo di S. Antonio di Padova: Studi Storici e medico-antropologici.* Virgilio Meneghelli and Antonino Poppi. Padua: Edizioni Messaggero, 1981, pp. 193–198.

Meneghelli, Virgilio. "La Revisione dei Resti Mortali di S. Antonio di Padova." *Ricognizione del Corpo di S. Antonio di Padova: Studi Storici e medico-antropologici.* Virgilio Meneghelli and Antonino Poppi. Padua: Edizioni Messaggero, 1981, pp. 153–156.

Purcell, Mary. *Saint Anthony and His Times.* Garden City, New York: Hanover House (Division of Doubleday and Company), 1959.

Stoddard, Charles Warren. *Saint Anthony: The Wonder Worker of Padua.* Originally published by The Ave Maria, Notre Dame, IN, 1896. Reprinted Rockford, IL: Tan Books and Publishers, Inc., 1971.

## Writings of St. Anthony

Anthony of Padua. "God's Love for His Children." Fr. Claude Jarmak, trans. *Messenger of St. Anthony,* May 1986: 4–5.

———. "Knowledge, Virtue, and Faith." Fr. Claude Jarmak, trans. *Messenger of St. Anthony,* Feb. 1990: 4–5.

———. "The Preacher Warrior Against Sin." Fr. Claude Jarmak, trans. *Messenger of St. Anthony,* Sept. 1989: 4–5.

———. *Seek First His Kingdom.* Fr. Livio Poloniato, ed. Fr. Claude Jarmak, Fr. Leonard Frasson, and Fr. Bernard Przewosny-Porter, trans. Padua: Grafiche Messaggero S. Antonio, Padua, Conventual Franciscan Friars, 1988.

———. *Sermons for the Easter Cycle.* George Marcil, O.F.M., ed. The Franciscan Institute. St. Bonaventure, New York: The Franciscan Institute, 1994.

———. "To See, To Speak, To Hear." Fr. Claude Jarmak, trans. *Messenger of St. Anthony,* July–Aug. 1988: 4–5.

———. "Washing the Feet." Fr. Claude Jarmak, trans. *Messenger of St. Anthony,* Mar. 1989: 4–5.

———. "You Will Find an Infant." Fr. Claude Jarmak, trans. *Messenger of St. Anthony,* Dec. 1990: 4–5.

## Additional References

Abulafia, David. *Frederick II: A Medieval Emperor.* London: Allen Lane, Penguin Press, 1988.

Augustine Fellowship, Sex and Love Addicts Anonymous. *Sex and Love Addicts Anonymous.* Boston: The Augustine Fellowship, Sex and Love Addicts Anonymous, Fellowship Wide Services, Inc., 1986.

Barraclough, Geoffrey. *The Medieval Papacy.* Norwich, England: Harcourt, Brace & World, Inc., 1968.

Barton, Lucy. *Historic Costume for the Stage.* Boston: Walter H. Baker Company, 1935.

Blanchard, Gerald T. "Sexually Abusive Clergymen: A Conceptual Framework for Intervention and Recovery." *Pastoral Psychology.* March 1991: 237–245.

Bonaventure. *Major Life of St. Francis.* Benen Fahy, O.F.M., trans. *St. Francis of Assisi: Writings and Early Biographies.* Marion A. Habig, ed. Chicago, IL: Franciscan Herald Press, 1973, pp. 613–787.

Brooke, Rosalind B. *Early Franciscan Government: Elias to Bonaventure.* Cambridge, England: Cambridge University Press, 1959.

Brown, Harold O. J. *Heresies: The Image of Christ in the Mirror of Heresy and Orthodoxy from the Apostles to the Present.* Garden City, New York: Doubleday & Company, 1984.

Carnes, Patrick. *Out of the Shadows: Understanding Sexual Addiction.* Minneapolis: CompCare Publications, 1983.

Cianchetta, Romeo. *Assisi: Art and History in the Centuries.* Narni, Italy: Plurigraf, 1985.

Coulton, G. C. *Life in the Middle Ages.* 4 vols. Cambridge, England: Cambridge University Press, 1967.

———. *The Medieval Scene: An Informal Introduction to the Middle Ages.* London: Cambridge at the University Press, 1931.

Cristiani, Leon. *Heresies and Heretics.* Translated from the French by Roderick Bright. New York: Hawthorn Books, 1959.

Cummings, Juniper M. *The Christological Content of the "Sermons" of St. Anthony.* Padua: Il Messaggero di S. Antonio Basilica del Santo, 1953.

Curran, Charles. *Absolutes in Moral Theology.* Washington, D.C.: Corpus Instrumentorum, Inc., 1968.

DeClary, Leon. *Lives of the Saints and Blessed of the Three Orders of St. Francis.* N.p.: Taunton Franciscan Convent, 1886–1887: 36–38.

Englebert, Omer. *St. Francis of Assisi: A Biography.* Eve Marie Cooper, trans. Ann Arbor, MI: Servant Books, 1979.

Francis of Assisi. *The Prayers of St. Francis.* Ignatius Brady, O.F.M., trans. Ann Arbor, MI: Servant Books, 1987.

Gregory IX. *"Speravimus Hactenus."* June 16, 1230. Unpublished translation by Fr. Claude J Armak. Granby, MA: n.d.

Habig, Marion Alphonse. *The Franciscan Book of Saints,* rev. ed. Chicago, IL: Franciscan Herald Press, 1979. 122–123, 912–913.

————. ed. *St. Francis of Assisi: Writings and Early Biographies—English Omnibus of the Sources for the Life of St. Francis.* Chicago, IL: Franciscan Herald Press, 1973.

## Works Consulted

Hastings, Margaret. *Medieval European Society 1000–1450.* 1st. ed. New York: Random House, 1971.

Holmes, Urban Tigner. *Daily Living in the Twelfth Century Based on the Observations of Alexander Neckam in London and Paris.* Madison, WI: The University of Wisconsin Press, 1953.

Isely, Paul J. and Peter Isley. "The Sexual Abuse of Male Children by Church Personnel: Intervention and Prevention." *Pastoral Psychology.* Nov., 1990: 85–99.

Jorgensen, Johannes. *St. Francis of Assisi.* T. O'Conor Sloane, trans. Garden City, NY: Image Books (A Division of Doubleday & Company), 1939.

Kantorowicz, Ernst. *Frederick the Second—1194–1250.* 1931. New York: Frederick Ungar Publishing Company, 1957.

Kunz, Jeffrey R. M. *The American Medical Association Family Medical Guide.* New York: Random House, 1982.

Laaser, Mark R. "Sexual Addiction and Clergy." *Pastoral Psychology.* March 1991: 213–235.

"A Lutheran Pastor." *Pastoral Psychology.* March 1991: 259–263.

Maitland, S. R. *Facts and Documents Illustrative of the History, Doctrine, and Rites of the Ancient Albigenses and Waldenses.* London: C. J. G. and F. Rivington, 1832.

Mandonnet, Pierre. *St. Dominic and His Work.* Sister Mary Benedicta Larkin, trans. St. Louis, MO: B. Herder Book Company, 1945.

Mann, Horace K. *The Lives of the Popes in the Middle Ages,* vol. 13. London: Kegan Paul, Trench, Trubner & Co., Ltd., 1925.

Moorman, John. *A History of the Franciscan Order from Its Origins to the Year 1517.* Oxford, England: Clarendon Press, 1968.

Mundy, John Hine and Peter Riesenberg. *The Medieval Town.* Princeton: Van Nostrand, 1958.

"One Priest's Reflections on Recovery." *Pastoral Psychology.* March 1991: 269–273.

Powicke, Frederick Maurice. *The Christian Life in the Middle Ages and Other Essays.* Oxford, England: The Clarendon Press, 1968.

Russell, Jeffrey Burton. *Dissent and Reform in the Early Middle Ages.* Berkeley and Los Angeles: University of California Press, 1965.

———. ed. *Religious Dissent in the Middle Ages.* New York: John Wiley & Sons, Inc., 1971.

Stanford-Rue, Susan M. *Will I Cry Tomorrow?: Healing Post-Abortion Trauma.* Old Tappan, NJ: Fleming H. Revell Company, 1986.

Strayer, Joseph Reese. *Western Europe in the Middle Ages: A Short History,* 3rd. ed. Glenview, IL: Scott, Foresman, 1982.

Stuard, Susan Mosher. *Women in Medieval Society.* Philadelphia: University of Pennsylvania Press, 1976.

Timmermans, Felix. *The Perfect Joy of St. Francis.* New York: Farrar, Straus, and Young, 1952.

Wakefield, Walter L. *Heresy, Crusade and Inquisition in Southern France 1100–1250.* Berkeley: University of California Press, 1974.

Walsh, James Joseph. *The Thirteenth, Greatest of Centuries.* "Best Books" edition. New York: Catholic Summer School Press, 1907.

Walsh, Michael. *An Illustrated History of the Popes: Saint Peter to John Paul II.* New York: St. Martin's Press, 1980.

Wiegler, Paul. *The Infidel Emperor and His Struggles against the Pope: A Chronicle of the Thirteenth Century.* New York: E. P. Dutton & Company, 1930.

**Madeline Pecora Nugent** has been writing for over forty years. She is the author of numerous articles, booklets, and columns, as well as the books, *Clare and Her Sisters: Lovers of the Poor Christ; Praying with Anthony of Padua; The Divine Office for Dodos;* and *Having Your Baby When Others Say No!* She also writes and publishes stories of patron saints distributed by mail through the non-profit organization "Saints' Stories," which she founded. Madeline has appeared on radio and television programs and has conducted retreats on the saints.

A vowed member of the Confraternity of Penitents, Madeline holds a graduate degree in English from Penn State University. She is a wife and mother of five children and has two grandchildren. She and her husband Jim live in Middletown, Rhode Island.

# Pauline
## BOOKS & MEDIA

The Daughters of St. Paul operate book and media centers at the following addresses. Visit, call or write the one nearest you today, or find us on the World Wide Web, www.pauline.org

**CALIFORNIA**
| | |
|---|---|
| 3908 Sepulveda Blvd, Culver City, CA 90230 | 310-397-8676 |
| 5945 Balboa Avenue, San Diego, CA 92111 | 858-565-9181 |
| 46 Geary Street, San Francisco, CA 94108 | 415-781-5180 |

**FLORIDA**
| | |
|---|---|
| 145 S.W. 107th Avenue, Miami, FL 33174 | 305-559-6715 |

**HAWAII**
| | |
|---|---|
| 1143 Bishop Street, Honolulu, HI 96813 | 808-521-2731 |
| Neighbor Islands call: | 866-521-2731 |

**ILLINOIS**
| | |
|---|---|
| 172 North Michigan Avenue, Chicago, IL 60601 | 312-346-4228 |

**LOUISIANA**
| | |
|---|---|
| 4403 Veterans Memorial Blvd, Metairie, LA 70006 | 504-887-7631 |

**MASSACHUSETTS**
| | |
|---|---|
| 885 Providence Hwy, Dedham, MA 02026 | 781-326-5385 |

**MISSOURI**
| | |
|---|---|
| 9804 Watson Road, St. Louis, MO 63126 | 314-965-3512 |

**NEW JERSEY**
| | |
|---|---|
| 561 U.S. Route 1, Wick Plaza, Edison, NJ 08817 | 732-572-1200 |

**NEW YORK**
| | |
|---|---|
| 150 East 52nd Street, New York, NY 10022 | 212-754-1110 |
| 78 Fort Place, Staten Island, NY 10301 | 718-447-5071 |

**PENNSYLVANIA**
| | |
|---|---|
| 9171-A Roosevelt Blvd, Philadelphia, PA 19114 | 215-676-9494 |

**SOUTH CAROLINA**
| | |
|---|---|
| 243 King Street, Charleston, SC 29401 | 843-577-0175 |

**TENNESSEE**
| | |
|---|---|
| 4811 Poplar Avenue, Memphis, TN 38117 | 901-761-2987 |

**TEXAS**
| | |
|---|---|
| 114 Main Plaza, San Antonio, TX 78205 | 210-224-8101 |

**VIRGINIA**
| | |
|---|---|
| 1025 King Street, Alexandria, VA 22314 | 703-549-3806 |

**CANADA**
| | |
|---|---|
| 3022 Dufferin Street, Toronto, ON M6B 3T5 | 416-781-9131 |
| 1155 Yonge Street, Toronto, ON M4T 1W2 | 416-934-3440 |

¡También somos su fuente para libros, videos y música en español!